Unbound

By J.A. Bullen

Also by J.A. Bullen

The Legends of Valoria series

The Last Paladin of Highmoore

Rise of the Divine Knight

The Shield of Aneira

Blood in the Rain series

Blood in the Rain: Chronicles of the Hunter

Tales of Anon series

Beyond the Amaranthine Veil⯑

Unbound

J.A. Bullen

?

For my love and my life. Without whom, I might have been sane.

To Mary,
Thank you.
Enjoy!
J. A. Bullen

To Mary,

Thank you.

Enjoy!

J.D. Butler

Chapter 1 – Coming of the World Storm

The storm winds blowing in from the icy waters of the Tyrda Fell, raged against the coast of Ulfrost Island, bending even the eldest of the mighty Wyrd trees. Planted by the ancient Norn, themselves, the trees proved the blessings of the Old Gods upon their island. Beyond their protective embrace, the hamlet of Ulfrost bared itself against the ominous, supernatural gusts of wind and bursts of sky crackling thunder. Every blade of heavenly light threatened to cleave the isle in twain.

Ulfrost island, nestled deep in the southern edge of the One Hundred Isles of Vala, represented one of the greatest and final conquests of the Vikings. Settled at the edge of charted waters, the island chain had proven itself a hard-won home to more than a score of wandering clans. Now, those who returned to the waters of the Tyrda Fell, whispered stories of an encroaching wall of fog, and those who vanished behind it. Lost even to the Aesir.

The only house in all Ulfrost village, which dared show light in the presence of such godly storms, lay furthest from the hamlet, within the forest. Kari, the young, blighted herbalist, sat before the roaring fire of her well-lit home. Her strong, skilled and well-worn hands, spun knots in the long flowing strands of her honey hair, as she remembered staring into the frightening, golden eyes, which had borne into her soul, from beyond a veil of cloak shrouded blackness.

The elder woman had appeared with the thunder in a flash of light. The sky had cracked above, only a moment before the woman's walking stick wrapped upon her door. As Kari opened it, her breath grew heavy in her chest, as though she were crushed within the maw of the earth. In her presence, Kari could no longer perceive the storm, the crackling of her hearth, or the air in her lungs.

Stumbling backwards, she moved from the tall and ancient woman's path. Her eyes were the color of gold. Her hair, long and silver, hung down to her chest. Her dark cloak wrapped around her, concealing most of her face and body. In each bronze colored hand, the elder carried a blanket covered basket, which she sat near the hearth.

"Your lady chief tells me that you, Kari, are the one, to whom I should entrust these babes." The woman, her voice deeper than the war drums on any of Ulfrost's longboats, sounded as shale, grinding upon personified stone, yet carried a distinct tenderness. She spoke with the power of the ages, the cry of the storm retreating from the sound, as she motioned to the linen covered baskets.

"High Chief Finna, is rather kind. I was blighted as a child and could never produce children of my own. Even when my husband, Gram, was alive. Though we tried, never did we manage." From the corner of the house, within one of the baskets, a shrill cry pierced the air.

Without pause or conscious thought, Kari floated across the room with elegant grace and cradled the crying babe in her arms. Pressing the infant, a small, milky white boy to her chest, she soothed him as she looked back to the woman. Seeing what she believed was a smile, she gasped.

"Please forgive me, elder. I did not think. I merely..."

"You merely sought to comfort the boy." The sound of shattering boulders in a rockslide filled the room. "Think nothing of it, child. I can see your chief has chosen wisely."

"Do you mean?" Kari began, her eyes watering.

"I shall leave these orphans in your care, if you would have them." She spoke, rising to her feet. Something primal within Kari, as though written into her soul, bade her to sit between the children, as the woman rose to her full height.

"I thank you, Elder. May the Ancient Ones smile upon you, from the realm eternal."

"Nothing is eternal, child, save time. Though even time, must change eventually." She felt an invisible force pressing down on the back of her head, averting her gaze, though she imagined she saw another smile. "The gods are falling, child, and their realms vanish with them. Surely, your clansmen have reported this?" She spoke with neither remorse nor triumph. Kari shivered at the woman's level of acceptance. From her, the event sounded expected. Necessary. As necessary as the change of seasons.

"They made mention of a great many peoples, vanishing beyond a wall of fog, and a storm of beasts, which writhed beneath its surface."

"Far to the east, from within the halls of High Lord Skjordsfell, have I brought to you, the last of their clan. A great beast had ravaged the lands there and laid waste to the Storm King's armies. On four red feathered wings and armored in the scales of its kin, the draconian harbinger of the fog, fell before Skjordsfell's throne. As they fought for the final threads of life within their death throes, I arrived.

"The boy was already dead, when I came upon him. With the persuasion of ways older than your gods and fables, he claimed victory over the great hound. The girl, whom I discovered beside the former High Lady, merely stared into my eyes, unafraid, as I collected her."

"They are not siblings?"

"Nay, though they must never be far apart. Not until they are ready to explore beyond your One Hundred Isles of Vala. Beyond the wall of fog."

"Why, Elder?" Kari asked.

~ 3 ~

"Do not question." The old woman roared with the gift of thunder in her throat. "Your warning, child. The children shall remain, never so far apart they feel the loss. Should one leave the One Hundred Isles, to journey beyond the wall of fog, so must the other! Swear to it, it shall be so!" The woman's thunderous voice continued its swell, until the beams and larders of the house, shook in such a way the storm itself had not caused. Staring deep into the elder's golden eyes, Kari confronted the stranger with all her courage.

"I swear it!" She growled, managing to rise from near prostration, to a knee. The woman's gaze moved from Kari's face, to her body and then returned.

"Then there is one more thing I must give you." She continued, reaching into the folds of her robes, which proved darker than the depths of the void. From within, she removed a sword in its scabbard, a rarity and sacred treasure among the Viking people.

The pair ran nearly the length of the Kari's thigh, a sword worthy of a High Lord, or his most trusted subject. The scabbard bore simple markings, providing no identification beyond its heritage. The handle, wrapped with thick leather cords, would defend the hands of the wielder as it was used in battle. The blade alone, would fetch a king's ransom.

"This belonged to the boy's mother. It was from she, I received both it and he. Be certain he cares for it." She ordered, placing the blade against the hearth.

"It shall be so, elder." Kari vowed.

"Then may their fates lie with you." She spoke and a moment later was gone, any sight of her swallowed away in the storm.

Now, nearly an hour since the old woman's departure, Kari stared out the window, watching the storm, trembling. A nearby sneeze capturing her attention, she stared down at the blue eyed, baby girl, who looked to her with large, intelligent eyes. She smiled at the babe and lifted her from the basket, cradling her tightly.

"Hello, my little Asta," she cooed, as the girl reached out with her left hand. Kari, noticed the mark on the youngling's wrist. Allowing the babe to grip her finger, she saw a birthmark shaped as a slaver's shackle. The sound of crying broke her transfixion on the mark, as she looked to the second basket.

"Don't cry, my little Vali. Mummy is here," she cooed in a loving tone, carefully lifting the boy. Her brow furrowed once more, noticing an identical mark on the boy's opposing wrist. Cradling both infants to her chest, she rocked them gently, watching the storm.

Chapter 2 – Came the Passing of Winters

Far off the coast of Ulfrost, the waters of Tyrda Fell, churned mischievously, swaths of emerald green at the heart of the great sea. The winds blew gently, carrying the smell of the bay, high up into Asta's perch atop one of the many ancient Wyrd trees, near her home. The azure eyed beauty sat upon the uppermost branches, eyes closed, daydreaming of wings.

Her long, blonde hair blew gently with the sway of the dancing wind. Her bared toes reached out from extended legs of silk, as she savored the smell and taste of the salty air. Her bow and quiver hung from a branch to her left. Her arms were wrapped around a series of sketches, which she grasped lovingly to her chest.

In the closing days of summer, each limb of the trees still bore large nets of greenery. Far below, tapestries of flowering plants and fruit bushes, painted her view. Above her, the sun shone high, though the reaching arms of the mighty trees, shielded her from its rays.

Hearing movement from below, her luminous eyes snapped open. Tipping her head down and to the right, she saw the proudly lifted head of a twelve-pointed Halla, beneath her. She smiled, as she watched the graceful and majestic creature step into the opening. Not a muscle trembling within her gentle frame, she watched as a doe and three yearlings followed close behind.

Each of the creatures was tall and slender. Their bodies were silver in color, with gentle tufts of leaf green hair decorating their hides. The yearlings bore ashen white marks on their hides, as well. Spots, which speckled their bodies, until their horns grew in.

The small group of grazing herd beasts stopped in the middle of the glen. Tipping their heads to the ground, they fed upon the rich, wild grasses. She continued to watch them from above, casually munching on the elderberries she had picked from the bushes, below.

The tart fruits burst in her mouth, as she chewed them. Her cherry lips puckered slightly at the taste, while she continued to watch the animals below. She smiled at them. They were free to go about and do as they pleased. She envied them.

"Asta!" She heard her name called from the direction of home to the west. Instinctively, the herd of Halla fled, causing a flicker of annoyance to escape the young woman's lips.

"Asta!" She heard her name called again. Leaning forward in her perch, she searched for her wilderness friends but failed to see them.

"Coming, Mother!" She called back, slinging her quiver over her lap as she rolled her sketches. Gently stowing them inside with her arrows and the staff of her bow, she strung her arms through the straps and began climbing down.

She moved with preternatural grace. Her limbs flowed with swift, fluid efficiency, giving as much the appearance of floating down, as climbing. The lower branches of the massive tree swelled, the nearer to the trunk she descended. The grass rustled beneath her feet as she dropped to the ground and sprinted toward home. She had spent her entire life in the valley with Vali and Kari. She could have run its entirety blindfolded and still easily found the front door of their home.

She could see her home in the distance. Its walls were constructed from thick logs, taken from the ancient forest. Ivy grew over top of the structure, rolling over upon lattices, where her mother grew many of her herbs. Laid upon simple stonework, as with the rest of the village homes, their house was built to withstand the harsh storms that came year-round. Standing outside of the longhouse, was her mother, glaring impatiently.

"Asta, where have you been, child?" Kari asked, eying her sternly, hands on her hips. Asta stopped and smiled at her mother. The woman had never taken a companion, so long as she had been in her care, though she could have her pick from any of the men her age. Her deep, hazel eyes glowed upon her smooth, tanned skin. Even with the streaks of silver in her long, lustrous hair, her mother was both beautiful and youthful.

"I was out in the valley, Mother. Nothing of note happened." She answered as Kari's gaze lightened.

"It is not safe for you to be out by yourself," she warned. "Any great number of things could happen."

"On Ulfrost?" Asta asked, eyebrow raised in a high arch.

"Even on Ulfrost. Just because the Ice Wolves, are no longer about, does not mean it is without its dangers. You could be attacked by a wild animal, suffer a bad fall, or..."

"Eat from the wrong berry patch and suffer a sour stomach?" She sighed in adolescent distress. There was a minor pause as Kari's eyebrows raised.

"What if the Kresh attacked?"

"The Kresh are not going to attack us, Mother. Even if they did, they would be hard pressed to gain more than a foothold in the shallows. You only fuss, because I cannot shape like everyone else. Surely, were Vali, the Old Ones or any other shaper around to repel them with their sorcery, it would not matter."

"Strength of arms and sorcery, alone, cannot stave off all of this worlds' dangers. And I would still worry, even if your brother was with you."

"Aye, Mother, that is why I carry my bow. Not even a Kresh Berserker gets up from an arrow in the eye." Kari's eyes narrowed as she shook her head at her daughter.

"Did you at least fetch the herbs I asked you to gather?" Without answering, Asta's eyes grew wide. "I might have suspected as much," she growled, turning back toward the house.

"I can run back now, Mother."

"No need. When I saw you trotting off in the wrong direction, I gathered the reagents myself. Come now, daughter. The ships will be returning soon."

"Yes, Mother," she groaned, following Kari. Moving around toward the back of their home, she stopped at the small stable where they kept their horses. Three horses stood in the stable, noses down in the tall grass. Two were brown, spotted with white. The third, slightly smaller horse, which belonged to Vali, was a pure chestnut brown.

They rode on horseback, through the valley, making their way into Ulfrost village. Far into the center of the village, Asta could already see the amassing crowds, awaiting the return of the fishing boats. As everyone watched for the boats, Asta stared into the sea, her great nemesis. Since before she was born, the people of her clan, had abandoned their explorative heritage. With the power of the old ways vanishing, travel outside the waters of the archipelago and Tyrda Fell had grown more dangerous than ever. As the ships came into view, she remained transfixed on the horizon, longing to venture beyond it.

"Is it not odd for the helmsman, not to stand behind the helm?" A young, strong framed, red haired woman spoke, looking back to one of her many peers.

"Come now, Halla," another, red haired Viking, joined in. "You know Vali prefers to keep the sails in sight." The tall, broad shouldered man in question, smirked as he held one hand forward. The other hand held a leather braided cord around his neck, tightly.

"We will be home soon enough, I think." Halla spoke back to her twin, enthusiastically. "Aegir has been good to us."

"The Old Gods are gone, remember?" Haldr grumbled. "Who knows what rules these waters, now?" Another young, tall, short haired man turned his head from the bow.

"Halla! Haldr!" He called. "Since Ulf and Vali are busy, might you two give me a hand with these baskets?" The red-haired brother and sister groaned.

"Do you really need us, Abel? Why not ask Agni? He is the muscle around here," Halla said, tilting her head toward the thick chested, broad shouldered man, tending to the fishing nets.

"Ulf asked him to tend to the cargo boat, which you two are supposed to be loading," Abel grumbled, carrying a large basket in his arms, which he sat with the others, at the bow.

Behind everyone, eyes still fixed on the sail and the ocean beyond it, was Vali. A strongly built, brown haired, green eyed youth, he was among a rare class of his people, who could wield more than one element. The old sorceries had proven a rare gift among their clan, its strength having dwindled in the past two generations.

He focused on the wind currents around him, his familiarity with the spirits surrounding his home waters, giving him a welcome boost in strength. His right arm remained extended toward them, the shackle birthmark on his wrist shown in plain sight.

"Halla! Haldr! Have you two finished cleaning up the damage, yet?" Ulf, the oldest and largest of the group; a physically powerful and imposing man, spoke.

"Almost!" Halla called back, leaning over the side of the longboat and wrenching aggressively against the haft of a spear. As the sharpened, bone tip of the lodged weapon pulled free, she threw it atop a growing pile of similar weapons. Gathering up the bundle in his large arms, Haldr carried them to a small boat, roped off to their own. Another large pile of weapons already weighed the vessel down, before Haldr tossed his bundle upon it.

The weapons had belonged to a wandering group of Kresh, whom had attacked them, whilst they charted the waters far to the north of their home. The last living threat to their civilization, the Kresh, were a mysterious and wild people. Though repelled countless times over the century the isles had been settled, the Kresh remained a constant, looming terror to the people. Even fifty years after the last major incursion by the blood thirsty natives, none dared voyage to the furthest of the northern isles.

The various axes, knives arrows and javelins were rather similar to those his people used. Many of them had iron heads and leather wrapped handles the same as what he carried. Others still, seemed foreign to him. Primitive tools, carved from bone or stone, which had proven no less effective at penetrating the hull of their ship. Still, he found the contrast between the distinctly different weapons unsettling.

Far from the northern territories inhabited by the Kresh, they had found themselves lost within a dense fog. Using his gifts for shaping, Ulf had discovered their ambush only a moment before it was sprung. He shuddered as he dwelled on the wild howl of their attackers, though the fog had kept him from seeing any of them.

With a silent nod, Ulf turned his attention back to Vali.

"You handled yourself ably, Vali. Your wind shaping held out acceptably. Jerold has taught you well enough." The man grumbled as though disappointed with the result. "However, I expect much more, should you hope to serve as captain in my fleet. Your earth shaping is still lax, at best. You must press yourself further than anyone else, should you wish to make your mark." Ulf said. Vali looked back to the man, nodding his head confidently. He released his grip on both the shaping and the necklace as he turned to address the man. The necklace, a dark stained, braided cord of leather, bearing a small, stone chipped symbol for protection, fell to his chest.

"Thank you, Ulf, I will try harder," Vali answered. "But what do we tell High Chief Finna? Surely, if the Kresh are assembling a war party, they are plotting an attack."

"That is chiefs' and warriors' business. We shall discuss the matter with Finna and the other warriors. A flier has been dispatched and the other clans have been called. Our current task is complete. Now, it is time to rest and prepare. Care for your mother and sister and keep practicing your shaping."

"Yes, Ulf." Spoke Vali in a low tone, touching two fingers to the braided coil around his neck. The necklace served as a constant reminder, and now he considered how much he missed his mother and Asta.

"Be sure to come to Finna and my house, tomorrow afternoon, once the warriors arrive, for the clansmeet." Vali looked up at Ulf, curiously.

"Ulf?" His head snapped toward the war chief of Ulfrost.

"Finna believes you have earned your place, boy. Be at the meet."

"Aye," Vali answered, as the boat, reaching the shore, came to a sudden stop.

"Excellent work, warriors!" Ulf roared. "You each have your assignments. I expect these boats made ready by evening." He said, stepping off onto the beach and marched toward the grassy hillside, where near the entire village had assembled.

Shouldering his pack, Vali followed behind Ulf, looking to his peers, who each smiled at him. Hands rushed from the beach, to help unload the boats, as Abel and the others, lifted supplies over the hull.

Looking up to the high tops of the hilly slopes, leading to the valley, he saw his mother and Asta, awaiting him. With a deep sigh of relief, he adjusted his pack and attempted to blot out what he had seen on the northern end of the archipelago.

Now, only a few days by sea from home, they had been assaulted by their ancient enemy. Had it not been for the talented, and experienced crew of Ulf's ship, the Sea Wolf, they would have been lost. It had been an act of luck on the old warrior's part, which had saved them.

Shaping, the gift of spirit crafting, given to the Viking people by the gods of the Aesir, had served their salvation. Ulf, a strong shaper of earth and water, had detected the enemy deep in the fog, moments before they struck. Combined with Vali's mastery of wind, they had saved themselves from the worst of the ambush.

"Show us, Vali!" He could hear several of the younglings, cheer. Called back to attention, he looked around and smiled, seeing a few of the young women his age. One among them, Freyja, stared at him with fluttering lashes.

The daughter of Ulf and the High Chief, Freyja was surrounded by scores of her peers. As Vali eyed her freckled face, long flowing, radiant red hair and strong, feminine figure, the woman smiled at him, forcing his lungs to constrict. While Freyja's entourage and the children each practiced shapings of their own, it was Vali's, they all desired to see.

"Please?" Another round of pleas from the children, came around. Vali let out another sigh.

"Again?" Vali asked, broad smile on his face.

"Of course." Freyja laughed. "That is what you get for showing off."

"Vali, can you teach me to shape as many elements as you?" One of the older children asked. "I want to shape them all, as well."

"Perhaps one day," he laughed. "Start with mastering your first, before you try to take on a second element, though."

"How do you do it? How do you not succumb to the spirit shift?" One of his female peers asked. His cheeks blushed slightly, as he placed his right hand behind his head.

"I cannot say for certain." He laughed, uneasily. "I just feel anchored, I suppose. As deep as I wade into the current of the spirits, I feel something holding onto me."

"Show us!" More children shouted, interrupting the conversation. Vali conceded with a smile, returning his attention to the younger onlookers.

"Just once," he said, holding out a single finger. The children cheered slightly, as Vali stared down at the sandy beach and gently twirled. The winds flowing in from the sea, whistled as they shifted in the direction he indicated. Sand slowly trailed up in a gentle vortex, ruffling the clothes of the children, who cheered, excitedly. Vali smiled at his audience as he released the wind and knelt beside a piece of long since dried driftwood.

Closing his eyes, Vali touched the tip of his finger to the piece of wood. A slight crackle, followed by a flicker of light, and the wood sparked to life. His smile only grew as he heard the cheers. Opening his eyes, he slowly pulled his hand out from the belly of the flames. Looking up to the crowd, he nodded his head and turning back to face his family, saw only his mother.

"Excuse me," he said, adjusting his pack as he climbed the hill and looked up at Kari. Quickly, scaling the hill, he dropped his things to the ground with a loud, "clang," as he hugged her.

"Hello, Mother," he finally whispered, before releasing the woman.

"My little Vali," she smiled, patting him on the cheek. "Showing off again, I see."

"I did not do anything so spectacular as the other Shapers manage," he sighed. "However, I did not want to disappoint the children."

"Nor the young maidens, of course." Her smile widened as her son blushed. "I know that you have a soft spot for Freyja, especially."

"Well that certainly is not going anywhere. Either Ulf would skin me alive, or High Chief Finna, would use her Earth Shaping, to see me ground into swaller for the hogs."

"Quite possibly," Kari let out a tender laugh." Though you are the first child in our clan, born in the past three decades, to have such a knack for the Old Ones' sorcery. To have the gift take such a strong root is extremely rare. Most can only manage mediocre shapings, in one element. I would sooner suspect they would work you half to death than see such gifts squandered."

"Then I fear Ulf may already suspect me." He groaned as he stretched his sore muscles. "Where is Asta?" He asked, looking around.

"You know your sister. She always basks with envy when you use your sorcery, or when you leave without her."

"The glade, then?" He asked. Kari smiled.

"You know your sister better than I."

* * *

"Big block head!" Asta growled through clenched teeth as she slashed her iron axe through the air. She ran her weapon through several swings, stances and forms as she did when practicing with Vali's sword. As beads of perspiration dripped from her brow, she growled in the back of her throat.

"Stupid, show off! So eager to impress with your special talents to every available girl in town, you cannot even say 'hello' to me." She spun in a half moon and threw her axe, piercing the head of her practice dummy, which was already ridden with arrows.

"I sure hope that is one of the Kresh and not your big brother." Startled by both his voice and the sudden gush of salty sea air she loved, Asta turned to see Vali, leaning against a tree, biting into an apple.

"Not only are we not related, but we do not know which of us is older," she glowered, plucking her items from the straw stuffed, burlap sacks. "Besides, it is a poor likeness to you. Its head is much too small and contains far too much matter between its ears." Vali grinned, swallowed and took another bite of his prize. Asta continued to glare at him and the fruit in his hand as he passed by.

"I am not sure," he said through a mouthful of apple, leaning against the worn practice dummy, strands of straw, bleeding out at every angle. "With that color and stature, perhaps it is your real, birth twin?" He smiled as he looked down into her squinted eyes.

"Are you going to share that, or greedily keep it to yourself?" She asked, pointing to the blood red orb.

"Oh, this? No, this is mine," he said, taking another bite in front of her and then turning his back, walked away.

"Seriously?" She called to him as another, perfect red orb was pitched to her, from over his shoulder. Reaching out, she caught the fruit and treasured the sight of it a moment, before taking a bite. Her eyes closed in sweet ecstasy a moment, until her irritation returned.

"I am still mad at you!" She called up to Vali, his pack slung over his shoulder.

"I know," he said, continuing to walk away.

"Where are you going?" She called after him, taking up a light jog to keep pace with his much longer strides.

"To the barrow," he answered. Asta stopped briefly as her eyes widened.

"Truly?" She asked. "I thought that Ulf or one of the captains had to go with us?" She asked, slowly following him.

"Has that ever stopped us before?"

"No, but..."

"Trust me, it will be alright."

"Last time you said that, you angered a pack of fenris wolves, with a stray act of sorcery."

"If you get scared, I will protect you." He teased.

"More likely, I will save you." She growled under her breath.

"I heard that," he called back, his control over the air, able to pull distant sounds.

"Stop wind shaping!" She growled, even as he laughed. "And if I am going with you just to keep the spiders off from you, I am going to be mad." She could hear him chuckle more.

"Are you going to be this way, the entire day?"

"We will have to see. Keep leaving me behind and see if it gets better."

"You know that I have had little say in the matter. Can you swim, yet?" Asta folded her arms and looked away, without answering.

"Awfully dangerous to take you out on the open water, if you cannot, Sparrow." She remained silent, staring down at her feet as they walked. "While I am here, I would be happy to help you learn."

"I thought I asked you to stop calling me by that silly nickname?" She grouched, ignoring his offer.

"And as I recall, you asked me to stop calling you, 'Little Sparrow,'" he answered. "Something about you being a grown woman, now."

Just ahead of them, the trees parted, revealing the high reaching hills. The hilltops leveled out at their highest point, providing a large, flat expanse, which nearly wrapped around the entire island. Far to the western side, resided the barrow, where their people were entombed, and they honored their ancestors. Facing them, only the grassy slope of a hill could be seen. Walking around to the other side, revealed the entrance to the hand carved, stone structure.

"Vali, are you sure that it is alright for us to be here?"

"Losing your nerve already, Sparrow?" He turned back and smiled at her. Narrowing her eyes at him, she threw her apple core.

"Do not be so worried," he said, laughing. "I have permission to be here, now, and by extension, so do you." Asta's eyes grew wide.

"You mean?" She trotted up beside him, staring up at him as he moved inside the stone semi-circle.

"Yes, I am a captain, now." Walking over to the back of the barrow, he knelt over a stone seal, bearing the Valknut. Asta remained both silent and still, as her brother gently pressed against the three inner shapes of the unicursal symbol. She could hear the stone shift beneath his touch and with a slow, smooth twist of his wrist, rotated the hidden mechanism.

Stepping back slightly, they watched as the seal shifted sideways, revealing a spiraling stone staircase. Without a word, Vali collected a torch from the sconce on the near wall. Placing the palm of his hand over top of the cloth wrapped wood and closing his eyes, he willed it to ignite.

"This way, Asta." He said, leading the way down, holding up the torch to provide sufficient light for both. He ducked slightly, allotting for the low, earthen ceilings inside the barrow.

The deeper they ventured, the more the tunnels opened, offering many different paths, leading to various graves and dead ends. Vali and Asta, having made several unauthorized incursions in the past, knew which paths to take and avoid. Making their way down the stairs and through the expansive, underground network of tunnels, he brought them to a room filled with large statues.

"The Old Ones," Asta whispered, eying the statues, each of which stood with a large kiln at their feet. Setting his torch in the empty wall sconce, he walked to the center of the room. Before the ever-watchful gods of the realm eternal, Vali knelt and offered his silent prayer.

She remained a few steps behind, eying her brother, whose head remained bowed. She took a moment to glance up into the faces of the many statues. She knew most by name; Thor, Sif, Freyja, Heimdall and such. The few she could not name, perhaps had lost their names, themselves, to the fallen histories of their people.

"Vali, is everything alright?" Asta asked, kneeling beside him, while he remained silent a moment longer.

"I am to attend the clansmeet, tomorrow afternoon," he whispered. "In part, so I may be recognized formally and given my command. Also, I am to report sightings of a mounting, Kresh war party."

"They are planning an attack?" Asta jolted, raising her voice louder than she had intended. Her voice echoed through the winding tunnels a moment, before Vali answered.

"It would seem so. I do not know what will be decided yet, but I thought I might caution you and offer my prayers."

"I can tell you exactly what is going to happen!" Asta snapped. "After the meet, you, along with every other warrior, will sail north and face the Kresh. During that time, I will still be trapped here, waiting for any chance to escape this island!" Again, Asta turned away from Vali, arms folded over.

"Come now, Sparrow. You know that I..."

"No, Vali. I am not going to try to understand or see reason. I want to go out beyond this island! To go with you, beyond the fog wall. I want to see where we came from. You should not have brought me here, just to try softening the blow!" She continued to growl as she left Vali behind. Staring down at the floor, he turned his head to eye his pack.

"I also wish for you to go, Asta." He spoke to himself, touching his fingers to his necklace.

Chapter 3 – The Clansmeet

Vali had risen before the sun that following morning. Many of the village houses still dark, Vali quietly made his way to the outskirts of town. Looking about cautiously, he ensured he had not been followed, before calling out.

A thick fog rolled in off the Tyrda Fell, further hindering his vision. Making use of the cover it provided, he chose to reach out with his senses, opposed to dispelling it. He walked alone through the barren streets, looking upon emptied food carts and closed trade shops as he searched.

"Freyja, are you there?" He projected. A moment later, the young, dark golden haired, rosy cheeked maiden, crept out from the shadows, her furs tightly bundled around her.

"I was beginning to worry that you would not come," she spoke, a gentle, soothing quality to her voice. Smiling, Vali moved to her and interlaced his fingers with hers.

"Of course, I came, dear Freyja." He whispered as he stared into her hazel eyes. "You must know how much I have missed you." Freyja, nearly one and a half heads shorter, leaned into Vali, burying her head into his chest.

"Is it true you must soon leave, again?" She asked, without looking up at him.

"I will find out, tomorrow. Have your mother or father said anything?"

"Not openly," she stated, shaking her head. "I overheard them discussing it, before they took to bed." Vali let out a gentle sigh as he held the young woman. A lamenting silence hung between the two. More than half of his fleeting thoughts while away, had been of the woman in his arms. Even more so could be said of hers. Gripping her tighter, he grimaced.

"I presumed as much might happen. Perhaps it will allow me another opportunity to speak with your father. Maybe even earn his blessing."

"Vali, I am scared. I do not want you to go." A gust of chill wind caught them before he could respond. It carried with it a reminder of the sea, and the claim it held over them. He gripped Freyja tighter, and sighed.

"I wish to stay here, with you and my family as well. If the Kresh are preparing a war party however, the best thing for me to do is crush their efforts."

"I know. Do you promise to keep yourself and my father safe?" She asked.

"Freyja, you know that I cannot…"

"Please, Vali. Even if it is only to ease my mind." He sighed, closing his eyes as he squeezed her tighter still.

"I promise to do everything within my power to bring him back safely."

"Thank you, Vali. I cannot wait for the day you return, and we do not need to meet in secret."

"As do I, Freyja. As do I. First, I need to earn your father's approval. Problem is, he does not seem to like me too much."

"Perhaps, Uncle Grom can convince him otherwise? He will be at the meet, I presume?"

"The Direwolves were summoned, as well. Maybe he could. Until then however, I will keep trying my best to impress Ulf."

"I know you will," Freyja whispered, burrowing her face into Vali's chest and squeezing him tightly. Not long after, Vali turned toward home. Slowly making his way back, he heard footsteps, not far to his left.

"I understand now, why you always wish to be on Ulf's good side." A fully-grown man, with short blonde hair approached, his heavily muscled arms crossed over his chest.

"Ah, good morning, Jerold." Vali spoke, nodding to the older captain.

"Ulf and Finna's youngling the reason you could not see fit to remain on my boat?"

"Jerold, we, I mean, Freyja and me. We wish to be proper."

"Smart lad; Ulf, Finna, or both, would be like to crush you should you go about any other way. Still, it was good to have a trustworthy second. A little foolhardy I might add, but plenty capable."

"Even without Abel and I, you still possess one of the best crews in the fleet."

"Ah, yes, Abel. That boy of mine holding his own? Not dragging his feet, is he?"

"No, in fact, I want to ask him to be my second. He helps keep Halla and Haldr busy."

"Ha!" Jerold chuckled, lightly. "As if the brood of that fool fisherman, could do a Viking's share of the work."

"They have both proven themselves quite capable, even if they need to be kept up on."

"Useful? Those two?"

"Not only are they excellent sailors, but they possess an uncanny knack for finding food. Their water shaping has proven itself useful for all the ways which make it unusual."

"That is useful." He agreed, looking up at the waning moon. "You best get home, Vali. Take care of that mother and sister of yours, while you still can."

"I will. Good day, Jerold. I shall see you at the Clansmeet."

"Aye...blasted Kresh. I do not understand why they cannot see fit to keep to themselves." The man muttered, walking away. Carrying a steady pace, the trek placed him back home within a short few moments.

"Late night?" Kari spoke, the moment Vali moved to open the door.

"Early morning. I stopped to visit Freyja. I did not have the opportunity last night."

"I presumed as much. Sun will not be up for some time, yet. I would get back to bed, were I you. The clansmeet is not going to wait for you, simply because you are asleep in the hall."

"Yes, Mother," he said, moving inside the house. Kari entered just behind him, as Vali stopped, eying the closed door to Asta's room.

"It will be alright, son. She is upset, is all. She still loves you and only wishes to go with you. Talk to her in the morning, once she has had the opportunity to settle down."

"I love you, Mother." He whispered, kissing her on the cheek.

"I love you, my little Vali."

* * *

"Before we begin discussing the situation on the northern islands, I wish to first congratulate Vali, on earning his own command," Ulf said, addressing the many gathered clans in the assembly. Vali looked around the room at the gathered faces. Every chief and captain from Ulfrost and several from the nearby islands were present among them. He recognized most but also grew aware that of all of them, he was the youngest.

"Congratulations, Vali," High Chief Finna, the small, yet powerful leader of Ulfrost and of all the One Hundred Isles of Vala, spoke. Though streaks of white had touched her otherwise long, straw blonde hair and lines of age and position, had wrinkled her fair features, Vali marveled at the striking similarities between the chief and her daughter, Freyja.

"Now, while we are all overjoyed at the prospect of a new captain, we must first discuss a great threat, which endangers all Vikings." There was a loud murmur amongst the assembly, which sprang up as High Chief Finna, waited. She, having given the group a moment's reprieve, allowed her words to sink into the crowd. Vali, looking around, curiously stared at the crowd and lowered his hand to the earth at the rumble he felt there. Within a breath, the trembling grew, gently shaking the assembly, who all flashed their eyes to Ulf and the High Chief.

"As I was saying," Finna spoke, the same calm, collected tone she had held, before the interruption. "The Kresh have long since been an enemy to the Viking people. While they are hardly our only enemy on the Isles of Vala, they have proven the most formidable."

"Until fifty years ago, when our forbearers broke them." Vali turned his head to see the short but broad built, red haired and bearded chief of Falkest, Freyja's uncle, Grom. "They have not dared to leave the northernmost reaches of the Isles of Vala, since. Why now, do they present such a threat?"

"My captains," Finna began, "alongside my husband, journeyed to the northern islands, as part of a regular scouting and fishing expedition. They were attacked, well beyond the Kresh borders, by barbaric, scarcely clad, Kresh warriors. If you require proof..." She stopped mid-sentence, motioning to the front of the room, where Abel, Agni, Halla and Haldr entered. Each of them carried an arm load of the Kresh carved weaponry, Ulf had ordered brought back ashore.

Various instruments of war, ranging from spears, daggers and hatchets, fell to the tables. Many were carved from bone and wrapped in taut leather, while others were made of iron. Of the blanch white of the weapons and tools was occasionally stained with blood and dirt from use. Looking upon the many weapons, each appeared to possess little of the wear Vali was accustomed to seeing upon battle ravaged weaponry. He understood this meant his enemy took great care of the way they practiced the art of death.

"Here is your proof, fellow chiefs and captains." Finna continued as each of the four, spilled their burdens out amongst the nine, long tables. "Whether we care to admit it or not, we may already be at war." Again, a chorus of murmurs erupted from the assembly. This time, Finna did not bother to call them to attention. After several moments of tension, a single member from each of the nine tables, stood. At the far end of their table, Vali watched Ulf stand. Across the room, Grom stood, again. It was then that the room grew ominously quiet.

"Well then, war chiefs, what say you?" Finna asked.

"The Sea Wolves are at your command, my chief," Ulf spoke, drawing his axe and laying it on the table.

"The Horse Clan gives you their blades," another, thinly framed, dark haired man drew out a long-handled axe and laid it on his table. One by one, the chiefs pledged their weapons, until it came to Grom, who shook his head.

"I am sorry, my brothers and sisters. I cannot offer you my aid." An uproar boomed from amongst the rest of the assembly, save two more chiefs, who remained silent. After a few insults and challenges were exchanged between the rowdier of some of the rivaling clans, Vali sensed the rumbling beneath his feet return.

"There is no need for threats and insults," Finna began, once order had been restored. "We are all independent of one another and are only bound to appear, by the pact. Grom, brother of my blood," she started, directing her attention to him, alone. "I do not challenge your right to refuse, however, I feel at a loss without your aid. The

Direwolves have amongst them, the most still able to draw upon the sorceries of the Old Gods. While my own clan possesses only seven who may be called strong with the old ways, there are others who have pledged their hearts, who have little gift for them. May you please enlighten us, as to why you refuse?" Grom eyed his peers carefully, before responding. Wetting his lips and drawing in a deep breath, he spoke.

"I appreciate both the compliment and your understanding, I also recognize the tactic behind it. Simply put, my clan are well known for our handling of the many beasts of our island and the earth sorceries we use to maintain our lands. Recently, we have come upon a sickness, spreading amongst our livestock. We have managed to quarantine many of our sick, but it will take every hand I have, to see to it we have enough crop and meat to see us through winter." No one spoke as Finna thought over his answer.

"I understand your reasoning. Is there naught, which you might offer this campaign, or that which we might do, to ease your burden?"

"Sadly, all I might give are a few of my vessels. Little good they do us, beyond transporting goods from one end of the island to the other. As far as aid, I thank you, but we shall manage."

"Thank you, Grom. Keep your boats." Nodding his head, Grom sat. "One final question, Grom. If I may?" Grom stood again, to address Finna.

"Of course." He groaned, the smile lines on his cheeks upturning slightly, as his brow furrowed.

"How fairs your son, Urs? I see he is not among your council."

"Ah yes, Urs is well. He manages the relief effort in my stead."

"Of course, he does. Thank you again, Grom."

"High Chief," he bowed his head respectfully, before sitting.

"As for Chief Rolf and Chief Allie, I have already taken council with them. The recent storms have ravaged Dumah Island, leaving the entire population sheltered within the caves along the coast. Clan Fenris has pledged their aid to their neighbor." Several saddened, yet kind eyes went to the bereaved Chief Rolf, while others raised their flagons to Chief Allie, the young woman barely three years Vali's elder.

"Thank you, High Chief," Allie spoke, placing a comforting hand on Rolf's shoulder. "Perhaps it is the youth within me, hungry for battle, glory and adventure, but I shall admit, I am remiss. I have long hoped to see your Vali, in battle," she spoke, smiling enchantingly at the young man.

"Hopefully, soon and on better terms," Chief Finna spoke. "To those who have pledged themselves, the Sea Wolves shall depart tomorrow morning. Send word ahead if you must. Our ravens are at your disposal. We will prepare a forward camp on Fangor Isle. Be prepared to meet us there, in no more than two weeks' time."

"My men shall meet you there," Chief Bjarke, another massive man, spoke. "My captains' seconds are already on standby. I shall send word to them promptly."

"Thank you. As for the rest of you, may the Old Ones watch over you." Vali eyed the many Vikings, which now poured from the hall. He stood to leave with them, as he felt a gentle touch on the small of his back. Turning about, he stared down at the leader of his village and people.

"High Chief Finna," he spoke, clapping his right fist over his heart. "How may I serve you."

"I need you to hurry home. Fetch your mother and Asta for me. I have special tasks for all of you."

"I will, my chief. I am sure that Asta will be most thrilled."

"Please hurry, child." Vali ran from the hall, darting passed, around and in between, occasionally shouting a warning ahead, clearing out those barring his way. Reaching his chestnut horse, Tof, he prodded the horse into a full gallop, taking advantage of all the speed the noble beast could muster. By the time he reached his home, he needed to reset his jaw, before he could speak.

"Mother! Asta!" He called, entering the house. Kari was quick to respond, rushing to the door.

"Vali, what is it?" She asked, worried expression on her face.

"It has been decided that we are shipping out, in the morning. The High Chief has requested for you and Asta to return with me." Kari's eyes widened.

"Go fetch Asta. She is in the glen."

* * *

Asta hung upside down from her perch, staring down at the birds she had been sketching. A pair of red tailed falcons, sat studiously, examining the nest they were building. They paid her no mind as she dangled by her legs, no more than four lengths of her body, above them.

"Asta!" She heard her name. The falcons turned their gaze toward the source and a moment later, Vali appeared, riding along the deer trail. Hearing him call her name again, she sighed and rolling backward, dropped down to the next branch with feline grace. Carefully stowing away her things, she quickly dropped several lengths at a time, being sure not to disturb the nesting falcons. Dropping down from the lowermost branches, she landed in a perfect, three-point stance and looked up at Vali.

"I was sketching the falcons," she snapped, setting her pack down beside her scarcely used, fur boots.

"I apologize for interrupting, but the High Chief sent me to fetch both you and Mother." Asta's eyebrows raised, as she stepped into her boots and laced them.

"The Chief has never requested my aid before? Was the assembly that catastrophic?" Vali's gaze drooped slightly.

"I ship out with my crew, tomorrow morning, to help prepare a forward camp for the campaign. Fangor Isle houses an old stronghold used in the last major campaign against the Kresh. We will be headed there."

"But surely you will need hunters, gatherers, trackers, foragers, scouts and the like!" Asta's heart leapt for joy. Not one member of the clan would prove as well suited for the task as she. Despite her size, she was nearly as strong as most of the men in the village, almost as skilled in combat as Vali and at least twice as quick and agile as any of them. Without thought or warning to either party, she leapt up against the side of the horse and into Vali's arms, hugging him tightly as she remained suspended in air.

"Asta, we have to hurry," he spoke, patting her gently on the back.

"Right, of course," she jumped down and ran to her own horse, which listlessly munched at the grass. Leaping onto its back, she caught the horse's attention as it looked up to her slowly, as though having long since grown used to her energy. Gently squeezing her thighs against the horse's ribs, she sped off.

"Sure Asta, just leave your things here," Vali muttered, staring back at the rest of her belongings. Dismounting, he walked to the base of the tree and collected them.

They took a steady pace back to Ulfrost village, which set Asta's urgently blazing nerves on edge. Eager to receive her orders, she bounced up and down impatiently in her saddle. Maintaining a clear lead on her mother and Vali, she constantly found herself staring back over her shoulder.

"Come on. The chief said it was urgent," she growled to herself.

"She wished for me to hurry. Not Mother." Vali called from behind.

"Stop wind shaping!" She yelled back, hearing him laugh in response. Eventually, if not finally, they reached the gates of Ulfrost and soon after, the chief's hall. Dismounting, she waited for the others, before going inside. Walking beside her, broad smile on his face, Vali handed over her abandoned belongings and approached High Chief Finna.

"Ah, thank you for coming so quickly," Chief Finna spoke, causing Asta to glance at her mother and Vali with narrowed eyes.

"Of course," her mother spoke. "What seems to be the matter?"

"Tomorrow morning, the Sea Wolves will be disembarking for Fangor, to make ready the stronghold there, for an incursion against the Kresh."

"You will need skilled hands, adept at hunting, tracking, scouting, scavenging and foraging," Asta blurted out quickly and somewhat cohesively.

"Quite." The chief resumed after a brief pause. "There is another problem, which I pray does not come to pass."

"What is that?" Vali asked, his broad smile fading.

"Chief Grom, has unfortunately decided not to join us," she sighed.

"On account of plague, spreading through his livestock," Vali added.

"So, he claims," Finna nodded.

"You do not believe him?" Vali asked.

"Nor should she," Kari added. Both Asta and Vali rotated their heads between their mother and the chief, at a total loss.

"Why?" Asta asked, breaking the silent tension.

"Because, were there a plague affecting the livestock of his lands, I would have been sent to aid in the effort. At the least, some if not all my friends on Falkest, would have sought some form of aid, even if it were simply helping to concoct a treatment. No one has sent word to me of any such malady."

"Perhaps they have the situation better managed than it seems?" Vali suggested.

"That is a possibility. However, a second possibility exists." Finna spoke. Vali and Asta both maintained worried expressions as their eyes continued to pass between their elders.

"You fear he may try and seize control of Ulfrost, while the warriors are away?" Kari asked.

"My brother was most upset when I was chosen to take the mantle of High Chief. I do."

"Then what do you propose?"

"I cannot afford not to send the Sea Wolves, on a whim. We would lose all respect with the other clans. Besides, Grom is a tactician. He will wait until our fighters are either deep in the campaign, or at their weakest. He will not dare risk an attack on the village, especially not when there are others nearby who could help. I believe that it is in our best interest to keep ourselves on alert. Do everything that we can to prepare. To anyone else, it would appear to be in preparation of the Kresh. To Grom however, if his intentions are less than honorable, it may well ward him off."

"What do you require of us?" Kari asked.

"Vali, I want you to assemble your crew. Last I checked, you were short a set of hands. Should you not have someone in mind, I shall have someone sent."

"I have a replacement pair of hands in mind," he said, flickering a glance at Asta, who tried with all her power, to suppress the brilliant grin she felt creeping across her cheeks.

"Kari, I need you to double your efforts, to produce as much medicine and healing treatment, as you can. I will inform the others to prepare as though we are already at war."

"Consider it done."

"I will get everything ready for the voyage," Asta chirped excitedly.

"A most generous gesture," Chief Finna spoke, "however, I need you to prepare the east watch tower. If Grom invades, it will be from the east."

"That is a large task for one person," Vali said. "I will go and help."

"No Vali, I need you to see to your ship and your crew." Asta's excitement and enthusiasm began to ferment inside of her.

"I would have Asta on my crew," he explained. "No one on this expedition could provide for us as ably as she. Especially in this terrain."

"I am sorry, Vali, but we simply cannot spare her." She said, turning and looking to Asta, who trembled, having grown so angry, she fought back tears amidst her frustration. "Asta, I need you to be our lookout. Without one, we will have no advance warning if we are attacked."

"I wish to go with Vali." Asta said angrily, balling her fists tightly to help restrain herself.

"I know, child, but the village needs you, here."

"Vali needs me out there!" Fermented joy changed to desperation and exasperation. "Any of the others my age who are not going, could manage a simple..."

"Asta, please," Kari spoke.

"None of the others are as well suited. It has to be you." Finna tried to explain.

"But I have to get off this island! We are free, yet I am trapped! I want to go with Vali!"

"You cannot!" Finna spoke with authority, a rumble of earth escaping her. "You will be needed if we are attacked. No one else could prove a proper defense. I am sorry, Asta. If you want to leave so badly, you must wait until after this Kresh incident. Afterwards, you may join his crew."

"Asta, Vali, go," Kari said, eying the chief.

"But Mother," Asta started.

"I said, go!" Heartbroken, Asta fled from the hall, while Vali stared at the chief another moment.

"You have your orders, captain." Finna spoke in the same calm manner.

"I shall see to it that the arrangements are made." He spoke, a light growl in his tone. "I pray you make this right by her. Respectfully, I believe you have wronged her, my chief." Forcefully throwing open the flap of the tent, he walked outside. Looking to the post outside of the hall, he saw only two horses. With a sigh, he mounted his steed and rushed for the harbor.

* * *

That night, Vali returned home, long after dark. Quietly stepping inside, he looked around and saw no one waiting for him. With a hard sigh, he crept through toward his room. Making note of his rucksack by the door, he opened it and dug inside. Removing two small, leather bound parcels, he set them upon the small table. Eying them a moment, he looked to his bed, undressed and fell upon it.

Come the first calling of the cock, Vali's eyes opened. Rising from his bed, he dressed and exited the room. Seeing an arrangement of items already set upon the table, he removed a wedge of cheese.

"Mother!" He called, before biting into it.

"She already left!" He heard Asta grumble from her room. Turning in that direction, he gently tapped on the wooden frame.

"May I come in? I have to leave soon."

~ 36 ~

"Just get lost!"

"Come now, Asta. I do not know how long I will be away." He could hear an audible sigh from within.

"Come in but make it quick. I am getting ready to leave, as well." Opening the door, he immediately noticed Asta across the room, bent down and turned away, gathering her things. She was bare chested and wearing nothing but her undergarments. Shaking his head, he averted his gaze and stood with his back to her.

"I do not know why you always fuss." She noted, placing her hands on her hips and shaking her head. "They are simply breasts," she continued to mumble as she fetched a shirt and pants.

"Just showing the proper respect."

"We have bathed together, swam…" she stopped. "I suppose you swam. I do not see the point in wearing so much clothing. Not only is it far too uncomfortable, it seems entirely unnatural."

"All the same, I shall not gawk at you, while you are exposed."

"It is not as though we are related."

"All the same."

"You are a strange Viking."

"I have never claimed otherwise." Asta and Vali both shared a broad smile as light began to creep through the window flap.

"You must be on your way. Soon, the horn will blow."

"I wanted to at least say goodbye."

"And you have. Please go. Your ship and your freedom await."

"Asta, you know I want to take you with me, right?"

"Please go." She avoided his gaze as he reached out for her. Reigning himself with an inaudible sigh, he turned, placed the leather pouch on her dresser and left. Being sure to leave his mother's gift on her rocking chair, he fetched his rucksack and left.

"Excellent timing," Jerold spoke as Vali neared and dismounted. "Ulf was just readying to blow the summoning horn."

"Good, I worried for a moment that I had missed it."

"A captain should arise long before morning. You should be the one blowing the horn, not the one listening for it," Ulf chided.

"Yes, War Chief. I shall do better."

"One can only hope. Your vessel was built for speed and long travel. I have assigned the captain, who might best utilize such attributes. You and your crew must sail ahead of the rest of the company. Scout out the island and secure a path from the southern bank, to the stronghold. There are a lot of people relying on you. If you fall short, or allow any of your crew to slack, it will come with a price of blood."

"I understand."

"We will see," he growled once more, placing the horn to his lips and blew. The horn's call rang out far beyond the village. Were he still there, he would have heard it's call echoing back from the glen. Within moments, those who had not yet arrived, stepped out of their homes, fully geared and made for their boats. Approaching his own, he smiled at the smoothly polished deck and to his crew mates, who stood upon it.

"Hail, captain!" Abel, Agni, Halla and Haldr boomed. Beside them, another young woman stood.

"Hail captain, my name is Thala. High Chief Finna selected me to your crew."

"Well met, Thala. Would you by chance be the child of Haulsen and Mildred?"

"Aye, I am she."

"Welcome. Take the forward position. Abel, I need you at the helm." As Abel and Thala moved into position, Vali paced across the deck. Running his eyes over every inch of his vessel, named the Valiant, he smiled with pride. The late-night light had done little justice to the longboat's beauty. Slender, swift and elegant, Vali was confident that he and his crew, would easily overtake the rest of the fleet.

"The rest of the Sea Wolves, along with the entirety of the One Hundred Isles of Vala, depend on us refortifying that fortress. If any of you hold any reservations, now is the time to disembark my vessel." A long silence filled the air, interrupted only by the bellow of Ulf's war horn. Walking behind the sails of his ship, he turned to face his crew.

"To Fangor!" He cried as the sails of every ship in the harbor, opened.

* * *

The moment she heard Vali ride away, she felt pangs of guilt in her chest from seeing him off the way she did. His last departure had only taken him away a few weeks and though he was not traveling more than a week away, the wait would be longer. Morose that she had not taken the time to see him and angry at her station away, she threw her boots across the room. The pair, thudding against the wall, landed beside her pack.

Resting on the edge of her bed, she ran her fingers through her hair and gripped it tightly. Staring down at her feet, she allowed her welled up tears to fall, wetting her toes. She did not bother to slow their descent, before brushing her hair from her face and rising to her feet.

Walking across the room, Asta lifted her heavy bag, quiver and winter furs. Checking that the straps were secured, she slung them onto her back. Seeing the leather pouch near the door, she added it to her rucksack, before leaving the house. Stepping outside, she felt the heat of the afternoon sun, the warm breeze, carrying upon it the smell of the ocean. With a heavy sigh, she walked to the stable and mounted her horse. At the sound of the war horn, billowing through the valley, she felt her tears falling, again.

~ 39 ~

She camped little more than halfway to her destination. Wrapping up tightly for the cold night, she took shelter beneath a strong oak with a well-known hollow. Between her and the watchtower, several more camping grounds yet lie, used traditionally by hunters or large groups on route to the site.

She sat in silence, eying her simple fire, chewing on a collection of the provisions she had brought. Leaning back against the tree, she stared up at the stars and felt a pang of jealousy as a nocturnal flier passed overhead, traveling north. Taking a drink from her wineskin, she pulled over her bag.

Shifting it to lie across her lap at an angle, she unlaced the leather woven holes in the sack. Flipping over the flap of the bag, she sifted through her belongings. Rediscovering Vali's leather pouch, she took it out, opened the pouch and turned it over in her hand.

A hard, heavy lump landed in her palm, a piece of smooth, cool, glassy stone. At the top of the stone, was a small hole, which had been bored through the stone and a leather cord, strung through it. A hard lump in her stomach grew to match the one in her hand as she leaned closer to the fire. The stone, a small piece of jade, glittered with light, revealing to her, a white shape carved into its face, a sparrow. She held the stone to her heart a moment, before laying it over her shoulders and binding the cord behind her head.

She admired the gem around her neck a moment, running its smooth surface between her fingers. Closing her eyes, she stole her will from her desires and set to turn in. Laying upon her side, she watched the flickering flames, until at long last, she was lulled away by sleep's embrace.

In her dreams, she saw Vali with his crew, sailing north. She smiled at the show off, his vessel pulling far ahead of the fleet by his manipulation of wind and sail. She knew had he so chosen, he could easily arrive a day or more before the rest of the fleet.

She could feel the cool winds on her face and smell the salt upon them as though she were there. The hot sun had long since passed and night settled in. She could see a mixture of excitement, merriment and fear, upon the faces of Vali's crew.

Abel stood proud, steering the ship as Halla and Haldr kept busy about the deck. Agni made use of his powerful arms, securing riggings, while a final member, her replacement, she growled, examined her fellows. Toward the back of the ship, she saw Vali, locked in focus, as he kept the sails filled.

"Vali!" Abel called, looking back over his shoulder. Keeping his hands in position, Vali allowed only his gaze to shift.

"What is it, Abel?"

"I think you should get some rest. Though I would not know, I can only imagine that shaping to such an extent, must be exhausting."

"It can be, but I can manage on a bit longer." He replied.

"If speed is your end, rest. The winds have dulled, and you are expending your energy without cause. Agni and Haldr can row for a few hours, until you have recovered your strength." On cue, Agni and Haldr approached, nodding their heads.

"I thank you," Vali spoke, releasing his hold. The ship lurched slightly from the sudden loss of wind and the sails sagged on their masts. Agni and Haldr set to work immediately as Halla and the new girl lowered the sails.

"Be sure to wake me the moment we have a strong head wind. Ulf wishes us to have the stronghold made ready, as quickly as possible. While our best two hunters will secure food and supplies, it will be up to the rest of us to make the fortress ready to house a host of Vikings."

"You wish to have all of that accomplished by the time the rest of the fleet arrives? It will take us at least three days!" She could hear Haldr complain from behind the oar.

"I am hoping that by manipulating the wind, I can grant us at least two. With you two rowing at night, we may seize three."

"Four days to the south end of Fangor Isle," Abel smiled. "I do not believe such a trip has occurred even in my grandfather's lifetime."

"Well then, let us be certain we do not disappoint. The fleet has high expectations of us. I wish to show them we are better than even they hope." Asta caught herself cheering and smiling along with the crew. "Abel, you are in charge," Vali spoke. "Remember, as soon as the wind picks up."

"Of course," Abel answered. "You heard him, Vikings! We have odds to defy. Halla, Thala, after you have finished securing that rigging, get some rest, as well. When the time comes, I may need you to rotate with Agni and Haldr."

"Right!" They answered and readied to rest, as well. Asta followed Vali, as with a smile, he pat Abel on the shoulder and made his way to the crammed lower deck, traditionally used for storing cargo. Barely large enough to house nets and a few baskets, Vali slid his body beneath.

Making himself a comfortable roost, Vali laid his head back, propped up his feet and closed his eyes. No sooner had Vali's breathing slowed, did her vision of him, ripple. Slowly opening her eyes, she moved outside to see the morning sun, rising over the forest.

Brushing the few loose hairs from her face, she bound it behind her head. Gathering up her things, she tied her bag to her saddle and mounted her horse. Prodding the horse into action, she steered her to the east. The path through the forest, once well traversed, provided a straight shot to the watchtower. She rode the entire day without rest, relying on the strength of her horse. By early evening, the watchtower came into view.

Eying the old tower, she dropped down from her horse and quickly relieved it of its burden. Setting her saddle on the post, she walked up the large, stone steps of the mighty tower and threw open the doors. Inside, the signs of abandonment were abundant. Dust and cobwebs decorated the entirety of its interior. As though a harbor for a group of smugglers; a table, chairs and several tankards lay about, recently used.

"My, boys," a man with the runes for cowardly, seared into his face spoke. "Njord smiles upon us, this day. Here, we have come to stow our goods and we find ourselves a new toy." Dropping her rucksack, Asta drew her bow and pointed an arrow.

"Come now, love." The branded man spoke. "We will be gentle. You will probably even enjoy it. Shower you with the finer things in life."

"The finer things cannot be given or stolen," Asta growled. "One can only seize them for oneself." She called back, arrow groaning against her bow string.

Chapter 4 – Fangor Isle

"Vali, are you certain that you do not need to ease up?" Abel asked, looking to his perspiring friend. The vessel traveled with reckless abandon as the shaper poured as much strength as he could maintain into the sails. The salty spray kicked up all around them with every wave they assaulted. Vali, brow pouring with sweat, forced a half smile as his crew eyed him.

"How long have we been friends, Abel? Have you ever known me to take it easy, simply because it would be less difficult?" Abel smiled without looking back to his friend.

"Since we first learned to crawl, and no. Not even when sailing to the edge, though I would hope you might consider it this time, purely out of good sense."

"Ha!" Vali chuckled as the Valiant crashed down on another wave, spraying the deck with salty mist. "Cannot afford to let up just yet. We are making good time."

"Vali, we lost sight of the fleet two days ago."

"Yes, the crew have each taken rotations at the oars and Thala manned the helm, while you rested. We are each doing our part to the fullest and I cannot be the exception."

"Just do not overdo it. I dare not wonder by who's hand, but I fear I would not survive my return trip home, should something happen to you."

"Asta would likely shoot you. Mother would shape the earth to crush you."

"And that is why I chose not to think about it. Now, I am going to have nightmares. At least take a breath and get something to eat. You are beginning to look pale."

"Fine," Vali sighed, releasing his hold. The ship slowed visibly but hardly as dramatically as it had the first night. Taking up a seat on the deck, he took a long draw from his wineskin, before picking at the meal rations Halla had brought him.

Stretching out his legs, he closed his eyes, savoring every bite as he rotated his sore muscles. He could not admit it to the others but the amount of shaping he had undertaken was taking a toll on him. For three days, they maintained their pace. Had he ever considered using his gift for the old sorceries, to such an extent, he would have practiced.

"Be plenty of time for practice, once we all make it back," he muttered to himself, thoughts drifting to Freyja, his mother and Asta.

"Thala, help me with these nets!" Halla called out, struggling to haul them over the side of the deck. Purely out of instinct, Vali opened his eyes and rose to his feet.

"Please stay put, Captain." He heard the young woman call as she glided across the deck. Leaning back, Vali rested his head against the railing of the stern. A moment later, he could hear the two grunting in unison as they pulled the net onto the deck.

"Well boys, looks as though we are not eating dried food, today." Halla cheered as the day's catch, flopped about on the deck.

"Excellent," Abel started. "Haldr can prepare and cook these after we break camp."

"Break camp?" Haldr grunted. Staring out over the deck of his ship, Vali's eyes traced along the shoreline. Small twinklings of refracted light filled his vision as wild spirits danced about in vast abundance. A thick swirl of amassing, green and bluish hues rose from the horizon line. He smiled, as he stared at the sight.

"Land in sight. Prepare to break ground. Fangor Isle awaits."

"Four days," he could hear a general murmur about the group.

Within the hour, their boat struck the beach with a "thud." Wasting no time, the crew made quick work, unloading the boat. As Haldr made camp, Agni helped Halla and Thala with supplies. Vali, finishing securing the riggings, turned to Abel.

"I am going to scout ahead. Abel, you are to remain in charge."

"Let me go, Captain," Thala spoke. He stared at the wilds. Trees, rivaling even those on Ulfrost pierced the skyline. Though he could hear the various creatures on the isle, no trace of them could be seen. Turning his attention to her, he grinned.

"How much combat experience do you have?"

"None, Captain, but I have been instructed in tracking and hunting."

"I need to explain something to everyone," Vali spoke, worrisome tone in his voice. "The reason that Fangor was chosen as our forward camp, is due to the likelihood of the Kresh appearing here. There exists a definite possibility that we may yet encounter a Kresh scouting party. For those of us who have not heard the stories..."

"Captain," Abel interrupted. "We have all heard tell of what the Kresh are capable of." As he spoke, Vali noticed the looks upon his crewmen's' faces.

"Alright then," he said, looking around. "I will be back by nightfall. I want a lookout rotation and shelter to be made defensible.

Be safe," he added. Dumping all of his unnecessary supplies and covering up completely, he took his bow, sword and a pair of hunting knives.

"You too, Captain," said Thala. "We will be sure to have dinner ready for you."

"Thank you. I will make for the stronghold and then head back. I will not be long." Vali turned to leave but was stopped by a strong grasp on his arm.

"And should you not return by morning?" Abel asked.

"We are Vikings. We all know what is expected of us." He answered, before running off into the woods.

"Abel?" Haldr spoke. Turning back toward his command, Abel bore a stern expression.

"You heard the captain. I want camp made, a lookout posted and two hands on prepping a defensible perimeter. Get a move on. Those Kresh could be watching us as we speak." Without a word, each member of the camp broke out in a hastened effort.

Vali crept away, following the overlapping trees and thickets as he made his way up the hilly slopes. Reaching out to the countless woodland and earth spirits, he fell beneath a veil of their protection. His movements nearly undetectable, he moved carefully, sensing instinctively where to walk.

The climb was steepest, along the enclosed pathways, though he dared not stray from them, only to be picked off by a Kresh scout. There was little knowledge of how the Kresh operated and he was determined not to learn the hard way.

Reaching the top on his stomach, he dragged himself across the earth and peered out onto the trails. The pathways lay clear, not a soul on the road. He could feel the embrace of spirits all around him. Reaching out for their aid, he formed their influence around himself, muffling his steps and blending into his surroundings.

He waited several minutes, the hairs on the back of his neck tingling as he stood in wait. The jungle around him had grown silent in anticipation. A loud bellow of a roar, confirmed something nearby, followed by howls of a nature resembling a cry for help.

Instinct drove him to his feet as he ran up the path. He could hear the terrified howl of yet another voice ahead of him, accompanying the first. Reaching a bend in the path, he saw a series of broken branches and matted growth, falling over the edge of the next turn.

Setting an arrow at the sound of another loud bellow, he sneaked to the trodden vegetation. Peering over the edge of the slope, his eyes searched for the origin of the sounds of desperation. Instead, he found blood, lots of it.

Easing his grip on the arrow, he allowed his bowstring to relax as he slowly descended the side of the slope, reaching back with his left hand, gripping onto anything to slow his fall. Debris kicked up around him as he skidded to a stop. Halfway down, he could hear what he imagined was a massive bear, far from an uncommon nuisance toward Fangor's winter season.

Steering himself to a tree growing out of the hillside, he leaned against it and trained his arrow. Down below, the amount of visible blood grew. Beneath him, thrashing about in the grass, he saw something large, agile and hairy, with a broad muscular body. Vali's eyes grew wide as he witnessed the large, grey, oblong snout, dripping with blood from its toothy maw. His heart pounded faster at the realization of the cave troll beneath him, and the massive tusks, which depicted it was male.

It charged through the tall, lush brush, murderous intent focused upon something fleeing further into the wilds. A lone figure burst through the tree cover, a young, tanned, female, barely clothed with red crowned hair, which bled to ashen blonde. One bloody arm hanged loose at her side, while one equally bloodied leg, dragged behind her.

A terrible shiver crept up Vali's spine as he watched the young Kresh's plight. The woman howled in her strange tongue, defiant and fierce. Battling against his own conscience, Vali groaned deep in his throat, aimed his weapon and released the arrow. A loud, angry cry of pain escaped the troll's mouth, as the arrow bit deeply into its left shoulder, near the base of its neck.

Spitting a curse to himself, he drew a second arrow as the troll turned to face him. Using the moment's distraction, the Kresh attempted to crawl away. Its nostrils flaring, the cave troll spun back around and latching onto one of the woman's legs, threw her back toward the hillside. Striking the base of a tree, she fell limp at its trunk.

Releasing the second arrow, while drawing a third, Vali watched as his arrow sank into the thick, fatty hide around the troll's neck. By the time the third shot struck the troll's throat, the beast had cleared half the distance between it and Vali. Quickly trading his bow for his double-edged sword and one of his knives, Vali braced himself and leapt into the air.

Passing over top of the blindly charging troll, Vali flicked his arm and wrist, releasing the hunting knife, which sank deeply with a ripping "oomph." The troll slammed into the trunk of the tree, shoulder first, bending and snapping it as Vali flew through the air. His momentum carried him forward, forcing him into a hard roll. Turning back toward the beast, he watched as the troll stumbled, trying to grab at the knife, buried deeply into the center of its back.

Though his control of such forces was limited, Vali reached out to the elements around him for strength. Tightly gripping the handle of a second knife in his left hand with earth infused strength, he stepped forward and threw as hard as his tired body would allow. Blade over handle, the weapon whistled as it cut the wind.

Sword held to his side, Vali charged as the knife moved slowly through the air. Likewise, the troll lifted its head laggardly as Vali rushed to face it. He watched the knife floating forward, maintaining its course, until it sank into the center of the troll's skull.

The troll lurched backward as time resumed pace. Within reach of the creature, he tipped sideways and using the momentum of his entire body, back slashed across the beast's torso. The heavy strike threw him off balance, causing him to fall forward.

Spitting out a mouthful dirt, he slowly rose to his feet. Grabbing his weapon, he stopped just out of arm's reach of the troll. The large black and white eyes had already lost their luster, though Vali thrust his sword down through its chest, to be safe.

Removing his blade, he flicked it clean and slid it into its sheath. Looking over to the tree line, he saw the young Kresh. Not far from where the woman lay, he saw a shredded collection of fleshy pieces. Staring down at the woman, his breath caught in his chest. Though covered in blood and filth, her features were remarkably stunning, both exotic and beautiful. Her angled cheekbones, refined jaw and slight tilt of her eyes, captured his admiration.

Kneeling beside the woman, he placed one hand over her mouth and felt the steady release of her breath. He examined her various wounds. A series of nonlethal scrapes and cuts blemished her strong and delicate features, while the bones in her right leg tipped sideways at an unnatural angle. What clothing she wore, nary enough to cover her feminine aspects, was in tatters, revealing more than what Vali could politely observe. Taking a deep breath, he slowed his heart rate and stole back his focus.

"I need to get you patched up and tend to your friends," Vali spoke aloud, looking back to the troll. "First however, where is your mate?" Removing his weapons and arrows from the beast's body, he moved toward the nearby cave.

Immediately, carried back by the flow of air, he caught the pungent stink of dried blood and filth. Shaping the air around him, he funneled the worst of it away as he moved deeper. Cautiously creeping forward, he stabbed his way through the cave, in search of the female troll.

Weapon held steady, he neared the tunnel's end and slowed his pace at the sight of a distant, flickering of light. At the light's source, he saw a lone torch, lying just out of reach of another young Kresh. Laborious breathing and pain rent what strength the boy had remaining. His eyes rolled sluggishly to Vali, who swallowed hard to keep the contents of his stomach contained.

The trembling boy stared at Vali, eyes already fading, yet seeking final comforts. The hand which was not reaching for the torch, was clasped atop a ruined abdomen, entrails partially spilled out already. The stench alone, told Vali the Kresh only had minutes. Lying in the back of the room, the second troll lay, in much worse condition.

"I will not hurt you," Vali spoke, sheathing his weapon. Several other Kresh, none of which he would consider warriors, lay in ruins around him. Approaching the dying boy, he knelt beside him. The Kresh's eyes followed him, as Vali gently moved the torch to his hand.

"There is nothing I can do for your wounds," he said, examining the boy. "I am sorry." Small tears fell from the eyes of his sworn enemy. Though Vali could not dare show sympathy to an enemy, his humanity, gave him little choice.

"How do your people honor their fallen?" He asked, voice hard as stone. Their eyes locked, and the boy's expression revealed acceptance. With a trembling hand, he reached to the necklace upon his throat; a series of hand shaped beads of various colors and a central tooth which bore runes Vali did not recognize. The boy, with a jerk, tore at the necklace.

"Let me help you," Vali spoke, aiding the boy. Removing the decoration, he held it in his hands as a slight grin, creased the boy's lips, before the light faded from his eyes. Vali eyed the boy a moment, before looking around the cave.

Beyond the piles of bones, both animal and human, and the bloodied corpses around him, Vali could see a second tunnel. Lifting the torch slightly higher, he could see he had yet to reach the depths of the cave. The flow of spirits was nearly discomforting as their colors blended together deeper within. He nearly stepped further, lulled by their alluring chorus.

"No time to investigate." He whispered to himself, looking back to the necklace in his hand. "Someone has to honor the fallen."

Several minutes and several violent wretches from his stomach, later, he left the battle site with a vile taste in his mouth. Vali now held five necklaces, each slightly unique. Calling a fresh gust of wind to cleanse the foul smell from his nostrils, he reached the cave exit. Threatening to vomit once more, he stumbled toward the wounded Kresh he had saved. The young woman stared at him with entrancing silver eyes as he approached. Eyes, made of stardust, though they were filled with remorse and fear.

"Both trolls are dead," Vali spoke, presenting the necklaces. "I believe that you need these," he continued, extending his hand. The young Kresh reached out with her good hand and accepted the necklaces as Vali looked over her wounds, once more.

"I promise I will not hurt you." He said, vainly, certain the woman could not understand him. Still, as he produced his wineskin and tore a cloth from his undershirt, she did not fuss as he began treating her wounds. Gently cleaning the wounds, he only stopped at the sound of rustling from behind.

Drawing his weapons, he placed himself between the wounded woman and the source of the sound. From the tree line, Vali caught a glimmer of light as an arrow propelled toward him. Quickly summoning a gust of wind, he flung his left hand up and away from his body, causing the missile to fly wide.

Two more arrows flew toward his chest, to the same effect. Beside him, still on the ground, the young Kresh shouted in her strange tongue, her voice shouting in short, abrupt bursts of melodious sound. Vali remained stationary, defending the woman as two elderly Kresh, broke the tree line. They stood, glaring at Vali, each with an arrow already strung.

"She is badly hurt," Vali said, kneeling beside the woman. Both Kresh, hissed at him through clenched teeth as the young woman continued to shout. As their eyes continued to pass from Vali, to the girl and back, the young Viking thought he understood.

"I am here to secure the stronghold," Vali spoke. "I will leave her in your care." He said, sheathing his weapons. "No one deserves to die as troll food. I pray that we do not meet, again." Stepping backward, the elder Kresh slowly advanced, putting away their weapons as they neared their kin. The red crowned woman, looked back to him briefly, shouting something in her strange, beautiful language, as she and the other two Kresh, passed through the brush. Reaching the path to the fortress, Vali took flight, having lost precious amounts of time.

Chapter 5 – The Keeper of the Tower

"Asta, lord of the freemen," she joked aloud to herself, sitting atop the watchtower, kicking her feet upon one of the plundered chests she had claimed from the smugglers. The sun was high in the sky, shining down on her back as she continued to ponder.

"High Lady Asta, queen of the smugglers?" She mused aloud, turning to glance at her three captives. Of the three, the youngest was the largest but most timid of the group. He possessed a head of unevenly chopped black hair but lacked the facial hair of the others. The elder of the group was also the best groomed, his long silver hair and beard neatly combed and braided. Of the three, the elder was also the smallest. Quickly losing interest, she turned her gaze back to the ceiling, to dwell on her new name.

"How about, Wretched Wench?" She heard one of the group call from down below. Turning her head back to where the three men below her were kept, she smiled.

"No. That just does not seem to fit as well," she muttered to herself. Rising to her feet, she walked inside from the balcony and stared down at the three men in the cages, which hung from the ceiling. The leader of the ill intending trio snarled at her, distorting the coward's brand on his face into a more disgusting shape.

"You just wait until we get out of here, you little guttersnipe! You might be feeling high and mighty, now but eventually, you will have to sleep. When you do, I will get out of this cage, tan your hide so well I could wear it and see how proud you feel after me and the boys take our fancy with you."

"I thought I gagged you?" She asked, seeing the cloth around his neck.

"Nothing going to keep me bound!" He spat. "I am getting out of here!"

"Out of curiosity, do you remember what landed you in that cage?"

"I will admit, you took me by surprise." He growled. "Not many women, what know how to fight where I am from. It will not happen, again."

"And is it not the reason your men each have a hole in their foot, because they tried to escape?"

"Won't be doing that again," one of the two henchmen grumbled. "She threatened to take gonads, next time. I would sooner face my maker with them than without."

"When they take you back to the village, it will be as slaves, not feed for the hogs. Gods only know what manner of rot you three are carrying."

"Lady Viking?" The third man spoke. Asta raised her eyebrows at the oldest of the three.

"Yes?"

"Is it to High Chief Finna's authority that we are to be surrendered?"

"Aye."

"And you have already sent word of our capture?"

"Aye." The man thought a moment, before speaking.

~ 58 ~

"Then I wish to carry a message to your chief." He said, alarming the branded man.

"You had better not, you old duffer," he growled, elbowing the man in the ribs. The old man sagged to the side from the force of the blow and then fell silent.

"Strike that man one more time and I will run you through, then spill your guts below you."

"Do it!" The coward growled. "Better to be killed by a shapeless whelp, such as you then unleash the fury of Helheim as he suggests." He said, jabbing his head in the direction of the man.

"What are you talking about?" Asta asked. The man turned away from her.

"You will see soon enough. Go ahead and keep us in this cage. We will be safer as your prisoners than we will be as his enemies."

"Whose enemies?" Asta demanded.

"Not saying a word." The man growled, turning his gaze away from his captor.

"Have it your way. You have told me enough to know that your master approaches. I shall be sure to send another flyer, praising your cooperation."

"You cannot!" He yelled, leaping at the bars of the cage. The elder man shook his head as Asta's lips creased in a smile.

"So then, you have an ally within the walls of Ulfrost? I shall be certain to personally address the letter to High Chief Finna and code the message. Thank you for your cooperation." She smiled, walking away. She could hear the leader groan, presumably from one of his fellows, striking him.

"Might as well tell her, now." The elder man suggested. "We are all as good as dead, unless we cooperate, now." She could hear an audible growl from below. A smile on her face, Asta sat on the ledge, just out of sight and waited.

~ 59 ~

"Grom knows the chief suspects him of an attack. He has no intentions of attacking this island. He plans to bide his time and wait out whatever it is that is to befall this land."

"And what is it, which is soon to befall us?" She said, eying the elder man.

"Even I cannot say." He said, looking down at his feet.

"Still afraid of the repercussions?"

"Of course. However, we do not know."

"What do you know?"

"Chief Grom and his daughter are often spoken upon the lips of those who serve in shadow." The elder man spoke. "Word is that his youngest daughter, the prophetess was granted a vision, which nearly killed her."

"What did she say?" Asta asked.

"I do not know. It had already been two weeks when we departed, and the lass had yet to awaken," the younger, unmarked companion spoke. Asta turned and stared back out the window, where the chief's raven waited.

"I will send my letter. Enough to warn the chief but not to raise suspicion. Perhaps we may all survive this threat. If Grom has decided to remain in his own land, why then, has he sent the three of you?" Now, it was the three men, who smiled.

"Grom did not send us. We saw an opportunity with all of your warriors away and attempted to seize it."

"Then perhaps you might have attempted a method, other than rape or murder."

"It is the way of his lot," the elder man spoke.

"I did not see you try and stop him."

"It is also the way of his lot to murder the elderly." The man added.

"I still could," said the coward.

"Well, as long as that is to be the case, I will kill you and have only one thief to contend with." Asta mused. "Well, I suppose you better get on with it, then."

"What?" The two arguing men gasped as the third stared.

"It is simple math, really," Asta said. "Transporting one prisoner back to Ulfrost is no problem. Three, on the other hand, might slow me down and I am not spending the night with you." The three continued to stare as Asta went about her business. Once her letter was finished, she tied it off to the raven's leg and watched jealously as it flew away.

It had already been four days, since she had to say goodbye to Vali again, but it already felt like weeks. Leaning over the balcony, she locked eyes with her mortal enemy, the sea and glared. She looked back to the westward bound raven, as it passed beyond her vision.

"Where were you lot planning on taking all this plunder, anyway?" She asked, gesturing toward the bags and chests.

"South," the coward grunted, averting his eyes.

"Any particular reason?"

"The Kresh are moving from the north. It made sense to us to get out of the way."

"A fair plan, I suppose."

"Why?"

"I am just bored. I was not planning on looking after you three when I was sent this way."

"Lady Viking, might I ask you a question?" The youngest man spoke.

"I suppose it cannot hurt."

"As capable a fighter as you are, why stay behind and not accompany the fighting?" An irritated growl escaped Asta's throat.

"I did not choose to stay behind. Chief Finna ordered me to come here. I was supposed to sail north with Vali."

"Why you?"

"The Chief thinks I would only be a burden to Vali, because I cannot swim." At this information, the coward burst into a fit of laughter as the other two, remained quiet.

"Ha, you call yourself a Viking and you cannot swim? How are you supposed to sail the Isles of Vala, if you have to remain below deck?" Asta looked over to her bow, which seemed to sparkle as though calling out to her.

"It is not so uncommon," the elder man spoke. "I have known scores of explorers, who could not swim or sail. How are you as a deck hand?"

"Vali has taught me everything I need to captain my own crew."

"Except how to tread water," the scarred man muttered.

"Who is Vali?" The young man asked.

"The boy I was raised with."

"Your brother?"

"No! Vali is not my brother. We were just raised by the same woman, from the time we were infants."

"Does that not make him your brother?"

"Not from the way I see it!" Asta spoke aggressively. Sitting in the cage, the elder man smiled.

"Please explain," the elder man spoke.

"Well, it is not as though we have ever called one another, 'brother' or 'sister.' Even saying it now, just seems wrong to me. I have to imagine he feels the same."

"Tell me, Lady Viking," the elder man began. "Is your Vali bound to another?"

"No?" She answered, an odd sensation behind the word. "Though he chases the chief's daughter."

"And does he treat you or this woman differently? Does he treat any of the other young women, in the manner he does you or her?"

"I have no idea how he acts. Vali is Vali, through and through. What does that even matter?" She asked, slightly agitated.

"Ash him some time. It is quite important." The elder man added.

"I just might," she snapped, before walking back outside, onto the balcony. Taking up her perch, she rested her feet on the railing, stretching her long, bare legs in the sun and stared out over the ocean.

"Vali…I wish I was out there with you. I miss you."

Chapter 6 – Unseen Threat

They set out in force for Fangor fortress the following morning, Vali lead the troop, who struggled to maintain his hastened pace. He smiled to himself, emboldened by the surge of energy provided by the wild spirits. Thala managed to keep close to him, though they were forced to stop periodically, while the others caught up to them.

Tales of Fangor's connection to the Old Ones' sorcery had been told long before the days of Vali's boyhood. The site, which had long held the interest of the Vikings, was infested with, more so than populated with wild spirits. Unlike those dwelling on long since inhabited islands, primal spirits had an ill habit of lashing out at those who sought to alter their natural habitats.

Also, in opposition to their docile relatives, wild spirits made long term settlements a nearly impossible task. These spirits, still retaining their baser, primal instincts, were by nature, devilishly difficult to work shapings with. However, there was no doubting the strength they might grant one, whom the fickle spirits had taken an interest in.

Fortunately, it appeared to Vali as though the spirits of Fangor fancied both he and the young shrine maiden. Unencumbered by the dangers of the previous day, he took the time to appreciate his surroundings, opposed to simply evaluating them. Their eyes searching, Thala pointed out several foreign sources of food Vali did not recognize.

Gathering what they could as they traveled, Vali stopped briefly upon the hill where he had spotted the Kresh. Noticing his unusually tense stature, his crew peered cautiously over the ledge. Taking note of the damage wrought in the struggle and the corpse of the troll, still at the base of the hill, they glanced back at their captain.

"Is this the place?" Abel asked, the answer obvious. Nodding his head, Vali forced himself to look away.

"Let's keep moving." He grunted. Thala remained behind briefly, eyeing the landscape and carnage only a moment, before moving on.

Near midday, they reached the old Viking stronghold, only to find the site in complete disarray. Among the many structures of the once proud fortress, only the walls and high towers remained. Through them alone, could the party imagine the former glory the historical landscape once held.

Long had it been since an excursion of Vikings had frequented the structure, and evidence to such lack of attention was evident. Within the stone walls, much that might have identified the area had been ravaged by time, and the wiles of the wild spirits. The few interior buildings, which had originally existed, were little more than broken down structures, long since left unstable. Setting down their belongings, they set to work immediately, their brothers and sisters in arms only a short distance away.

"Let me be clear, you deviated from your given task, to fight a cave troll, who was in the process of mauling a young Kresh woman, with the intention of saving this woman's life?" Abel whispered that night, on their way back from the evening hunt. Constantly, he looked about for eavesdroppers, as his own voice battled between monotone chiding and cries of hysteria.

"No one deserves to die that way. Not even the Kresh." Vali sighed, having given up withholding the telling of his first contact with the Kresh.

"True enough, but then to tell them where we are headed. Do you not think that you could have left that part out?" Vali grumbled at Abel's point. He was unsure himself, what had possessed him to warn them of the incoming troops.

"I might have, alright? These Kresh were not warriors. Some of them were too young, others, too old. The red crowned woman was likely the only one our age. She was in my opinion, the only one who was not out of place."

"But why would the Kresh send such untested tribesmen, into the wilds of a place as dangerous as Fangor?" Abel asked as they continued to rise along the high reaching trail.

"I do not know," said Vali, shaking his head as the fortress came into sight. Already, Haldr and Halla, had lit the evening torches for their night watch. Agni stood within, Thala beside him, tidying up the stronghold for the arrival of the clans.

"But you are just now, bringing this to my attention?" Abel asked, as though disappointed.

"I did not know how to tell you. I thought it would be best to wait, until after we had a defensible foothold. We were already on the lookout for an attack. The information could not have helped us any."

"True, but it's me, Vali. You know you can trust me."

"I do," Vali said, clapping Abel on the shoulder. "But I can also depend on you to worry unnecessarily."

"True again," Abel answered with a smirk. Approaching the stronghold, they acknowledged Halla and Haldr, who were both staring out, vigilantly, bows held in their hands. Looking about at the amount of work they had managed, thus far, Abel sighed. "Well, Vali, I think we have done well for two days."

"The fleet should be here, tomorrow or early the morning after." Vali groaned. "There is still much to be done."

"I wouldn't worry about it too much," Abel shrugged. "We managed much more than anyone else could have. You still have your trophy to show?" He asked, looking down at Vali's hip pouch.

"Yeah, front fangs of a Fangor troll. I placed them with my things in the bunkhouse."

"That's bound to impress Ulf and the others. Arrived two days earlier than expected, prepared a defensive point for use against the Kresh, and managed to slay a cave troll, which would have proven problematic for the campaign. All in all, I would call the past two days quite successful."

"Yeah, but you are not Ulf and it is not your daughter, I hope to take as my companion."

"True. Would not matter though. You still would not get my blessing," Abel smiled at Vali's wounded expression and laughed, as he was slugged in the arm.

"A blight on your blessing, then." Vali smiled. Abel held up both hands in surrender.

"Hey, save it for Ulf. He is the one you need to impress."

"Wish we had another day."

"Ah, story of the world. Best to make use of the ones you've got. Never know how short lived they will be." Reaching the center of the camp, both men sat near to the cooking fire and rested themselves against the short wall, dividing the road from the campfire.

"How did the scouting go, Captain?" Thala asked, carrying a bundle of wood in her arms. Depositing it atop the already gathered pile, she stopped and waited.

"Well. We saw some game, though we failed to catch anything, since yesterday. Hopefully, they are only spooked from the trolls that were here and not from another pair. Were I to never again see a cave troll and its...habits, I would live happily."

"Asta would be looking for another one," Halla commented. "She is quite possibly the craziest Viking I have ever seen."

"She has her moments," Vali smiled. "She wanted to come with us." The others near the fire, save Abel, stared at him.

"Why didn't she?" Haldr asked. "We could have used her help."

"High Chief Finna had other plans for her. Beyond that, I cannot say."

"Does your sister often stay behind?" Thala asked. Vali nodded.

"Much to her chagrin, yes. However, I warn you. Do not refer to us as siblings around her. She hates that."

"But is Kari not your Mother?"

"Adopted. Asta and I are both from another land, beyond the fog." Again, everyone, save Abel, tuned in, scooching closer.

"From beyond the fog?" Halla spoke, mystified tone in her voice. "What lies out there?" Vali shook his head.

"Nothing as far as I know. Mother was told we were the last to escape. We were only infants at the time."

"Do you think your Mother knows more?" Thala asked, leaning over Halla to gain a better vantage.

"It wouldn't matter if she did. Mother has asked me not to venture out, without Asta. Though she is like to handle it better than I, I could never bring myself to place her in so much danger."

"Odd thing for a Viking to say?" Haldr commented. "I thought the thrill of the adventure came from the danger it presents. Have you never wanted to see what is beyond?"

"I have no opposition to danger," Vali smiled, ignoring the question. "I am simply protective of Asta."

"Why?" Haldr asked. "We have seen the way she fights. She is easily better than the rest of us. Probably holds her own against you, too."

"That she does," agreed Vali. "She also tends to take viable threats for granted. She often acts as though she were invincible. As though the Aesir themselves, brought her into the world."

"Now that, I have seen firsthand." Abel laughed, rising to his feet. "Have all of the preparations for the stronghold been made?" He asked.

"Everything Vali asked." Thala confirmed.

"Good," Vali spoke up, grateful for the diversion of topic. "Tomorrow, I want everyone not on guard duty, to join in the gathering of supplies. I need one volunteer, to take the southern edge, near to where we expect our troops. Your job will be to guide them here, once they arrive."

"I will do it," Thala stood. "I will signal once they are in sight."

"Thank you. Everyone else, finish eating and then lights out. Abel, go ahead and get some rest. I would like you to relieve Agni on the next watch."

"Very well, Captain." Abel confirmed, returning to his plate.

"Same goes for everyone else. Make sure to get some rest. We still have a lot of work ahead of us."

"Aye!" They called as Vali, cleaning his plate, rose and walked to the gate, where Agni stood, both his food and drink, untouched. He remained in an awkward light, his large figure barely noticed amongst the light shadows cast by the flames of the nearby torches.

Looking out over the downward slope of the hill face, Vali took in the high trees, their lush greenery, filled with nighttime ambience. Fireflies lit up the night in small clusters, while the creatures of the night, called out to their brethren as they searched for prey.

"Aren't you going to eat something?" Vali asked, eying the massive man.

"Afraid I haven't much of an appetite, Captain." He responded, eyes forward, watching the road.

"Are you feeling ill?"

"Nerves, I fear. Don't much care for killing. Fancy myself more of a builder, or fisherman."

"I am not too fond of it, myself. However, it becomes necessary if you do not want someone or something else to kill you." He allowed the comment to hang in the air. The reply, he felt, came after too long a hesitation.

"Aye. You needn't worry about me. I will not let you down, even if it comes to that."

"I am counting on you," Vali said. "Do you need anything?"

"To know that all of you are well and good, behind me," he replied.

"With you at our side, we could be no other way." He smiled, gently clapping his stalwart friend on the shoulder. "Wake me at the first sign of trouble," Vali said, turning back toward the camp.

"The Kresh?" Agni called after him. Vali stopped and looked back over his shoulder.

"What of them?"

"They are our enemies, right?" Now Vali, his thoughts clouded with uncertainty, hesitated.

"That is what everyone says. As far back as any stories go, the Kresh have always been a threat to the Vikings on the Isles of Vala."

"What do you think?" He asked. "I am not interested in what the oral stories say. We are not on Ulfrost. Away from our own clan, the captain dictates the law. What do you think of the Kresh? I have never seen one, though I am sent to kill them." Vali did not answer for quite some time. He had no explanation to offer him. His first encounter with the Kresh and he had found himself trying to save them.

"I think that in the past, they have tried to kill us, take from us and destroy what makes us Vikings. I think that makes them my enemy."

"Is that what we are doing here? Setting up a war party, so we can wait and see what they do? For the sake of what was done half a century ago? Or are we merely on our way to spill blood, unnecessarily?"

"We will find out once everyone arrives."

***

The following morning, Vali, dressed in hunter's garb and made his way through the forests of Fangor. Haldr, Halla and Thala, each had taken separate routes from the stronghold, to scout the trails. Vali walked the northern route, eyes wide, for any signs of food or the Kresh.

Into the thick of the island forests he ventured, carefully avoiding the many broken bits of wood, which covered the forest floor. Dipping and swaying, he avoided the low hanging vines, until he came upon an old tree, which towered above the others. Looking up to it, he chose his vantage.

His senses tingled from the haunting caress of the wild spirits of Fangor. They tickled at the edge of his consciousness, an unnatural, electric hum, which left the hairs on the back of his neck, raised. Despite this, he confidently carried himself forward. For now, they were only curious.

Bow on his back, he climbed into the old tree, eyes searching for signs of danger. Reaching the lowermost branches, which were as thick around as he, Vali pulled himself atop and looked about. An uneasy calm silenced the forest around him. The hair on the back of his neck stood on edge as his eyes scanned for that which he could sense watching him.

Vali placed his hand up against the old tree, sending out his presence through the ancient monolith's roots. Life tingled all around him, sensed by the deeply buried network of limbs. Sensing a large flicker among the rest, he turned his eyes northeast and saw a rustle in the far thicket.

Before he could draw his bow, or even yell, the presence vanished. With a shaping of earth and wind, he dropped down from the branch, landing with little more sound than the displaced crunching of the leaves and crept forward. Peering through the bushes, he saw nothing but more forest.

Curiosity guided his steps. He followed the direction the presence had fled, swimming his way through the thick vegetation, which threatened to suffocate anything venturing off from the road. He could feel uneven ground beneath his feet, as the earth slowly slipped down and away. Ahead of him, the trees parted slightly, allowing several rogue rays of sunlight to press through their grasp.

Stepping toward the source, into the opening, Vali found himself standing over top a large canyon, which cut through the forest. Staring down passed his feet, he saw a flowing river, cutting through the heart of the forest. His eyes searched the entirety of the expanse, but he saw no one.

Shrugging his shoulders, he turned back and walked toward the ancient tree. Pressing his way back through the thick bushes, he came out to the clearing and made to take up his perch. A distant sound came to him, muffled by the vastness of the forest. Curious, he resumed his climb, rising halfway up the tree with such speed, Asta may have been impressed. Rising to the top of the tree, he turned toward the sound of another distant booming. Far out to sea, he could see the fleet.

***

"I see that you and your crew have indeed managed to reach Fangor, before the rest of us." Ulf grunted his approval as he followed behind Vali and his crew, as they led the Sea Wolves up the path to Fangor stronghold.

"Yes, Ulf. We have been quite busy, these past few days."

"Few? You managed the voyage in four days?"

"Yes. There were even cave trolls, which had to be disposed of." Ulf snarled distastefully at the news.

"Perhaps everywhere you might go, where others ignore, you will find trolls. Blighted beasts they are. The filth of Helheim. You should have waited for more to aid you. Trolls have been known to overrun and dismantle entire squads."

"I should know," Vali whispered under his breath.

"It was foolish of you." Ulf added.

"I shall be certain to await help, next time."

"I do hope that you do. The next time could quite easily become your last time. The clan would be worse off, with one less shaper in their number."

"Is there anything more I can do, Ulf?"

"Have there been any sightings of the enemy?" Ulf asked. Vali's throat dried and any words he could think of, slipped through his fingers. He paused a moment longer than he feared he ought to, before looking back to Ulf, who stared impatiently, awaiting his answer.

"The trolls had killed a number of people. I found pieces all over the cave, though I could scarcely identify them from anyone else." Ulf thought a moment, pulling at his beard as he thought.

"Then it is possible that some Kresh survived. Did you see any when you encountered the troll?"

"I am unsure," Vali murmured.

"Pardon? Did you, or did you not?" Ulf spoke, his tone growing more threatening.

"There was a lot of chaos around the troll. It charged straight from its cave, nearly taking me off guard. A number of creatures fled from the beast. I cannot say as though I paid any particular attention to any of them." He lied, of course.

"You have never seen chaos like it before?" Ulf raised an eyebrow at him. "It was my understanding that you have fought off wild beasts on numerous occasions."

"I have. However, I have never seen chaos such as that. I will admit, it came as a surprise."

"And yet you still managed to fell the beast."

"Yes, I relied on the training I have received, along with my own instincts, guts and shaping."

"Add in some sense and you may yet go far." Ulf grunted, turning away. "As you were, Vali. Tend to your crew. Thus far, it looks as though you have done well."

"It was a group effort."

"You would have failed, otherwise. Be ready by dawn. We will begin sending out forward forces along the waterways. Should there be any Kresh in the area, we will find them close to water."

"Of course, we will be ready." Vali said, moving back down to the courtyard, where his crew awaited him.

"Do we have new orders?" Abel asked, the rest of the crew behind him, eagerly listening.

"We make for the waterways, come morning. Ulf wants us to accompany him, while the others make final preparations and get some rest. We are to scour the waterways, in search of the Kresh."

"And should we find nothing?" Abel asked.

"Ulf will not stop until we have." He saw Agni's gaze drop. A silence fell upon the rest of Vali's crew, tired, hungry and as uneasy as they were.

"Should we find nothing on Fangor, we will fortify this forward camp, while a party sails forward to the next location."

"And when will we stop?" Agni growled. Vali and Abel both, looked around, eyes in search of anyone listening in.

"I...do not know." Vali answered, though no one was fooled. War was the Viking way. The way they grew. The way they proved themselves. The way they defended their homes. Whether they found the Kresh on Fangor, or any of the other One Hundred Isles, they would not stop, until they found the Kresh war party and crushed it.

"It would be best that we all rest up, while we can. We set out, first thing in the morning." Without another word exchanged between them, they walked to the mostly repaired bunkhouse. Vali rested his head and propped up his feet. Though he closed his eyes and relaxed, sleep eluded him.

"Asta..." He whispered into the darkness of the bunkhouse, the sound of snoring all around him. "I pray to the Old Ones, you are safe. Please be safe."

***

"Vali, it is time to wake up." He heard a whisper near to his ear. Vali's eyes opened slowly, as he saw Thala, her hair still down in long flowing strands, hiding all but her luminous ember eyes.

"Is it?" he asked, rising to a seated position and planting his feet on the floor.

"I have yet to wake the others, but yes," she answered, moving from him and approaching Abel's bunk.

"Thank you, Thala."

"Of course, Captain." She said, gently waking Abel. Vali was unsure when he had fallen asleep, though he wished that he had not. Within the hour, they had boarded the few ships, which would venture out. Vali stood at the bow of his ship, guiding Abel and the others, through the foggy channel as Haldr, Halla, Thala and Agni, rowed.

They followed close to Ulf's ship, as the man steered them through, nearly blind, without incident. By midday, they reached the place Ulf had earlier described as the most likely point for the Kresh to camp. Their boats touching the bank, Vali lowered the anchor and jumped to the bank. Already, he could feel the ever-watchful gaze of Fangor's oldest denizens, tickling at the hairs on the back of his neck.

"Come now, Vali. Do keep up!" Ulf growled, already half way to the top of the hill. Trotting after the man, Vali readied his arms as he followed behind the man. He could hear his and Ulf's crew, not far behind, hastily moving about as they readied their boats and attempted to catch up to them.

"Ulf, slow down." Vali called ahead, his eyes desperately searching for any sign of an ambush. "The Kresh could be anywhere. We could walk straight into a trap."

"Have heart, Vali. The Kresh know better than to show their faces in the presence of a Viking. We have seen to it, since the days of my father and grandfather before him. You have nothing to fear from them. Should they choose not to flee, then they will be crushed." Vali's heartrate only hastened as he attempted to follow the man.

Vali could hear a rustling about him, though his eyes caught not the slightest trace of movement. Ulf stood, chest held out, axe in his left hand, long, double edged sword, in the other. Behind them, his crewmen caught up to them.

"Vali, this is unwise," Thala whispered in his ear. He realized, she too, could sense the spirits closing in around them, obscuring their vision. The fog they formed was meant for them, alone. He turned to see her glowing eyes and nodded in agreement.

"Fan out. Stay close to each other but be sure that we know exactly what we are walking into." Silently, his crew did as asked and a moment later, he could only see Thala at the end of his vision to the left and Abel, to the right.

Ulf remained in the lead, every step, daring to charge out to battle the Kresh, alone. Vali carried the hastened pace, doing his best to keep his eyes open. Sifting through the fog, he caught the end of his boot on a large root, snaking through the grass and let out a begrudging curse.

"Hold," Ulf spoke, stopping abruptly. As everyone came to a stop, Vali stood firm, chest puffed out, keeping a wary eye on his surroundings.

"Tend to yourself, Vali," Ulf spoke.

"I am alright. I shall manage until we are back behind cover. We are too exposed, now for me to worry."

"We are not exposed." Ulf whispered. "You will be alright."

"Ulf?"

"I am not so certain that there are any Kresh on this island." He grumbled. "At the least, we are not in danger."

Abel, who had loomed in close, nudged Vali, discreetly.

"Come on, Vali, let us look at that foot." He urged. Nodding his head, Vali knelt and unlacing his boot, slid his foot from it. Already, he could see blood, staining the ends of his woolen wraps.

"I have a bandage in my pack," Abel spoke, pulling his ruck sack over his shoulder and shuffled through it.

"War chief," Thala began. "How can you be certain that there are no Kresh, here?"

"I do not sense any malicious presence. The presence a Kresh war party bears is not simply an imposing sight. It is almost palpable. It hangs in the air as thickly as charred brew. Besides, even with their gift for blending into the land, they cannot hide an entire attack force. It is clear we will be forced to press on ahead, if we hope to find a band of warriors."

"How can you be certain?" Vali asked, accepting the bandage from Abel and started wrapping his foot. Ulf froze for a moment, searching for the proper words.

"Are you ready?"

"Yes," Vali answered, pressing his swelling foot back into his boot.

"Then we need to keep moving. I wish to have this island cleared, as soon as we possibly can." He grumbled, as he resumed his quick pace. Vali and his crew, followed closely behind, still adding caution to where the war chief provided none.

"Does this have something to do with the village?" Vali whispered, trotting alongside Ulf.

"I wish to end this campaign, swiftly. It is unlikely that a large force of Kresh, would have already made their way, so far south. Unless they have recently discovered navigational skills, they should be forced to stick to the bridges and roads." Vali's thoughts drifted to the young Kresh woman, her fellows and the elderly, which had taken her away.

"Ulf..." He began, though the man kept his pace.

"What is it, Vali?" He asked.

"What of the Kresh, who were attacked by the trolls? If they made it this far, could there not be more?"

"You said that each of the bodies, was of a young Kresh, correct?"

"Yes?"

"Then they were not warriors." Ulf said. "I am unsure as to why their young were out so far. Perhaps a rite of passage. Perhaps something else, entirely. We know too little of their culture to be certain. Beyond that, I have no desire to slay the helpless.

"The fact remains that if these younglings were allowed to be slain, then none of the warrior caste were present. My best guess is that they were scouting ahead for the main force, when they encountered the trolls. It will take a few days, before anyone comes after them. I would prefer to keep them from gaining ground on this island at all."

"Of course. What can we do to help?"

"Just as soon as we can be sure that this island is secured, I will send you and your crew back to Ulfrost to gather supplies."

"War Chief?" Vali asked.

"You have been having difficulty securing food, these past few days. This will become problematic, should we wish to maintain a prolonged campaign against the Kresh."

"I understand." Vali answered, another lie, as he eyed the chief's odd behavior. Continuing forward with no sign of the Kresh, they managed through the fog. Looking about, Vali followed Ulf toward a nearby overlook. From their vantage, Vali could see clear to the beach on the northern shore of the island.

"Do you see anything?" He asked, crouching down beside the chief. His view was filled with the white sands of Fangor, enshrouded by the deceptively calming lull of forest. Somewhere, within the harmonious canvas, they sought out a race he had always be told were naught but brutal savages.

"No, but then again, that is partly the problem. Whether the Kresh are here or not, we cannot see them. The other problem, which you are already aware of, is that Grom could attack us at any moment and we would be hard pressed to stop him. It is also entirely possible that he will not and that the Kresh, are nowhere near us."

"But could we see them, we would know." Vali commented.

"Precisely."

"That is why you wish for my team and I to head out. You wish us to return to Ulfrost and make certain that things are alright."

"Aye and if they are not, I will need you to alert us. I require someone who can make the journey from Fangor to Ulfrost in record time yet maintain a viable excuse to be shuttled back and forth."

"You wish to know how things are going back home, then?" Vali concluded. "Very well. When do you wish for my crew and I to set sail?"

"Just as soon as..." Ulf trailed off as his eyes locked onto something in the distance. Vali, moving closer to the man, eyed the distance from his vantage. Far to the north, beyond the beach, he saw a large blur, forming. Squinting his eyes to gain a better vantage, he tipped forward ever so slightly.

The black mass in the distance, continued to loom in closer, judging by the rate that it grew. Both men continued to stare, unmoving. Curious, Abel and the others approached he and Ulf.

"What is that?" Abel asked. "A ship?"

"There is no way that is a ship," Halla spoke. "It is much too large."

"Do we move in to get a closer look?" Thala asked.

"Not until we have more Vikings," Ulf spoke. "They may not turn out to be our enemy, but I would much prefer a thousand or more men at my side, before I am forced to decide which." Ulf stared a moment longer, before turning his head back toward the stronghold.

"Come, let us return. The others should be arriving soon." Ulf said, standing and walking back to the boat. Abel and the others followed Ulf as Vali remained a moment longer, watching. In the distance, surrounding the massive blot at the edge of his vision, he witnessed several smaller black spots webbing out.

"Vali, come on. Hate to leave behind the captain." Agni called. Snapping back to his comrades, Vali rose to his feet, took one last, long look at the south bound mystery, and followed.

As they made their way back, the fog, which had slowed them before, made finding their boat, nearly impossible. Warier than he had been previously, Vali walked carefully, though he occasionally heard the others groan with discontent.

Their progress only slowed as the fog thickened, the further they marched. Moving about blindly, many of his crew grumbled under their breath. Abel tripping with a curse slowly rose to his feet and felt around for his weapon. Walking up beside Abel, he gripped the young man's shoulder carefully.

"Give me a moment," Vali said, closing his eyes. Reaching out to the elements around himself, he focused on the thick, damp air.

"It is working, Vali," said Abel, collecting his axe. "The fog is thinning." Vali continued his work, trying to disperse the fog, as he felt fatigue, quickly catching up to him. He continued to pull from the swell of spirits around him, which allowed him to perform beyond his limits. In the distance, a high-pitched wail of a scream, seared into his mind, causing him to falter.

"Easy, Vali," Abel gasped, catching him. "Are you alright?"

"Did you not hear that?" Vali groaned, his head throbbing from the sudden attack to his senses.

"Hear what?" Abel asked.

"Never mind," Vali spoke, shrugging off the fatigue, along with the ringing in his ears. Thala was quick to his side, helping to guide him back to the boats.

"Try not to overexert yourself shaping," Ulf warned. "You will soon be needed to spirit everyone back to Ulfrost."

"Of course, Ulf. I shall use more discretion in the future."

"Be certain that you do. It is a poor practice for the captain to lose consciousness, while walking through suspected enemy territory." Vali remained silent as they continued toward the boat. Sitting back, Vali rested as Ulf took command of his vessel.

Chapter 7 – The Attack

"Come on, you three!" Asta called, looking back at the men following behind her. She pulled on a collection of ropes with disarming strength, which were fastened to the men's bound wrists and ankles.

"We are!" The scarred man growled, begrudgingly leading his pack as Asta kept her bow trained. Outside of the tower, three younger Vikings and Freyja, waited on their horses. At the sight of Asta, they jumped down, ropes in hand. Checking the bindings on each of the prisoners, Freyja rode beside Asta.

"How has the watch been?" She asked, a tone befitting the High Chief's daughter. Eyes traversing the landscape, her gaze rested on Asta.

"Eventful, as you can see," Asta grumbled, gesturing to the three. "Did the High Chief have anything to tell me?"

"Other than be sure to keep up the good work? No. There has yet to be any word from my father or Vali." She added with a frown. Asta mirrored the expression. "None of my ravens have brought word of any developments, either."

"What does the chief have planned for us?" The eldest scavenger interrupted.

"She intends to put the three of you to work. Try to escape and we have been ordered to cut you down." Freyja spoke in her mother's authoritative tone, the earth trembling beneath her. None of the three spoke as the young woman's shaping rattled their bones.

"Freyja." One of her entourage whispered, gently. "Please be careful. Your shapings tend to be unstable." Nodding her head, she released her grasp on the environment as Asta cleared her throat.

"Did she at least say how long I am expected to remain, here?" Asta sighed irritably as the words left her lips. Freyja eyed the sulking youth, sympathetically, before shaking her head.

"I am sorry, Asta. She did not. Would you like for me or some of the others from the village, to come visit you, once we are done with these three?" Asta let out an aggressive sigh, before walking back toward the tower.

"No, it is fine. If I do not need to watch after these three, at least I will be able to practice my bow arm." Without looking back, she listened to the sound of the horses as Freyja and the others rode away. Glancing about, she took in the encroaching forest. A ring in the tree line had been cut long ago, making room for the surrounding grounds. It only added to her feelings of isolation.

Asta walked to the front of the tower and moved to the edge of the cliff. There, she looked out over the sea, the sight of it alone, leaving a bitter taste in her mouth. Drawing her bow, she turned, set an arrow and immediately fired, the arrow piercing her target, the dummy mounted fifty paces away.

"Why do I have to stay here?" She yelled, launching another arrow, which struck the target in the left side of the chest, beside the first. "It simply is not fair!" She fired a third, which striking again in the same place, caused the shaft of the arrow to dig deeper into the target.

"Freyja and the others are free to come and go as they please, yet I am to remain trapped here. What have I ever done to anger the High Chief so?" Her fourth arrow, tore through the back of the target, sailing several paces beyond. Asta growled angrily. Stalking toward the target, she made sure to strike it several times in the head with the staff of her bow, before collecting her first three arrows.

Seeing her arrow sticking out of the ground ahead of her, she approached and plucked it from the ground. Sliding all four arrows back into her quiver, she stood upright and caught a glimpse of the beach over the edge of the cliff. That, and the boat the smugglers had used to move about the island.

Asta turned her head, looking around for anyone else. Calling out, she listened for an answer, before looking back to the scooter. The vessel was small, barely large enough for the three men who sailed her, plus their plundered cargo. Again, Asta looked around, before slowly venturing toward it.

"I am still keeping watch, so long as I stay close, right?" She asked her conscience as she descended the hillside. "It is not as though I am abandoning the watch. I will still be watching the south side of the island. Any boats coming this way, I will be certain to notice." She continued to sway her own guilty conscience as she neared the bottom of the slope.

"What would Vali say? How would he feel about me shirking off my duty, or making compromises against it?" She stopped at the foot of the hill and stared at the small vessel.

"Of course, he would be upset, but then again, he is free to go and do as he pleases, while I am trapped here." She paced back and forth, neither scaling the hill or moving nearer to the boat. Staring at her freedom, an imaginary beacon of light, crafted around it, beckoning her forward, she clenched her fist and growled angrily.

"It will still be there, tomorrow. Perhaps tomorrow, I will go." She told herself, as she marched back up the hill.

That night, as she lay back in her humble cot, staring at the ceiling, Asta's thoughts continued to drift back to the allure of freedom. Her only light, the candle by her bedside, Asta rolled onto her side and stared at the flickering light.

"Vali, you better come back soon. I want to get off from this island." She groaned, rolling onto her back and closing her eyes.

That night, she dreamt of seven tall, hooded figures, walking through lush green meadows, leaving nothing in their wake, save ash. The figures maintained a slow, constant pace. All that was green, festered and died as they passed. Looking down the path of the trail they made, she saw Vali and the rest of her kin.

She focused her vision on the rows of men, standing in wait, staring at the creatures, which loomed nearer. Vali was panting aggressively, sweat pouring from his face. He looked ready to collapse on the spot. Never before had she seen him so downtrodden.

Near to him, she saw Ulf, shouting out numerous commands to the men, who stared boldly ahead. Each and every one of them, were covered in dirt, weary faces all around. Despite their ragged appearance, they maintained disciplined ranks, waiting for Ulf to sound the charge.

She could feel the wind upon her face, hot from the flames below. She could feel the dirt of the battlefield beneath her fingertips. Her nostrils flared as the smell of charred flesh, blood and sweat congealed as a single, pungent aroma.

The ravine descending from the stronghold was streaked with scorches and craters. Entire patches of the green hills lay barren, the life from their soils eradicated. Of all the brave fighters, none among them looked unscathed, unafraid.

A trek of fire ran in front of the Vikings, used to light the tips of their arrows. The line of bowmen, missiles alight, fired in unison. The seven men continued their slow crawl toward Vali and the others, paying no mind to the arrows flying to either side of them.

Asta cried out, the words unclear, even to her as they poured from her throat. The garbed men loomed nearer, not a single arrow fired, touching them. A moment later, Ulf sounded the charge. More than one thousand Vikings charged forward, weapons drawn, ready to slaughter the seven men and all those who stood behind them.

The seven, stood firm, watching the coming tide from behind their veiled robes, metal, featureless masks upon each of their faces. Asta continued to watch, eyes wide with terror as one of the seven, raised its right hand into the air. From the tips of its fingers, existed several small twinklings of dancing light. With a loud crack, the sky split apart, and a beam of lightning rained down in the center of the advancing ranks. Several men fell to the ground, after having been thrown through the air and moved no more. Ulf continued to shout, men continued to charge and the other six robed men, raised their hands.

The earth came alive all around the Viking horde. Some were propelled backward by shifting walls of dirt, while others were sucked beneath the ground by them. Ulf shouted new orders, which Vali helped relay. Men continued to charge, and men continued to die.

Again, Asta caught herself shouting out to the men. As pointless as she knew the effort to be, she carried on all the same. As she did so, all seven forms turned their heads and stared directly at her.

She not only saw, but felt their lifeless eyes, hidden beneath the metal plates, watching her. She could hear their somewhat labored breathing, could smell the stench of the battlefield. The creature that had called down the lightning, lifted its right hand into the air toward her.

Asta screamed, trying to wake herself from her dream. As they had previously, the fingertips glowed, the earth around it began to die and light surged forward. Asta rolled from her bed, screaming. Her shoulder struck the floor as she continued to move away from the bed. Nearly toppling the table as she knocked into it, she stopped and slowly rose to her feet.

"I have to warn the chief!" Asta yelled aloud, as she scurried about the watchtower. Flinging the clutter from the nearby table, she scrounged about, until she found a clean piece of parchment and unfurling it, reached for her quill. Scratching out her message, relaying everything she had seen in her dream, Asta rolled her letter and ran to the balcony.

Looking around, she searched for the raven that usually visited, her only contact with the village. Walking around the balcony in its entirety, she realized that the wise bird was nowhere to be seen. Spitting a curse to herself, she continued to look around for another option.

Panic flooded her veins. The men on Fangor needed her help. Vali needed her. Asta looked to the northern coast, where she knew her boat would be waiting. Looking behind her, she saw the readied trough of oil, which she was to ignite, should the enemy be spotted. With a heavy sigh, Asta reached out for her nearby candle and holding it to the edge of the oil basin, ignited the flame.

Bolting down the stairs of the watchtower, she passed through the open doorway and ran out into the evening light. Racing down to the beach, she threw her belongings onboard and pressed against the side of the boat. With a heavy grunt, she managed to shove the vessel into the water and climbed aboard.

Having spent countless hours at the docks and having been personally tutored by Vali, Asta's hands moved with muscle memory, releasing the sails and steering herself east. Though the breeze provided her with little more than a gentle push, the vessel was small enough, she could rely upon her own strength. Grabbing hold of both oars, Asta set them in place, making use of her entire body.

Looking back to the watchtower, she saw the brilliant flames of the beacon fire, fanning out for leagues. The waves gently rocked her boat, tipping her from side to side. She could not place the feeling, but within the well of her stomach, an unfamiliar churn presented itself.

Asta continued to row, having little difficulty maintaining the pace thanks to arduous hours of conditioning she forced herself through. The further she ventured around the island, the more her stomach panged in disagreement. Refusing to slow, even as the waves grew rougher, Asta wrenched her head over the side of the boat and hurled.

"Now, is hardly the time to be getting sick." She growled at her rotten luck as she continued to work against the contempt her innards currently felt toward her. She threw up once more, before she pulled away from the island and was able to rely solely upon the sails. With a great deal of unease, she shifted herself into position and grabbing hold of the rudder, steered around the outskirts of the island.

Where she had spent more than a day, riding from Ulfrost village to the eastern watchtower, within a short few hours, long before the sun's first rays shone over the horizon, she rounded the bend. Less than an hour more and she would be able to see her village, even in the pitch black. Trouble was, the village was not pitch black; it was alight with flames.

Chapter 8 - Home

"Vali, you are acting insane!" Abel shouted from behind the helm of the Valiant. "You could actually kill yourself, exerting yourself to such an extent!" Vali stood, both hands pressed forward, forcing the boat to move at full speed. Laying into the air currents, with all the shaping he could muster, had been strenuous enough. Far from the strange influence of the spirits of Fangor, his fatigue had quickly been recalled. Having been holding the shaping for nearly an entire day, the effort quickly ate away at his dwindling strength.

"We have no choice." Vali groaned. "Ulf and the rest of our kin, are still on Fangor, waiting for us to return with good news and supplies. At any moment, those things we saw in the waters north of Fangor, could arrive, and there is every possibility that they will not be friendly."

"Surely, they represent one of the other clans," Haldr suggested. "Who, other than the Vikings, could possess such mastery over the seas?"

"Who indeed," Vali answered. "I would just assume be able to lend them a hand, in case they are not."

"What good will you be to them, if you collapse, or kill yourself?" Abel added.

"I only need to hold out a little bit more. We still have a strong wind, to lead us where we need to go. I will release my hold the moment it is beyond us." Vali grunted through his words, the strain of speaking, leaving him without breath.

"It is a wonder the ship has not fallen apart." Thala mused, earning her an irritable glance from Abel and Vali both.

"As soon as the head wind moves beyond us, be sure to get some food, and some rest." Abel growled. "We may not manage as powerful a shaping, but we will push as well. Haldr, please prepare a place in the storage hold."

"I will likely drop where I now stand," Vali choked on the last word but maintained his grip on the shaping. Receiving a nod from Abel, Haldr returned to his labors.

"Abel, please let him work," Thala whispered to him. "He can do this."

"I suspect he still would, even if he could not." Abel smirked, turning back to the steering oar. "Alright everyone, begin rotations. I want everyone bright and ready to row, the moment the captain releases the wind." A burst of activity rushed about the deck of the ship. As Halla and Thala, made for the cargo hold to rest, Haldr and Agni prepped themselves to manage the oars. Within minutes, everyone was where they should be, waiting.

Another hour went by, before Vali's supply of natural wind, diminished and the strain of channeling its power, increased. As his hands shook and his eyes shuttered from the piercing pain in his temple, Vali released the shaping. The boat lurched violently, causing everyone onboard to stumble. Vali, unable to muster any more strength, fell to the deck.

"Captain," he heard call, as he felt a shifting of wind and Haldr was at his side. "Are you alright?" He asked him, stern, concerned tone in his voice.

"I will live," he grunted, placing his hands beneath himself. With Haldr's aid, Vali managed himself upright, where he leaned against the bow, gently tossing side to side from the waves.

"How far do you think you have brought us?" Haldr asked.

"Ask Abel...I have no idea." He answered, before laying on his side. "I dare not attempt a water shaping, now."

"My guess is that we are already half way home." Abel answered, eyes closed, his left hand held toward the stern.

"Is that possible?" Agni gasped as Haldr looked to the captain.

"With a shaping, no. With the Old Ones' sorcery, I suppose so." Abel said.

***

Vali awoke, to bright beams of sunlight, striking his face. Deliriously, his eyes worked about, searching for any sign of sense or purpose as he attempted to slow his spinning head. Pain immobilized him at his first attempt to roll, and a second attempt was delayed.

"Vali, there is no need for you to get up, just yet." Thala spoke softly.

"I should. Need to make certain we arrive by tomorrow morning." Taking several deep breaths, Vali attempted to rise once more.

"At least grab something to eat." The newest member of the crew chided. "Halla, could you please help the captain?" Before Vali's vision had unclouded, he felt a strong shoulder, pressing beneath his right armpit.

"Come on, Captain. We need you at your best." Halla spoke, guiding Vali behind the sails and helping him into a seated position. Placing several items into his hands, she walked to the front of the boat to check the anchoring lines. Too tired to complain, Vali took a long draw from the wineskin in his hand, before biting into the dry ship biscuits in his other.

"Has everyone had a chance to rest up?" He asked, voice still sounding dry and weak.

"The others are resting, now. Abel suspects that we will still manage to reach home, tomorrow."

"Glad to hear it," Vali said, setting his things aside and slowly rising to his feet, which still felt more liquid than flesh and bone.

"I am guessing that you should not be doing that yet." Halla warned as Thala snapped her head around.

"Captain, attack or not, Ulfrost has little use for you incapacitated." The fiery eyed youth growled.

"Ulf and the men we left behind, have little use for people taking their time, or taking it easy." He responded. "I can take a day to rest, once we are on the return voyage. Until then, I have my orders to reach Ulfrost as soon as the Old Ones allow me."

"I wonder how Asta and Kari will feel about that defense, when they see what sorry shape you are in?" Halla teased.

"You wouldn't?" Vali protested.

I hardly think that she would need to, but I wouldn't test her." Thala chimed in. "Part of our job is ensuring that the Captain stays alive."

"I will rest a bit longer, but once the winds pick up some more, I will resume."

"Your pyre, not mine," Thala laughed. Vali sat back, gently attacking the light meal in front of himself. Eyes fully adjusted, he stared out to Tyrda Fell's bright, blue water and attempted to chart the distance they had yet to travel. He had been too busy filling the sails that he was unable to account for how far they had traveled.

"Did Abel happen to mention how far out we are?" He asked, still staring down at the deck.

"Captain," Halla called.

"Yes?" He asked, though looking up, he knew before she had a chance to answer. At the horizon's edge, a thick plume of black, fanned out across the skyline. Rising to his feet, Vali drew from the water skin, once again.

"Halla, I need you to tie me off!" He demanded, reaching down into his gut for the strength he required.

"What for?"

"I do not want to fall unconscious and wake up in Valhalla," he growled. "I am getting us to those clouds by evening." Thala and Halla both turned to eye him, before looking back to the smoke.

"Right," Halla spoke and made haste upon his request. Holding his grasping hands out in front of his body, he reached out with invisible feelers, latching onto every last gust of wind he could perceive. The boat jerked violently, causing Thala and Halla both, to stumble forward.

"What happened?" Abel asked.

"Look," Halla called, pointing to the blackness far ahead of them. Abel turned his head, noticing the smoke.

"Haldr! Agni! Get up, quick. Everyone ready to help Vali! Ulfrost needs us!" From below, the two men scrambled up on deck and ran for the oars.

"Halla! Thala!" Find anything we might use as an additional sail. We need more speed!" Vali called.

"Will the boat be able to handle it?" Abel asked.

"We will make it." Thala and Halla made haste, gathering every spare piece of fabric and working to fit it into a large sheet. Next, removing some of their spare riggings, they fastened lines to bind the makeshift sail and worked to rig it to the masts.

As Thala and Halla climbed overhead, Vali focused his attentions forward, pressing the boat to the point the wood groaned beneath his feet. Already he felt his body shake, but such pleas fell on deaf ears. Vali would not be stopped.

***

By nightfall, they had neared the coastline, the sight of the fires lighting Ulfrost, reaching out from behind the cover of the trees. Vali released his hold on the winds, before they had drawn near, allowing a slowed approach to the village. Vali maintained a four-point stance on the deck as his insides wretched violently. Halla helped to hold him up as Abel steered the vessel close.

"Captain, are you going to be alright?" Halla asked him. Vali panted heavily, barely able to catch his breath.

"I...will...live." He gasped. Halla tipped him back and forced the water skin to his lips.

"We will be at the cliffside, north of the village, soon." Abel whispered. "What are your orders, Captain?"

"We use the high ground...gain an idea of what has happened. If needs be, we strike, without mercy." He continued to gasp, dabbing the edges of his mouth with the back of his sleeve. Unnervingly, there was a heavy taste of copper in his mouth, though he dared not tell those in his charge.

"I am none opposed with that approach," Agni answered, gaining him a number of stares.

"Truly?"

"Attacking a foe, who has not been seen to be a threat, bothers me. Answering the call of war, to lay waste to an enemy attacking my home, merits a more hostile approach. Savaged will be the corpses of any who threaten my own." The longboat came to a gentle stop as the hull struck the beach.

"By all means then, Agni, son of Argus and Branka. Fetch your weapon. Tonight, we go to war." Vali spoke into the night, slowly rising to his feet, sword already at his side.

As Haldr and Agni stepped off from the boat, Vali, still trying to keep his balance, followed. Haldr quickly strung his bow, while Thala, spear in hand and sword on her back, trotted up to the front of the ranks. Halla, bow in hand, walked beside her brother.

Keeping to the cover of the shadow, they kept their eyes on the flames. Moving up the hilly slopes, they made for the edge of the forest, Halla and Haldr forking out ahead, in search of threats. Agni and Thala stood in front of Vali, who supported himself on Abel's shoulder.

Though it strained him, Vali placed his hand to the trunk of the nearest tree and felt through its roots. A gentle hum traveled through his body and with his left hand, he reached out to the spirits of the air. A gentle stirring came to him from within the earth and with it, he could hear the gentle rise and fall of shallow breathing.

Placing one finger to his lips, Vali silently signaled for everyone to move back behind the cover of the trees. A moment later, he could hear the crack of wood as a bowstring was pulled back tightly. Twisting his body into position, Vali, nearly blind in the darkness, reached out with his senses and only hoped he was not wrong.

"Asta?" He whispered, using the power of the wind to carry his voice, in the direction of the archer. A moment later, a rumble in the bushes and a dark silhouette confirmed his guess.

"Vali?" Asta whispered back, bow pointed into the darkness.

"Praise the Old Ones," he whispered, limping toward her and wrapping his arms around her. "What happened here?" Asta pulled herself from Vali's grip and turned her head in the direction of Ulfrost village.

"We fell under attack, while you were away."

"Do you know who lead the attack?"

"They came unidentified. At first, I thought that it was Grom."

"What?" Thala asked. "If not him, then who?" Asta shook her head rapidly.

"I am not sure. I do not recognize any of their ships, nor their fighting techniques."

"You were at the watchtower," Vali spoke. "If it were Grom, he must have attacked from the north?" He guessed, turning his attention back the way he had come.

"I do not know," Asta said, shaking her head. "I came back this way to warn everyone..."

"Warn everyone of what?" Vali asked. "Asta, did they pass by the watchtower?"

"No, it is not that." She replied, shaking her head. "How did you manage to get passed those black robed people?" Everyone stared curiously at Asta.

"What black robed people?" Vali asked.

"I had a vision. In it, you and the others stood against an army of seven men, garbed in black robes."

"An army of seven men?" Thala asked.

"Is that even possible?" Haldr joined in.

"Did it not happen?" Asta asked. Vali shook his head as the sound of more people, entering the forest, came to him on the wind. Again, finger to his lips, Vali pointed toward the source of the noise and stalked behind a nearby tree. The others followed his lead, each taking up concealed positions of their own.

Their breath froze in their lungs as they waited. Bodies vibrating with nervous anticipation, Vali kept one eye out in the direction of those who approached. Placing the flat of his palm to the trunk of his hiding place, Vali felt out toward those not by his side.

At first, he only perceived the six beside him. A moment later, five more presences entered his area of perception. He focused harder, relying on the tree for its support as well as its roots, as the strain from the day, weakened his body further. He heard the light crackle of a bowstring as Asta trained her arrow.

"Wait," Vali whispered with the subtlety of the wind. Turning his head, he aimed his voice. "Freyja?" He whispered once more. The sound of the footsteps halted abruptly. Remaining motionless a moment longer, Vali and his crew waited.

"Vali?" He could hear the young woman ask. Signaling forward, Vali stepped from cover, feeling Asta's hand on his shoulder as he moved out of her reach.

"Freyja, what happened here?" He continued to whisper as he stepped forward.

"By the Old Ones, Vali, it is good to see you." Freyja said, hastily clearing the distance between them. Wrapping her arms tightly around him, she burrowed her head into his chest. Weeping as he held her, she tightened her grasp around him. Patting her gently on the back, he placed his chin atop her head.

"Freyja, what happened?" He whispered again. Eyes filled with tears, she stared up at him, shaking.

"We were attacked by men from the south. I do not know what happened. One moment, we were gathered about the evening campfire and the next..." She looked away, back to the village.

"What? Not Grom?" He asked, clearly announcing his suspicions toward the man." Freyja's eyes widened at the implied accusation.

"By the nine, no!" She stammered. "Mother believes that they are a band of exiles. They just started to attack everyone!" She sobbed. The other four, stepping from the darkness placed a hand each on Freyja, tears in each of their eyes, as well.

"The Fallen Brotherhood." Vali muttered, turning his attention back toward the village, which lie to the south. He had not considered the band much of a threat, their lot having remained unseen since the days before his birth. Exiles of the clans of Vala, they had long been thought banished beyond the fog, never to return. "So, they were not lost in the fog."

"Vali," Abel interrupted, gripping his friend's shoulder tightly. "We need to move quickly." Vali nodding his head, drew in a deep breath. Placing both hands on Freyja's shoulders, he pressed her back gently and stared into her eyes.

"Freyja, I need information. Is there anyone left in the village?" She paused for a moment and nodded.

"Yes. Mother and several of the others, barricaded themselves in town. Kari and those who managed to flee, were headed for the barrow."

"Why are you not with them?" Asta asked. Vali shot her a sharp glance, forcing Asta to shiver as he waited for the frightened woman to answer.

"I was scared. I did not run away when I was told to. I was left behind. So were they..." she added, turning her head back to the other women. As Asta stared at her brother, she could feel a palpable heat, rising from him as he stared toward the quite real fires ravaging their home.

"Abel." He growled deep in his throat, the sound remnant of a pack of scorned fenris wolves.

"Vali."

"Take Freyja and the others with you back to the Valiant." He told him. "Take one deckhand with you. The rest of us are going to the village."

"Vali, you cannot!" Freyja started to cry once more. "Those monsters will kill you!"

"I swore an oath, to High Chief Finna and to the rest of Ulfrost." He continued to growl. "Asta, chart me a path." Without a word, the young huntress stalked into the darkness.

"Vali, are you sure about this?" Abel asked, the others having grown completely silent.

"There is little other choice." Vali's low toned growl vibrated his clenched teeth. Abel nodded his head.

"Haldr, I will need both a strong set of hands and an archer. Halla will better serve a quiet approach than you." The male twin changed direction, walking back to the boat.

"Go." Vali spoke, eyeing Freyja. "We will take care of the rest." Drawing in a steadying breath, the chieftain's daughter lifted her chin and nodded her head.

"Be careful," she ordered, puffing out her chest, slightly. "Return with the others, without fail." She turned away from him and followed Haldr. Abel, merely patted Vali on the shoulder once more, before he too, turned back.

"Everyone left," Vali stated, eyeing those before him. "Let us take back our people." He said, testing his grip on his sword as he led the way south.

As he cleared the tree line, the flames scattered around the perimeter of the village, grew ever more present. From their position, fifty paces away, the heat radiating from the flames, caused Vali's forearms to perspire. Ahead of them, nearly invisible, Asta waited, crouched down in the short thicket, watching.

"What do you think?" Vali whispered to her, the power of his windspeak, smothering his words, before they could travel to prying ears.

"We do not have enough boats, for everyone," she whispered back, pointing toward the beach. Turning his gaze, he saw the few boats, which had been left, alight.

"We will need to do our best, to get everyone out of the village." He began. "After we have taken them a safe distance, we can swing back around and attempt to liberate the others."

"But Vali, what about mother?" Asta asked, trembling in her voice.

"Mother can care for herself." He spoke in a low tone. "Were we to go to her, first, she would only remind us that our duty is to the village, not her. The barrow is better defended than the Chief's house. It is clear who has a chance of outlasting and who does not. Besides, the barrow rests atop a vast array of tunnels. Mother knows them better than any I know of. She may have already escaped."

"You do not know that." Asta sneered.

"I do not, but I have faith. It is all I might have, now, should I wish to avoid despair." Asta's gaze trailed off a moment and she sighed.

"I only see a small number of people, pacing about the beach. It appears as though the main force is concentrated closer to the town's center." Vali turned his attention to the southeast, where the Chief's house stood.

"We would do well to pick off silently, as many as possible." Vali spoke, drawing his bow from behind his back. Nodding her head, Asta stepped from the cover of the bushes, arrow resting on the shaft of her bow, primed for firing.

Vali followed close behind her, his comrades beyond him. They quickly moved along the edge of the trees, until they were concealed from sight by the face of the main slope, leading to the village. Dashing forward, Vali signaled out to either side, commanding his forces to split up.

Though the foot of the slope was only thirty paces ahead, the sprint left him winded. Dropping to a knee, he panted heavily, arm over his face to help conceal the sound. Asta eyed him, concern worn over the entirety of her face.

"Vali, are you alright?"

"I shall be." He forced out. "It took a great shaping to bring us back here so quickly. I did not have time to recover my strength."

"You need to hold back, then." Asta grumbled. "You are only going to get yourself killed in a battle, if you can barely stand."

"I fear I have no other option. Should I do nothing, many will die."

"You probably will, if you do."

"One for many. What must be done, shall be done." He gritted his teeth as he forced his legs to bare his weight. Rising uneasily, he reaffirmed his grip on his bow and stalked forward. He could hear Asta sigh with agitation from behind, followed by the sound of her slow pursuit.

Not much further over the hillslope, Vali counted three figures pacing back and forth along the beach, torches in hand. Pointing to them, he looked back at Asta, who nodded. Shifting course, they continued toward the Chief's house.

The deeper into town they approached, the fewer flames lit the way. Numerous small lights shone ahead of them, slowly crawling along the outskirts of the village. Asta at his hip the entire stretch, they hastily moved between the many cairns and stood only a few dozen paces from their destination. Trouble was, so did the enemy.

No fewer than twelve, black robed forms stood before them. Each of them had their backs turned to Vali and Asta, instead focusing their attention onto the Chief's house. Looking upon the structure, Vali smiled at the stone constructs, enormous walls, the height of trees, which had risen from the ground, in defense of the home.

"Are these the same black robed ones you saw in your vision?" Vali asked, using a concentrated wind shaping, so only her ears could sense the words. Asta leaned to the side, staring passed her brother. Of the twelve, she could only see the faces of three, which were made of flesh. Looking back to Vali, she shook her head.

"We wait for the others to get in position, before we strike. You shoot from the right. I will take the left. Force them to form in the center and it will be easier for the others to come down on top of them." As they waited, Vali and Asta both, prepped for the ill deed ahead of them. Removing several arrows from their quivers, they gently stabbed them into the ground, ready to be fired.

A moment later, as they waited, Agni and Halla appeared in the shadows across the road, to Vali and Asta's left. Vali nodded to them, to which they nodded back. Using a quick series of simple hand signs, Vali relayed his intentions to them, before turning his head to the right, and noticed Thala, standing at the ready, beneath a tree. Through the same process as with Agni and Halla, he signaled to her.

"Are you ready, Asta?" He asked, plucking an arrow from his quiver and setting it to his bowstring. Though she did not speak, he heard the subtle graze of an arrow being fletched. Drawing back his arrow, Vali eyed Asta out of the corner of his eye, catching her attention a brief second.

"Go," he wind shaped once more as he released his grasp on the arrow. The bowstring snapped forward, launching the arrow, which guided by Vali's wind shaping, did not even whistle. The head of the arrow lodged itself into the back of one of the twelves skulls, causing the figure to go rigid, before slowly collapsing to the ground. A split second after, as Vali drew up his second arrow with speed and precision, Asta's target fell, arrow piercing its heart through the back.

By the time the remaining invaders turned, four more fell. Halla and Haldr added in their own fire as Asta and Vali launched a second attack. Vali winced slightly as he heard a call amongst the figures, the sound rough as gravel, bellowed forth. He quickly adjusted his aim and fired through the throat of the one who had yelled as Agni and Thala, weapons drawn, charged forward.

Their coordinated attack left little chance for the invaders, who were quickly toppled by the ambush. Vali, hands still shaking, watched as Agni brought his axe head down upon the final man, dropping him in one stroke. Turning his head to Asta, he signaled the advance as he too, ran to the Chief's house.

"We will have to climb over!" Agni called to Vali as Halla looked down to pick at the line of rope on her waist.

"Asta," Vali called, squatting down and cupping his hands low to the ground. Smirk on her face, Asta took up a running start, charging straight at her brother. The simple wraps she wore on her feet to protect the pads, made no sound as she charged him, leaping at the last moment.

Both feet landing in his grasp, Vali wrenched with his entire body, launching the much smaller woman skyward. Asta, using her hands and feet, continued to propel herself up the wall, narrowly grasping its edge with her outstretched hands. Using her well-balanced strength and unrivaled predacious abilities, she pulled her body over.

"You are especially tired, Vali. Normally, you would have no issue launching me to such a height."

"Just go, gather everyone. I will contact the Chief now, so you are not attacked." He growled at her, placing his hand against the earthen fortifications and closed his eyes.

"Vali, we cannot stand out here in the open, for long. More of the enemy will be on their way." Agni whispered, pressing his back near Vali's as he kept a watch on their surroundings.

"We must buy him time," Thala answered for Vali. "It takes concentration to pull off a shaping such as this." She continued, sword still in hand.

"That brings a question," Halla spoke, bow already trained, ready for the first of the invaders to surface. "Where did you come upon a sword? It takes some families generations to afford one's make."

"It is the family blade," Thala answered. "Passed down from one defender of the Ulfrost shrine, to the next. As you know, my family has long served as the altar guardians to the Old Ones."

"You do not bury your swords with your dead?" Halla asked.

"Not many altar guardians leave far beyond the shores," Agni commented, sharp, almost disapproving tone to his voice. Thala winced slightly out of her left eye and an equally sharp, wolfish sneer, spread her lips.

"I assure you, I am no less formidable, despite my lack of experience. I will not let any of you down." Vali, having thus far remained silent, opened his eyes and turned.

"She is in." He sighed. "I made contact with the Chief. It seems as though only she and a few of the elders are inside. Mother managed to flee to the barrow with all the younglings and their mothers."

"What is the plan?" Thala asked.

"I want for all of you to take them to the ships. Sail them to Canor, to the north. From there, they can manage on foot, long enough for us to get the others to safety. We will meet them at the northern bank, once we have Mother and the younglings."

"And once we are all gathered with nowhere to hide in case of attack?" Halla asked.

"We will be able to make much of the journey on foot." Agni commented. "You mean to make for the main force, do you not?"

"I mean to get these people to safety. If I must, I will take them to the stronghold, east of Canor's northern bank, on Throst Island." Thala, Halla and Agni, all perked up at the mention.

"We could easily move from there, to our allies north of Grom's isles." Thala commented.

"We have to escape from here, first." Vali groaned as a figure crept out of the shadow and stood atop the hill. Turning its head back, it called out, only to be silenced by Halla's arrow. As the body slumped to the ground, Vali readied his own bow.

"Vali," he could hear Asta call from behind the wall. "I have them, Vali. They are moving for the north shore, now. I have a boat near to there, as well."

"How many?" He called.

"Ten."

"Take them to Abel. Tell him to sail north, to Canor and return for us on the eastern slopes, near the barrow. We will have more survivors there."

"Alright."

"Agni, Halla, go with them. I need you to guide them to the spot I mentioned, earlier."

"Will you be alright?" Agni asked, hand grasping Vali's shoulder.

"Thala and I will manage. Be certain that Asta knows to meet us at the barrow with her boat, as well." With a nod, Agni and Halla sped off, returning to the concealment of the darkness.

"Then what does that leave for us?" Thala asked. Vali turned his head to the east.

"We have some running to do." He commented, before sheathing his sword and taking up a brisk pace. Thala followed beside him. A moment after, as they fell under the protection of the trees, lights appeared beyond the slope. Several more figures, holding swords and shields drew up next to others holding torches.

"Let's go," he whispered to Thala, leading the way toward the barrow. The young woman followed close behind, her footsteps completely silent. Vali shivered at the thought of the young shrine maiden moving quieter than the dead. Even with the spirits heightening his senses, he could not hear her.

It was not long until the light provided by the burning village faded, leaving them stumbling through the darkness. Looking back, Vali saw a vast number of flames, flickering along the hills, moving slowly away from Ulfrost village. They were being followed by hopeless numbers.

"By the gods themselves, Thala. Do not slow." Vali spoke through hard fought, shallow breaths as he faced back to the east.

"I will try but are you certain that you can see the way?" She asked, her breathing normal, even though she matched pace with him.

"I can. By gently reaching out, I can sense the roots and branches of the trees around me. They will help guide the way." Vali again, narrowly out of breath, forced out. Reaching out, Thala placed her tiny hand on Vali's upper shoulder blade.

"You will tire yourself too quickly if you continue to rely on your shaping."

"It is worth the strain." He could feel his lungs burning and for a moment, feared he had been run through.

"Allow me to take the lead. My eyes adjust much more easily to the dark." Thala offered, moving alongside him.

"Thank you," Vali conceded. "Be sure to stop at the edge of the forest. We do not want to wander into the middle of the enemy. I will restrain my search to look for signs of the enemy." With no word to the contrary, Vali refined his search, looking only for the trees to show him where the invaders might be.

"We are there," Thala whispered, halting abruptly at the edge of the tree line. Vali bent in half, resting his hand against the trunk of the nearest tree. Attempting to catch his breath, he waited for Thala to relay her observations.

"I do not see more than a few torches." She stated. "Do you suspect that the invaders have moved inside?"

"Let us hope not." Vali, slightly recovered, stood straight. "It will be difficult for us to overcome an enemy force by ourselves."

"However, little choice remains..."

"I never said that we would wait." Vali clarified. "We do need to be sure to avoid as many threats as possible, however. I hate to admit it but Asta might be right. I am unsure how long I will manage in a full-on battle."

"I see." Thala whispered back, without looking to Vali. "It looks as though we will need to use a different entrance to the barrow."

"I do not know of any other." Vali said.

"There is one, near the shrine, to the north." Thala said, pointing a short distance down. "We can follow the edge of the forest and work our way just short of the shrine. Hopefully, these invaders have not taken over it, yet."

"Lead the way." He said, motioning forward. Thala nodded and rising from her hiding place, ran ahead of Vali. He followed close behind her, blind otherwise, without her aid. Hugging the tree line, they sprinted through the short vegetation, while dodging in between the trees. Several minutes later, having reached the northern edge of the forest, they cautiously stepped out into the open.

No lights gave any hint to the enemy's presence. The sound of the sea as it struck the sides of the cliff face, filled their ears. The broken quiet provided a sense of ease as the smell of the salty air, reached them.

"This way," Thala spoke, shaking herself from the moment and led Vali through the opening toward the small arrangement of stone constructs ahead. Though he had not frequented the shrines in some time and the dim light of the moon bore him no clear image, he knew his way.

Spread about in a circle, the shrine laid out before him, a monument to those who once dwelt in the court of the Aesir. A monument stood for each of the Old Gods; the mighty Thor, with his wife, Sif, Baldur and many more. At the center of the shrine, stood the all father, himself, Odin, Frigg beside him. Charging to the gates of the shrine, they came to face the guardian of the one hundred isles, Valkyr.

The maiden stood tall, sword in hand as she watched over the shrine. As they approached, Thala made certain to bow in the goddess's presence, before entering. Vali repeated the gesture, as he followed behind her.

"This way," Thala whispered, guiding him forward. "The entrance lies at Odin's feet."

"The way to Valhalla, lies beyond the will of the all father." Vali muttered to himself, nodding his head as he kept his eyes open for danger. All around them, the statues of the old gods watched, their eternal vigil concentrated at the shrine's center.

Ahead, he saw Odin, strong, noble features, upon the face of a wise elder. In his hand, he held a staff. Ever flowing sagely robes wrapped around his shoulders. Ravens, both carved and alive, decorated his statue, perched upon his shoulders and staff, also staring at Vali and Thala.

"All Father," Thala spoke, kneeling before the lord of the Aesir. "It is I, Thala of Ulfrost, guardian of this shrine. I have brought with me Vali, a warrior who fights in your name, against a faceless enemy. There are those we call kin, who are trapped within the barrow. I ask permission to enter, so that we may save them."

A silence filled the gap between them, only the sound of the sea breeze rushing over the grounds and the occasional "caw" of a raven, broke it. The ravens cackled amongst themselves a moment, before the sound of stone, sliding upon stone, sent a shiver down their spines. Slowly standing, Thala brushed off her knees, before walking toward the back of the statue.

"Come, Vali, the way has opened." Vali stared at the young woman's back a moment, before remembering his purpose. Moving to the back of the statue, he watched as Thala disappeared through a gap in the robes. Moving to the place where she had vanished from, he saw a slight trace of darkness, where an opening awaited.

"Vali, hurry! We may not have much time." He could hear Thala's voice echo from within. Seeing a small light through the crevice, he followed the sound of her voice. Pressing his torso through the tight fit, Vali stepped out into the mouth of a cavern. Thala stood before him, torch in hand, casting a light on the stone carved stairs at their feet.

"How did you light the torch?" He asked. Thala turned her head to the torch in her hand.

"Oh this? We always keep one lit, just in case. We have to swap them out regularly but at a critical moment, such as this, it pays off. Are we going, now?"

"Of course. Please, lead the way. I have never been to this side of the tunnels, before." Thala, nodding her head, turned and hastily traveled down the stairs, the sound of her boots even quieter than the crackle of the torch in her hand. As Vali followed, he noticed the gentle thud of his boots, striking the stone.

Thala, with hastened steps, turned around the corner, the map of the tunnels well embedded in her mind. Vali attempted to reach out for any sign of his Mother, the younglings, or the enemy. Touching his hand to the stone walls, he felt for any vibration the stone might carry.

"Shaping will do you no good down here." Thala spoke, still moving forward.

"Truly?" Vali asked, looking further down the path of the winding caverns. Wooden beams and stone were raised in places, adding additional support to the structure within. The deeper they traversed, the more coffers lined the walls, housing the remains of those who had first settled the Isles of Vala.

"Yes. These caverns were rumored to have been forged by the ancient kings, by order of the old gods. The Isles of Vala, have many secrets, which are well defended from outside influence. You will be hard pressed to find much of anything, within these halls."

"Do you know where we are going?"

"Yes. I would guess that Kari has taken everyone to the burial room or one of the burial chambers. Either way, we should head for the central chamber, where the bodies are prepared."

"Not sure that I enjoy the sound of that, but you are right. A location such as that would be far easier for Mother to defend herself and the others in. Do you think that she knows that shaping the earth will be difficult?"

"I am surprised that you do not."

"I have never attempted to shape the earth, while I have been underground. Earth is about the only element Mother can shape, since her illness."

"Well, as you stated, tactically, it is a defensible location. We can be thankful for that much. However, since we are underground and in an enclosed location, I would advise against fire shaping or wind shaping on a large scale."

"Wind shaping is nearly impossible beneath the surface," Vali stated. "With fire, do not worry. I have no intentions of cooking us alive."

"We are almost there, now," Thala dropped her voice to a whisper. "Be ready for anything." Vali carefully drew his sword. Brushing away another net of cobwebs, Thala extinguished her torch and slowly crept into the next chamber.

"Vali!" He heard his mother call, before he had seen her. As his eyes adjusted to the dull light of the room, he noticed near twenty people, mostly young children and a few of their parents, gathered in the room, each huddled close to one another, tears in their eyes.

"Vali!" He heard his name again and saw his mother, bloodied, covered in dirt and bruises, walking toward him.

"Mother!" He called back, slowly making his way to her as Thala knelt near some of the unaccompanied children, smile on her face as she attempted to calm them. As Vali and Kari made their way to the center of the room, they wrapped their arms around one another, tightly.

"Vali, my child, are you alright?" She asked, ignoring her own wounds to carefully look him over.

"Yes, Mother, I am fine. You are wounded."

"Do not worry. These wounds are more than a day old. What is going on out there?"

"Ulf sent my crew and I back to Ulfrost. He had a terrible feeling that Grom might attack us. It seems that he was right to be worried."

"This certainly does seem like Grom's doing." Kari spoke.

"Mother, did you manage a good look at the invaders?"

"Closer than I wished, to be sure. Had this been Grom's work, I would suspect that he would have been among them. I will not rule out his guilt, but I suspect this attack was made by an outside force."

"What outside force? The Kresh? What of the Fallen Brotherhood?" He asked. "Could not they have returned?"

"It is not impossible, though they would have needed help. This was certainly not the work of the Kresh. Perhaps someone else, within one of the clans, operating on their own or with the exiles. Were there any at the clans meet, who seemed to harbor any ill will, other than Grom?" Vali thought back, trying to remember everything, which had transpired.

"No. Only Grom caused an uproar. Chief Rolf and Chief Allie, were both pardoned at the clans meet, since Dumah had been stricken so badly. Chief Allie and her clan were spearheading the relief effort."

"What did Grom do, which caused the uproar?"

"The High Chief asked about his eldest son, Urs, after his refusal to give aid. He was not at the clans meet." Kari's eyebrows raised.

"And this is what led to the confrontation? Finna failed to mention that."

"Not entirely, no. However, I believe that it was the matter, which started it. Grom did not arrive at the clans meet, prepared for any engagement. He never intended to offer aid, even before the summoning."

"An internal struggle, perhaps. Finna and I had not considered that." She thought a moment, before looking back to Vali and Thala.

"How did you two manage to slip passed the invaders?"

"There is an entrance at the shrine." Vali pointed out. Kari turned her head up to Thala and smiled.

"I thought I recognized you, young Thala. How have you been? Are you still working on your shaping? I have not seen you for some time, now."

"I have been well, thanks to you, Teacher. I miss Mother and Father, but I do well on my own and continue to practice at the shrine, every day."

"I understand. I have a feeling you will be well accompanied here for a time. Vali, do you have a plan to escape from this mess?"

"Yes," Vali jolted upright, returning to his mission. "Abel and Asta, are both steering ships to meet us just beyond the shrine, along the northern beach, beneath the cliffs. We, all of us, will leave through the passage Thala and I took to arrive and head for the beach.

From there, we will sail to the northern edge of Canor, where Agni and the rest my crew will have taken High Chief Finna and the others." Kari thought a moment, running her thoughts through her mind.

"Very well, then. Let's be on our way. I suspect that it will not be long, until the invaders attempt to break through the walls, again." She forced a smile to spread her lips as she looked at the worried faces of the children eyeing them.

"Come now, children. It is time for us to be on our way. Who is excited about riding on a boat?" A few chirps amongst the crowd rang out between the younger ones, reality having yet eluded them.

"You all know my son, Vali, correct? He is here to take us away from those mean men. We are going to go and meet with your parents and everyone else. Are you ready?" The gathered children and adults all nodded their heads, before rising. Amongst the group, he heard many murmurs of thanks and praise to the gods, for their deliverance. However, Vali continued to eye the passage, which he was most familiar with.

"Vali, let's go," Thala pressed, urgent tone in her voice.

"You are right," he mumbled, hearing the scuffling of metal from beyond the chamber. "Asta and Abel are going to grow worried, should we keep them waiting overlong. Go ahead and take the lead. I will cover the rear." Thala nodded her head and moved down the passage.

Vali stood back, watching as everyone slowly moved beyond the burial chamber. As the end of the line came up, Kari placed her hand on her son's shoulder. He smiled faintly at her and placed his hand on the cavern wall.

"We need to seal off this exit." He suggested. Kari eyed him and nodded.

"Earth shaping is quite difficult in here. I had quite a deal of trouble burying the other tunnel, before you arrived. Come then, give your mother a hand." Kari placed her hand beside Vali's, closed her eyes and focused. Beneath his hand, Vali felt the gentle thrumming of his Mother's shaping. Reaching out for it within his mind, he added his own strength to the pulse.

A moment after, he felt a strong surge rumble the chamber around them. Bits of dust and debris fell from the cavern ceiling as the ground beneath his feet shook. He could hear a distressed call from further down the passage, though he continued to press against the wall.

He could feel as his mother leaned on him, little more with each passing breath. Even with her aid, he could feel himself weakening, as well. Silently, he cursed his lack of preparation with such massive shapings.

As sweat poured from both of their brows, he felt as the stone beneath his hand chipped and cracked. He felt his extended presence, forcing itself forward, wedging into every earthen imperfection, and expanding. The crack widened, giving him more space and then some, until the crack split through the ceiling.

"That is enough, son," Kari panted. "We need to back away now, before we become entombed, as well." Vali's eyelids flickered open, as he felt his internal self, retreat from the wall.

"Of course. Let me help you, Mother." He said, sliding his shaky arm beneath his mother's, helping to support her weight.

"I am not so old that I cannot pull off a simple earth shaping, every now and then."

"That was no simple shaping and your health has been poor enough that such shapings are like to steal your strength." He fought against his own fatigue, keeping a brave face for his mother and the others, as they came upon everyone.

"Such a good boy," Kari whispered, patting her son on the chest as she allowed him to approach Thala.

"We collapsed the tunnel. At the very least, they will not follow us from behind." He saw as Thala's face winced slightly from the news.

"I suppose it could not be avoided," she sighed. "Come, it appears as though we are still in danger." Vali again squeezed through the narrow opening, which Thala had passed with ease. As the smell of salt returned to his nostrils, he tilted his head from side to side, keeping a watchful eye on the grounds.

"I will take the lead," he whispered back, drawing his blade and stepping out into the open. He moved beyond the all father's robes, battle ready, as their charges followed behind. Passing through the gates, he looked back to the forest and stopped. Signaling for the others to charge north, he knelt and placed his hand to the ground.

"What is it, Vali?" Kari asked, as Thala ran with the others. Vali gently shook his head as he reached out through the roots of the vegetation, each one connected to the next. In the distance, he felt a faint flicker of foreign life. The enemy was marching toward them.

"Run!" He spoke softly, yet urgently as he gently pressed against his mother. Without hesitation, they both spirited away the best they could, neither one caring to look back.

"Quickly!" Thala called from the edge of the cliffside leading down to the drop off. "I can see the longboats coming in and the enemies' torches in the distance behind you!" Unfortunately, Vali turned his head back to see.

Marching up the hill toward them, from beyond the barrow and the trees, he saw them. Hundreds, if not thousands of torches flickered in the distance. Several of the younglings had been fetched up by their parents, who sprinted for the coast. Many of the parentless however, trailed behind the others.

"Vali, archers!" Thala called, pointing to the southwest. Vali turned his head and saw as a dozen or so invaders, stepped from the tree line, bows in hand. As each reached behind their backs to pull an arrow from their quiver, panic flooded Vali's veins.

"Run ahead! Grab as many as you can!" He cried out as he heard the bowstrings release. With a heavy growl, he felt his knuckles pop from his grasp on his hilt. Reaching deep into the pit of his stomach, he reached out for every spirit he could sense. Pouring all their might into a single stroke, Vali back slashed with a growl, channeling the power of the wind. It was not nearly enough.

His eyes filled with horror, as three, four, and seven, of the younglings fell to the ground, the arrows driven off course only in part. He heard his own voice, amongst others, cry out in horror at the sight. Several of the children, who had been missed, stopped and tried helping their friends to their feet. Thala dropped to a knee after having attempted a similar shaping.

Vali could hear music. A chorus of disembodied, inhuman voices called for him. He felt dizzy and sluggish, though the world moved slower than his staggered steps. Feeling himself losing synchronicity with his physical body, only the sensation of a lead tightening around his wrist kept him focused.

Kari, doing her best, grabbed onto one of the injured, who was rising to their feet. A moment later, Thala was slinging her arms beneath the shoulders of two more. Vali, his awareness restored, saw the archers preparing a second volley and charged, shield raised, voice erupting with fury.

Managing to capture the attention of a few of the archers, they turned their gaze upon him and fired. Shield raised high, he felt the impact of the missiles as he attempted to channel another gust of wind. The singing voices continued to breath just beside him as the strain of his shaping grew. Releasing it, he stumbled and fell, narrowly avoiding another bolt, which grazed his ear.

As he bit a mouthful of dirt and rolled, he heard another cry from the fleeing civilians. Vision blurred by the murderous intent flowing between he and the spirits he continued to draw upon, he slammed his fists into the ground with rage. With another loud bellow, he rose to his feet, only to feel pain flooding through his body. Glancing down as he raised his shield, he saw an arrow planted into his left thigh and another, in his right shoulder.

"RUN!" He bellowed again, growling as though a deranged beast, signaling to its brood of an enemy's death. Two more arrows struck his shield, while another nicked the side of his right shin. He buckled only slightly, channeling all his anger and outrage, into a single point. The point, the thicket at the mouth of the forest, burst into flame, immediately surging across the dry brush and grass, lapping at the legs of his attackers.

The pained cries of his enemy, the first sign they were made of the same flesh as he, echoed back. Vali stumbled, having given too much of himself to the spirits, he nearly collapsed. His head swooned as he felt himself drifting from his body, which began moving on its own. Suddenly, his right wrist burned as something ethereal squeezed tightly, shackling him to himself.

He screamed within his own mind, his voice, echoing one hundred times over. He grew delirious a moment, his temples thrusting outward as his skull threatened to crack. In an instant, the pressure had subsided and adrenaline again, coursed through his veins.

His vision clearing slightly, he looked upon his enemies. Stumbling from the fire, they attempted to put out their flames and recover as Vali, enraged beyond the brink of sanity, charged. Four remained still as Vali pointed himself to a cluster of three. Blood heated beyond its boiling point, Vali's blade bit through the armor, which lie beneath the nearest invader's robes.

He felt a surge of sanguine, splashing his face as he hobbled beyond the first man and struck a second, cleaving his arm from his body. The second man groaned in pain, until Vali brought the heel of his boot, sharply down upon the man's throat. The third attacker, having recovered, swung at Vali with a short sword.

Dragging his right leg as he shifted backward, Vali avoided the overstepped blow and tipping his aegis, swung his shield arm. The heavily damaged, wooden shield, shattered as it crushed the man's throat, dropping him. Vali stumbled backward, wincing, as a fourth arrow struck him low in the back. Allowing the crumbled pieces of his shield to fall, he lifted one of his hatchets from his left hip and with a well-trained throw, sent it haft over handle toward his attacker.

Blade wedged between his eyes, the soldier fell, skull nearly split in two. Patting out the last of the flames, four more soldiers, each a considerable distance from Vali, rose and took notice of him. Vali, opening his maw wide, released an inhuman howl and charged the best he could as he felt the spirits tugging against him, once more.

Taking notice of the enraged Viking, the four men drew up their weapons. Vali, with what little strength remained in his body, reached out to the elements to further bolster him, prolonging his death and opening himself to the spirit shift more. As he neared the soldier at the center of his red hazed vision, he saw his enemy drop of its own volition. Stopping abruptly, he saw as the other three, each crumbled to the ground, as well, arrows planted into the backs of each.

"VALI!" He could hear Asta's familiar scream from the north. The sound broke through the clouded sensation in his mind, forcing his attention to return to his body. His shackle gripped more tightly, forcing the intoxicating embrace of the spirits from his body. A moment later, blood rage fading, he felt his knees buckle and collapsed.

"Come on, Vali," he could hear Abel's voice as two sets of hands grabbed onto him.

"By the nine, he is in bad shape!" Haldr shrieked from the side opposite of Abel.

"HURRY!" He could hear Halla and Thala call in unison as Vali's vision cleared, slightly. He was being dragged through the field, his boots grazing against a small form lying on the ground beside him. Rolling his eyes to the side as he passed by, his eyes watered at the sight of one, far too young to have died.

"May the mother goddess, herself, collect you swiftly to her breast," he murmured as he felt himself lifted.

"Vali, we are almost there!" He could hear Abel speak.

"The children?" Vali moaned. He could hear Haldr let out a sharp wince at the question.

"More alive than dead, my friend. We managed most of them."

"Can we collect their bodies?"

"I am afraid not," Abel choked. "The invaders were too close when we reached you." Vali felt himself forced down onto the hard, rocky surface of a longboat.

"VALI!" He could hear his mother and Asta call as they descended upon him.

"Mother, is he going to be alright?"

"Quiet," Kari hissed. Vali felt a gentle pressure on his chest as a pair of soft, feverishly warm hands, touched his skin.

"Vali, I have to remove the arrows, before I can treat your wounds." Kari whispered to him. "I do not need to warn you that this will be painful." As she spoke, he felt a small hand sliding into his own, running its gentle fingers through his.

"Freyja, is that you?" He asked.

"I am here, as well," he could hear Freyja from the opposite side, as another hand grasped his other.

"I am here, Vali," he heard Asta from the side in question. "We are not leaving you."

"How many did we lose?" He asked, wincing as he felt the first arrow break and removed from his thigh. A short pause followed.

"Four. Mother saw to another, who we are not certain will last the night." Vali winced again, the stab he felt through his heart, more painful than any of his physical wounds.

"Please pray for them." He whispered with a fractured tone. He looked up to Freyja, who nodded her head, her tears peppering him as they fell. He felt Asta's trembling hand within his own as she too, nodded. Closing their eyes, they drew in a deep breath and began to speak.

"May the mother goddess lift them to her bosom," he heard Freyja whisper as he felt another arrow wrenched from his flesh.

"May they find peace in the realm eternal." Asta added. Kari continued to work on Vali, for several, haunted moments. Filling the vast expanse, were the cries of those who had survived.

"We have just lost sight of the coastline," he could hear Abel call from a distance. "The second boat is following close behind."

"Good work, Abel." Vali groaned, another arrow pulled from his body.

"Do not speak, son." Kari grumbled, her skilled hands working bits of herbs and cloth against his wounds. "I am almost finished. Be sure he eats and gets something to drink, once I am."

"Of course, Mother," Asta whispered.

"We will see to it, he rests," Freyja added.

"It will take at least a day, to reach the northern shore of Canor," said Asta.

"We can cut that time down, if we set up a rotation at the oars." Vali suggested. He felt Asta on his right, shifting her weight as she turned her head.

"Abel. The captain suggests a rotation at the oars, to reduce our travel time to Canor." Without another word, Abel bellowed out to several of the people on the vessel, calling for volunteers. With nothing passing between the passengers and the man beyond their brave faces, several of the unwounded took position behind the oars.

"No one objected?" Freyja mused.

"They would not, even if they were the ones wounded," Kari answered. "Each and every one of us, be they farmer, herbalist, warrior, or fisherman, are Vikings. We will die, before we allow the enemy to catch us, or our young. What must be done, will be done."

"We are stronger than I thought." Freyja commented.

"Let us hope the enemy has also underestimated our spirit," Kari added. "It will make all the better for us to drag them to Helheim and watch them barred from the gates of the honored halls."

Several minutes later, body throbbing in pain and heavily bandaged, Vali sat propped up against the side of the deck, Asta and Freyja at his side. Still delirious, he laid his head back as waves of ship biscuits and water, were poured down his throat. The entire time, he felt their presence beside him. He was unsure when it had happened, but eventually, he fell fast asleep.

Chapter 9 – Those that Remain

"I assure you, I am fine." Vali grumbled as Asta, Freyja and Kari, continued to fuss over him.

"The Old Gods themselves could declare it and I would still not be swayed," Kari chided. "You are not yet fit to perform any shaping, especially not a wind shaping to make the boat move faster."

"Stop trying to act tough, Vali." Asta chimed in. "You are not going to impress anyone, by passing out, again."

"Besides," Freyja started. "You risk reopening your wounds, should you make such a foolish attempt. I will not allow it. There are other wind shapers among us. This burden is not yours, alone." Vali, continuing to growl at the three, dagger glancing women, turned his head.

"Abel, help me out, here?" He called.

"No can do, Captain," Abel answered. "I already warned you once. Around them, I fear for my life."

"Coward."

"I prefer to think of it as a sign of sagely wisdom." He laughed from the safe distance between the helm and the quartet.

"Thank you, Abel," Kari scoffed. "I would hate for both our captain and his second, to be out of commission when we reach Canor's northern shore."

"Let it go, Vali." Asta whispered, gently stroking the uninjured side of his back.

"Try to at least enjoy the scenery." Freyja suggested. "Canor has a beautiful countryside." Vali rolled his head to the side and stared out at the western coast of Canor. Tall, lush green trees flooded the coast, their trunks thickly packed together. Birds could be seen, flitting above the tops of the trees. Beside the view of the landscape, sat a child, tears falling from her eyes as she clutched a bloodied bandage on her leg.

"What will we do once we reach the northern shore?" Asta asked, causing Freyja to throw her a sharp glance.

"We will need to rejoin the others. Afterward, we will have to make our way northwest, making our way closer to Dumah's southern edge. At the same time as we cross for our neighbors, others of us, will need to head toward the front lines on Fangor. Ulf and the others need to be informed of what has happened."

"I volunteer to go with you to Fangor," Asta told him.

"Vali cannot go to Fangor." Freyja cut in. "He needs to return to Dumah, with myself and the others, where he can rest."

"I am sorry, Freyja but as Captain, it is my duty to report to the war chiefs. I guarantee that your mother would have it no other way." Freyja stared at Vali, partially in disbelief and in part, out of disapproval.

"Do what you must, then." She grouched, folding her arms and turning away. "I am placing my reservations out in the open, now. I think that you are still at risk of rot and illness."

"Well, provided that I remain in good health, until then, I will have less of an excuse not to go."

"Lay your head back," Kari barked as she pressed back on Vali's forehead.

"Ow, Mother," Vali protested in vain as his Mother sat beside him, pushing Asta to the side.

"Quiet," she demanded, working her way across his wounds, checking his bandages. Seeing the dark circles, which had formed beneath her eyes, he did as he was told. Vali looked back to the second boat, from which Kari had just returned from tending to more wounded.

"Mother, you need to rest." Asta said.

"As do we all," the herbalist grumbled. "As long as I have patients to treat, I can afford a few lost hours of sleep."

"Did the child...?" Vali muttered. Kari shivered, then released a sigh as her son turned his gaze over to her.

"Everything I could do, was not enough." She let out, faintly.

"If you did everything that you could, then there was nothing that could be done." Freyja said, gently grazing the tips of her fingers across Kari's shoulder.

"That matters little, to the child or her parents." Kari growled, pulling away as she turned away from Vali. "Be sure to clean those bandages, before long. I do not want to lose any more than I already have." She walked back to the far side of the boat and knelt beside another of her patients.

"I am sorry," Freyja said. "I only meant to help."

"It is not your fault," Vali sighed. "Mother is always this way, when she loses a patient. She is grateful in her own way, to be certain."

"Vali, you need rest," Asta urged, caressing his shoulder. "Lay back. Rest. We will see to everything, while you recover." Vali eyed both Asta and Freyja, who nodded their heads.

"I suppose I am little good to anyone, dead on my feet."

"There's the spirit," Asta laughed. "Now, stop talking and sleep."

"Do not worry, Vali," Freyja cooed. "Everything will be fine, sooner or later."

"We need to send word to the others." He grumbled, allowing his heavy eyelids to slowly close. "They need to know what has happened."

"We will," Asta spoke, from a distant place. "Once we have reached the others, we will."

***

"Vali," he heard someone whisper into his ear as they gently shook him. His mind was a blur of color, flashes and impressions, a summary of his many, recent, dreamless nights and his near shift into the river of spirits. Boats, the sea, flame, blood and anger; all raced across his vision. A red crowned woman, with wild, canted eyes, silver as the silhouette of moonlight.

"Vali, it is time to wake up. We are nearing Canor's northern edge." His eyelids slowly fluttered open. He lay with his head resting on something warm and soft. He peered through half lidded eyes as he adjusted to the bright, midday sun.

"How long?"

"Just over a day." He heard the same, feminine voice answer. Rolling his head to the side, he saw Freyja, kneeling at the edge of the boat, one of High Chief Finna's ravens, perched near. She tipped her head to the noble bird and tied a small piece of parchment to its leg, before sending it skyward. As Vali followed its eastward flight path, he turned his head to see Asta, looming over him.

"Do you feel better?" She asked as he slowly sat upright. Vali's muscles wailed with discontent as he willed them to move.

"Maybe a little clearer," he moaned, pressing the heel of his right hand to his throbbing forehead. "How far out are we?"

"Abel believes we shall see the others, before evening. By nightfall, we should be able to make our way east, while a small party sails to Fangor."

"Allow me a moment. I will get us there quicker." He pressed his opposite hand to the deck, lifting himself to his feet.

"You will do no such thing!" He heard from multiple sources. Looking about, he came to realize the three scornful stares he was receiving from Asta, Freyja and his mother.

"Stay there, until we are ready to disembark." Kari ordered. "We all know you intend to reach Fangor as swiftly as your body will allow. I would have our rescue party leave here, somewhat rested." Vali allowed his head to hang low as he turned his gaze to Freyja.

"Did you send a raven to the war chiefs?"

"I did, while we were still on Ulfrost. Had you not arrived as quickly as you did, I would have suspected father had received my message."

"Have the ravens ever failed to deliver a message, before?"

"Sometimes on the battlefield, messengers are killed." Kari spoke, as the second boat sailed close by.

"Mother, do you suspect that the battle has already begun?" Vali asked. "There was little sign of the Kresh, before our departure, and no sign of any warrior caste." Kari and the others eyed Vali. Abel, lifted his eyebrows, sending him a subtle warning.

"You have seen them?" Kari asked. Vali's heart froze, realizing what he had nearly admitted to. Taking a moment, he noticed every eye upon both boats, directed at him.

"When we first arrived, I forged ahead to the stronghold. On my way, I encountered a group of Kresh, which had been attacked by a pair of cave trolls. From what I saw, the only Kresh, were young and old. Not one of the group, would I consider to be a member of the warrior caste. Elders, perhaps, but not one fit for battle." Kari thought a moment, before answering.

"It is apparent that not everything is as it seems." She muttered.

"Mother?" Asta asked.

"Younglings and elders beyond their home borders, left defenseless in the wilds. Surely, the Kresh are not so savage and primitive, they simply leave flocks of their youth to be slaughtered." As Kari spoke, Vali thought of the silver eyed woman, again.

"War Chief Ulf made a similar mention. He could not place it but assumed that the main force could not be more than a few days behind."

"Then be prepared for a battle." Kari warned. Vali turned his head toward Asta, remorseful smile on his face. Asta lowered her gaze at him, as well, already accepting her position.

"Asta," Kari spoke.

"Yes, Mother?" Asta muttered.

"Please accompany your brother. He may have great need of you." Asta's eyes widened as a smile spread across her lips.

"Are you certain? You may need me to help traverse the slopes."

"We shall be just fine. Should we take this second vessel, we shall manage quickly enough." Finna spoke.

"By all means do with it as you will. I took it from those grave robbers anyway."

"We appreciate that. Be sure to travel swiftly to our fighting men."

"Certainly, Mother." Vali answered. "I shall see that we make good time."

"To do that, you shall first need to rest." Kari chimed in.

"Might I at least stand? My flank is beginning to grow rather lifeless." Asta snickered lightly as Kari, gently shaking her head, nodded.

"Do not for an instant, think that you can hide your shaping from me." She threatened as she too, rose and moved away. Once she had returned to the second boat, which drifted back in place behind them, Vali slowly rose from the deck. Standing upright, he stretched his tired limbs and looked about at those in his charge.

A variety of tired, hungry and frightened faces stared back at him. He held a bold expression on his face, relaying confidence to his fellow villagers. Turning his eyes to the coastline, he smiled at the sight of a small, low flame.

"Abel, I see our heading." He said, pointing. Several of the villagers, turned their heads to see, as well, while Abel adjusted the helm. Thala and Asta made quick work of lowering the sail, as they eased the boat to a halt along the beach shore.

"Everyone stay on board, until I can determine that we are safe." Vali whispered back, as he, Asta and Thala, each stepped over the side of the deck, weapons drawn. Eyes carefully studying the coastline, they paid little attention to the soft, malleable silt beneath the waters of the bay, crawling up the ankles of their boots.

"Asta," Vali reached out with his wind shaping. "Do you see anyone?" Though she was only a few paces off from his left side, he could barely make out the gentle shake of her head.

"Vali," he felt an impact on his eardrums, carrying the word along with them. A shaping, which pressed into him, words only he could hear.

"High Chief?" He wind shaped back in the same direction. A moment after, black forms appeared from the ground.

"It is good to see you all." High Chief Finna spoke, wiping away a collection of mud, dirt and tall grass, which had been piled on top of her. "Is your mother and the others with you?" Vali's head dipped toward his boots. Asta, eying him a moment, opened and closed her mouth twice, before responding.

"We lost some of the younglings along the way. Everyone else is safe on the boats." Chief Finna did not respond a moment, wiping at her eyes with the inside of her robe's sleeve.

"I understand. You did your best. That is all that can be asked. I thank you for this service, Vali, Asta and Thala. Without you or the others, I fear we may have lost them all. How is Kari?"

"As can be expected. It has been some time since she lost a patient, let alone, so many in a single eve." Asta spoke.

"I understand. Please, follow me. The others are waiting."

"You stood watch by yourself?" Vali asked, following behind the elder.

"Of course not. Your friends are positioned around the other elders. Come now. The sooner we move out, the sooner we make our way east, while you and your crew return to secure a route to Fangor."

"Freyja has already sent a raven toward Fangor." Vali spoke. Finna turned her head to him, eying him curiously.

"I do suppose that was good thinking on her part. Has any word come back, yet?"

"None."

"Then it is safe to assume they do not yet know. Must be that the Kresh have attacked." Finna drew silent a moment longer. "It will be safe to assume that your journey back, will be hard fought. Be sure that you are prepared. Both of you." She said, turning her gaze toward Asta.

"High Chief?" Asta asked.

"I can only assume that your mother wishes you two to go together. I have no place to deny you, at this point. Perhaps in my old age, I missed something. I am grateful to all of you, however, for seeing to so many, in such short notice."

"We can speak of this later, my chief." Vali added. "First, we need to see to it that everyone begins the journey east, so that we might reunite with the main force."

"Of course. This way if you please." Finna spoke, leading them further away from the fires, toward a hilled slope. As they reached the height of the hill, Vali saw numerous familiar faces, pointing weapons in their direction. The moment their eyes registered what they met, their limbs eased, and their weapons lowered.

"Thank the gods, you have come." He heard one of the elders sigh, as Agni and Haldr made their way toward them.

"Everyone," Chief Finna spoke, eying her flock. "We must make to leave, quickly. There exists no telling how far away the enemy is. We need to move quickly, across the channel to the next island.

"Vali and his crew, will take us across, before leaving for Fangor. They will leave us one longboat, two of their crew and shall return with some of our warriors. To do so, we must be swift to find ourselves far from harm." A general murmur rose up amongst the group as they slowly moved their aged bodies. Agni and Haldr assisted those who fell behind, while Chief Finna turned to Thala.

"Shrine maiden, I need for you to be sure that everything is prepared for the journey."

"Of course, my chief." Thala spoke as she ran back down the hill slope.

"Agni, Haldr, would you two be willing to continue on with the chief and the villagers?" Vali asked. Both men, without a word, nodded their heads, as they continued their work.

"Come now, Vali, Asta. Let us make ready to see each other off, then." Chief Finna spoke, a slight drag to her right leg as she walked.

"Are you wounded?" Asta asked, observing the walk.

"Shaping takes a toll on me, I am afraid." She managed, before succumbing to a lengthy coughing fit. They waited patiently, hands ready to catch their chief should she fall. As the fit subsided, the woman stood with her back straight and continued where she left off.

"Not to mention lying on the cold, damp ground for a long stretch. No dear, I am afraid this is simply a result of age. Hurry now, we need for you and the others to make swift work to reach the others. The longer we delay here, the more perilous our situation grows. Please hurry."

"Yes, my chief!" Asta chirped, turning and hastening her return to the longboat. Vali was already waiting for her, below. Kari and the others worked to make ready the boats.

"Agni. Can you please fetch the second boat?" Finna asked.

"I can make it ready, my chief." Asta called, pointing toward her boat.

"No, not that one. The one we made while we were waiting." She added, pointing further down the coast.

"You work quickly," Vali added, impressed.

"We have shapers among us but more importantly, years of skill and experience. Your second was most helpful. Added with some muscle provided by your two friends, we managed. With two vessels, we can make for Dumah much more easily." A moment later, a boat, nearly the size of Vali's, floated from around the bay. Vali and Asta both smiled at the sight.

"Resourceful as always, I see." Kari commented, peering from off the deck of the second ship. Abel, Halla and Thala, each worked in the background to divvy various necessities between the two boats.

"We have to be." Finna commented. "Please take a moment to see to your children, Kari. The journey will be difficult for both of our parties. I fear for what our brave, young Vikings yet face."

~ 136 ~

"Of course," Kari nodded, a crack in her voice. "Just give me a few minutes with them." She said, dropping to the shallows of the beach and strolling near to them.

"Everything will be alright, mother." Vali spoke, wrapping his arms around his mother and holding her tightly. He extended his right arm, allowing Asta to squeeze between them and gripped around her tightly.

"Mother, please do not cry," Asta whimpered, gently stroking her mother's back.

"It is my right," Kari protested, her tears dripping freely on Vali's vest. "It is my job to worry about my children."

"I promise, Mother," Vali began. "We will be alright. We have each other. Asta and I will protect one another and bring back help, just as soon as we are able."

"Do you remember what I have told you?" Kari asked.

"Do not travel beyond the fog, unless we've no other choice." Asta answered as Vali felt a pang of guilt.

"And always stay together. The gods themselves, do not dwell out in that world. I dare say, I have long feared the day when you two might sail beyond the Isles of Vala."

"We have no need to go so far. It will be alright." Asta said. Kari gripped tightly onto her children's shoulders, nodding her head and steeling against her own emotions.

"Of course, it will be," she said. "You are Vikings, and more importantly, my children. Together, there is nothing that you two cannot accomplish. Should you be forced into battle or should things grow rough, you must promise me something. Both of you."

"What is it, Mother?" They both whispered.

"Always take care of one another. Do not once, for even a second, forsake one another."

"I will not," said Vali.

"I could never," replied Asta. Kari pulled away, moist eyes staring at her children as she smiled proudly.

"I love you both, with the entirety of my being. Do me proud."

"We will." They whispered into the night, before departing, only a short few moments later. They were quickly rejoined by their comrades, each of which piled silently onto the deck of the Valiant. Staring forward off from the stern, Vali eyed the dark, rolling clouds. The boat shifted as Agni and Haldr, behind the oars, pressed the boat into open water, before Thala caught the wind in the sail. They were on their way back to Fangor, where an unknown enemy awaited.

Chapter 10 – The Return

The waters proved rough that evening and their hearts heavy. The wind, having died down, provided little aid through the cold, starless night. All around, the sound of thunder boomed, off in the distance. Vali and his crew guided their vessel without the use of their celestial guides.

"How can you be certain that we will not lose the way?" Halla asked.

"I understand that voyaging is difficult under such circumstances, Halla, but we are hardly in uncharted waters." Abel grumbled. "Fangor is due north of Canor. It is only a matter of venturing to the next island and making our way around it, to the next."

"That hardly seems a fool proof plan for success," teased Asta. "Are you certain that we venture north?"

"Speak to our shapers. It is their water shapings, which guides us." Asta and Halla both turned their heads toward Vali and Thala, who smiled.

"Do not worry. I do not need to exert much force, in order to determine our heading. We are on the right course. Should the weather turn against us, I can draw from the power of the storm to press us faster. We will not be caught in unfriendly waters." Asta looked down to her waist, where the lifeline she had secured sat. Checking the knot, she sighed.

"And you are letting Thala help you?"

"I assure you, Asta. He is not in this alone." Thala replied, eyes closed in concentration as she pressed both hands to the deck of the ship. Asta nodded her head.

"Just so long as you both know what you are doing."

"We have prepared for this. It will hardly be the first or the last storm, which Abel and I have sailed through. We are ready for this. It is what we face on Fangor, which has me concerned."

"The Kresh?" Halla asked.

"At the least," Abel muttered. "By the Old Ones, I would like to know who else we are facing."

"As would we all," Asta sighed.

"Such thoughts will do us little good, if we cannot warn the rest of the warriors. We need fighters, not worries." Vali started. "Once we are sorting the enemies' corpses, we can determine who from whom."

"Of course," said Asta. "I suppose it does little good to worry about something we cannot change."

"The mountain is not felled in a single stroke, but by the conquest of one stone, upon another." Thala murmured.

"Then from one stone thrower to the next, let us pray for pebbles and not boulders." Abel groaned.

"Where is your sense of adventure, Abel?" Halla asked. "Should we not revel in the thought of a daunting task ahead? I say let the enemy come. Come at us with their ships, their blades and their godless ways. We shall crush them all. The Old Ones will guide us." No one said much, either to bolster or deter their companion's encouragement. They simply accepted it, allowed it to mull in their hearts, and allowed it to settle.

By morning, the isle north of Canor, Canus, was off their starboard side. They had thus far navigated the storm, without incident, though the wind still provided them with little aid. Vali took his turn at the oars, Asta working across from him as Thala and Halla, rested.

"So, Sparrow, is this everything you hoped it would be?" Vali smiled, grunting slightly against the oars, with every pass.

"Even more so," she replied excitedly. "I could not have imagined how enthralling this could be. I only wish that we could go beyond the fog wall. See what has not been seen yet. Chart new islands, discover new things. Just like our ancestors."

"Try not to get ahead of yourself," he laughed. "Where we are headed is most definitely known, but no less dangerous. We could be sailing into the center of a battleground."

"I know that." She snapped. "I am attempting a bit of positivity. Not everything needs to be about gloom and death."

"True. I am simply being realistic."

"Well, keep it to yourself, a moment." Asta continued to chide. "This is my first, large adventure. Let me enjoy what I can."

"Of course," he conceded. "I do wish it was under different circumstances, however."

"And weather," Asta grumbled, the rain running down her spine, causing her to tremble, periodically.

"I might manage a shaping to ease a bit of it," Vali proposed, turning his head up to face the sky.

"Do not even think about it," Asta warned. "Bad enough, you have been splitting your focus between rowing and wind shaping, as it is." Vali eyed her curiously, without directly confirming.

"What gives you that idea?"

"Do you always tire so easily, when you are at sea?" She smirked dangerously at him. "That is not just the rain on your skin."

"Well, if it sets you at ease, I am only managing a slight shaping. Just enough to guide a few of the wayward spirits to the sail. It is one, which is not that difficult."

"But likely the best that you could manage, without fully concentrating." Abel added from behind.

"The helmsman should focus on steering." Vali called back, as he pressed with his legs, moving the oars through the water in rhythm.

"And the captain should listen to his crew," Asta glowered.

"I will admit, I wish I could pour everything I have into this one," Vali stated. "Trouble is, I have not fully recovered from the last and do not wish to be useless once we are ashore."

"Are you that worried about what we might find?" Abel asked.

"Not scarcely as much as I am for what we left behind."

"I think you may wish to reconsider that statement." Abel muttered, faint, worried tone in his voice.

"What is the matter?" Asta asked.

"I can see smoke in the distance, rising over Fangor Isle." He answered, pointing in the distance. They each turned their attention where Abel pointed. High in the sky, floating up above the southwestern peak, Vali saw a massive plume of smoke.

"Must be a battle, then." Asta chimed.

"Asta, please wake the others," Vali asked, rising from his bench and walking to the bow. "We may not arrive to all friendly faces." Eyes widening, Asta shook her head and moved to the stern, where the others had tucked beneath the deck.

"What is it?" Halla asked sleepily, rubbing her eyes as she surfaced.

"Appears as though the Kresh have arrived." Thala noted, her eyes fixated on the sky.

"Ready your weapons. We may be under attack, before we ever reach the shore. Full battle gear." Vali called, sliding on his belt and equipping his axes and bow. Asta, fully armed with axe, bow and buckler, stood at the ready, hand already upon her quiver, bowstring already strung.

"The moment we strike the beach, I want us to break for the channel. I need a volunteer to scout ahead of the boat." Vali called.

"I will," Asta offered. "I can easily move about the hills and ensure that no one attacks the boat."

"Alright. We will not be able to reach the stronghold strictly from the boat, if there is a battle about. With the elevation and the narrow pass, we would be slaughtered before we ever sighted help. We need to find someplace safe to hide the longboat, until it is needed. That way, we do not lose our only way back, while we move toward Ulf and the others."

"How can we be certain that the boat will remain undiscovered?" Halla asked.

"Along the channel, there is a spot. A small, inlet cave, which runs along the face." Asta spoke. "It was marked on mother's maps. Her husband, Gram, used it during a visit to Fangor, years ago."

"Are you certain?" Halla asked.

"If it is on the former High Chief's maps, then it is there." Abel interrupted. "Asta, can you guide us there?"

"I should be able to. So long as I follow the channel, I should be able to guess where it might be."

"And I can use shaping to search for it." Vali suggested.

"Well then," Abel sighed, gripping the steering oar and clenching his teeth. "I suppose we best be ready. I am taking us in." Asta, holding firmly onto her lifeline, stepped up onto the railing of the deck, leaning gently to the side as she awaited her chance to scout out ahead.

The boat neared the tight, rocky edges of the channel. Abel, keeping a careful, well-trained eye on the bow, maneuvered around the jutted rocks, as he steered through the island. Reaching out for the nearest jagged slope, Asta propelled herself from the deck of the boat, Vali, cutting the line as she crawled hand over foot.

The line snapped back toward the mast, where it was still secured. Asta, reaching the top of the stones, slid the remains of the rope from her waist, tossing the small bundle back down to the boat below. Charging forward, she leapt from one jagged tipped rock, to the next, making her way down the channel, pulling slightly ahead of the slow-moving boat.

"Follow close," Vali called back to Abel.

"Not for lack of trying, Vali, but easier said than done." Abel called back, straining with concentration as he continued to steer, using the rear oar. Vali nodded his head, eying the young woman worriedly as she continued to pull further ahead of them, bow in her hands, arrow strung, a second in her teeth.

"We are nearing the cave," Vali called, seeing a series of waterfalls just up ahead. "We must be close to the halfway point. Once we are there, we can stow the boat and make our way up the backside of the cliffs."

"Vali?" Thala spoke softly, concern in her eyes.

"Yes?"

"I am still a bit unclear on two things. First, why did we not use these caves on our first trip to Fangor? Second, doe using them now not place us behind what would likely serve as the Kresh frontline?" Vali sighed as he considered what she had said.

"First, we need to be certain that the route to Fangor, which our fleet would use, is made clear. Had we used these caves from the beginning, we would only have had to backtrack to the opposite side of the island to begin our search.

"Second, we may be needed to secure a route through the enemy. Should Fangor have fallen under attack, the trail up the mountain will be entirely inaccessible. Asta will find us a way through, while we hide the boat. If possible and we manage to rouse some of the fighting men to our cause, we will need to create a path for them to reach the beach."

"Vali, the cave!" Abel called, motioning up toward Asta, who was signaling the all clear.

"Right then, everyone, be ready to get wet." He called as Abel pulled against the oar, lurching the vessel starboard, until the crashing downs of the waterfall splashed across the deck. Being sure to lean overtop any of their cargo, which might come lose, they tipped their heads down, passing through the sheet of water.

Lifting their gazes once on the other side, they searched within the small confines of the cave. The cave was barely large enough to house the Valiant, its ceiling narrowly reaching down to the uppermost heights of the ship masts. Were they not careful on their way out, they could easily lose one of them to any number of the large stalactites, which decorated the ceiling.

"Are we certain the Kresh do not know of this place?" Abel asked.

"Not remotely. However, if we are all to advance on the stronghold, it is a better option than simply abandoning our boat on the beach. We might have hope of returning to it, this way." Another moment passed as a silhouette appeared on the opposite side of the water sheet.

"We need to move," Asta urged them, breaking through the curtain.

"The Kresh?" Everyone on the other side asked. Asta shook her head as she looked back at the veil.

"Only if the Kresh are like to burn the forest down in their path." She stated, hopping down to join them on the shore. A long pause fell between the group as they quickly shifted into position. Vali however, found himself wondering what enemy they truly faced.

"This way everyone," Vali said, accepting the torch Thala offered and with a brief flicker of focus, brought it to life. Holding out the makeshift torch, wreathed in flame, Vali illuminated the cave, his eyes searching for the passageway to the surface.

"Over here," Thala called. The young shrine maiden crouched low to the ground. "There is a tunnel leading out this way." She spoke, jumping down into a small crevice with a splash. Vali and the others followed close behind, jumping down behind her. Asta, submerged nearly to her chin, tilted her head back to keep above water, while Vali and Abel, bowed their heads before the low ceiling.

Torch held against the low ceiling, Vali lit the passage Thala walked, while the others followed close behind. After the first several paces, through the watery tunnel, he nearly smacked his forehead on the ceiling, the floor slanting upward slightly. Turning back to look over his shoulder, he eyed his companions.

"Be wary, the passage shortens from here." He warned, turning and following the shrine keeper. As they marched further down, only a small gap between the flame, the ceiling and the water level, remained.

"There is a set of steps, leading up." Thala whispered back. "I think it leads up into the hills."

"Lead on then," Vali spoke, handing the torch forward to her. Nodding her head, Thala accepted the torch as Vali and the others climbed out of the water and closed in behind her.

"Just give me a moment." Vali spoke, placing his hand in the air in front of the entourage and willed the water to shape to his command. As demanded, the water ran from their clothes, drying them rapidly. Releasing the shaping, Vali stumbled slightly, before turning back to face up the stairwell, acting as though nothing had happened.

"Conserve your energy, Vali." Asta growled. "Dry clothes will help us little if you find yourself too tired to fight your way out of a Kresh ambush."

"I agree," said Abel. "We can handle a bit of discomfort, if it means we will be at our best during an enemy attack."

"Noted. However, wet leather and wool makes much more noise and is harder to navigate than dry." Thala turned her head back down from the stairwell. "I believe I can see the exit, up ahead." She told them, handing back the torch as she began her climb. Through the same force he had conjured, Vali now doused the flame, before dropping the torch upon the steps. Pulling out his bow, he readied for an attack, as they stepped out into the light.

All around them, the wilderness swarmed in upon an abandoned building, the walls long since giving way to the natural forces of root, rot and vine. Vegetation covered every conceivable, stone surface, while saplings and fungus decorated the floor. Vali looked around carefully as the others swarmed out, gathering his bearings. It did not take him long. To the northwest, clouds of smoke billowed from out of the trees.

"We need to get moving." Vali called, looking to Asta. "Run ahead. Scout the way. We will cover you from behind." Asta, with a nod of her head, took flight, charging into the cover of the forest.

"She will be alright, Vali." Halla said, patting the man on the shoulder after seeing his disgruntled face.

"I know she will be. I am more worried about what she is going to find, than whether or not she will be alright."

"Is she that good?" Thala asked.

"He picked her, before we were assigned you." Abel pointed out blankly.

"I am glad to have you along, as well, Thala. Both you and Asta are assets to this crew. As for Asta, she is the best scout I know. She will find us a path or, she will make one." He gripped his bow tightly, before following into the thick of the forest.

Pressing their way through the concentration of trees, the air grew thicker, reeking of the flames burning on the high slopes. Vali, eyes fixated on the small blur of Asta ahead, moved cautiously. His crew marched in a spread formation, each keeping their eyes locked in a different direction.

"Vali!" He heard the call from up ahead. Crouching down lower, he could see Asta fanning for him to approach. Carefully, he answered the summons, trotting lightly to avoid making any noise. Asta did not once turn her attention from what she was seeing. Instead, she remained motionless, watching the horizon as Vali came up beside her.

"What is it?" He asked, gently cupping his hand over her shoulder. Asta merely pointed forward. Vali reached out at the low hanging greenery, which detoured his vision and gasped.

Below them, much of the forest had been burned away. Devoured stumps and burning logs, formed a sea of smoldering coals. The destruction branched out into a large cone, pointing toward the stronghold's mountain path.

"What could have done this?" He asked, staring in awe at the devastation. Vast trenches were scraped into the valley floor. Slick, greasy tar coated much of the ground in and around these unnatural formations, flames still burning upon much it. Smoldering ash sent trails of smothering smoke from the ground where it did not.

"Could you have done this?" Asta asked. Vali considered the questions a moment.

"Were this a shaping, they must be much more powerful than I am."

"Or much more practiced," she whispered. "But a shaping could have done this?" Vali slowly shook his head from side to side in astonishment.

"I do not know as though even the High Chief has the strength to perform such a feat. In the old days, there were tales of Shapers utilizing fonts, to increase their energy pool. In the end however, the size of the shaping depends on the availability of spirits and the shapers manipulation of them. It is possible. I just cannot conceive how. Even if I were to manage to do everything properly, I would still risk spirit shifting."

"Could one of the old fonts still exist?" Asta asked as the others approached. Halla, upon seeing the sight, fell onto her backside, as Abel slid down the side of a tree, eyes wide in terror.

"That is the only way I can imagine," Vali said, looking over his shoulder. "Thala, do you have anything to add to this? You said before you knew a little of the old ways, being the shrine keeper and a highly shaper. Could a powerful shaper, possessing something to enhance their control over the spirits, have done something like this?" Thala, seemingly uncompromised by what she saw, nodded her head after a moment's deliberation.

"The old stories would suggest so, yes. I believe a powerful Shaper could have done this. However, such a Shaper should no longer exist. Not one member of the clans has ever managed to conjure so many spirits."

"Or at least talked about it." Abel muttered under his breath.

"The arc of the cone is not that wide." Vali commented. "What or whoever did this, was not concerned about moving any large number of troops. Should we rejoin the others, we will likely hold the advantage there."

"If they can do this again, I suspect it will be our only advantage." Halla grumbled. Vali nodded his head. To his horror, so did the others.

"Alright that is enough consideration. We need to meet up with the others. If we run into trouble, we eliminate it. No sense in leaving an enemy at our backs, simply so we can arrive more swiftly. Asta, I need you to scout ahead, again."

"Alright."

"Take the right path, circle your way down toward the backside of the trail. Report back here, once you have found us a way in." He said, rising to his feet.

"Where are you going?" She asked, looking back at him.

"I am heading down there." He said, gesturing toward the carnage below. Something sat in the back of his mind, bothering him. He needed to know what happened.

"Out in the open!? Have you been stricken with madness!?"

"Vali," Abel spoke up. "That is probably the worst idea you have had in some time."

"I will cover you, Vali." Thala said, bow in hand.

"Thala?" Asta and Abel spoke as Halla gripped her bow tightly.

"Me too."

"Seriously?" Abel and Asta shrieked.

"Asta, Abel, I need to go down there. If I can commune with the spirits, should any remain, I can determine what we are up against. With any luck, I might be able to gleam how this was done."

"It would not hurt to have something like that on our side," Thala muttered. "Shapers always learned from one another in the past."

"That, or we communed with the spirits, who taught us." Vali added. Asta growled, a low tone, rattling deep within her throat as she glared at the trio.

"Fine, but the first sign of trouble, run."

"Are I not the captain, here?" Vali laughed.

"I am with Asta on that one," Thala said.

"As am I," Abel and Halla agreed.

"I will be alright." Vali sighed, stowing his weapons and slowly working his way down the steep slope.

"You better come back in one piece!" Asta growled threateningly as she sped off in the opposing direction.

He could hear the others behind him, only for a few moments, dropping several lengths at a time as he worked his way down to the valley. Once the sound of their voices left him, he peered back. A flicker of light, breaking through the ruffage, told him they were still watching.

The stench of the destruction below, reached him before the heat. The smoke, still rising from the ashes, burned at his eyes, making them water. Reaching the edge of the greenery, he cautiously reached out and tapped the nearest of the ruined trees, wrenching his hand back quickly.

"Still a long ways from the epicenter." He muttered to himself, eying the gap between he and his destination. Closing his eyes, he reached out into the open air, feeling for any spirits still in the area.

Probing out, he attempted to reach through the air, though nothing revealed itself to him. Confused look on his face, he instead knelt and holding his hand as near to the ash as he could bear, searched, again finding nothing. Standing upright, a haunting realization came to him.

"Was this done by killing the spirits, opposed to borrowing their energy?" Stepping back, he placed his hand on the trunk of the nearest tree. Sensing the spirits within, he reached out to them, staring curiously as they buzzed beneath his touch.

"Do not be afraid," he spoke softly, sending soothing feelings of ease and comfort, through the tree's trunk. "I wish to know what occurred here. I am not here to harm anyone." The spirits eased slightly, curiously grazing against his consciousness.

"Please, show me. What happened here?" At the request, the spirits "buzzed" at him, hiding away from him, once more. Vali poured more of himself into the oak, reaching deeper for the spirits.

"Please do not hide. I seek knowledge. If I am to face the forces which did this, I must know how to combat it." At the far reaches of his conscience, he felt a gentle nudge, as some of the smaller spirits returned.

"Thank you," he said, opening himself, allowing the spirits to reach into him. Vali felt himself being pulled from his body, the spirits integrating his mind with theirs.

A blur of color and sensation whirled through him, the wood spirits' gentle humming sway, moving him as leaves in the wind. As his vision stabilized, he saw himself standing in a ravine, lush with forest life, a gentle creek flowing through its center. Looking about, he saw a looming figure, far at sea.

A loud "boom," split the sky. A moment later, a great burst of dirt, wood and stone, erupted from the ground as a volatile fountain. A great, destructive ball, comprised of debris from the carnage, bounded across the ground, producing similar geysers of earth, with each strike against the soil.

Vali, despite knowing he was walking through a memory, jumped back out of reflex. On edge, he pulled his shield in front of his body, peering out beyond it as he moved to cover behind the trees. Another explosion split the earth, following the same destructive path as the first.

He continued to watch in horror, hearing through the spirit's delicate senses, as its brethren cried out around them. The massive figure, still gloating over everything in the distance was no longer alone. A series of smaller figures, crept steadily forward, approaching the beach. Vali watched as what he recognized as three small boats, struck the shore.

From within the boats, a score of dark figures stepped out, vibrant, dark aura swirling about them. A sound neared from behind him. Vali turned his attention to the noise and saw as several brightly illuminated figures charged into the ravine. Though their shapes were indistinguishable, the light wrapped around them possessed a bright greenish blue, with swirling bouts of red.

He recognized the calls of the men, identifying them as fellow Vikings, though of which clan, he could not be certain. They charged forward, their auras slowly glowing redder as they drew near. One of the dark figures, stood afore the rest, hand raised. It was what happened after, which stilled the breath in Vali's lungs.

All around the figure, spirits were forcibly pulled toward the swirling vortex, which formed around its arm. Gritting his teeth as he listened to the wail of the captured spirits, Vali watched as the swirl of energy swelled. The other lights slowed their approach, their hesitation well-earned as they bore witness to the bizarre shaping, which took place.

The figure flung open its hand and swung its opposing arm, so the two hands clapped together. The result, a large, scarlet burst of flame, scoured forward, scorching everyone in its wake, the other figures included. Vali shuddered, his knees buckling slightly as he watched the auras of not just the men, but the forest, the creek and the stones, vanish.

Vali's vision swirled once more, as he felt the spirits releasing his senses. His vision returned, his mind adjusting to his eyes, more so than his eyes to the light as he took in his surroundings. Sitting, he placed his hand back upon the tree, gently patting its trunk.

"Thank you for showing me. Might you impart to me a way to combat such a force?" Though he knew his chances were slim, he still found himself disappointed, when the spirits did not but shudder. His eyes traced the path of carnage, which ran up to and broke apart along the mountain trail. Moving nearer, he watched as the odd, earthen spirit or two, poked out at him.

"Resilient beings, earth spirits," he mused, pulling himself entirely from the trees network and rose to his feet. Looking back up to the tree line above him, he signaled to the others that he was going to move forward.

The path up the ravine was steep. Halfway up the climb, he could already feel fatigue setting into his thighs. To his left, the land was scorched away, leaving behind glassy, cragged hillside. Following the trail of green, he scouted behind Asta, covering the young woman's back. Pulling further from the dead zone, he felt some strength seeping into his body.

"Vali." He could hear Asta call from a short distance ahead. Speeding his pace, he rose up the hillside to see her looking to him, eyes filled with fear.

"What is it?" He asked.

"Our forces are no longer under attack, but the fortress has taken a lot of damage. Come look." Vali rushed forward, running up beside Asta, who pointed to the source of the plume of smoke.

The walls of Fangor fortress were heavily charred, black staining most of its entire face, wherever the stones had not been knocked away. The gates held firm, though he suspected just barely. The land all around was charred, while much of the landing afore, was no longer.

"I will signal the others!" He said, tapping the awestruck blonde on the shoulder and turned back down the path. Stowing his bow and unsheathing his sword, he knelt beneath the warm sun and caught the glare on the side of his blade. Gently turning the blade up and down, he sent a series of flashes to the others. A moment later, he saw a series of glimmers return.

Vali! Hurry!" He heard Asta call again. Quickly charging back to her side, he stopped to look where she pointed below the fortress. In the waterway to the north, numerous figures fled from the fortress.

"Could be our men chasing after the invaders!" Vali said, moving forward, his muscles suddenly tightening in preparation on their own.

"What do we do?" She asked. Vali's eyes scanned the valley and the direction the stream flowed. Though the figures were north of the stronghold, there direction was west. Sending a gentle pulse down into the earth beneath his feet, he felt the spirits of earth, still bolstering him.

"I am going to cut them off. Wait here for the others. Have them report to the war chiefs and come for me." Before he managed his second step, Asta had her hand cupped around his forearm.

"This is not a good idea, Vali," she said sternly, eyes filled with worry.

"I know that. There is not much else I can do. You know what to do. I am counting on you." He said, gently pulling his arm away and taking flight. Asta stood, watching him a moment, gripping her fists tightly as she turned and ran to meet with Abel and the others.

The downward slope leading back into the valley still held a plethora of life, having been untouched by the invaders. Reaching down into the soil, Vali felt for the spirits of the earth to guide his feet. His steps felt lighter, even as he could feel himself anchoring to the ground. He smiled with relief. The wild spirits of Fangor were with him.

Charging through the vale with the spirits' aid, Vali moved as swiftly as though he were riding his horse. The earth, seemingly shifted him of its own accord, propelling him faster than he would have ever dared move before, on such terrain. Charging to the next roll in the valley canyon, Vali took up a position at its opening.

Drawing his bow, he stuck three arrows into the ground, a fourth in his teeth and nocked the fifth to his string. Waiting patiently, bow tipped casually to his side in ready position, Vali reached through the earth. Five figures approached, two in front and three behind, moving toward him. Standing firm and bringing his bow up to shooting position, he placed a small amount of tension on his bowstring and drew in a deep breath.

The spirits of the wind carried the frightened voices of those ahead of him. They spoke in a familiar, yet foreign tongue. One voice masculine and the second, female, he immediately picked up on the melodious language of his old enemy. Vali felt an annoyed tug in the pit of his stomach. The Kresh had women and children with them. Easing on his bowstring, he knelt to the earth and placed his left palm to the ground.

"Please slow the Vikings." He whispered, a thrum from the earth, answered his request. A moment later, he could hear the agitated groans of the three in the back. From out of the ravine, he caught sight of a red crowned woman, one hand clenched over her chest, the other, to her spear.

The young boy at her side could not have seen more than twelve winters. His face was painted with dirt and blood. His clothes hung in tatters. Signs of abuse were apparent on his body as they drew near.

They slowed as they drew closer to Vali, the woman from the troll cave, staring at him curiously. Her spear was pointed out at him as they passed with a wide berth. Drawing close enough, he could see the bundle, clasped so tightly to her chest in a leather sling was a small, ashen skinned babe. Vali dropped his bow to his side and nodding his head, moved away from the beautiful, exotic woman.

Retrieving his arrows, he slowly moved into the ravine. Taking his gaze from the woman, he again cursed himself for allowing an enemy to leave. Without bothering to look back, not wanting to know where it was that she was going, he continued his walk, being sure to take his time. Ahead of him, he could hear the angered bellows of the struggling Vikings. He forced down a laugh, at seeing them waist deep in thick, viscous mud.

"Aye, boy, come quickly." One of the three, older Viking men called. Vali moved up to them hastily, recognizing their red and silver clan colors.

"You are Arne's men, are you not?" He asked, looking at the middle aged, red bearded man who had called to him. The men, all three, were balding with only red beards and hazel eyes to decorate their pale, blemished faces.

"Aye, from the Storm Callers of Vaengr Isle." Spat the younger of the group. "Can ye get us out of here?" Vali looked them over once and twice, to ensure he seemed surprised.

"A moment, if you please. I will ask the spirits to release you." Vali knelt and placing his hand to the ground, gave his thanks, before silently asking them to release the men. The ground beneath the three, eagle crest wearing men, rose, pressing them from the pit. Scrambling away from the pool, they looked up at Vali.

"I recognize you, now. You are one of Ulf's Sea Wolves, are you not?"

"Aye, they call me Vali." He said, extending his hand.

"You did not happen to see some Kresh just now, did you?" The man said, motioning his head back down the pass, accepting Vali's hand. "One managed to sneak under our noses and free two prisoners.

"Have the Kresh arrived?" Vali asked, turning his head to face down the ravine.

"Aye. You should see the damage they wrought on the fortress." The man spoke as the younger two in the group, stared at Vali angrily.

"You mean to say you did not see them?" One of the two growled. "You came down the same path as they!"

"I did not see any sign of the enemy. I only happened down this way, because I heard your calls for aid." He said, turning back to face the trio. "Had you not been so loud, I would never have known."

"That is unfortunate," the older man spoke. "I have never seen such destruction wrought upon our lands. The Kresh have in their possession, some new, magical weapon. It is far more destructive than any shaping I have ever seen."

"I was on my way to the fortress. I have seen at a distance the damage. The plume of smoke touches the sky, nearly blotting out the sun." Vali added, pointing to the blackened cloud, which still rose high above them. "I find it difficult to believe the Kresh could have done such a thing."

"Well, they did. Best you accept that fact." One of the two younger men spat, again. "While you settle into disbelief, those three

Kresh are getting away. Gods know what they might bring back with them."

"Well, if it as you have said, they are gone, now. Let us hope that they simply turn back." Vali sighed.

"What? You simply wish for the enemy to retreat? What sort of Vikings do they bring up in Ulfrost?" The younger man continued to glower at him.

"They raise the sort who value life as much as death." Asta seethed, bowstring fully drawn as she approached from behind Vali. "I suggest finding your feet and making your way with us to the stronghold."

"Cowards, you lot!" The two young men turned and slowly walked back as the elder eyed Asta and Vali, apologetically. As Vali turned to ease Asta, the young woman released her hold on the bowstring. The arrow, soaring between both Vali and the elder, settled into the ground, only a breath from the right foot of one of the rude duo.

"Asta!" Vali growled sharply. "Now, is not the time!" Asta sighed, slowly lowering her bow and easing the second missile from her string. As the younger two men sneered, she returned the arrow to her quiver.

"Keep your mongrel on a tighter leash," was the last of the words they spat as they moved on. Vali, turning on a heel, placed both hands in the air in front of Asta, warning her not to proceed.

"Please, forgive them," the elder of the trio spoke. "Sometimes it is the way of the young to be ignorant, stupid and thoughtless. Some suspect it makes them less than Vikings to be otherwise. I am ashamed to admit, it is common practice as of the last few generations."

"I am certain the tension from the latest attacks has not helped. Are you alright?" Vali asked.

"Ah yes, quite. Strange, being sucked into the earth that way. It would seem the spirits were favoring our prey. I dare say, I hope that the occurrence does not repeat itself."

"Prisoners? Were there Kresh being held at the stronghold?" Vali asked.

"Aye, a young boy and his sister." The man's eyes dropped to the ground, slightly.

"What?" Asta asked.

"It was our men who captured the boy, who was carrying the babe. I am ashamed to say they were keeping the boy as a slave, of sorts. Keeping his sister for safe keeping."

"And the Kresh are the barbarians." Asta scoffed as Vali shook his head.

"How did he manage to escape?" The older man smiled as Vali carefully chose his words.

"Cunning tongue," the man commented. "There was another Kresh, about your age, I would guess. She had a crown of red hair, which flowed over a golden mane. It was she, who snuck beyond our guard and rescued the boy and his sister. She managed to incapacitate several men on her escape but killed no one."

"And you were sent with those two ruffians?"

"Rather, I ordered them to take me with them. Keep them from anything too rash, at the least. I am Throm, second in command to Arne." The man said, extending his arm. Vali reached out, clasping the man's forearm in return.

"Well met, Throm. I am Vali, and this is Asta. Please accompany us back to the stronghold. I suspect my second is already delivering a report to the war chiefs. It seems this campaign has met with ill ends on all sides."

"Oh?" Throm raised his eyebrows quizzically. "A bit more ill fortune could not hurt the campaign, I suppose." He spoke with a chuckle as he turned to follow the vale back to the stronghold. As the three of them walked, Vali held back slightly, his eyes at last tracing back to the path the Kresh had taken.

"Vali?" Asta whispered, her shoulder pressed against his. "What is going on?" She asked, glancing back toward the valley. "I saw everything." She maintained a whisper so as not alert Throm.

"I am not quite certain what is going on, yet. However, it will be best that we keep from any infighting. Please keep your temper in check." Asta's eyes narrowed as she scowled at Vali but said nothing. After a moment, she drew a deep breath and sighed.

"I just hope you know what you are doing."

"I know, Asta. Believe me, I know."

***

Their trek through the vale seemed to take quite some time, especially to Vali, who had recently discovered how to move at an incredulous pace. However, eager to keep the elder Throm in their good graces, they walked alongside the man. As they climbed the steep hill, they saw numerous fighting men and women, already standing outside of the gates, arguing.

"I do not care if there are other problems. What has happened here, effects much more than just Ulfrost." Another of the chiefs, Gunnar, a thin, yet firmly muscled man growled, staring eye to eye with Ulf. The green sleeves of his brown and emerald clothes, tattered and soiled from their recent excursion.

"I have already lost many of my mounts and a number of my riders to these invaders. Kresh or not, this campaign is not over, until we push them back for good. We only barely managed to repel them through the strength of our shapers. The Sea Wolves will be needed to finish the campaign."

"Aye, you have lost many a fighter, but not your home." Ulf growled back. "When all is said and done, the Horse Clan shall return to Vinland. My people are in amidst a battle to reach our distant neighbor."

"By all accounts of the young lad, they shall arrive within the next day or two. Once all is said and done, I will gladly pledge the clan horse to reclaim your isle." Gunnar turned his attention to Vali, Asta and Throm, as they entered the crowd.

"Ah, it seems that your young captain and the rest of his crew have arrived." Gunnar said, patting Ulf on the shoulder in parting.

"It is good to see you, boy, Asta." Ulf said, massaging the ridge of his nose. "As you can see, things have not been progressing well here, either."

"Gunnar will not support an effort to reclaim Ulfrost?" Vali asked. Ulf shook his head.

"Nay, and it is not just Gunnar. None of the chiefs are willing to back down, as of yet. They wish to finish this business with the Kresh, first."

"War Chief Ulf, they do not honestly believe the Kresh possess such shapings as this enemy, do they?" Vali asked in disbelief.

"Aye. As much as it pains me to think it, they do. Each of the chiefs believes the reason the Kresh have chosen now of all times, to attack, is due to the belief that they now possess such magics. Superstitious fools, the lot of them. We have seen naught but babes and children. There is not a warrior to be found, who carries the Kresh blood." Vali checked his surroundings carefully, eying over his shoulder. Noticing the two younger men who had been at Throm's side, glaring at him, Vali turned back to his war chief.

"Ulf, is there somewhere we might speak in private?" Ulf turned his head slightly, tipping his gaze from the horizon to Vali.

"What seems to be the matter?" He asked.

"There is something I must speak with you about, but not in front of the other clans, or more importantly, some of their blood hungry fighters."

"This way," he said under his breath. Pressing passed Vali, he moved toward the other end of camp. "Each of the clans has set up a small camp, within the stronghold. We can speak privately in my quarters. I do hope that what you wish to speak about, is well worth the time. There is an unknown enemy out there, preparing to strike as we speak."

"I understand, Ulf. Do you wish for me to take my crew and patrol?"

"Perhaps it will come to that. For now, however, we wait. When the enemy returns, we will fight them back, again."

"The other clans are already growing restless though, are they not?"

"Aye, they are. Hiding behind stronghold walls is not typically the Viking way. To say there have been disagreements, would put it mildly."

"Any dissention?"

"They came together by oaths of loyalty alone. They will not dessert us, nor will they battle us. Each war chief may still command his own. Should they grow restless enough, they will head out alone. Until then, what they have seen so far has sufficiently scared them into staying put."

"Cannot say as though I blame them. Ulf, the spirits have shown me what happened to the valley. All this destruction, at the hands of seven beings? What exactly are we up against?" Ulf simply stared back, sunken, almost lifeless gaze in his eyes.

"I do not know." He answered as they reached the other side of the encampment, where Ulf guided Vali inside a small building. Looking inside, Vali saw simple stone floors, leading to a lit fireplace. He could feel the warmth of the flames reaching out for him. Walking in, Ulf secured the door behind them and motioned for Vali to take a seat. Tapping his ear gently, Vali nodded and willed the air around them to conceal their conversation.

"Well then," Ulf began, taking a seat near to Vali. "What seems to be the urgent matter?"

"Ulf, I need to tell you about the Kresh on this island?" Vali let out lightly. The man's eyebrows raised slightly as he looked upon the young captain.

"Arne's men had two young Kresh captive, but they have since escaped. Poor lad. Even were they our true enemy, they need not be treated so." He growled angrily, once more making Vali question the man's true feelings about the Kresh.

"Ulf, I helped them escape, twice." The much larger man continued to stare at Vali with imposing intensity, even though sitting, his presence loomed over him.

"Explain." He answered. Vali sighed, partly from relief that he was not being chained, and part in horror that he was revealing his secret.

"When I first arrived on Fangor," he started, the words clinging uncomfortably to the back of his throat, he forced them out. "As I said, there was a Kresh party, which was slaughtered by cave trolls."

"Yes, I remember. You kept some of the fangs as proof. What of it?"

"Not all of them were dead."

"So, you lied in your report." Ulf stated, no tone of surprise in his voice.

"Aye, war chief. I mislead you." Vali said, turning his gaze down to the floor.

"For what purpose?" The man continued in absolute monotone.

"I had initially intended on leaving the Kresh to die. However, a young, female Kresh caught my attention. She was in trouble and I could not stomach letting her die at the hands of that creature."

"To die by any troll, is a pitiable death, even for an enemy," Ulf agreed. "Yet, you went out of your way to save an enemy and later lied to your war chief."

"I know. I am sorry. All that were left was the young woman and a few elders. I could not bring myself to killing them, nor could I stomach turning them over to..."

"Be butchered by myself?" The man asked, eyebrow raised. Vali's throat clenched tightly, and his mouth grew dry. He agonized over his next words far too long to attempt redemption. With a hard swallow, he broke his guilty silence with a betrodden groan.

"Yes, war chief."

"I understand your reasoning. It is a difficult thing, taking a life. Even though it is our way, to pillage, conquer and explore, it is never easy to take without purpose. There would be no glory, no honor or fame, to be won from such slaughter. I suppose I cannot see fault in such thinking."

"Thank you, War Chief."

"However, such actions may have also proven catastrophic for your crew, had other Kresh been alerted to your presence. Do not allow a soft heart to comfort you against reason. You are responsible for the lives of those under your command. Better yet, you might have endangered the lives of the rest of the fleet. Never spare an enemy, without first considering the consequences."

"Of course, War Chief." Vali sank closer to the floor. An uneasy silence drifted between the two men a moment, before Ulf continued.

"What of the two escaping Kresh? What involvement did you have with the young boy and his sister?"

"The woman was the same that I allowed to flee after the trolls. It was she who rescued the boy and his sister. I came upon them down in the valley. I used my shaping to hinder the progress of Arne's men, when they attempted to capture them. I am the reason they managed to escape the valley."

"A grave offense," Ulf sighed. "Were you seen?"

"No."

"Praise be to the Gods for that. Should you be suspected, alone, would be enough to challenge you to combat. Were any accusations made?"

"No, however, I would not put it passed two of the men I encountered, to blame me." Again, Ulf sighed.

"Boy, you best continue to earn your merit." He said, shaking his head. "A fair number of problems may have been resolved, had you allowed the Kresh to be at either opportunity."

"I cannot apologize," Vali grumbled.

"I am not asking you to. Perhaps the Old Ones shall show us one day, what will they enacted to provoke such actions from you. I am glad that you confessed. To be honest, I had hoped we would not encounter any of their kind. Perhaps it was the former High Chief's influence, but I loathe such conflict, as our youth seek."

"I am afraid I do not understand, war chief." Vali responded. The man eyed him wearily and shook his head.

"When you are older, you will see truths, which were once lies. You will also find that the closer one reaches toward death, the longer they stare back at life. Neither, however, is here or there. For now, I need for you to return to our people. See to it they arrive on Dumah."

"What about the enemy?"

"Stopping this enemy will matter very little, if there is no one to return to."

"If all we can afford our people is a prolonged death, nothing matters much." Vali sighed. "How many shapers amongst the clans?" Ulf lifted his head, staring at the wall, the other side of which lead to the rest of the encampment.

"Plenty, though no more than a score of men, between all of the gathered clans have any strength for it. Not compared to this enemy, at least." He said just above a whisper.

"Ulf! You need me here," Vali stammered, having hoped the number would be higher.

"Keep your voice down, boy." The war chief thundered, his body humming with the quake of fear and anger in his being. "Do you not think I know that?" He spoke, his tone much softer, quieter. "There has to be someone left, just in case things..." Ulf trailed off a moment. Vali listened, hearing the stirring of a commotion outside. A moment later, they heard a rapping at the door.

"Enter," Ulf boomed, before Vali heard the door swing open. The moment the midday light crept into the room, did the pressure from Vali's shaping dissipate. A wind shaper himself, Jerold stared curiously at the two but did not question as he delivered his news.

"War Chief." Jerold exclaimed, pressing the doors closed behind himself.

"What is it?" Ulf and Vali both stood abruptly. Jerold, noticing the young captain, nodded his head to him, before continuing.

"That massive ship is still in the distance, to the southeast of the island, a fleet of smaller ones, floating about it. It appears that our revenants are back."

"Revenants?" Vali asked.

"It is what we are calling the black garbed shapers, on account of not being able to inflict lasting wounds."

"You have not managed to wound even one of them?" Vali asked.

"Not so far as we can tell. A week ago, when they first arrived, Iver managed to shoot an arrow into one's eye socket. The damned thing wedged into the metal faces they wear and dangled there. The creature beside it, merely plucked the arrow out and the undying blighter stood back up. It took everything we had to get them to leave."

"But you managed to knock it down?" Vali asked.

"Only briefly," Jerold pointed out, as though he were trying to explain it to a youngling. Vali continued to mutter quietly to himself as he considered Jerold's information.

"Vali, what are you getting at?" Ulf asked. Vali stood, eyes staring through an invisible void, his mind whirling.

"I am not yet certain, but there is something there." He muttered, continuing his train of thought. "They cannot be killed, so far as we know, but they can be incapacitated by a mortal wound, perhaps." He looked back to the other two men, who eyed him curiously.

"Vali, do you have an idea?" Jerold asked.

"Maybe, but I need some time to think." He could hear the other two growl under their breath.

"We may not have time!" Jerold snarled. "War Chief, what exactly are these things?" Ulf looked over to Vali, who shook his head.

"We do not know."

***

An hour later, having laid out his thoughts on the matter of the Revenants to Jerold and Ulf, Vali reentered the camp. No sooner had he left the private quarters of the War Chief of Ulfrost, did the eyes of many of the other fighters, lock on him. He concealed a shiver that struck across his spine as he passed Arne's encampment.

Setting his sights beyond the walls of the stronghold, he noticed the slightest flicker of movement in the uppermost branches of an old oak. Marking that as his destination, he set out to learn what had captured his scout's interest.

"Asta, what do you see?" Vali asked, climbing up behind the young woman, who was perched atop the tree, nearest to the valley's gorge.

"Those things are coming," she whispered, giving no other acknowledgement of his approach, her eyes fixated. Taking up roost beside her, he swung one leg on either side of the branch and stared over her shoulder.

Three boats drew near to the shore, the rest of the fleet waiting behind them. Vali squinted his eyes, trying to make out the forms on the boats. Leaning forward slightly, Asta took note of his scrunched face.

"There are seven of them, as the other clansmen said," she relayed.

"Black robes?"

"And metal faces," she nodded. "There is more though," she trailed off.

"What?"

"I am not sure. Perhaps it is my imagination, or fatigue, but I get a sense from them. Something foreboding, yet familiar; terrible and yet, I find it inviting." Vali turned his gaze to the distant boats and the black specks upon them. Though his senses were not nearly as keen as Asta's, he too felt their palpable aura.

"It is as though the spirits are quivering." He said, reaching out a hand.

"What do you sense?" Asta asked.

"Almost as though I hear their voices, quavering. They are retreating from the coastline," he spoke, eyes closed as his sister observed. Though she could not see the spirits, the grass swayed against the direction the wind should be blowing. A moment after, she felt the shifting wind, blowing her hair back.

"They are terrified," he confirmed, opening his eyes. "Asta, by the Old Ones, what are we up against?"

Chapter 11 – The Revenants

Vali and Asta formed up atop the hills, overlooking the valley, across the gorge from the stronghold. They, along with the rest of Vali's crew and several fighters from the clans, watched the hooded figures as they approached the stronghold. None spoke. They barely dared to breathe, before the stalking stroll of the deathly apparitions.

Seven forms, in phantasmal robes, slowly walked through the valley. The sun was beyond its zenith, though still impossibly radiant for a concealed approach. The valley had grown quiet and still. Vali could only feel a few remaining spirits of earth and wood, though they maintained a constant vigil.

The small troop carried forward, climbing from the valley floor. Up above, the clansmen stood at the ready, guarding the stronghold. Even in the distance, Vali could see Ulf, arm in the air, waiting to signal their attack. As they stood, waiting for the man's signal, Vali felt a strange tremor, flowing through the earth.

In the valley below, all seven figures came to an abrupt halt, turning their gaze toward them. Ulf flung out his hand, signaling the attack. A roar sang out from the Viking lines, its voice, mighty and all encompassing. Its echo traveled far beyond the confines of the valley.

A flurry of arrows soared overtop the stonewalls, plummeting down upon the wraith like creatures. They staggered in place as the volley rent their bodies, but none fell. They merely hovered over the ground, neither collapsing or displaying any permeable nature. The matter of their undying status however, was of little concern to Vali. Their eyes were still upon him.

"Abel, I need you to ready the boat." Vali whispered. Thala, Asta and Abel, all snapped their heads to face them as Halla maintained her watch.

"Vali, you cannot be serious," Asta replied. "The warriors are all counting on us. We cannot abandon them." Her voice accidentally heightened, fetching the attention of a few other warriors.

"I am not. I want you to go with him," he added. "Thala, Halla and I, will see our task carried out." A few of the onlookers shifted their gazes away, nervously gripping the hafts of their axes.

"I am not leaving, either." She snapped.

"Asta, those revenants are creating a shaping as we speak. They are dipping their minds into the earth, now, feeling out the entire island. I can feel them, tracing every edge with the tip of a long, bony finger.

"They already know where the stronghold is weak, where the defenders' formations will falter, and where our strongest shapers are positioned. Worse yet, they know we wait to ambush them. Despite all of this, the spirits of the earth are vibrating strongest around you and I."

"He is right." Thala confirmed, opening her eyes. "I can also sense it."

"Why?" Thala asked, while the others stared in disbelief.

"The spirits are attempting to hide us," he thought aloud. "They are producing a blind spot. However, to shapers this powerful a blind spot could easily serve as a beacon." No sooner had the words left his lips, did the seven figures, still under fire change direction, shrieking as they approached.

In the distance, Ulf howled again drawing his sword, ordering the charge. No fewer than one thousand Viking warriors descended from the stronghold. Of the seven figures, three turned their attention to the horde. The other four remained on target.

"Abel, Asta, go!" Vali ordered, taking up his bow. Asta shook her head.

"No Vali! You need me here, fighting beside you."

"Not this time, Asta," he grunted. "This time, it is better that we separate. Take the Valiant and go. If I am right, our enemy will disperse, part for you, and the rest for me." Abel, dutifully nodding his head, gently grasped Asta's arm.

"You know he is right, Asta." Abel said. "We will have a better chance if we hurry and Vali will have fewer of the devils to worry about." Asta stared hard at the man, a moment longer, before nodding her head and retreating.

They moved south of their position, cutting through the wood leading to the stream. A sigh of relief left his lips as Asta vanished from sight. Turning his eyes back toward the enemy, he found his suspicions confirmed. Of the four black robed devils, two broke away, traveling southwest at a walk, toward Asta and Abel, while the other two stayed on course.

Beyond them, Ulf and his warriors drew within one hundred paces of the enemy, slinging arrows and shapings. Three of the enemy awaited. They stood, side by side near enough to reach out and grip one another's shoulders, but not so close they brushed together. Slowly, they spread their arms out from their sides, a dim light radiating from between them. Their hands grasped the air, gathering fistfuls of dark energy in their palms.

The men and women to either side of Vali, eased. Three mortal men stood no chance of fending off an army of angry Vikings, their bellies filled with hate, anger and battle lust. Unfortunately, these were not men, and they were far from mortal.

The three staring down the oncoming horde, flung out their hands, unleashing a terrible volley of wind, lightning and flame. Arrows were stricken from flight, falling back upon the men, whose advance they were meant to strengthen. Those struck by the branching forks of lightning, were hurled backward, their bodies twisting and contorting as the light jumped from one warrior to the next. Where the flames touched however, there was naught left but ash.

The blood lusting men and women in the lead, charged blindly through the chaos. Their own shapings of earth, wind and water, poured into the cascade. Those bearing witness from behind wavered, until called back to ranks by the angry bellows of the war chiefs.

"Vali, they are still coming," Thala warned, drawing up her bow. "I can still see those other two in the glen, stalking Asta and Abel. What should we do?" Vali turned his head toward the commanders of their band, Jerold and his second, Alfhild, a strong, freckle faced, red haired woman, no more than a decade Vali's elder.

Their forces formed up a shield wall on all sides. Many of their bowmen, stood just within the outer circle, awaiting a target for their arrows. Others still, had taken up roost in the trees, anxiously staring down at the events below.

"We wait for them to draw within range of our bows," Jerold and Alfhild agreed. "Once they are close enough, we can engage them with arms. I will require all of my shapers to strike in unison from the cover of the trees."

"Aye, but what if those devils use their flames to set the entire forest ablaze?"

"We will all be roasted alive!" Another of the men called out.

"Do you lot not remember the first battle? Each of the revenants commands a single element. Wind, fire and lightning are not ours to worry about. The trees shall defend us from attacks of earth or ice. Without those, our greatest worry shall be from the pack master. We ought to be far enough from the stream that the water devil cannot drown us."

Vali listened intently as Jerold continued relaying orders to the warriors. Maintaining his attention on the man, he could not help but flash the occasional glance at the fighting in the ruined valley. His comrades below, steadily gained ground against the elemental wielding invaders.

A loud, piercing howl split the air. The wind died out with a shiver as the bestial calls continued. Vali, Halla and Thala drew nearer together, weapons drawn as the others looked about.

"Fall in," Jerold called. The men and women gathered, all formed into lines, eyes facing ahead. "Watch our flanks. No one knows where those enchanted beasts might attack from."

Another round of howls rang out. Vali's eyes searched about for the feral creatures. Instead, he saw one of the two revenants still approaching, the other two, nearing the edge of the valley. One lone robed figure remained behind, kneeling to the ground with outstretched hands, fingertips buried in the soil.

"Thala, Halla, watch out for me." Vali whispered, kneeling himself, mirroring the revenant. He felt Thala's thigh brushing up against him as she covered for him. Closing his eyes, he felt the pulsing of the earth spirits in the soil.

"They are forcing the earth to take shape," he observed. "All around us, roughly ten paces apart. The howling must be a trick." As he spoke, he heard a distant cry, though they were packed together tightly.

"Thala, I need to clear a line to the shaper." Another cry rang out. Vali turned his senses toward the source as one of their own was clipped from the outer rings. He could feel numerous lifeless forms dashing about, circling their party.

He felt the embrace of the beasts against the earth from which they were shaped. Every moment the creatures were allowed to roam, was agony for the spirits they trampled. Their existence was a pox on the planet, and the spirits sought his aid.

"Help me," he whispered to the spirits beneath the earth. "Help me stop them." He felt a gentle vibration under his palm; a calm strength flowing into him. Gripping tightly onto his bow, he slowly rose to his feet.

"Thala, I am ready," he whispered. He could still hear the cries of those around him, as they fought to stave off the stone-shaped beasts. Standing at his full height, Vali pulled back on the bowstring and took aim.

Of the two revenants focused on Vali, the one nearest to them stopped, standing in wait, watching as their kneeling companion performed its terrible deed. Beyond them and their kin fifty paces to the south, the remaining three wraiths stalked a horde of fleeing Vikings back toward Fangor stronghold. Vali's bow groaned beneath his grasp. He could still feel a soothing pulse from the spirits at his feet filling him with strength. Eye on the enemy earth shaper, Vali exhaled and released his arrow.

A pained howl pierced the air as Vali's arrow struck the revenant, who fell backward. All six of the standing revenants snapped their attention to their comrade, shrieking in rage as their fellow thrashed about wildly.

"The beasts are melting back into the earth!" One among them cried out as the Vikings cheered. Without hesitation, Vali drew up another arrow and pulled back on the string. Surprisingly, the effort strained him greatly and he found his knees buckling.

"Vali, what is the matter?" Halla asked, doing her best to support him as Thala stood in the lead.

"There was a large shaping behind that attack. Do you have strength to do it, again?" Thala asked.

"Aye," Vali grunted, slowly rising to his feet. Drawing up his bow, he trained his eye upon the revenants, who had thrown themselves over their writhing companion. Pulling back on the bowstring, he could feel the power of the spirits pouring through his limbs. He exhaled and released the arrow.

The second time he channeled the power of the spirits through his weapon, he nearly collapsed. Only together, did Thala and Halla manage to keep him on his feet. A sound of two great forces colliding, or of two boulders rolling down a hill, only to crash together, echoed through the forest and the valley. Vali's eyes trailed up as a gasp escaped those around him.

"What are they?" He asked, seeing his arrow, pressing against a once invisible barrier, only able to be seen due to the rolling currents of wind between the opposing forces. As one of the black robed figures held the arrow at bay.

The three who attacked the stronghold, ran at full sprint toward them. The third and fourth wraith were tussling on the ground, one desperately trying to pin the other, while holding the arrow back. All of this happened as the two, who had been following Asta and Abel, charged toward their evil kin.

The first of the wraiths to reach their fellows, batted Vali's stationary arrow away. It was in that moment, Vali became aware of something far more troublesome. As the two who stopped Vali's arrow turned back, the restraining revenant was thrown backwards. Then, Vali saw what had become of the one he had fired upon.

The metal mask had been discarded, revealing patches of darkened fur, an elongating snout and feral eyes. The robes of the wraith split apart as the figure collapsed on all fours. The black fur grew out from the ripped seams as the body swelled. The six remaining revenants, all backed away, slowly stepping from their comrade.

"Jerold! Call the retreat!" Thala yelled confidently, her voice void of the faintest, nervous tremor. The man, broken from his gawking stare, nodded his head.

"Everyone, fall back further into the trees! We shall loop back around to the fortress!" Without delay, the men and women gathered, charged deeper into the woods. As they brushed passed Vali, Halla and Thala, they huddled together to keep from being washed away in the sea of bodies.

As the way cleared, they saw again, where the revenants had been. Now, they saw a half dozen fleeing forms and one massive, black, shaggy, four-legged beast. It's tail, the length of Vali's horse, whipped back and forth agitatedly as it snarled. They listened in silent horror as it sniffed the air and the ground, having not noticed those fleeing it. Then, much to their chagrin, it turned to face them, with the long snarling snout and luminous yellow eyes of a wolf.

"It turned into a Fenrir?" Halla gasped as the three of them backed away.

"Halla, I am scarce to believe it, but it might be Fenrir." Thala said softly. "The stories say that he is dead. Felled by Tyr's hand, during Ragnarok. How can he be here, now?"

"We have to get out of here," Vali whispered, returning his bow to its proper place. "If we hurry back, we can still signal Abel and Asta. Neither of them would have ventured far, regardless of what I told them. We can sort out the details of this beast later." Moving away from the tree line, they could hear the loud howl of the creature, both murderous and hungry.

"Quickly," Thala urged, pulling firmly against the young man. "Shaper or not, you stand little chance against Fenrir. In the end, even Odin fell." The words left her lips, as though they pained her. Vali, drawn forth by the incredibly strong woman, found his feet and carried on through the woodlands.

***

"There it is again," Asta called down to Abel, who held the steering oar, firmly in hand.

"I still cannot hear it," he called up to the woman, who had clambered the main mast of the Valiant and stared out at the island.

"It is like the howling of a great wolf," she sighed, clutching tightly at her breast. "It is calling out, angry and fierce." She shuddered, closing her eyes as she sorted her mixed feelings.

"More the reason for us to wait out here in the shade of the bluffs. No wolf is going to bare itself to the deeps and the large, jagged rocks will hide us from the enemy's ship."

"I want to go to it," Asta said, her voice meek.

"Are you crazy?" Abel gasped. "You hear the call of a massive beast and you want to run toward it?"

"Vali could be in danger."

"Vali will be planning on coming to us, in case they are overwhelmed." The wind picked up, blowing Asta's hair about furiously. She held the mast tightly but refused to move her eyes. High above, the cliffs overlooked the bay. Trees covered its top and ran down the slopes of its back. Only the tallest towers of the stronghold could be seen over the tops of the trees. From the level of the water, beyond the edge of the cliff, a monstrosity of a ship, large and terrible, loomed into view.

"Abel, we might have a small problem." Asta called down to the man.

"I am not so sure I would call that small." He muttered, his eyes locked on the vessel. As the massive boat sailed along the other side of the jagged rocks, Abel looked about for options. "I am going to try and take us further inland. A ship that size, they will not be able to follow us."

"We still have to find Vali and the others!"

"We will, but we have to be alive, ourselves." Abel grumbled from behind clenched teeth.

"It may not matter," Asta yelled back, pointing as a number of smaller boats were lowered into the water. Upon the boats, several figures, dressed in black, stood upon the boats. Their bodies were heavily armored, their weapons massive.

"An invasion force?" Abel asked, steering the longboat away. Asta quickly poised herself near the top of the mast and drew her bow.

~ 181 ~

"I can tell you they are not friendly." She replied, gripping tightly with her thighs, to free up her hands. From the boats, one of the many armored men lifted a hand, pointed and shouted in a foreign tongue. Despite not understanding the man's words, she knew their meaning. "The enemy! Attack!"

Without pause, Asta released her first arrow, which struck one hapless warrior in the middle of his neck and shoulder. Before she had a chance to fire a second arrow, men ducked, and shields were raised to cover the many bowmen, who all stared angrily her way.

"Abel, take cover!" She cried, doing her best to conceal her entire body behind the wooden column. She could hear nearly a dozen twanging sounds, as a flurry of arrows was released. Dipping her head back, she silently screamed as the missiles skitted to either side, while others, thudded against the wooden column.

"Asta, are you alright?" She could hear Abel call.

"Yes, you?" She answered, dropping to the deck. He eyed her, his shield held up, three arrows embedded within it.

"I'll manage," he grimaced, nodding his head toward the bloody patch on his thigh. "We are almost in the channel."

"You're wounded!" Asta exclaimed, kneeling to see the wound.

"It's just a scratch! Get ready for the next volley!" Asta turned her gaze to see the archers in their now lowered boats, pointing their weapons skyward. After a brief glimpse, she felt her legs swept out from beneath her.

Again, she heard the arrows being released. Rolling to the side, she tucked up against the railing. Abel, hand still on the steering oar, held his shield high, as he tucked his body behind. Asta watched as the arrows came. They crashed down all across the deck. With a heavy groan and a thud, so did Abel.

"Abel!" She yelled from behind cover as the young Viking collapsed to a knee, an arrow embedded into his exposed thigh and oblique.

"We are entering the channel, now. Take the oar," he groaned, slowly sinking to the deck. Asta sprang to her feet and seized the oar, her hand grazing over his as she did so.

"Good, keep us off the bank. I have to tend to my wounds." Asta nodded, trembling slightly as the man broke the arrow shafts with a snarl. She focused her eyes upon her work, blotting out the man as he took to task.

The channel was narrow, barely wide enough for her to guide the boat without scraping the hull. With little wind and no extra hands to row, however, the going was slow, and she could soon hear the shouts of the foreign tongue behind her.

"Vali!" She called out. "Where are you?"

Chapter 12 – Terrors of the Old World

"Do not look back!" Vali yelled to Halla, who had turned her head in an attempt to see the beast behind them. They charged through the forest, the constant low looming branches providing countless obstacles, which tore at their faces. Thala, being the smallest, had pulled ahead of them. How far, Vali could not tell in their half-blinded flight.

The trees groaned and cracked as the monstrosity behind them clamored with predatorial excitement. Vali heard a tree uproot and collapse not far from their backs. Every instinct told him to look over his shoulder, to look upon the thing which stalked them. Only the focus and discipline, which had long since been engrained into him, kept him from embracing such urges.

Another tree shattered; loudly enough, it could have been beside him. He felt a gust of wind and the panging of debris against his back as the tree toppled sideways. He could feel a series of tiny tremors trailing behind him, with each successive bound.

Vali veered left at a slight angle, steering himself through a few leaning trees. He again heard and felt as the wood was reduced to splinters. Preparing himself, he placed one hand on the hilt of his sword. The path steep to his left, he propelled himself over the downward drop and swung to his right.

His blade slid effortlessly from its sheath, hungry for the taste of flesh and blood. He felt the blade bite, sinking deep into the beast. A pained shriek of confirmation and a trail of blood proceeded as Vali passed off the massive wolf's left shoulder.

"Umph!" He grunted, the collision of the two bodies spinning his own, while propelling him further over the drop. Vali braced himself, tucking his legs and shielding himself with his empty hand.

Another groan escaped him as the first of the branches below, rushed up to greet him. The first branch cracked and faltered as he passed, though his left arm and side sang with pain. A second branch, nipped his hip spinning him as a third, struck his ribs.

His mind whirled with pain and a moment later stopped, with a sickening "crack" to the back of his skull. Far off in the distance, he could hear his name. Even closer, he could hear the delirious wail of the predator that searched for him.

The world still spun with nauseating speed as he again, opened his eyes. He unconsciously gripped the soil in his hands, instinctively afraid he might renew his fall should he release his hold on the ground. In the back of his mind, it occurred to him he had lost his sword, though he did not know when.

He heard his name yelled again, just as he began to make out the shapes of trees. He felt something collapse beside him and focused on an urgent pressure that he felt on his right shoulder.

"Vali, praise the Aesir you are alright." Halla whispered, her eyes flitting about, cautiously.

"Where is it?" He groaned, slowly attempting to rise with Halla's help.

"Still up on the slope," she answered. "You took one of its eyes, before you fell. Thala is leading it away, now."

"My sword," he croaked, slowly turning his head from side to side.

"I have it. Hurry, we have to go!" The urgency in her voice only grew as she wrenched assertively. Placing his free hand beneath himself, he slowly found his feet.

"Which way?" He asked, now feeling the steady flow of hot sticky fluid down the back of his neck. Halla's eyes grew wide a moment, before she placed his sword in its scabbard.

"Follow me. Thala will meet us along the channel." She said. Vali slowly placed one uneasy foot in front of the other, stumbling beside her. Relying heavily on Halla's aid, he saw the water off to the side, hearing it through the whining in his ears.

"Hide here," she urged, pushing Vali down into a small drop off in the shallows. "Keep your eyes open," she ordered, wading down the stream, already waste deep.

Vali shivered, the chilly water of the shallows resting at his chest as he knelt. His senses slowly trickled back to him. The ringing in his ears dulled. His distant vision grew less hazy. Another shiver escaped him as he heard water splashing.

"Vali, hurry. Thala is making her way down and the others have returned with the boat." He nodded, rising to his feet. Wading, half floating, he guided his weightless body downstream, in the direction Halla had come from.

"Vali, give me your hand," he heard Halla call to him. Turning his eyes to the source, he saw the young woman still with him, struggling against the current. The chill of the icy water sinking deeper than bone, he reached out lethargically and felt her grab hold of him.

"Here! Over here!" Halla called, waving her hand. Though the distance was still difficult to gauge, he could see a boat. Upon the vessel, two figures moved about. Only as the Valiant moved closer, did he recognize Asta and Abel.

"Vali is hurt," Halla called, pulling him close to the bow. "Help me get him in." Before Halla had finished delivering her request, Asta was at her side, both arms extended over the port side of the deck.

"What happened?" Asta grimaced, her contorted expression a combination of anger, relief and terror.

"We were preparing to engage the black robed ones," Halla began, pressing against Vali's back. "Vali used the spirits to strike back at one, which was summoning earthen beasts. When the attack landed, the revenant started into a fit. For a moment, it looked as though the other black ones tried to restrain it, until they fled."

"Why would the black ones flee?" Abel asked, while Asta laboriously poured over Vali's wounds. Another roar shattered the natural ambience and echoed through the hills.

"That is why," Halla continued. "Thala should be here, shortly. She ran off to lead it away from us." No more than a breath later, a splash in the water forced everyone to rear their heads. The ripples in the water, converged quickly as Thala's tiny frame half emerged, kicking and sputtering wildly.

"I lost it, but only just. I would suspect it to quickly regain my scent." She called out to them, swimming toward them.

"Hurry, Abel," Halla looked back over her shoulder as she pulled Thala from the water. "We have to get back out into open water."

"That might prove a slight problem," he muttered, eyes still locked on the narrow walls of the channel. Vali continued to look about deliriously, fading in and out of consciousness as Asta shook him, periodically.

"The stream opens up ahead," Thala said, pointing beyond the next bend. "We can row back if we need."

"That is not the issue," Asta said.

"Then what?"

"The black ones have seized the waterway. We hoped we might avoid their attention, but they are not far behind." The crew fell silent. Quiet enough, Vali could hear the almost non-existent murmurings of the spirits around him. He closed his eyes as he reached out to them, escaping Asta's vigil.

They stirred restlessly, spirits of wind and water, carrying with them an infinite wisdom, crude warnings and a fathomless presence. He probed out with his mind, his shackle, restraining him from falling in too deep. He touched the shallows, allowing his consciousness to flow into the smallest of ripples within the massive network.

"Spirits of the wind and endless sea, I beseech thee. By the grace of the Old Ones and in reverence of their kingdom, please guide us to safety." At once, as his request reached them, he felt a collective glance, acknowledging him. Vali felt countless probes, touching against his consciousness with maddening abandon. Curiosity radiated from the spirits, as though seeing him, or anyone, for the first time. A moment later, he heard a gasp and pulled against his mind's shackle.

"Abel, what is it?" Halla asked.

"The oar and the sail, they just...took over." Asta turned her eyes down to Vali, who smiled weakly, holding up his right wrist, jostling it gently.

"Can you help me to my feet?" He whispered. Asta nodded, tilting her head away to hide her tears. Vali rose unsteadily, relying heavily on Asta. He stumbled along, placing his hands on the mast and looked forward, where Halla and Thala kept watch.

"The spirits of Fangor are guiding us. They will take us to open water."

"Vali," Thala turned her head to face him. It was the first time he could recall seeing fear in the young woman's eyes. "Are you going to be alright? Using the will of the Old Ones goes far beyond a shaping." Vali smirked without further response or acknowledgement.

All about him, the spirits whirled, carrying untold knowledge, which tempted him with more than just madness. He gripped ever more tightly to the mast and tighter still, to the shackle on his wrist, which felt to carry the entire weight of a life.

There was something else there, as well. Something far more vast. Perhaps as large as the network of spirits. It too, tempted him. Taunted him, even as it clung to the earthly edge of his shackle. He dwelled on this new presence a moment, too afraid to raise his eyes to it. Instead, he blinked and allowed his senses to refocus on the physical world around him.

"Vali," Asta cooed warmly. "Are you sure that you can do this?" All around, the spirits shifted their gaze. Vali slowly turned as not a word but a series of impressions, touched his consciousness. Danger. Peril. Death.

Guided by the force he now found himself slave to, Vali drew his sword. A loud "clang," and a heavy rebounding force, became ever present as Vali's blade struck at a large javelin. He only barely glimpsed at the smooth, dark, metallic handle as it was propelled over the side of the deck.

"They've caught up to us!" Abel called, looking back at the small boats, filled with armored bodies, each baring one of a various number of weapons.

"Can we outrun them?" Halla asked as Asta and Thala both looked to Vali, who had returned his attention to the channel.

"Vali?" Asta prodded. "Can we?"

"We will make it," he said faintly, keeping his eyes trained on the horizon. Another javelin soared into the air, falling a distance short of their stern. It was then, eyes staring in disbelief that Asta realized what Vali was up to.

"The current is ceasing behind us?"

"Only slowing," Vali grunted. She noticed his shallow breathing and intense focus. "Holding the current, while moving us." He explained, each word slithering onerously between his lips.

"Would it be too much strain?" Halla asked. Vali failed to answer. Asta turned her head, sensing the meaning.

"It would kill him, in a sense," Thala confirmed. "He could shift at any moment, as it is."

"How so?" Abel asked, not once taking his eyes from their pursuers, who now trailed far behind them. Another guttural roar echoed through the mountain peaks.

"He is allowing the spirits to work through him, as their catalyst," Asta explained, without knowing how she knew. Her own senses felt the touch of the spirits at work and strangely, she found herself hungry for the connection. Shaking herself free, she turned back to face Halla.

"The more of himself he opens to be used as the channel, the more vulnerable he is to being washed away in the coursing flow."

"So, even now..." Abel began.

"He is wading against a raging stream, holding naught but a thread." Thala said, placing a hand on Vali's forearm. He jolted, causing the others to jump back. The boat slowed, while Vali walked to the bow. Waves crashed over the bow, dousing everyone on board. Wiping the water from their faces, each turned their eyes to their captain.

"What is it?" They asked, eyes trained on the channel walls.

"The enemy has routed us." He replied, faintly, the words sounding distant in his fatigue. "Asta?" He said, turning his head slightly to the side, a tormented look on his face. Asta straightened, tightly holding her breath.

"I will not let you wash away," she whispered as the man knelt and placed both hands to the deck. As the Valiant and her crew passed through the end of the channel and into open waters, the enemy ship drew near.

At first, nothing. After a moment, a series of dark, metal projectiles began to fill up the sky. The boat lurched suddenly, causing near everyone on board to fall sideways.

"Vali, do not dive too deeply." Asta urged, arms wrapped around his shoulders. They heard another roar from off the island. Though they were still sailing through the shallows between overlooking cliffs, it seemed too distant to be of bother.

Another volley loomed high above them, leaving a shadow over the water. The boat jostled once more, tipping everyone about, unmercifully. Vali sank a bit lower to the deck as the bottom of the boat flattened against the water's surface.

"Hold on, Vali. We are almost through." Asta urged.

"They are pulling away from me," he grimaced, hands attempting to grip on invisible leads. "They are fleeing. Panicking. Something has pressed them on and they want me to go with them."

"Stay here," she commanded, tugging against his arm. "Do not go with them. Do not abandon me." Vali shivered at the words. He could never abandon her.

"Danger," he whispered. "Must stay," he continued as a third volley, soared skyward. "Cannot stop it," his eyes suddenly flashed open as everyone braced themselves against the descending javelins. Spinning about, Vali thrust toward the sails with both hands. The masts groaned threateningly as a strong gust of wind billowed from Vali's fingertips, filling the sails and pressing them back toward the rocky, tree filled cliffs.

As the wave of projectiles grazed the side of the boat, Vali stumbled to the side. Asta gripped onto him, wrapping an arm around his waist as he caught himself upon the port side of the deck.

"I have you..."

"Another volley!" Abel cried out, interrupting Asta. Though the next several seconds passed with languid sluggishness, it was not enough for her to fully understand.

Abel was struck to the deck, a javelin through his shoulder. Thala and Halla, both threw themselves to cover. Asta gripped protectively onto Vali as she attempted to turn her body.

Only, she felt a great force, thrusting her in the opposing direction, toward Vali. The sudden sensation of falling, accompanied the pain in her arms, body and neck, from being wrenched about. Then, there was the bitter, bone biting cold and the taste of salt in her mouth.

Instantly realizing where she was, Asta kicked with all her strength, while releasing a terrified cry. Bubbles poured from her mouth as she sank, and the salty water burned at her eyes and nose. Something else dawned on her. She had been holding onto Vali.

A new surge of panic swelled within her. She vainly tried calling out for him, producing nothing more than a second stream of bubbles. Whirling about, she noticed a stream of crimson, leading down to the sinking man, javelin through his lower torso.

Asta attempted to move to him, awkwardly kicking to the side as she pushed back with her arms. She began to sink but not so fast as the man beneath her. A silent scream of desperation filled her, even as she felt her chest concaving.

A pair of arms wrapped around her, pulling her up and away. Asta resisted helplessly, unable to swim on her own and already feeling her consciousness slipping. Vali faded from sight beneath her as she felt herself breaking the water.

"Save Vali! I have to save Vali!" She screamed against the bitter wind, weeping as she felt the pull behind her.

"I have run out of rope," a solemn voice said from behind her. Asta turned her head to see Thala, hair matted over her face, which stared on in shock. Beyond them, she noticed a thick cord of rope, which held taught to the mast of their vessel, carrying them from the larger ship.

"I am sorry, Asta." Thala said, her voice quavering. "I only had enough time to save one of you." Asta, at that moment, lost any restraint she had previously salvaged. Her left arm and body ached terribly, her wrist in particular, felt as though it burned with cold fire.

A surge of raw emotions flowed through her. She ached for Vali, felt enraged by those who had taken him and felt angrier still, at her inability to save him. Halla had begun to pull them to the deck as Abel steered the Valiant, leaning forward, barely clinging to the oar as his right shoulder bled heavily. Asta's eyes fell upon the black ship.

"I am going to kill them all!" She growled, tugging against Thala's grasp. The surging of emotion continued to swell. She was filled with desire. Desire to kill. A hunger for destruction, filled her belly and somewhere, a possessive instinct stirred.

"We will, Asta, but first, we have to survive."

"Vali was mine!" She growled. "I want him back!" Flailing her body in a fit.

"He is gone, Asta," Thala spoke, struggling against the wriggling woman. Asta slipped from her grasp, Thala barely managing to grasp hold of her left wrist. The shrine maiden's eyes flashed with fear as she gazed at her friend's birthmark.

"Asta, the mark on your wrist is fading! The chains are breaking apart!" She cried out, watching as one after another, the links on her slaver's shackle mark, vanished.

"He belonged to me! His life was mine, alone!" Asta snapped her head back to Thala. The young woman gasped, even as she heard Halla above them. Asta's eyes had yellowed, now belonging to a serpent, instead of a woman. Even Halla froze in place, horrified by the sudden change in the woman.

"I shall destroy everything, before I allow anyone to take from me!" Her left arm pulled free from Thala's grip, grasping the port side of the bow. With inhuman strength, she pulled herself from the water, landing with both feet on the deck. Rearing her head, she stared beyond Abel, who grew motionless as Asta's skin, slowly morphed.

"How dare they take from me!" She roared again, crazed smile on her face. The lustrous, milky flesh had taken a greenish hue, her skin had begun to dry and flake. Not flake but turn to scale. Scales, which flowed in patterned lines.

Asta continued to stare out over the stern. Slowly, she walked to the back of the ship. Abel, releasing the steering oar, attempted to slide from her path.

"Asta!" Thala screamed, managing to pull herself onto the deck. Asta snapped her head back, a confused look spreading across her face a moment after. A single tear rolled down her cheek, made out of place by the murderous, twisted grin she still wore.

"If they covet that which is mine, I shall take away all that is theirs!" Asta bent at the knees and leapt. In an instant, her flesh rapidly expanded, ripped and burst into a massive, tangled mass of scaly, coiled flesh and folded, red and gold feathered limbs.

"By the Old Gods! What is that?" Halla cried as the draconic lord uncoiled. First, a pair of magnificent red and gold feathered wings spread wide, followed by a second set, which stretched diagonally away from the first.

Glimmering blue and green scales, covering a silvery underbelly, stretched out at least four times the length of their longboat. The tail, ending in a fork, was tipped with more of the red feathers. As the body unfurled, a long, slender and elegant serpent's head, white as ash, peered from behind one of the wings. The large, yellowed eyes stared out at the massive ship as a sea of darkness rose up into the sky.

Large fangs appeared from within the angular maw as the beast that was Asta roared. The emitted shriek, both beautiful and terrible, shattered the sky. As the darkness loomed in closer, the godly beast shrieked once more, and the darkness dropped to the surface of the water.

Her wings flapping in unison, Asta loomed over the ship. Despite their considerable distance, Thala and the others could still hear the call to arms from the ship. Floating above the vessel, she rose higher.

~ 195 ~

Again, the sky began to grow dark. This time, vast clouds loomed overhead, casting both ships into darkness. The crew of the Valiant, stared on in unadulterated horror as thunder, rain and lightning, traveled with the clouds.

"Vali told me of a great dragon that destroyed his home beyond the fog." Abel said, his voice quivering.

"What did he tell you?" Thala asked as Halla looked on in horror.

"He told me that the woman who left he and his sister with Kari, told her of a beast with feathered wings. A survivor from the age of the Old Gods."

"What do we do, then?" Halla asked. Swallowing hard as his eyes remained fixed, Abel coughed.

"Lower the sails," he croaked, as the winds picked up and the waves began to roll. Thala and Halla rushed to their feet and working to release the riggings. As the sails were secured, their eyes turned back to the source of the dark clouds, which rolled in a swirling vortex above Asta.

A bolt of lightning struck the boat, which did not take fire. A second bolt lit the sky. Thala's eyes strained as she sought distance.

"There is one of those black robed ones on that boat," she said. "It is trying to redirect the lightning."

As a flurry of weapons soared into the air, Asta let out another shriek, which scattered them. A third bolt reigned down, as though thrown by the hand of Thor, but to no avail. Thala's eyes could scarcely make out what was happening, now that they had gained some distance.

The calls, shouted by their enemy grew more distinct. Their counter attacks, at least from a distance, seemed to come more swiftly. The enemy had organized.

"Abel, we need to bandage your wound." She decided, peeling her eyes away. "Halla, can you take the oar?" The other

~ 196 ~

woman did not speak, though she moved to Abel's side. Without peeling her eyes from the scene, she took up the steering oar. Thala knelt beside Abel and poured over his wound, which had seeped out from beneath the cloth he had pinned in place.

"Asta," he whispered, wide eyes on the true form of his childhood friend. "By the guidance of the Old Ones, be safe." Thala continued to dress his wounds, with a highly trained, routine proficiency. The keepers of the shrine, though rarely leaving the island, were often required to assist the village healer. To their great fortune, she had found herself a most able student for Kari.

"Until I see you again, my friend," Abel murmured, staring at the unforgiving sea and the spatter of blood off the port side deck. "Drink up and be merry in the halls of the All Father."

"May the halls of Valhalla take you warmly," Thala added.

"May we all be reunited, when our days are done," Halla chimed in, a small tear rolling down her cheek.

"Abel, you have lost a lot of blood." Thala said, securing another length of cloth. "You need rest and sustenance. Halla and I can manage the Valiant." Abel nodded his head and weakly pointed to the west.

"I want to see this through." The others slowly turned their heads as Asta again, roared in the distance.

Char marks had begun to appear upon the hull of the ship. While the enemy still resisted, even from the distance, they could tell that the battle would soon be over. An elemental force, liking to a beam of ice, shot back at the winged serpent. A glistening, glossy shell, slithered along the long tubular body.

Asta shrieked in pain and frustration, rearing her head as lightning continued to strike at and around the vessel. Steam surged from her angular face as a light radiated from her mouth. As the ice melted away, a plume of multicolored light, shot from her gaping maw and struck at the ship, along with the lightning.

"It is over," Abel sighed, as they heard the ship's back, breaking. The fires remained unabated this time, slowly spreading across the deck. Another rage filled cry smothered the sound of the thunder as the dragon unleashed a second blast of the destructive light. Each of them watched, too horror struck for applause and far too disturbed to feel relief, as the ship sank beneath the surface of the water.

"Abel? Halla?" Thala whispered as the creature in the distance loomed over the wreckage.

"What is it?" Halla asked.

"Has it occurred to either of you that may not be our Asta anymore?" Two heads snapped to face her as the hovering monstrosity turned its head to face them.

"Do you think she sees us?" Halla whispered. A loud, terrible, beautiful cry, caused each of them to startle.

"Lower the sails!" Abel gasped, pushing weakly against Thala. "If the wind shifts again, we can use it to push ourselves away."

"Or destroy our longboat." Halla pointed out.

"We are dead if we do nothing!" Thala called, rising to her feet and sprinting to the mast. Another shriek rolled from the creature's forked tongue. As she drew near, the swirling vortex reformed above her.

Before the edge of the storm reached them, the sails filled and they were propelled forward. They heard an angry call from behind them, followed by a massive impact, striking the water's surface, not far from them. As a geyser of salty spray, splashed over them, Thala used the support of the mast to rise to her feet.

"She is attacking us?"

"Can we outrun her?" Halla asked, visibly trembling. No one answered. Four red and gold feathered wings beat in tandem, supporting the large, blue and green scaled body. Upon her ashen white face and silver underbelly, several, shallow wounds were present. Another bellow escaped her as she quickly cleared the distance between them.

"Asta!" Thala yelled. "We are your friends! Try and remember! We have all fought together! Vali's death hurts all of us!" At their fallen comrade's name, the serpent halted its advance.

"Asta!" Abel and Halla called out, as well. The creature stared at them a moment, seemingly confused.

The waves continued to roll, pressing them away from the threat. As they pulled away, the creature shook and bellowed with rage. The rain and the wind picked up intensity as her wings beat violently.

"She is really going to kill us, isn't she?" Halla asked. Rearing its head, they saw another stream of swirling rainbow light, forming.

The surface of the water broke as thick, twisting tentacles rose up. Asta lurched backward, flapping her wings defiantly. The tentacles continued to reach higher, attempting to ensnare her. Asta released a beam of her violent light, which struck the water's surface at the center of the tentacles.

"We have to get away," Abel groaned, watching as a column of steam rose from the surface. "One of those two things are going to win. I would prefer to be on dry land and well away from here, when they are finished."

"We cannot head back to Ulfrost or Fangor," Thala said. "Where do you have in mind?"

"We need to reach Dumah," Halla said. "We need to report what happened here. Anyone who manages to escape the stronghold, will be heading either there, or to their own island."

"You are right," Abel agreed, glancing back at the battle between the monsters. "Either way, we need to regroup." Noticing Asta's necklace lying upon the deck, the cord broken, he lifted it into his palm and gripped it tightly. "We need to mourn and recover our strength." The longboat sailed free from the storm, bringing them to calmer waters. The three of them stared back, watching the battle as it, and Fangor Isle, slowly vanished from sight.

Chapter 13 – The Savage Lands

The smell of lavender, cinnamon and smoking firewood wafted into his nostrils. He stirred gently, wincing as his body recalled the pain it was in. He slowly opened his eyes, seeing folds of leather, which hung above him, supported by a series of encircling branches at its center. Pushing the woven blanket covering him away, he found that he only wore his breeches.

He tried to speak but his throat was too dry. Glancing down at his partially uncovered body, he gasped at the many bandages wrapped around his torso. Removing the covering across his waist, he saw the bloodstained strips of linen.

His head turned with only minor difficulty and he managed to gather a sense of where he was. A modest fire burned just outside of his reach. Reaching to his throat, he carefully clasped the braided cord around his neck.

"By the gods, please be safe." He willed silently.

Slowly, Vali worked his aching body and limbs, before rolling to his side. He managed to reach his knees, before pain robbed him of breath and sweat dripped from his brow. He took a moment to catch his breath and allow the beating of his heart to slow. Once again in control of himself, he turned his head up.

All around him, he saw pelts and leathers, strewn about, providing some padding and warmth to the dwelling. Another, empty bedroll occupied the lonely space. A quick search of the room found his tattered clothes.

His sword was not among them. His axes, knives and bow were also gone, lost to the waters of Fangor. Lamenting the loss of his most trusted companions, his weapons, he continued his search. A few clay pots sat at the far side of the tent. Inside them, he found dried meat, fruit, and water in the third pot.

Cupping his hands, he drew out a small amount of water and took a slow drink. He turned back and looked at the pots full of food, which caused his stomach to churn. Moving beyond them, he rose to his feet and peeled back the flap of the tent.

The cool, nighttime air rushed in at him, causing him to shiver. Despite the chill and the embrace of dusk, he carried on, wandering through the center of what could only be a campsite. Tents, identical to the one he had just exited, formed a ring leading to his own, which lay at its center. Beyond the tents, rows of trees rose up around what must have been a bowl-shaped glade. He saw a waterfall resting just beyond the first rows of trees, which fed a stream that ran just outside of the circle.

Vali focused, reaching out for any nearby spirits, wishing for warmth and direction. His eyebrows furled as he failed to find anything. Kneeling, he placed his hands to the earth. He sensed nothing.

"The water then," he whispered to himself as he stumbled on. He could hear the gentle roar of the water, splashing against the rocks. Something else caught his ear, a soft, enchanting melody, delivered in a foreign tongue. A swell of intrigue took over, driving his steps.

He followed the sound of the song, which led him to the stream's edge and a little further down along its bank. He found the woman's voice enchanting, a siren's call, drawing him nearer. The water splashed over his ankles as he walked along the bank, surprisingly warm, despite the chill air.

At the center of the plunge basin there lay a thong tree, which bowed over the pool. Upon the trunk, sat the form, which shaped the song. Slowly approaching, Vali gently cleared his throat.

"You have a beautiful singing voice. Might I ask what..." Vali stopped abruptly as the figure on the perch sprang up in surprise and turned to face him. As the woman rose, the beams of moonlight falling over the tops of the trees, illuminated what he had before missed. The woman, divinely formed, tanned skin glistening in the pale light, was completely nude.

"Please forgive me," he stammered, turning his head away as the young woman spoke to him in her foreign tongue. He could feel his entire face burn, enough so he might serve as a signaling beacon to ships at sea. "I did not think. I did not know you were...so..." He continued to ramble in panic as he stepped away.

His foot slipped from the surface of a rock, causing him to topple. Letting out a loud grunt as his head struck another stone in the stream, he floated listlessly. His vision blurred as he reeled in pain. A "splash" several feet away and a pair of soft hands on his torso were his next sensations.

"You alright, Viking?" He heard the woman ask, her voice like a note from her song, her accent, rough and exotic. The sound of her voice, tickled in the back of his mind, sending an enticing chill down his spine. He only found himself further flustered.

"I think so," he answered, slowly opening his eyes, to see the now shadow darkened silhouette of the naked woman. "Ah!" He jolted, shielding his eyes as he turned away.

"You are strange. Even for your kind," she mused, a slight giggle in her statement.

"I did not mean to approach you," he said, eyes tightly closed, head still turned away.

"You did not?" She asked, layers of confusion behind the question. "You no hear me sing?"

"No, I did. I mean I just wished to listen." An involuntary groan echoed out from his throat as he searched for the proper words.

"I no understand. What trying to say?" His head and hands floated in air, having vainly translated his words.

"I did not mean to see you," he strained, nearly turning his head back toward her, while again flailing his arms, attempting to reach his point.

"I still no understand," the woman said, pulling on Vali's arm. "Come stranger, you need rest and warmth. There is chill in the air." She said, pulling against him.

As she pulled, he felt two somethings, soft, firm and cushiony. He stumbled worse than he had previously, trying to avoid gazing upon the woman. Reaching the central tent, where he had awoken, he looked briefly as the flap was pressed passed him.

In the dull light cast by the low flame in the tent, Vali at once recognized the young Kresh, whom he had encountered twice before. Her long, red crowned and white hair was pulled over her right shoulder. She wore only a breech cloth, which barely concealed her lower, feminine features. He eyed her toned and tanned, bare back a moment, an awkward indecency stirring within him.

"I did not realize it was you." He spoke in disbelief. She turned to eye him, curious look on her face.

"Others would have killed you." She answered with no real attachment to the words. She knelt on the second bedroll in the room, looking away from him.

"Why didn't you?" He asked. The woman's toned shoulders sagged forward slightly as she sighed, lifting a makeshift brush.

"You not the same." She answered, running a comb made of animal bone through her hair.

"True, but our people have been enemies ever since we first met. Different, the same; none of that has ever mattered to the Kresh or the Vikings."

"I also different." She said as it occurred to Vali that even broken, she spoke his language.

"Do all of the Kresh speak my language?"

"No." She spoke solemnly, slowly crawling into her bedroll. "Sleep. You need rest." Vali moved to his own bedroll, staring at the now covered woman, who eyed him blankly.

"What do I call you?" He asked, lowering his head, eyes locked on hers.

"Does not matter. We are enemies."

"Please," he asked. "My name is Vali." The Kresh sighed.

"Aya," she answered. Vali lipped the name, allowing the syllables to roll off from his tongue.

"Do you know what has become of my other belongings? My sword? My bow?" He asked.

"Only saved you." She whispered. Again, a pain seared into his heart at the loss of his possessions. His sword, the last proof of his lost heritage. With a sigh, he patted his necklace and his body. He was still whole.

"Thank you for saving me, Aya." She rolled away from him.

"I have not saved you. I have delayed your death."

"What do you mean?"

"Sleep, my enemy. You do not die, now. Once you are strong, we will see."

"Aya?" He whispered.

"Yes?" She answered, an irritable tone in her voice.

"Thank you."

"You are welcome." She muttered sleepily, pulling the blanket over her shoulder. Vali eyed her a moment, before rolling onto his back and closing his eyes. Then the dreams came.

His vision was filled with the blurring lights of spirits, flailing about him playfully. Their current ran all around and through him, guiding him, pressing him along their path. Fear of the spirit shift sent him into a panic, as he desperately wretched himself from the grasp of those who pulled him.

Stumbling forward, he stepped out onto the clouds, bursting with whirling light, a continuous cycle of sunrise, sunset, moon rise and on. More clouds flashed by at incomprehensible speed. He stood, watching, attempting to understand what it was he bore witness to.

Far beneath him, the surface of the world shifted as rapidly as the sky. Great, torrential storms blew onto the land from endless bodies of water. Great rings of fire, erupted from the earth. Massive windstorms left behind nothing more than blasted plains. Entire continents and island chains, moved about across vast bodies of water. Islands crashed together, forming continents, while continents became islands. Over time, entirely new masses appeared from beneath the sea.

"The memory of the spirits?" He asked himself. Shaking his head, another thought came to him. "Perhaps of Midgar?"

Tearing his eyes away, he focused them back upon the sky, where his mind found some ease. He sighed with relief, looking about for something which still made sense. He closed his eyes, which opened him to new sights.

He looked down on himself as he floated weightlessly in the dark, icy water. Asta and Thala were both gone, pulled away by an unseen force. He was not alone for long however, as he was joined by Aya.

He watched as she pulled him toward the surface. Standing atop the water, he watched as the mysterious Kresh woman pulled him ashore, examining his wounds. Next, she looked up to his face and placed her hand beneath his nose.

A worried expression gleamed within her silver eyes. She pushed her wet hair from in front of her face, bent down over his body and...kissed him. Vali felt heat rising in his face as he watched Aya at work. She backed away from him, staring down as she straddled his waist. Next, he watched as she pressed against his chest repeatedly, before returning her lips to his.

The process repeated multiple times, Aya bringing her lips to his and then compressing his chest. He saw three more Kresh, all older than the woman who pulled him from the water. He was unsure if they were the same as those he had seen before, though Aya bowed her head before them as they approached.

She did not rise from his waist, but continued her work, shouting in her strange, coarse speech as she pressed his chest. One of the three elders, a small, shriveled, silver haired Kresh, spoke back. Aya shouted something back to her elder, thrusting a finger at Vali's chest.

"Kanadesh." The elder spoke with authority, the vowels pronounced with a masculine tone. Though they themselves possessed some power, the woman's features sank from the weight of her words. Aya snapped her head back, seemingly in shock. Her eyes were wide for but a moment as she slowly turned her gaze back on Vali's fragile looking form.

Her face softened, followed by a few, gently spoken words, before she nodded her head. The two other elders stepped forward, shouting what could only be words of protest, before the silver haired Kresh raised her hand, silencing them. The other two quiet, the eldest approached Aya.

Aya slid from his waist, settling on his right side. The elder planted her staff in the sand near Vali's head and leaned against it as she spoke to Aya. The young woman nodded her head and placed her right hand over Vali's heart, while taking his right hand in her left. Placing his palm over her left breast, she began to mutter inaudibly.

A strange hue formed around both he and Aya. Both of them were cast into an odd, emerald green shadow as the elder tapped her staff rhythmically against the sand. The light around them flickered periodically, further prodded along by both the increasingly fast taps of the elder's staff and Aya's chant. One final tap of the staff caused the light to fade as Vali rolled to his side and spat mouthfuls of water out onto the sand.

Slowly, he opened his eyes, again seeing only the tent above him, illuminated by the dimly lit flame. He rolled his head to the left and saw Aya, her back to him, seemingly asleep. Pushing his blankets aside, he rose.

Shuffling to the back of the tent, he found his pants, woolen socks, boots and bloodstained shirt, hole torn through it. Sliding into all but his shirt, he carefully crept from the tent, afraid of waking his sleeping savior. His heavily bandaged torso still pained him, though he ignored it as he pulled back the flap of the tent.

Daylight struck him like a hammer, causing him to duck back. He winced as the wound in his stomach sparked with pain. He tipped his gaze to Aya, who stirred in her sleep. Releasing a light sigh, he pushed the flap of the tent away and stepped outside.

He narrowed his eyes as he looked out over the campsite. Several Kresh, very young and old both, sat gathered about, talking amongst themselves or playing children's games. Vali took no more than a few steps from the tent, when silence befell the entire camp.

The eyes of every man, woman and child, fell upon him. Somewhere in the distance, a baby's cry disrupted the unnatural quiet. Out of habit, Vali reached out to the spirits but once more, found none. A young, brown haired Kresh, no more than five years younger than Vali, stood, gripping a spear in his left hand.

Angrily, he jabbed the weapon at Vali, growling threateningly in his tongue. Recognizing a young Kresh holding a baby several feet away, he watched the child dash away. While many of the other Kresh grinned, a few stared apprehensively as Vali eyed the boy, one hand over his wound, the other raised at shoulder level.

"I mean you no harm." He said, staring at the boy. "I only wished to enjoy the sun and the breeze." The boy, unabated, continued to stare angrily, slowly advancing.

A sudden, sharp sound like a heavy branch pounding on stone, caught the attention of the entire camp. Vali looked across the camp, near to where he had found the stream. There stood the diminished, silver haired elder who had helped save him in his dream. Standing next to her, again, he saw the boy and his sister the babe.

"Stranger, follow," the woman beckoned, before turning and walking to a large tent located near the back of the camp. Vali peered around at the variety of mixed looks he received, before proceeding. Taking another look at the young boy, he gently pressed down the tip of his spear.

"Looks as though you will not be killing me, just yet." He smiled at the boy as he shuffled passed. Pulling his necklace back to its proper place on his chest, he brought the protection symbol to his lips and kissed it. Feeling the eyes of the entire camp still upon him, he carried on.

The elder stood, holding back the flap of her tent a moment, waiting for Vali to catch up. As he drew near, she entered the tent, the flap closing behind. As Vali drew near, he could smell piney incense, burning from within.

"Enter," he heard the elder speak. Her use of his language was harsh, half croaked, as though she knew the words well, but they resisted her refined tongue.

Vali entered the tent, finding it much the same as the one he had first awoken in. The smell of pine grew ever more pungent as the flap closed behind him. The tanned, silver haired Kresh sat upon a mat, near to another dim fire pit. A pile of furs and leathers resting in front of the mat across from her.

"Sit," she commanded more so than offered as she gestured toward the mat. Before the mat, he recognized clothing similar in fashion to those his people might wear. A fresh shirt, fur coat and trousers, all stained a dark brown. He did as he was told without protest, slowly lowering himself to the floor. He grimaced slightly as a small stain appeared on his bandage.

"What are you plans?" She croaked at him. Vali eyed her a moment, before answering.

"I do not even know where I am. As far as my intentions, I need to find my crew, my people." Thoughts and images of Freyja came to him. "There are those dear to me that I must seek out. Make certain they are safe." The elder nodded her head a moment, before speaking.

"I understand the desire to see your loved ones." She said. "Few in my care know not of loss and separation. Though the youngest of us do not know it, even they have experienced it. Only before they learned the faces they lost."

"You speak of the war between our races." Vali presumed.

"I speak of loss and separation, Viking." She spat the title, disgustedly. "Neither is subject to your people. We lost many, long before our races first met. Death has merely adopted a new face, since."

"Why save me? Why bring me to your camp?"

"A debt was due. A life for a life. Just as ours were left to save themselves, after your aid. There is little I may do for you, once you have regained your strength. I offer you clothing, but little more, can I give." He bowed his head in thanks to her, touching his hand to the pile of clothes.

"I thank you." He replied. "Aya said something similar," continued Vali. "She said that only I could save myself. What did she mean?"

"In a few days, when you are stronger, we will move on."

"Am I to accompany you?"

"Unless you would rather be killed here, or face the wilds, alone, yes."

"And what awaits me where you are heading?"

"Likely death, but one even your people would approve of."

"So, I am to be thrown into combat, then? Die with a sword in my hand, sun on my back?"

"More or less. I advise you to stay behind. You should likely not last more than a..." The elder stopped as her gaze shifted behind Vali. He too, turned his head to see Aya in the entrance, eyes narrowed and hair a mess.

"Good light, Aya." Vali said, slowly rising to his feet. "I did not wish to wake you." He did not manage to reach a knee, before he was forced back down by Aya, who stormed into the tent.

The tone in Aya's voice was one of cornered aggression, an animal, gone berserk after being toyed about. The Kresh tongue flew from her lips in a fury of harsh syllables. He knew not their meaning but felt their intention. He was to be left in her charge.

She continued her tirade, waving her hands sporadically, while frequently motioning toward Vali. Confused, Vali continued to view the exchange. As Aya's outburst started to fizzle, she placed a gentle but affirmed hand on his shoulder.

The elder, still seated, showed no sign of hostility toward the younger woman. Unfazed by the outbursts, she calmly met her gaze, until she paused for breath. The elder's reply was short, yet Vali felt a sheet of ice flow with the words . Aya stood trembling, her face red and wrinkled from anger as she looked to Vali.

"Come," she commanded, holding out her hand. "Not leave you." Vali accepted her hand and slowly rose to his feet. As Aya made to leave, Vali turned and bowed his head to the elder.

"Thank you for the gift," he said, raising up the bundle of clothing.

"Take care around the others, Viking. You are still kin to the enemy." Aya shot the elder one last, angry glance, before she and Vali left.

~ 213 ~

"Would you please explain to me what that was about?" He asked once they had moved several paces from the tent. Moving toward the tree line, Aya continued to blaze forward, threatening to leave him behind.

"Come with me," she grumbled, still angry but not with him, he supposed.

"Where are we headed?" He asked. She looked at him, curiously. She tilted her head from side to side, staring blankly at him.

"Headed?" She asked, tapping her own temple.

"Going," he clarified. "Where are we going?" She pointed to the bloodstained bandage on his stomach.

"Needs cleaning," she responded, turning back toward the thickening greenery and lead on.

"Your chief told me I would be killed whether I stayed or went. Why?" Again, Aya looked back at him.

"This word, Chief. How is it meaning?" Vali thought a moment, before answering.

"Leader. The Chief leads the clan. We have peace chiefs and war chiefs, where I am from. Does that make more sense?"

"I lead you," she answered, a puzzling look on her face.

"Yes, and I follow you," he added. "But you," he said, pointing at Aya. "You, follow the chief, or leader," he continued, pointing back to the elder's tent. Aya nodded her head, pointing to the same tent.

"Damaruhk" she said. "Damaruhk say where to sleep. When to move." He nodded his head thoughtfully, aware that his survival depended upon his understanding of his newfound rescuer.

"The same as our village chief, or peace chief." Vali explained. Aya nodded in understanding.

"Follow. I your chief." She said, leading him to the stream.

"May I ask you a question?" Vali asked as he sat upon the branch he was steered to.

"You have been." She retorted bluntly. He smiled at the response.

"Are you and the Damaruhk the only Kresh who understand me?"

"There are others," Aya answered, picking at the knot in his bandage.

"Where are they?" He asked.

"Not here," she responded.

"Is it forbidden?"

"I do not know, 'forbidden.'" She said. Vali placed his fist before his face and his thumb under his chin.

"Something you do not talk about. Are not allowed to say." Aya stared at him a moment longer.

"I do not understand. Why can I not say it?" Vali felt a slight twinge of frustration as he struggled to find the appropriate words.

"Never mind. Can you tell me where the others are?" Aya knelt in front of him as she peered at the wound, setting the bandage aside.

"Who are the others?" She asked. Vali groaned.

"Do you know where I can find the other Kresh, who speak my language?"

"I do. Is that what you wanted to know?" She asked.

"Yes, how many others are there?" He answered, in exasperation. Aya placed a small wad of plants into her mouth and chewed them. Standing, she walked to the stream, where she rinsed the bandages. He watched her carefully as she dunked and rang out the cloth, several times.

"Not many," she answered, after plucking a matted, half chewed ball of herbs from her mouth. "Most Kresh need not learn."

"Why is that?" He asked. Aya stared at him, disappointedly.

"You speak my language?" Vali's demeanor dropped.

"Why would you ever need to speak with someone you intend to kill?" He answered, immediately understanding her point. Aya nodded in agreement as she returned to his side, the tiny ball in her hand.

"This will help the bleeding," was the only warning Vali was given, before Aya reached inside his wound with two fingers. He squirmed uncomfortably, as pain seared through his torso. He continued to grimace as she plucked out one matted ball and inserted the fresh one. Her work done, Aya discarded the old ball and moved to the stream.

"Why did you learn, then?" He asked. Aya froze for a moment, her eyes dropping to his wound.

"Damaruhk's...mate," she said after a moment's contemplation. "He was of your kind."

"The Damaruhk bonded with a Viking? I cannot imagine that was a popular idea."

"Popular?" She asked.

"Well liked." Aya nodded her head in understanding.

"It was not." She said, dipping the bandage again.

"Did the Kresh come to accept him?"

"Some," she answered, ringing out the bandage. "Others tried kill him."

"How?" Vali asked, curiously. "Did they come to accept him that is?" Aya looked at him with amusement twinkling in her silver eyes.

"Does kin of my enemy wish to be accepted?" She smirked, raising an eyebrow. Vali jolted slightly at the question.

"I was just curious, is all. It would be nice to at least know what I am getting myself into."

"You will face the Comartok. As did Damaruhk's mate."

"And should I face the Comartok, will the rest of the Kresh still want to kill me?"

"Probably." She stated blankly, slowly wrapping the wound.

"What is the Comartok?" Aya sighed, pulling tightly on Vali's bandage.

"You ask many questions, Viking." She groaned. "Even in sleep, you talk." She complained, using her right hand to imitate a rapidly flapping mouth.

"I am sorry," Vali said. "There is so much I do not understand."

"Enough, for now," Aya said, securing the knot. "You need strength, first." Gently, she pulled on his arm, helping him to his feet.

"The Damaruhk said we will leave in a few days. That or die, here. I suppose I should make ready for then."

"Stay here. Wash. I will grab food." She walked away, leaving Vali alone. He looked about a moment, before kicking off his boots. Removing his pants and under breeches, he tossed them aside, before wading into the water.

Taking up a seat, Vali submerged himself to his chest and closed his eyes. Senses dialed in, Vali focused on the stirring of the water; its chilly breath on his body, the light grip on his limbs. As he delved deeper, he found something more, the stirring spirits, which felt far off to him. Their lights seemed dull to him. He focused harder, reaching out for them, until he felt a hand on his shoulder.

"Do not drown, again." He heard Aya say as she crouched behind him in the water.

"Aya, I am not wearing any clothes?"

"I know. I will wash them."

"Thank you, but that is not what I meant." He shuddered as Aya ran her hand across his back.

"What do you mean?" She asked, innocently splashing more water onto him.

"Umm...you are pressing up against me."

"I do not want you to drown. You are my...problem?" She said, clearly unsure of the word. Vali's eyes narrowed.

"You did not have to save me." He grumbled.

"Are you upset?" She asked, bringing her head beside his ear.

"Never mind that. Aya, do you know why there are so few spirits here?" Aya lifted her head away and stood. He turned to face her as she stirred about in the water.

"Spirits are everywhere. They are a part of you and me. Can you not see them?" She asked, a sympathetic tone to her voice.

"Only barely," he sighed.

"But you move spirits. Can you not feel them? I do." Vali, again, closed his eyes and extended his senses.

"I can only faintly sense them." He grumbled with frustration. "I do not understand. Something seems different, wrong. I cannot seem to place it." He lifted his hands in front of his face and jolted. Holding out his right arm, rotating it in the light, he stared at his bare, milky flesh.

"What is it? Something on your arm?" Her eyes grew wide with panic. "Leeches?"

"No, Aya. It is nothing." He sighed, shaking his head. The Kresh's expression eased, but not the tension in her body.

"I do not understand. You hold arm like so," she spoke, mirroring him.

"I used to have a birthmark on this wrist. I do not understand." He continued to stare in confusion.

"Was this birthmark so important?" Aya asked, emphasizing birthmark as she slowly sat beside him.

"It was the one thing that Asta and I had in common."

"Was this Asta, your mate?" Vali looked back at her and shook his head.

"No, nothing like that. What is your word for girl, who shares a mother?"

"I know the word, sister." Aya responded, raising her eyebrows.

"Well, what is your word?"

"Kasha." She said, almost with a sigh.

"She was similar to my Kasha, then." He said, lifting his braid from his chest. "She and my mother, gave me this. This symbol here. To my people, it means protection.

"What happened to her?" Aya asked, leaning in slightly, which placed her closer than previously. Vali shifted uncomfortably, before answering.

"I am not sure. We were both in the water. Another of my friends, Thala, was there. I suppose that she made it to safety."

"I hope you find her." She said. Vali smiled, looking back at her from over his shoulder.

"You have my thanks." He smiled, gently patting Aya's hand. "I suppose I should get stronger, so I can complete the Comartok." Aya's gaze dropped as she nodded.

"Strength, first. Then we leave and learn what happens."

"Any thoughts?"

"Ah, a great many, stranger."

"I meant about the Comartok."

"I have not taken it."

"Seriously?" He asked. Aya nodded her head. "I thought that it was required in order for you to become one of the people?"

"I was born Kresh. Until I complete the Comartok, I may not stand with Damaruhk."

"Stand with?" He whispered to himself.

"I can only follow. I cannot lead."

"So, after the Comartok, you will be the Damaruhk?" Aya shook her head despairingly, as though Vali had made a grave error.

"No. Be respected. Hold voice with the Kresh. I no be Damaruhk."

"Everyone here seems to hold you in high regard. What do you mean by hold voice?"

"Kresh here, all elders and younglings. I hold voice with them, because they depend on me. Next to braves, I am less than..." She pointed at their faces in the water.

"Reflections?" Aya shook her head.

"In light, darker." She spoke. Vali thought a moment.

"Shadows?" Aya stared at him and nodded, the word fitting.

"Less than shadow." She confirmed.

"I understand the feeling. So far, everything I have done, has been part of an effort to make Ulf recognize me."

"Would this Ulf, recognizing you, give you freedom?" Vali eyed Aya curiously.

"Are you not free?" He asked. "You have come so far from the rest of the Kresh." Aya turned away. He stared at her back a moment, before she spoke again.

"No Kresh is free. We are all of one people, but the people are not one." She stood and walked toward the shore. "Food is ready. You cannot gain strength without food." She said with a frail tone in her voice. He watched her walk away, before returning to the bank to dry himself.

Sliding into his new pants, socks and boots, he turned his attention to the village. The distrustful stare and uneasy glances returned the moment he came into view. Again, paying them no mind, he moved through the village. Seeing Aya across the camp, kneeling before the fire, he made for her.

"Here, stranger. Eat. Drink." She said, holding a wooden bowl out to him.

"Thank you," he said, accepting the bowl containing a soupy brew. He watched as the Kresh around him blew the steam from their bowls, before sipping from them. Gaining a small level of understanding, Vali mirrored their process as Aya rose and walked away.

The soup was strange, but good. Though it contained spices he did not recognize, he could tell that the meat was rabbit. As he sat, appreciating his first true meal in what might have been more than a week, a shadow loomed over him. Vali glanced up slightly, only to see a sandaled foot, striking him in the chest.

He fell to his back, spilling stew on himself and filling his world with pain as the young, dark haired Kresh from before, stood over him, spear in hand. The young man yelled in the tongue of his people, words Vali did not yet understand. He did however understand the intense pain in his head and torso, in addition to the weapon pointed at his chest.

Slowly, Vali dug his hands into the soft soil, feeling the natural thrum of nature, licking at his fingertips. He extended his consciousness toward the sensation, reaching out to the spirits for aid. He felt their answer, a gentle wave of strength, which flowed into his body.

With the haft of the spear, the Kresh jabbed at Vali's head. Tilting his head out of the way, he allowed the weapon to slide over and passed his left shoulder. As the young man staggered forward, planting the end of his spear, Vali chopped from right to left with his good arm, shattering it.

As the hopeful, over eager Kresh fell forward, Vali rolled to the side and kicked, knocking the smaller warrior away. His body screamed out in pain and a sudden wave of nausea, nearly crippled him completely. Instead, he choked down the rising bile and pressed against the ground with his arms.

The other Kresh in the camp, now on full alert, swarmed about, each shouting. A shadow loomed over Vali, who turned his head to see another kick rising toward his ribs. He moved his arm in place, blocking the kick with his augmented strength. It was not nearly enough.

The Kresh staggered backwards, limping on a leg bearing a bloodied shin. Again, Vali bit back the urge to vomit and was tackled. Dust flew up around them as they tussled and rolled.

Vali landed on his back with a grunt as the air was forced from his lungs. The Kresh were incredibly strong for their size he learned as a knee pressed into his ribs, causing them to creak. Next, he felt the hands of a skilled metalworker, not a young man, clasp around his throat.

He struggled against his attacker, trying to tuck in his knees as he wrapped his arms around the Kresh's. The young warrior resisted, even with his enhanced strength. He could feel his lungs collapsing, his eyes began rolling into the back of his skull as a distant commotion erupted. There were shouts, a woman screaming fiercely and then, air.

On your feet, stranger," Aya spoke to him, hovering close enough for him to smell her sweet breath. He opened his eyes to her standing, staggered over top of him, knife in one hand and a short, bladed spear with a bludgeoning ball on the end, in the other.

Vali groaned as he found his feet, placing his hand over his wound, which had bled lightly. He grew light headed as he rose, his entire body still trembling from the shaping. She glanced back at him over her shoulder briefly, before turning back toward the youngling.

Aya chided the youngling in her strange tongue, her voice a low toned growl, her lips pursed into a snarl. Upon her back, was slung her bow. Her glaive however, was held in her hand, tightly gripped and poised.

He watched the confrontation in part out of curiosity, though it was taking all his strength to remain standing. Rather, he balanced himself on teetering legs, while Aya thrust her weapon at her kin. The younger Kresh sighed angrily and lowered his broken weapon, never once taking his eyes from Vali.

"Come, stranger," she barked, walking passed the fire pit. The young man continued his spiteful chattering, pointing at Vali as he did so. He walked alongside Aya, who stopped briefly at the drying rack, where she removed several strips of dried meat.

"Try to eat," she ordered, tossing him a chunk and placed the rest in her leather pouch. He eyed the meat as they walked, his throat already clenching uncomfortably. Placing the dry, salty meat in his mouth, he attempted to chew.

The meat was tough, and it pained his jaw, but he continued working his tired mandible. He continued his agonized mastication, through the length of their trek. As soon as they had both entered the forest, Aya turned on him.

"You have grown frail, stranger. The Comartok will be your death." She said, taking up her peculiar weapon and using it to lop off a dried, low hanging branch. Cutting the branch down and into two different sized pieces, she threw one to him.

"What is it for?" He asked, catching the branch.

"You need to regain strength. The Comartok is not for one who is bested by younglings."

"I attempted to use a shaping to strengthen myself."

"And what result?"

"I felt a gentle infusion, but you can see how it left me."

"Is that what normally happens?"

"No, I should have easily overpowered him. Like I said, something is different. My birthmark, losing my ability to shape, I do not understand."

"Instead of relying on spirits, you rely on yourself?" She suggested, moving through the brush ahead of him. Vali looked down at the stick and nodded his head.

"And will you teach me more of your language?"

"Would be easier if you understood a few things." She turned back and nodded, as well. "Fine then, you practice, I hunt."

Chapter 14 – The War Conference

"There it is, Abel. Dumah Island." Shouted Halla from the bow of the longboat. Abel nodded, seeing the rolling hills and the small mountain range, where last he heard, housed the people of Dumah.

"Thala, Halla, once we break land, I need you two to take care of the boat and our remaining supplies. Have us ready to redeploy if necessary. I need to speak to Chief Rolf and learn what the situation is here." Thala and Halla both nodded, returning to their labors as Abel steered them ashore. As the boat sank into the beach, Abel quickly bounded from the deck and ran up the beach.

"Hail, kinfolk," a female warrior called from a slight distance. He slowed as he drew near, stopping near enough to see her. She had long red hair, which was braided back and fell over her right shoulder. Upon the milky flesh of her angular face, was a series of light freckles, which peppered around her luminous, green eyes.

"Hail, kinfolk. I am Abel of Ulfrost. I have two others with me, here to see that our clansmen arrived safely."

"Well met, Abel of Ulfrost. I am Katarina of Skald. You and your crew may follow me. Your clansmen arrived a few days past."

"Thank you," he answered, running back to the beach. As he drew near, Thala and Halla both eyed him curiously.

"What is it?" Thala asked, setting the last of the riggings in place.

"One of Clan Fenris's is going to take us to the others." There was no hesitation from either of the women as they disembarked and left Abel behind. Anxious himself, he gave chase.

Beyond the beach, Dumah opened into a series of rolling green hills, offset only by the small mountain chain, which broke through to the west. They rose in stark contrast to the green fields, a series of grey stones, shale.

"The village is still under repairs, so we have not yet moved everything from the caves. Chiefs Allie and Finna will wish to speak with you, however. Though it has been rather dull out here, we have heard much talk of things out in the world."

"I have a feeling you have yet to hear the half of it." Abel muttered as they walked. Katarina eyed the man, staring intently at his weary, color drained face, before turning to the two, equally exhausted women in his party.

"I had suspected you might have tales to tell. I shall eagerly await to hear them, tonight." She said, leading them to the mouth of the cave. Walking out from within, another brown and green clad Viking, this one, an older, salt and pepper haired man, neared.

"Warriors from Ulfrost, come to speak with the chiefs of the campaign." Katarina said, gesturing toward the others. The man nodded his head stiffly.

"Follow me," he rumbled and walked back inside.

"Thank you, Katarina," said Abel as he passed by.

"Of course. Perhaps you may tell me of your adventures, this evening?"

"Perhaps I may," he smiled, before receiving a carefully placed elbow from Halla.

"Come on, you flirt." She chided softly. "We have kin waiting for us." Thala said nothing as she followed the guard of the cave's entrance. Surprisingly, the stone caverns were filled with the remnants of the evening sunlight, though shadows had begun to creep along the edges of every tunnel.

"There are a number of holes burrowed every ten to fifteen paces, allowing the light in." There escort explained, neither stopping or looking back. "We still light torches at early dusk, or when the sun fails. Finally, there are patches of cave moss throughout, which glows in the night." Even as the man spoke, a flame came to life down a side path, followed quickly by another.

"The people of Dumah have made excellent use of the terrain." Abel commented. "No wonder they sought shelter from the storms, here."

"These caves have long defended our people, but they cannot provide everything," a young, raven haired beauty in a cloth dress, spoke.

"And what do they lack?" Abel asked, earning him another gentle prod.

"Oh, a number of comforts; tales of the outside world, the sound of the sea and the like. It is also difficult to produce much in the way of food. We still rely on the fields."

"Understandable," Abel agreed, the woman walking alongside them. "Perhaps after out meeting with the three chiefs, I can tell you of our adventures?"

"Ahem!" Thala coughed into her sleeve, capturing his attention.

"Are you well, Thala?" He asked. The raven-haired woman giggled lightly.

"There will be no need to regale me, later, Abel of Ulfrost." She replied. "I am Brina, daughter of Rolf and Signe." Abel paused a moment, lost for words as his companions shook their heads.

"Brina, are you here to take us to the chiefs?" Thala asked, flashing an agitated glance toward Abel.

"I am. It is not much further to the meeting place." She said, leading the way further in. They continued to follow the future chieftain through the glow moss covered tunnels. As they traveled further, the fewer ventilation holes they encountered and the more they seemed to rely upon the moss and torch sconces, to see.

The loud murmurings of a heated discussion echoed down the halls to them, before they rounded the final turn. Reaching it, they found themselves in a large, well lit, open room. Gathered around large, round tables, sat many ship captains and chiefs, who had gathered to defend Fangor. Though not all had arrived, among them, he noticed Chief Finna, seated near to Rolf and a lovely older woman, who could be none other than Brina's mother.

"I bring Captain Abel and crew of The Valiant." Brina said loud and clearly, introducing them to the room. All heads quickly snapped around, while Freyja, Finna, the rest of The Valiant's crew and Kari, stood.

"Captain Abel?" Kari called, the middle-aged healer gasped as she quickly raced across the room toward them. Brina inclined her head slightly, as she stepped to the side and moved toward her mother and father. "Where are my children? Where are Asta and Vali?" She spoke frantically, though Abel could tell from her face, she already suspected the worst.

"I am sorry, Kari." Abel said, slowly lowering himself to the stone floor, his side and thigh, still paining him. "We lost Vali to enemy fire, while fleeing Fangor. Asta, well," Abel paused, finding an explanation impossible to deliver. "Is another matter to discuss. Privately." Kari nodded her head as Finna and Freyja approached.

"Abel," Freyja began, tears already streaming from her eyes. "Where is Vali?" There was hope in her voice. Abel shook his head; the question having deflated his defenses. Glancing to the others for help, they each stared at the ground, unable to voice what all now knew to be true. Lips trembling, breath frozen in her lungs, the young girl turned to her mother for comfort, her tears pouring onto the ground.

"How did it happen?" Chief Finna growled, her tiny demeanor making the sound of the resulting rumble in the earth no less terrifying. "We have received some reports, but none which we have found conclusive." Abel took a moment to compose himself. He opened and closed his mouth several times, before a gentle prod from behind caught his attention.

"You can tell them, Abel." Thala assured him. "It was not your fault." He drew in a deep breath and relayed their story. Throughout his recollection, several loud gasps interrupted his otherwise, unchallenged monologue. Freyja sat, shocked in silence, tears pouring from her eyes. Kari and Finna however, sat listening, their gazes unchanged.

"What of the rest of our warriors?" Finna asked, her tone sunken slightly. Kari stared down at the wooden table beneath her, the power of her earth shaper's grasp, denting the wood in her anger. Noticing this, Abel could not help but gulp.

"Our orders were to escape. The plan for the others was to hold the stronghold. If they determined that they could not, they were to flee and come here." Finna and Kari both sat back down, silently contemplating the situation.

"Then all we can do is wait." Finna muttered, turning her head back to Rolf, Signe and Allie. "Might we continue this discussion at a later time? It seems that our war chiefs have yet to arrive. Though the objective is to reclaim Ulfrost, we will not know what we can manage, until they return." The other chiefs glanced at one another, before nodding in unison.

"Of course, High Chief Finna." Allie spoke, bowing her head and clasping her fist to her chest. "May we drink to those lost, and again, for those who have yet to return. May the All Father's halls be blessed by those who have fallen." There was a general murmur in the room, as many heads bowed. A moment later, as the room started to clear, Finna and Kari pulled Abel aside.

"What did you wish to speak with us about?" Kari asked. Abel twitched with nervous energy as he formulated the proper words to describe what he had seen.

"This will not be an easy story to tell, and even more difficult to believe." He began, looking around the room for any sign of eavesdroppers. "Are you certain that this is a safe place to discuss sensitive issues?" Kari knelt and closed her eyes as she placed her hand to the ground.

"There are none within ear shot." She confirmed, before standing and fixing her gaze on Abel. "Tell us what you could not before." Again, Abel gulped as he took up a seat at one of the many, vacant tables. Thala and the rest of the crew gathered around. Agni and Haldr, having yet to hear the story, leaned in close. Thala patted Abel gently on the shoulder as he wrung his hands.

"First, Vali determined the black ones were somehow tracking he and Asta. He did fully explain how he knew or why he suspected, but he ordered Asta and I away from the rest. We returned to the Valiant and waited to pick up the others.

"After the shaper Vali wounded became a great beast, worthy of the name, Fenrir, we collected the crew and set out to sea. Thala trailed behind, having led the creature away from the rest of us. Once she rejoined us, we moved further into open water. It was then that a massive vessel belonging to the black ones, attacked."

"How massive?" Finna interjected. Abel considered the question a moment, before Thala answered.

"No fewer than three decks, at four times the length of our average longboat." Kari and Finna's eyes both swelled at the information.

"Go on." Kari spoke.

"We did our best to outmaneuver the massive vessel, but they kept upon us with a hail storm of projectiles. Vali used his shaping to its fullest to defend us, at no small risk of spirit shifting but was overcome. He and Asta were struck from the deck and fell into the water. Thala jumped in after them but only managed to reach Asta.

Once we managed to get them onboard, there was something different about Asta. Something wrong. I must admit, I am still in disbelief myself, but what happened to her, I..." Abel trailed off, not sure how to break the news to Kari and the High Chief. It was Thala who answered.

"If I may," she began. "As shrine maiden of Ulfrost, I feel confident in picking up where Captain Abel has left off." She looked to Abel and then the chief and Kari, for permission. Abel looked to her gratefully.

"Very well, Thala. Please proceed." Finna answered.

"Just as Abel explained with the Fenrir of Fangor, a shaper changed into a beast of the old world." She paused a moment, allowing her listeners to absorb the horror of that thought. "While we fled those 'wraiths' aboard their giant vessel, a similar change overcame Asta."

"But Asta cannot perform shapings?" Finna said in disbelief. Thala nodded.

"No, as had been my understanding. However, what became of Asta is very much the same as what happened to the shaper on the island. She not only performed indescribably powerful shapings, she transformed into a four-winged, draconian beast." Kari and Finna collapsed further into themselves, tears falling freely from the eyes of the healer.

"Next, she attacked the black ones' vessel, engaging in battle with another of their shapers. After sinking the ship, she turned her sights upon us. We narrowly avoided destruction, as another of the wraiths, transformed into some tentacled sea monster, and attacked Asta's new form."

"High Chief." Kari said softly, her voice quivering as she spoke. "It is as I told you. The beast from the old world, which ended the

High Lord Skjordsfell." All eyes save Finna's opened wide in horror. The High Chief however, sighed wearily.

"I fear you are right, my child. Captain Abel?"

"What became of my daughter?" Kari asked.

"I cannot say. However, I can say with a manner of certainty, that she survived the confrontation."

"Thank the Old Ones for that mercy." Kari muttered.

"Right now, we need to determine our next course of action." Finna began. "However, there is little we can do, until the rest of our warriors arrive. Until then, rest. You all look miserable with weariness. Recover your strength. We will see you later for the feast." Finna said, turning her head away.

"I believe that Brina can show you toward the sleeping quarters, as well as where to find food and washing. We shall see you later. For us, there is much more to discuss with the other chiefs." Finna walked away. Kari, though hesitant, followed. Turning back toward the end of the hall, where Brina had retreated, they quickly found the young woman.

"Is there something I can help you with?" She asked, raising an eyebrow to the group.

"Yes, can you please show us where we might bathe, eat and rest?" Abel asked. "It has been a long time since we have had a decent supply of either." Brina smiled to them, kindly.

"Of course. Please follow me." She said, leading them further into the tunnels.

***

Abel awoke that evening, to the sounds of merriment. Lazily opening his eyes, he rolled from the cot he had taken up, and slowly rose to his feet. Brushing the sleep from his eyes, he stumbled out into the tunnel, following the many voices.

He had not walked far, before Thala and Halla joined him. Agni and Haldr both, were waiting for them, near the end of the tunnel, smiles on their faces. The three weary travelers stared at their comrades curiously a moment, before asking their shared quandary.

"What is happening?" Abel asked. Agni smiled broadly, stroking his beard and patting his stomach.

"It is time for the feast." He said enthusiastically, rubbing his belly again. "There has been quite a deal of hardship, but there has been plenty of food."

"I have gone to bed with a stomach ache, nearly every night since we arrived." Haldr smiled, sniffing the air. "Tonight, will be no different." He continued to smile as he walked away. Halla followed behind her brother as everyone else gathered, smirked.

"Those two are the same as ever." Agni laughed.

"That is a good sign." Thala added. "Perhaps we can all take a cue from them. Keep moving forward." She paused briefly. "We never know when our last meal together will be." A sobering silence passed between them as they followed Agni's lead to the banquet hall.

Torches blazed in their sconces, forming a broad, illuminated circle around the room. Tables filled with food and ale sat in the center of the room, surrounded by salivating people. That night, they ate, they drank, and they cried for those and others whose fates were still unknown.

In the middle of the night, there second day on Dumah island, Abel awoke to a loud chorus of voices. Rising with a start, he stumbled through the opening to the main tunnel and looked about. Through the light provided by the torches, he saw Thala running toward him.

"What is going on?" He asked, sleepily. She came to an abrupt stop and looked at him with a proud smile on her face.

"Lights out on the sea. The rest of our comrades have arrived!" Abel's eyes grew to match the young woman's.

"Show me." He gasped. Thala spun on a heel and charged back the way she had come, Abel quick to follow her. They were joined by many others, some faces new and others old, as they made flight through the narrow tunnels. Up ahead, Abel could see the natural light from the moon, beginning to shine through the ventilation holes in the earthen formation, until at last, moonlight.

Stepping out into the light provided by the light rays, he and Thala both, made their way toward the hilltop. Climbing the slope, they stood high above everyone else, who continued to step out from the tunnel mouth. Staring out over the sea, broad smiles crossed their lips. Nearly one hundred lights shone back at them, each resting upon the bow of a longboat. Their comrades had returned.

Chapter 15 – One With The Kresh

Vali slowly opened his eyes and stared at the ceiling of their tent. He rolled his head to the side and saw Aya lying near, sound asleep. He watched her light, gentle breathing and listened to the soft cooing of her breath.

"It has already been three days," he whispered, groaning as he rolled to his side. The pain in his torso throbbed, though not as it did in his arms, legs and shoulders. Pressing away his blanket, he slowly pushed himself to his feet.

Stretching his body, he breathed deeply, feeling the tension in his body ease. Gently, he rotated his torso, easing himself through the movements. Already, he could feel his strength returning, no small part in thanks to his new companion. Making his way to the entrance of the tent, he pulled back the flap and stepped outside. The morning sun had just barely begun to rise over the treetops. As he looked out, the other Kresh only turned quickly enough to glance at him, their minds otherwise occupied.

He moved toward the center of the camp, where the early morning fire had already been squelched. Naught remained in the pit but dimly lit coals. Looking about, he noticed several tents were already collapsed, lying upon the dirt, ready for their journey out.

He knew little of their destination, only that he could not stay. Aya had warned him that once the Kresh moved on, the terrain would again, turn to wilds. Instead of surrendering to the moving environment, he walked toward the Damaruhk's tent. She met him just outside.

"Still here, then," she muttered, her voice both tired and coarse.

"I am." He answered, stepping inside behind her. "When do we leave?"

"Soon. It will take some time, before everyone is packed and ready. Once preparations are completed, we will be on our way."

"I want to help. What may I do?" The elder eyed him suspiciously, examining him for any sign of insincerity. "Please, if I am to attempt to become one of the people, I might at least share in their labors." Again, the Damaruhk stared at him.

"If you insist. Follow me," she said. Exiting the tent, he watched the elder as she addressed her people. Vali received numerous startled glances from the tribesman. The crowd of people parted slightly, as two older Kresh, a man and a woman, spoke.

"What did they say, Damaruhk?" He asked, staring back against the sea of eyes.

"You may help them. They also suggest you might help the younger ones carry what little we travel with. It will not be much, but if you desire to lend aid, you may."

"I accept," Vali said, cautiously approaching the two. They lead him to the opposing side of the camp, where their small tent awaited. Within, the couple possessed only a few earthly belongings a piece, in addition to the light clay urns and woven baskets, which were common around the camp. Within the hour, Vali and the two had everything collapsed and prepped for travel.

"What are you doing, Viking?" Aya asked as she drew nearer. She held all of her equipment over her bare shoulder, again tilting her head to the side, curiously.

"If I am to become one of the people, I must start somewhere." He answered. Aya stared at him curiously.

"Do you want to be one of the people so?" Her tone, skeptical, though nearing the edge of surprise.

"I see little option at this venture. At the very least, once I complete the Comartok, you can stop calling me stranger or Viking." Aya stiffened upright, before glowering at Vali with the faintest hint of irritation.

"Many Kresh ways, we ignore for you. Do not complain."

"I would not. It is merely one more thing to look forward to."

"Then you find your Freyja?"

"Her and Asta both. My mother, as well."

"Do you miss them?"

"Very much so." Aya looked back toward the rest of the camp and sighed.

"I will help you as I can. I must make ready to leave," she said, turning and walking away. Vali took this opportunity to look upon the many different Kresh. Young, old, and those he and Aya's age, all working together.

Those with children, carried the smallest members of the clan, carefully wrapped in leather slings around their torso. The younglings flocked around them, each carrying a small burden from the whole. The eldest, barely managing to carry themselves, stayed within the center of the group, along with the children.

Aya remained at the lead of the pack. Damaruhk and those old enough to wield weapons, followed behind. Vali had seen similar behaviors in wolves. Warriors who know the way, lead the group, while scouting for threats.

Those too weak, or otherwise unable to defend themselves, follow at a distance. This left the alpha, along with the rest of their strong, to protect the whole from the rear. Vali nodded with appreciation at the Kresh's method. They insured no one was left behind.

Looking up ahead, he noticed the young boy from Fangor, his sister held closely to his chest. The babe's skin had tanned slightly in the short time since he last saw her, better resembling the rest of the Kresh. Her hair growing head of hair however, remained ashen white. The babe smiled as she peered out from her carrier. Vali smiled back at her, before the young boy covered her.

They spent most of the day trekking through the woodlands and marshes. As they walked, Vali took in the scenery. Though they walked through the wildest parts of the jungles, the path seemingly unwound for them. Finally, as night began to fall, they stopped along the river.

Exhausted, Vali lowered his burden to the ground and aided the elders. Finished, he looked about and saw many of the younger Kresh, who sat collapsed around the circle of tents. A gentle nudge on the back of his shoulder catching his attention, Vali turned to see a bowl-shaped cut of yellowish fruit.

"Is that for me?" He asked of the elder Kresh woman, who nudged him a second time, extending her arms.

"Thank you," he smiled, accepting the piece of melon. He watched as the couple turned and walked away, then bit into his fruit.

"You did well," Aya commented, stopping to his side, testing the string of her bow.

"Heading out?" He asked, seeing the weapon and woven shawl around her shoulders. Aya nodded.

"I keep the people. It is my place." She said, stepping forward.

"Here, I will go with you." Vali said, rising to his feet.

"It is my place, not yours. Rest. We will have more walking, tomorrow." She said as she walked out into the forest. Finishing the last few bites of his melon, soft rind and all, he walked about the camp.

All around, the Kresh worked as one to make camp for the evening. Looking upon the many erected tents, he noticed Aya's was not among them. Moving through the clearing, Vali walked the familiar paths, finding them to be nearly identical to those he had walked the past few days.

Sitting upon the ground, exactly where it had been in the previous camp, a bundle of cloth and traveling packs, marked the location of their tent. He looked about some more, watching as a wave of younger Kresh, carried bundles of sticks and dragged branches from the forest.

Following them, he watched as they deposited their burdens onto the ground in front of boys and girls, four or so years older. These early adolescents in turn used the sticks and branches, to erect the many tents of the camp. He did not have to wait overlong, before a small group of children made way to Vali, carrying more construction supplies. They slowed their approach as they noticed him. He stared into their youthful, tanned forms and their innocent, curious faces.

"Are those for me?" He spoke in as soft a tone as he could manage, while lowering himself to a crouch. The children's eyes remained locked as they lowered their bundles. Another of the Kresh, emerging from the forest with a bundle in her arms, called to the children, who fled toward her.

"Now, what must I do?" Vali muttered aloud to himself, staring at the piles of wood. Looking up from his feet, he watched as the group assembling the dwellings, moved on to the next one.

His eyes narrowed as he observed them. They worked in a well-choreographed, rhythmic flow, each Kresh working in tandem with the others, placing branches into the ground, laying them against one another, and securing them with leather straps. As they finished, they wrapped the stitched leather sheet around the angular dome and secured it.

As they moved on to the next tent, Vali blinked his amazed eyes and turned back to his bundle. Quickly, he lifted two of the largest branches and watching the children, attempted to mimic their movements. Working to hook the tops of his support beams, the one in his left hand slipped and fell to the ground.

Somewhere in the distance, he thought he heard a light giggle. Ignoring the sound, he reached for his branches and attempted again. Eyes trained on his task, he furrowed his brow with concentration as he transfixed on his objective.

He growled with frustration as the sticks came free once more. Hearing the giggle once more, he looked over to the children. However, they had already moved on several plots away, paying him no attention.

"You are too accustomed to having your spirits aid you." The Damaruhk spoke, her gaze peering back over her shoulder. Turning back to face Vali, she sighed. "Allow the children to tend to it or wait for their aid."

"I wish to do this." He said, adamantly.

"The Kresh work as one people. To be one of the people, you will need to work as one of the many."

"There must be a better way." The Damaruhk nodded her head.

"Aye, for a lone hunter there is. I shall not spoil it for you. Try to remember that while my duty is to lead the people, the children have an equally important responsibility." Vali considered what she said. The fact that each Kresh, whether designated by age or gender, performed on a daily basis, set chores.

"It is not so different from my people. Each of us has a role. My role was like Aya's. I hunted, foraged and scouted ahead for my people. You could say I was a pathfinder. I helped find our way. Whether we were exploring or returning home."

"Aya's role is her own. It is not yours." She answered adamantly.

"Then what is my purpose?" He asked. The Damaruhk stared deeply into Vali's eyes. Her gaze felt disapproving to him, harsh and cold as winter iron.

"There is no place for you among the Kresh. You are not one of the people."

"And after I face the Comartok?"

"It will not matter. You will be dead." She spoke in a tone, which carried no emotion.

"I may yet surprise you. An outsider has faced the Comartok before."

"Aye, they have, but even then, it did not matter."

"Why not?"

"Because you will never be one of us. An outsider cannot simply become what they are not. You cannot become Kresh, no more than an elk can become a bird." Vali chose to bite his tongue a moment, carefully considering his words. As the Damaruhk turned to leave, he drew in a breath.

"I may yet surprise you." The Damaruhk stopped and turned her head slightly to the side.

"We shall see." She said as she walked away. Waiting until the elder had gained some distance, Vali turned back to face the tent. Again, taking up the branches, he took a single leather strap and wrapped it around the tops of the two.

Lifting the conjoined branches, he planted the ends of both into the ground. Stretching the distance between the two branches, he burrowed the edges into the ground. Releasing them, he stepped backward and stared at them.

"Now, I just need," he muttered to himself as he reached out for two more of the tall branches. Carefully lifting his branch, he aimed for the loop of his leather strap. As his branch fit through the loop, he positioned and planted it firmly into the ground.

"What are you doing?" He could hear Aya laughing as she drew near. Startled, Vali spun on a heel and tripping on his branch, brought the pieces of his structure down on top of himself. Again, he listened to the melodious giggle of the Kresh woman. Furrowing his brow, he slowly rose to his feet.

"I am trying to set your tent." He growled to himself as he nudged a stray branch with the tip of his boot.

"That is the place of the younglings. Not yours."

"I have no place among the people. I thought I might at least do this." Aya eyed him, her features taking on a sympathetic look.

"Will be among my people soon."

"Then the Comartok." Vali murmured. Aya nodded her head.

"After, we find your place, your Freyja and your sister." Vali nodded his head, sighing deeply.

"What will you do after the Comartok?" He asked her. Aya's shoulders rose as she shifted, uncomfortably. Pausing a moment, her tension abated.

"I will help you." She stated, blankly. Vali whipped his head around.

"But you cannot go back with me. The other Vikings will not understand."

"If my people can be made, so can yours."

"Do we know if your people can understand?" Aya looked away from him, having taken sudden interest in her sandals. Slowly, she looked back to him, resolute expression on her face.

"The Comartok, then." She spoke, turning her head back to the southeast, where their mysterious destination awaited.

"The Comartok." Vali agreed. The group of children returned, stopping just shy of where he and Aya stood. A small girl within the pack, pointed to the pile of branches and the two, which Vali had

~ 246 ~

strapped together. Talking in her tongue, she stared at them. Aya nodded her head, speaking a series of kind, soothing words. With a smile and a nod, the children giggled gleefully, before starting their work at setting the tent.

"Come, stranger. You follow." Aya said, turning away from the children and walking toward the edge of the camp.

"What did you say to them?" Vali asked, looking curiously back at the joyous children, who were among the first, to not seem too scared to near him.

"I say you hit your head. Think you are child." Vali's eyes narrowed as Aya giggled ahead of him. "Do not worry, stranger. We will find your place." She said, stepping into the tree line. As Vali approached, he happened to stare down at a stray twig on the ground and realized something. The tree line was just that. A line, where on one side were trees and on the other, the camp. Suddenly, it occurred to him that the clearing had been made.

"Aya, do the Kresh navigate between campsites?" The Kresh turned back to him, pressing her red and blonde hair over her shoulder to better stare at him.

"How else might we travel? Do your kin not travel as such?" Vali thought a moment, realizing she did not understand.

"Sort of. What I mean is, are there specific places you travel to, where you can set up your camps?" Eyes trained straight ahead of her, Aya continued to search through the forest.

"Yes, camp best by rivers and streams." Again, Vali sighed as they walked through the thick, jungle brush. They moved slowly, though he did not understand why. Aya's head turned from side to side, carefully searching the tall grasses and up in the trees as she carefully tipped her head back from time to time...sniffing.

"Aya, why are we out here?" He finally asked, after they had walked nearly until dusk. She stopped, holding up one hand sharply. Slinging her bow over her back, she peered up and with the agility and grace of Ulfrost's most nimble tree dwellers, scaled the lower branches.

"Come, stranger." She called down, wrapping her thigh around the branch, anchoring herself as she extended her hand to him.

"I can manage," he said, reaching up to the lowermost branch and pulling himself to meet her. "Asta and I would climb frequently back on Ulfrost."

"Ulfrost?" Aya asked him.

"My island. Where my people are from."

"The Aesiryn." She commented, climbing higher.

"Aesiryn?" He asked.

"Where your people come from. Your gods, the Aesir. Come. We go higher." She said, continuing to rise from the ground. As they climbed, Vali glanced downward, watching as the few branches which peeked out from the ground, shrank to twigs.

"Aya, why are we climbing this tree, in the middle of the night?"

"Show you something."

"What?" He asked, hands reaching just beneath her feet as she continued to climb.

"Many things. Many answers." He again could feel the wind upon his back and his muscles began to ache from the exertion. Still, he followed the vexing woman, until he felt the very sway of the uppermost branches in the wind and they came out above the other trees.

"Aya, what am I looking at, exactly?" Vali asked, staring out over vast expanses of forest. From his vantage, not a single clearing could be seen, save the narrow pathways, where the streams and rivers flowed through.

Far off in the distance, his eyes followed the green slopes of the hillsides, leading to rocky slopes, which were topped with yet more trees. Far beyond the green capped hills, he saw where the channel opened and guessed another island lie beyond. Rotating to the south, he stared toward home, though he could only envision it and not actually know that he looked toward Ulfrost.

"There," Aya said, pointing far downstream toward the coastline. Vali trained his eyes on a series of barely visible, white topped domes, in the distance.

"What is that?" He asked.

"That is where my people wait." He had expected some excitement in the words but found none. Instead, he thought he heard the sound of dread, stirring beneath the warm cusp of Aya's voice.

"We will reach them tomorrow, then?"

"Yes." She answered. Vali sat quietly, staring at the domes.

"Do you think that I am ready?"

"Does not matter." She said, pointedly.

"I do not know what you mean?"

"Either you face your death and die, or live. Ready or not, it comes. The Comartok may kill us both."

"You keep saying that, but you forget something." Aya's face transitioned from distraught to confused.

"What?"

"We are still alive." He breathed as he took in one last glance toward his home. "I am going to head back down." He said, lowering himself from the tree tops.

Silent contemplation accompanied him on his walk back to the campsite. For nearly a week, he had worked with Aya, or rather, at her behest, to build his strength back. The Kresh methods were not entirely different from the Vikings, battle play, stone throwing, climbing and the like. However, where he had grown accustomed to sport and attempts at beating one another in various games, the Kresh viewed their exercises as a way of deepening their resolve to the people.

As amusing as he found the differences between his people and the Kresh, he could not help but feel they were too different. He could not imagine a peace being formed between his people. Their history had long been forged in blood, iron and glory.

He still remembered the stories of his youth, spoke upon the lips of every war chief and only slightly different, upon those of the peace chief. The Vikings had first conquered the One Hundred Isles of Vala centuries ago. The people before they or the Kresh had been of a wholly different race, with beasts, which breathed fire and spears that could kill a man by pointing it at his breast.

These people had built high walls, which long protected them from the earliest of his kin. However, with the aid of the Old Ones, his ancestors had managed to take root among the ashes of the old race. He pondered upon his own thoughts, realizing his own mistake.

"I am not of the clans of Vala." He mused to himself, stepping back into the clearing of the Kresh camp. Looking back toward the tree in the distance, where a slight, angular shape gave away his mysterious new friend, he smiled.

"If my people can be swayed to take in Asta and I, perhaps." He sighed once more, before walking to their tent, which stood proud at the center of the camp.

Chapter 16 – The Cana

They left earlier that morning than the one before. The Damaruhk was insistent they make the final stretch of the trip, within the day. Vali, as before, helped pack the camp and carried a Kresh's share of it upon his back. Now, they followed the streams, Aya in the lead beside the Damaruhk.

Sweat dripped from Vali's brow as he carried more than he had the first day. The elders had been insistent to help him, but he had smiled, while he asked Aya to translate for him. He looked to either side of himself, seeing the other young Kresh, hauling their own burdens. From them, he did catch a variety of glances, ranging from confused, indifferent, happy, and from his black-haired friend with the penchant for violence, disgust.

He paid them little mind, concentrating most of his efforts to following Aya. He was grateful for the general, downward slope of the terrain, which made traveling easier, however, more than once did he catch Aya, staring back at him and smile. He smiled back to her, breathing heavily as he was, shifted his burden and carried on, feeling slightly renewed.

By evening, the streams began to fork out into a tangle of webbing waterways. The forest broke apart slightly as they stepped into a new, marshy area. The damp, swampy ground of the floodplain, reached up around them, as they crossed. Vali stood, water below his chest, watching as the smaller Kresh worked to cross.

Many of the children, simply swam, while the elders, clung to large pieces of fallen wood, helping them to float across. Those to either side of him, who carried the weight of the camp on their shoulders, were all mostly tall enough to keep their heads above water, even if not their burdens. Looking forward, he saw Aya, submerged passed her breasts, arms spread wide to her sides as she waded through to the other side.

With little to look at beneath his eyes, Vali took a moment to examine the surroundings up above. Trees rose from out of the water, their limbs stretching out wide, though bearing little color besides the brown of wood. Atop more than one of these trees, did he spot something unnatural, a small platform, or perhaps a large nest, with bits of dried flora serving as walls.

Ahead of them, Aya stopped. The pack followed her example and froze. The children treaded water or swam in small circles, while the elders floated in place. Vali, ignorant as he was, crept forward and stood beside the Damaruhk.

"Is there trouble? I will help you in a fight."

"Silence, stranger and be still." The Damaruhk said with a voice likened to a cat's hiss. "You know not of what you speak." Confused and slightly taken aback, Vali remained quiet, watching carefully as Aya glanced back once, bearing an admonitory expression.

She turned back to face the direction she had lead them and raising her weapons above her head, called out in the Kresh tongue. Now, Vali felt the weight of the tension among those he traveled with. The children huddled into one another, conjoining with the circle of elders. Of the Kresh, only Aya and the Damaruhk remained in front, Vali beside the elder.

Again, Aya called out across the waters and to the trees. No answering call returned. She turned her head back to the Damaruhk and nodded, before stepping forward.

"We may proceed, stranger." The silver haired elder spoke. Turning to cast him a sharp, disapproving look, she grimaced slightly. "Be wary and try not to do anything rash or foolish. You are in enemy lands. Even among the Dama clan, there are enemies here. Do not provoke any of them, under any circumstances." Vali simply nodded his head as the pack moved forward.

The bank of the floodplain was not much further from their stopping point. Soon, Aya was stepping out of the water, where she gently shook herself, before returning her bow and quiver to her back. Her glaive however, she still held protectively to her side.

Each of the tribesman followed Aya's lead, taking a moment to wring themselves of as much of the water as possible, before shifting their respective burdens and falling back in line. Vali noticed more of the strange, unnatural man-sized nests and realized what it was they were. Guard posts.

The first of the new Kresh, he saw long after it had seen him. He relied on his peripherals to gaze upon the tall, muscular warrior. He had a braid of long, golden hair, which was pressed behind his bared torso, where Vali eyed the many tattoos and hand painted marks upon his flesh.

The thickly corded muscles of the man were relaxed, though he held an arrow nocked to his bowstring. He could not help but wonder if the arrow remained trained solely on him, even after the young warrior left his field of vision. He could feel the hairs on the back of his neck prickle and had to consciously stop himself from reaching for his weapon that was not there.

At this point, he noticed the redoubled tension of those he traveled with. Everyone, save he, Aya and the Damaruhk looked on worriedly, their eyes darting from one nest to the next. Vali suddenly realized how very little he knew of the Kresh and their world.

Blue and ash painted warriors, armed with long, feathery plumed spears, rushed out from the trees to meet them. Aya took up a protective, predatory stance reminding Vali of a certain, ebony colored jungle cat. He had only once seen such an animal, prowling one of the northern isles, during his first expedition under Jerold's command.

She half crouched, body poised and ready to strike. Her spear was held at an angle, which would serve her adeptly for thrusting or striking. Another thing became abundantly clear to Vali. Where the Viking clans of the Isles of Vala, had grown in relative peace with one another, the Kresh had not.

Of the Kresh staring them down, one, far larger than the others, stepped forward. He spoke to them in the Kresh tongue, a guttural growl seething from between his pursed lips. He jutted a finger passed Aya, straight at Vali.

Aya, again, sprang protectively, this time placing herself between Vali and the Kresh as though she were hiding him. Aya, in her own melodious rendition of the Kresh language, answered back. Her tone was no less fierce than the large warriors. Where a lion is feared for its sheer size and might, Aya was an eagle; swift, cunning and more prone to tearing another's flesh and organs from their body than tolerating the slightest of discourtesies. The warrior before her, by Vali's reckoning, was not the courteous type.

Vali's hand twitched instinctively as he witnessed the exchange. The Damaruhk however, placed her hand over Vali's and tapped it gently to caution him. He sighed, gripping his fist tightly as Aya continued to stare down her enemy.

The far larger Kresh sprang forward, weapon raised, eyes burning with the fires of Hellheim. Aya, roared as a lioness and mirrored the aggressor's action. The large, blue Kresh thrust his weapon out at Aya, who moved swiftly enough, she seemingly vanished.

Like a primal flash of lightning against a cloud of blackened storm clouds, she jutted in and out of line with the Kresh's weapon, whirling her own as she did so. The back haft of her glaive struck the side of the spear, the pommel knocking the weapon against its holder's body. In the same motion, she slashed wide, cutting into the large Kresh's thigh, dropping him to a knee. The final, gracefully executed move, brought the glaive's pommel crashing down on the Kresh's elbow and planted the blade gently upon his left shoulder from behind.

Another deep throated yell came from behind the line of warriors. At the sound, Aya looked back over her shoulder with narrowed eyes. The Damaruhk stepped passed Vali, gently pushing against his chest, while calling toward the source of the voice.

The voice called back as two figures stepped forward from beyond the lines of warriors, encircling Vali and those he traveled with. Turning her gaze on Aya, the Damaruhk spoke, once more, causing a flick of irritation from the young woman. Hesitantly, she lifted the blade of her weapon from the subdued warrior's shoulder and stepping backwards, lowered the weapon to her side.

The lines of Kresh warriors parted as Aya turned and walked backwards toward her people, glaive still held at the ready. The Damaruhk stood near to her, placing her hand on the young woman's shoulder. As a tall, broad chested Kresh stepped forward, the Damaruhk stopped. Beyond the massive warrior, another equally large Kresh, chest covered with scars moved to meet the Damaruhk.

He had long silver hair, which was pulled back in a braid. His chest and arms were decorated with various scars, proving his status as a warrior. He carried no weapon and despite his limp, he walked with a sense of proud stature the likes of which Vali had seen amongst the oldest veteran Vikings. Those, who had fought in the old wars with the Kresh. Patting his escort on the shoulder, he stepped with two paces of Damaruhk. Tilting his head down to eye the dwarfed woman, he grinned at her.

"Damaruhk," the man called with the bark of a large dog and extended his arms in a welcoming gesture.

"Canaruhk," the old woman replied, nodding her head without lowering her gaze. Vali watched the exchange anxiously, attempting as he may to understand each of the words the two spoke. He understood none of it, no matter how hard he tried.

The two continued to exchange words, their tones as gentle as Aya's might be when discussing matters with Vali. As the thought came to him, both Dama and Canaruhk turned their eyes upon him. The elder man's gaze was hard. Vali imagined the man was deciding where best to plunge a knife, or of the color Vali might bleed.

"Stranger, come." The man called, nearly causing Vali's jaw to drop. Aya flashed a worried glance from Vali to the two elders. As she stared at the Damaruhk however, the old woman merely nodded her head. Vali stepped forward, stopping before the Damaruhk and with the best of intentions, bowed his head and saluted. He waited several minutes under the man's hard gaze, awaiting acknowledgement.

"I know the custom of your people," Canaruhk said to him, his voice again harsh, unlike it had been with Damaruhk. "It is not our way, but I understand you do so with respect. You should know, I have slain many of your kin. Why do you travel with the Damaruhk? Why have you come to the lands of my tribe?" Vali shifted his gaze to Aya and the Damaruhk, silently pleading for instructions. Aya, looking just as worriedly, did the same.

"Answer, stranger." The Damaruhk nearly spat, her tone much coarser than it had been in the past. Vali was beginning to understand why he was going to die in this place, far away from his home. He suspected he may die within the minute, yet alone see another sunset or smell the salt on the ocean. Nervously tapping the cord on his neck, he cleared his throat.

"I traveled with the Damaruhk and her clan, because I am lost. I wish to return to my people."

"So, you might lead them in battle, to slaughter our kin?" Canaruhk spoke angrily. All around them, the Kresh hissed and snarled. Vali shook his head and cleared his throat.

"No, Canaruhk. I do not wish for more pointless bloodshed between our peoples. I was wounded by an enemy and tossed from my ship, off from the coast of Fangor. The Kresh whom I am traveling with saved me. They pulled me from the sea and," he thought to his dreams. "Breathed life into me. Kanadesh." He muttered, remembering the word he had heard in his dreams.

Both Aya and the Damaruhk jolted backwards in surprise as Vali spoke the word. Equally surprised by their reaction, he nearly did not notice as Canaruhk leapt with more grace than a man his age ought to possess and placed a knife to his throat. Vali froze, standing perfectly still as he heard Aya shout in protest.

The Damaruhk spoke calmly to the other elder, in their tongue, so that Vali could not understand the words. After a brief exchange between them and several gestures toward Vali, knife still to his throat, the Canaruhk eased. Vali eased, as well, gently feeling the light trickle of blood on the underside of his chin.

"It seems that you speak truth." The Canaruhk spoke, seemingly angrier than before. "The Damaruhk has also told me that for a time, you fall under her protection. She is Rukh. Despite my objections, I shall not kill you, yet. The second question, stranger. Why do you travel here, to my lands?"

"I wish to become one of the people. I have loved ones, whom I have left behind. I fear a fate worse than mine awaits them."

"You face death." Canaruhk reminded him.

"To my people, there are things worse than death, and many, worth dying for. As I said, my loved ones face worse than I." The man's gaze did not soften, but something else appeared within his eyes, Vali thought it might be empathy.

"What do you hope to gain from my tribe?" The old warrior asked.

"I wish to undertake the Comartok." Another roar of disapproval erupted amongst the ranks of the Canaruhk's clan. The man himself, however, simply stared at Vali, in part, surprised, the other, amused.

"You wish to take on the Comartok." He repeated, nodding his head slowly as he considered it. "Damaruhk, is the last of the Kresh to undertake the Comartok and live. She and her mate." At this,

Vali noticed the Damaruhk look down toward the ground, a glistening tear in her eye.

"I wish to undertake it." Vali spoke more confidently than before, staring directly into the eyes of the proud chief. The older man looked about a moment, thinking of the proposition.

"Does the Damaruhk sanction this?" He asked. The elder woman, allowed the tear to fall to the ground and looked up at Vali, anger in her eyes. Vali eyed her alarmingly as she turned to Aya, who nodded gruffly. Looking back from the young Kresh, she appeared weakened, her shoulders slouching forward.

"Yes." She spoke in Vali's tongue, allowing him to hear how much it pained her to say it. The Canaruhk closed his eyes and nodded his head, before turning to face his tribe. As he spoke in the Kresh tongue, the gathered warriors took turns gasping and acting out of shock as those he had passed the last several days with.

Canaruhk continued to speak to his tribesmen, who Vali had begun to notice, were all men. As the uproar died down, the old Kresh warrior turned to face Vali. Aya stood beside the Viking, her hand on his shoulder, gripping tightly.

"Stranger, do you truly wish to become one with the people?" His tone had suddenly become less threatening. The nervous tensions lifted lightly. Squaring his shoulders, Vali resumed his brave face.

"Yes, Canaruhk." He spoke with conviction.

"Then with the consent of the Damaruhk, you are to prepare for exile, until the Comartok has been completed." Vali's eyes flashed wide, while Aya's dropped to the ground. To him, it was as though the final stone on a burial mound had been laid.

"I go with him!" She yelled. Neither the Canaruhk nor the Damaruhk seemed surprised by this, though the elder woman's head fell in despair as the rest of the assembly gasped.

"Damaruhk?" The elder spoke. She did not answer, only nodding her head. Canaruhk made a low, rumbling tone in his throat.

Vali did not understand its meaning. However, he had learned his time would be wasted should he ask.

"Prepare for your exile. Come the fall of the next moonless night, you shall be stripped of all that makes you Kresh, until you return, having defeated the great enemy."

"Canaruhk, what is this great enemy?" Both of the Rukh shot Vali an irritable glance. Realizing he had clearly spoken out of turn, Vali lowered his gaze again. Aya's grip on his shoulder tightened, and he felt the small woman's body trembling through it.

"The Comartok. Great enemy." The man began his explanation. "In every generation, a great beast arises, in the name of the gods of death. It is the duty of the Rukh, to slay these beasts. The Rukh are a rare breed and our numbers are nearly wrought.

"Many of our braves, who might have become Ruhk, are dead. Slain by your kin, Viking. Of the Ruhk, Dama, Cana, Gara and Tha remain. Alas, it seems the gods of death have again given form to another of the Comartok.

"Viking, the next moon cycle begins in two weeks by your kin's calling. Be sure that you are ready by then. Those you travel with shall provide what they may for your journey, while my warriors shall be happy to test you. Return without proof of your deed, then you and this woman will be killed."

"The Comartok is death, or conquering death," Vali whispered to himself. Nodding to the Canaruhk, he turned to face Aya.

"You do not have to do this, Aya. You should stay with your people. They need you. My loss would be of no consequence to them." Aya's eyes narrowed, the trembling he felt from her stopped.

"Do not speak of what I should do, stranger. Of things, you not know." She growled at him. "This my choice. Way of my people. Not your decision." She turned back to and approached both elders.

She saluted to them, an open palm, pressed over the center of her chest as she presented a half bow to each. Never once, did she break eye contact with those she lowered herself to. He suddenly understood the reverence she held for these warriors from a former life. They in turn, nodded back to her and shared a few words in their tongue, before Aya returned to Vali's side, still glaring at him. Both Rukh, as Vali had learned to call them, spoke in private.

After their brief discussion, Canaruhk turned to his people, while Damaruhk addressed hers. They both spoke to their charges in their own language. The warriors, lowering their weapons, walked back from the direction they had arrived. Those Kresh he had traveled with followed them as the Damaruhk turned to Vali and Aya.

"We shall stay here. The Cana shall not harm us. Regarding the Comartok, we will discuss it, tomorrow night. Make use of your last remaining days among us, stranger. I most now rely on you to defend not just one of my own but the last of my bloodline. I believe your people use the word, granddaughter." Vali looked at Aya, who averted her gaze.

"Come, stranger." Aya barked at him, gathering up her weapons. "Return these belongings and rest. Tomorrow, we prepare." She left both Vali and the Damaruhk behind, as she moved beyond the tree line.

"I did not know she was your granddaughter." He spoke, obvious lamentation in his voice.

"There was no need to tell you." The old woman growled. "I had simply hoped that you could be swayed."

"Is Aya taking on the Comartok for my sake?" The Damaruhk sighed.

"No. This was her choice. You were simply an excuse. I wish she had never found you." The woman nearly spat, the level of disgust in her voice clearly depicting how he appeared in her eyes.

"I wish we had found each other under better circumstances."

"Your people will always be an enemy to the Kresh. You enjoy war and conquest, too much." She brushed passed him, moving toward the tree line, leaving Vali standing alone with only the guards in their nests, still holding their bows.

"By the Old Gods, I hope things can change." He looked up at the half moon and sighed. "Asta, Freyja, everyone, please be safe."

That following morning, Vali awoke, every muscle fiber in his body aching. He rolled to his side and to his surprise, saw that Aya was gone. Slowly rising to his feet, he stretched his body and dressed. Pulling back the flap of the tent, he stepped outside and took in the morning breeze.

Even between the two clans, few Kresh moved about the camp. Quickly however, their eyes turned to gaze upon him. None reached for their weapons, which he noticed remained nearby, even as he approached. Setting down in front of the fire, he warmed his hands, doing his best to ignore his onlookers.

Daring a hastened glance or two, he attempted to gain a sense of his surroundings. Several warriors sat about the fire, weapons at their sides. Noticing each was male, he scanned a second time. Several, smaller forms moved about the camp, their clothing and stature betraying their feminine forms.

He watched them longer than he thought polite, though he noticed another difference between the two clans of Kresh. While the Dama clan, shared their daily burdens, it appeared the Cana still practiced gender specific roles. Vali considered his observations, withdrawing his own judgments.

Each of the males was far larger than those of the Dama clan. Even the young, appeared bigger than those the same age. Of the women in the clan however, he could not distinguish any signs of combat training. Where each of the Dama held a fierceness in their gaze, he only saw such a trait in the Cana males.

He knew little of these people. Their ways or their lives. While life with the Dama, had proven itself quite similar to his own. He found other areas of Cana life to be familiar.

"Stranger, come." He looked up at the sound of Aya's voice. He saw her, standing across the campfire, her glaive, bow and a long, leather wrapped parcel on her back. Glimpsing at the tanned hide, nearly the length of her glaive, he followed his caretaker obediently.

"Is something the matter?" He asked. The other Kresh stared at Vali, equally as confused as Aya.

"What does that mean?" She responded. Vali let his head sag a moment.

"Is something wrong?"

"We are to be exiled and sent to our deaths. Everything is wrong, Viking."

"Fair enough," he said, slowly rising to his feet. "What do you need?"

"You to practice." She said, turning away. You will need cunning and strength. I help with cunning. Follow." She continued walking toward the tree line as Vali looked back to the Kresh.

"Good light, then." He laughed to himself. The Kresh, unable to understand his words, still smiled, having fully understood the exchange. He walked after the young woman, shaking his head nearly the entire time.

The camp, just as had been the case with the Dama camps, was nestled in the center of a clearing. The glen, no larger than to support the camp, was surrounded on all sides by thick entanglements of greenery. Vines wrapped around many of the trunks of the trees, which were all partially sunk into the earth.

The major difference he could tell between the camps was the amount of moisture in the soil. The Dama had always been certain to camp along the rivers, the Cana seemed to make their camp within the heart of a great swamp. This floodplain, he decided, offered them a tactical advantage over anyone who might invade their home. Stepping through the tree line and into the untamed forest, he saw Aya waiting for him.

"Take these," she said, tossing him a dagger and a small leather pouch. He caught them both and stared curiously.

"What are these for?"

"You need bow to face Comartok." She said, removing her own from her back. "Good for hunting, good for fighting." Removing her bowstring from the pouch on her hip, she plucked at it playfully, leaving her shaft and arrows in their quiver. Vali nodded his head in agreement as he looked around.

"I have never made a bow from these trees." He said, running his hand along the trunk of a nearby elm.

"It will serve you well," she answered, looking deeper into the forest. "Can you use it?" Vali looked up at her with a smile.

"I will manage." He continued to smirk as he lopped off a branch.

"Make later," Aya said, jumping down from her perch. Removing the leather parcel from her back, she held it out to him. "Need more than bow. Strength and practice." She said, gesturing for him to take the gift.

Vali reached out for the object in her hand. Accepting it, he found it to be well weighted and was slightly longer than the length of his arm. A leather strap ran from the top to the bottom of the parcel, with a flap folded over and secured on the opposite end.

"You found my sword!" He said, removing the flap and drawing the weapon. He held the familiar blade in his hands a moment, testing out the weight of it.

A series of complex emotions flowed into him. A Vikings weapon was their lifeline, their most trusted companion. Even in death, they were buried together. Without it, he had felt incomplete.

"The waters where you fell were not deep. The children helped find it."

"Thank you, Aya." He said, a slight choking sound in his throat. "It means a lot to me. Thank you." Without thinking about it, he closed the gap between them and wrapped the startled young woman in a tight embrace.

"Let me go, Viking." She squirmed against him, unable to utilize either of her arms. He pulled away from her, smile on his face.

"I mean it, Aya. Thank you." He said, releasing her.

"Very strange, Viking. I no understand your kin." She grumbled, smoothing out her disheveled clothing.

"I was just giving you a hug, was all. I am sorry. I have no other way to thank you."

"Warn me, next time." She grumbled, walking passed him. "I might have stabbed you."

"Well, I am happy you did not." She looked at him, grumpily and shook her head.

"You need practice. Else we both die." Vali eyed Aya, feeling sympathetic to her situation, even though he did not understand it.

"Why did you decide to go with me?" Aya looked as though she were going to say but instead turned away.

"I wanted to. I wish to become Rukh."

"Will defeating the Comartok, the great enemy make you a Rukh?"

"Yes."

"What of me?" Aya eyed him curiously.

"What you mean?"

"If I do not die, will I become Rukh to your people, as well?" Aya stopped for a long time, contemplating the question.

"Ask too many questions. Practice, now. Or we both die." Nodding his head, he turned back to face the rest of the forest. Running his weapon through a series of practice swings, Vali placed his hand over his sore abdomen as he fell back on the training of his youth.

Aya watched him some time, learning his movements, studying his steps and his attacks. She hopped down from her perch and drew up her bow. Leaning her weight down on the shaft, she bent back the wood as she pulled tightly on her string. Setting the loop of the bowstring in place, she tested it, before pulling an arrow from her quiver.

"No stop, Viking." She said, drawing back on the arrow. "Your target is tree trunk." Nervously, Vali turned back toward his invisible opponent, slashing, thrusting and striking as he continued through each of his poses.

As he continued to work through his forms, he felt a flash of wind, fluttering passed his right ear. Before he could stop from the shock of it, he heard a hard "thud" against the trunk of the tree, where Aya's arrow was planted. Vali turned his head slowly to look upon the woman, only to be scolded.

"Keep going!" She yelled at him, loosing another arrow, which embedded itself beside the first. "We need be one. Work together." She said, reaching behind her head and drawing another arrow with trained ease.

Reluctantly, Vali returned to his training. He made a backhanded slash and followed through with an upward stroke as another arrow struck the tree, forming a triangle between the three arrow heads. From the height of his swing, he shifted his feet and struck once more, with a fourth arrow glancing over his left side. Having again, struck near to the first three arrows, Vali turned.

"What is it?" Aya asked, standing across from where she had been. "Work together. Take turns at Comartok. Keep beast distracted." Lifting the sheath Aya had made for him, Vali slipped it over his shoulder and sheathed his weapon.

"Should we take the Canaruhk up on his offer." A smirk appeared on Aya's lips.

"They hurt you." She warned.

"Probably. They appear much more experienced than I and I have yet to recover my shaping."

"May need it." She added, kicking at a stray twig lying on the path.

"I realize." He looked back to the elm branch and lifted it from the ground. "Shall we, then? At least we can learn when we are going to hear more about the Comartok."

"Come, stranger." Aya said, plucking her arrows from the tree trunk and walking further into the forest.

"But the camp is that way?" He said curiously, pointing back toward the encampment.

"Too early return, now. I want hunt." She called back. "I teach." Vali continued to stare at her backside as she foraged through the brush.

"I already know how to hunt." He called after her, following.

"You know Viking way. Loud, clumsy. Rely on spirits for everything. For Comartok, must learn be silent." He could hear her call back, seemingly from a distance. He pressed his way through the brush, where she had vanished through and looked about.

"Aya?" He called gently, slowly spinning. "Where are you?" As weak as his gift had grown, Vali had spent every spare moment, attempting to regain his prowess for commanding spirits. Even now, as weak as his connection was, he could detect a few lesser ones.

Gently touching upon them, he knelt and closed his eyes. Reaching toward them with his consciousness, he felt their chaotic flow of energy. The lesser spirits, he found, lacked the refined nature of their more powerful brethren.

They twitched anxiously bucking and kicking at his outstretched consciousness as an unfriended or unbroken steed might. More than once did he wince as he felt their retaliation through the connection. As sweat decorated his brow, he managed to latch onto one, which begrudgingly granted him a glimpse of its sight.

The imagery provided was inconsistent, fuzzy he thought. It seemed the younger spirits lacked an interest in the physical world, making the information they provided of little use. Before he released the connection however, he caught a flicker of movement and glowing, feral eyes.

"You are dead, Viking." Aya whispered in his ear, her knife to his throat, her torso pressed against his. Vali carefully eyed the weapon at his throat as he drew the still contained spirits strength into himself.

Both still assuming a four-point crouch, Vali kicked back his right leg as he rolled his throat away from Aya's blade. The Kresh made a high-pitched sound of surprise as Vali gripped her wrist with his free hand and swept against her legs, tackling her to the ground.

Vali landed on top of the young woman, who remained still, silver eyes filled with shock as he pinned her wrists behind her head. He felt her thighs to either side of him as he smiled down at her, his face hovering just over hers. He could smell her sweet breath, feel her rapidly pacing heart beneath her bosom, thundering against his chest.

"You might be invisible, but it appears as though I may possess a few surprises." He smiled at her again as she continued to eye him, part of her aggrieved, another elated. He felt her powerful thighs twisting against his hips, rolling him off from her body. In the blink of an eye, Aya had rolled herself free of his grip and planted the knife just to the side of his left eye.

"Much to learn, Viking." She grumbled as she rose to her feet and walked away. Vali, without turning his head, looked to the knife and sighed. Rising to his feet, he pulled the knife from the ground and followed the powerful woman.

They continued through the forest, Vali following Aya as she led him deeper within. Though she was no more than two bounds out of reach, as she crouched lower, she again vanished from his sight. He froze a moment, unable to determine where she had gone. Settling lower to the ground, he peered through the tall grasses, toward the clearing.

Walking through a small meadow, a lone deer passed by. He stood on all four legs, twelve points spread upon its broad antlers. Vali looked back over his shoulder, wishing he had already made his bow.

He listened carefully, unconsciously tapping into the presence of the lesser wind spirits around him. He could hear their dancing, the sound of their movements, peeling through the tall grass, blowing against his face. They whistled gently as they passed through an old log, lying in their path. Then, there was a sound of someone blowing out the gentle flame of a candle.

The arrow soared through the tall grasses, invisible until it struck the deer, high under its ribs. The animal lurched upwards but Vali could see in its eyes that the creature was no longer for this world. Next, he saw Aya, bounding through the tall grass, having been just outside of arm's reach from him.

In the split instant it took for the capable hunter to clear the distance between her hiding place and the deer, she had returned her bow to its quiver and drawn her long hunting knife. Catching a glimpse of the blade, Vali found it similar to the one currently in his possession.

Before the body, not yet realizing it was dead, had fallen to the ground, Aya plunged her blade into its heart, to assure a swift kill. A profound silence filled the jungle, as Vali watched the woman embrace her prey. He did not understand the exchange; only enough to know that something important had been lost to him.

Gently lowering the majestic beast to the ground, she knelt in front of it and bowed her head before the downed deer. Too stunned to react, Vali watched in awe as she spoke a few gentle words in the Kresh tongue, gently touching the beast's brow and stood. Pulling her arrow from the deer's ribs, she turned her head and stared directly at Vali, who was still crouched.

"Come, stranger. Work to do. Then, we bring to camp." Vali nodded his head and rose to help her.

That night, all the Kresh of both clans, gathered around the large fire they had built. While many hunters and gatherers had returned with various offerings for the evening meal, Vali was sure to partake in the venison Aya had provided. He sat in wonderment at the people around him and stared at the young woman whom he had come to know.

He sat across the fire from her, watching as she danced to music, which was played somewhere he could not see. The notes were something he could not hear. He found himself at a loss for his lack of perceiving them.

He stared down at the bowl he had been given. Stew made from the venison, with even more being made into strips of jerky. He ate his meal absent mindedly, taking his time with it, not to savor the flavor of the rich, gamey meat, but its purpose. What was Aya doing, before she claimed her trophy?

Numerous passerby glimpsed and pointed at him, laughing and speaking in their native tongue. Vali did not notice. He continued to drift along a river of thought, about a people whom he had long been taught were his enemy, but whom he had found little he did not enjoy about them.

Their angular features, their tanned skin, exotic eyes and hair; all of it seemed beautiful to him. Their way of life, set him at ease; the same way sitting alone on the coast, smelling the sea as the sun sank beneath the waves did. He felt a pain in his chest. Something was missing there, and he wished to know what.

"What do you see, stranger?" He heard just behind him, breaking his concentration and sending his drifting vessel ashore. Vali turned his head to see the Canaruhk and out of respect, moved to rise.

"Stay. I will join you a moment." The elder said, taking up the seat next to Vali and watching his encampment with pride. Vali turned his attention away from the old Kresh and those who stared at their exchange.

"It is hard to explain." He answered, at first not possessing proper words to answer the Rukh's question. "It is not unlike our gatherings on Ulfrost, but there is something else at work, here. I cannot place it." The old warrior nodded his head, providing nothing to guide the young man's thoughts.

"You are enemies, are you not?" He asked the Rukh. The elder nodded his head.

"We are."

"And yet Aya is dancing. Children from both clans are playing together. Your warriors are talking with the young of Damaruhk's tribe. I do not understand."

"The Kresh are not as simple, or as complex as you believe, Viking. I will not take the time to teach you as I might a youngling in my tribe. Would your kin turn away an infant, because of its sires?" Vali considered a moment, everything in his being telling him 'never' but a solemn, broken voice buried deep, whispered differently.

"It is not uncommon." Vali admitted. "I have heard of it and have done nothing. My sister and I were an exception. Our mother took the both of us in, even though we came from beyond the Isles of Vala." The Canaruhk raised an eyebrow at Vali, who stared down into the smoldering embers of the high reaching flames.

"You are not from these lands?" Vali shook his head.

"No. Our elders tell of a time, when a fog settled about the world, slowly suffocating all life it touched. Slowly, our ancestors began to vanish from the known world and things which were once known to us, became lost.

"Our fisherman, our hunters and explorers, all stopped venturing outside of the Isles of Vala. The fog settled at the far reaches of the Tyrda Fell, looming just beyond the reach of its emerald waters. My mother told me that during the night, when the final kingdom of the world outside of our isles fell, a woman with golden eyes delivered my sister and I."

"I do not like you, Viking." The Canaruhk said, drawing in a deep breath as he surveyed his clan. Vali gently rolled his head to the man, who hesitated to continue. "However, if you do return as one of the people, I shall accept you. Perhaps it has come with my age, or from witnessing the decline of my people, but I do not wish to war with your kind, any longer."

"I have been thinking, ever since I first met Aya that not once, have I ever known a truly valid reason for the fighting." Vali answered. "It was as if our ancestors chose for us."

"As though it was never our decision to begin with." The Canaruhk added in his low, rumbling tone. "To that, we can agree. Spirits guide you, Viking and be sure to look after the one who walks with you. She is important to the Damaruhk. That makes her important to the Cana, as well." The elder Kresh rose from his seat without another word and moved amongst his own people. Vali smiled as small children flocked to him, clinging to his clothes playfully and older Kresh, saluted him.

"What troubles you, Viking?" Aya asked, dropping to a seat beside him, platter of various meats and fruits upon it. He observed her a moment as she placed a large piece of melon to her lips and bit into it.

"Just thinking, I suppose."

"Think too much." She answered, grabbing another piece of reddish orange fruit and holding it out to him.

"What is this?" He asked, eying the juicy, sour smelling fruit.

"Cana fruit. I not know." She said, continuing to hold it forward. Vali, cautiously leaned forward and opened his mouth. The moment Aya deposited the object on his tongue, he felt his lips pucker.

He backed away out of shock as his tongue tingled and heard the sing song giggle of his peer. After a moment, the shock of what he was ingesting, subsided and he enjoyed the sweet taste, which followed the extreme initial tartness. He savored the fruit, nodding his head in approval as Aya, tipping her head back, eyes on him, deposited another slice into her own mouth.

He laughed back at her as her eyes closed, nose wrinkled and lips puckered, while she shivered fervently. As he imagined he had, her expression softened, and he saw in her eyes, enjoyment. Reaching out, he waited for her to nod to him, before he repeated the process.

"It's delicious," he confirmed, provoking a smile from her. A series of loud knocks against a skin covered drum, cut their conversation short. Both he and Aya, looked up to see both of the Rukh, standing beside one another, eyeing the entirety of the camp.

Canaruhk began by speaking in the Kresh tongue, followed by Dama. Vali leaned in closer, attempting to catch one or two of the sparse words he knew. He relaxed as he felt a gentle touch on the top of his hand and turned to see Aya, looking forward.

"It is about the Comartok." She told him. "I speak you their words." He sat back as Aya listened intently. As if understanding her purpose and intention, both of the Rukh waited momentarily, as she turned to Vali.

"They make clear to all the Kresh, they help us. They wish us success in facing the Comartok. They warn Kresh of punishment, if they try to stop us." As she finished, she looked back to her elders and nodded.

As prompted, both Rukh, continued their story. Vali watched the exchange, often stopping to stare directly at Aya as he eagerly awaited her aid. After a series of hand gestures, which he could not imagine as good, he tapped the woman impatiently on the thigh. Gently slapping his hand, she remained focused forward, until the elders again paused.

"They say great enemy has appeared to the north. On Fangor. They say is Comartok for certain and must be slain. At next moonless night, we are exiled. Cannot return, until great enemy is slain."

"Is the Comartok still on Fangor? How are they tracking it?" Aya motioned for him to calm himself as she continued to listen.

"One stays on island. Other, travels east. Your kin call island Dugat."

"That is just north of Dumah. My clan are there, now." Though it was the Rukh, opposite the fire, who spoke, all eyes were now on them. The looks upon the faces, took on grave appearances, which sent chills down Vali's spine. Worriedly, he turned his head to Aya, to see she too, bore an expression of shock.

"What did they say?" He asked. Aya nodded her head, taking a moment to gather herself, before translating.

"They say Comartok has taken shape of great wolf. Wolf is among most revered of Kresh guardians. Strong, cunning. Say after slaying all at Fangor, it searches for food. It has only one eye." Now, it was Vali's turn to seize with shock.

He remembered, too well, the black robed one, who had attacked his people and scorched the land. Of the one, which he had struck with his full power as a Shaper that had turned into the being Thala had named as Fenrir. He reached behind his head and drew his sword and rested it upon his lap.

"I was the one who claimed Fenrir's eye," he whispered to her, staring down at his blade.

"This good news, then." Aya said, placing her hand on his shoulder. "We know it can be wounded." Vali shook his head, eyes still on his weapon.

"It took all of the strength the spirits could lend me, to do that much. Without my shaping..."

"We find a way." She said encouragingly. "Practice not hurt, though." He nodded his head as the Rukh's announcement continued without them. An hour or more passed, before Aya tugged at Vali's collar. Looking up at her, she motioned toward the tent they had come to share.

"You rest. Tomorrow, we practice. Braves help us." She motioned her head toward a group of five, rather large, thickly muscled Kresh, covered in painted symbols. Vali glanced at them and rose to his feet. Among them, was the large, dark haired man who had wished his death only a short while ago.

"Good night, Aya." He said, gently touching her elbow.

"Sleep well, Viking. Much work ahead." Vali could not help but imagine how much nicer the prospect of roughing it in the savage jungle looked at this venture.

Chapter 17 - Awakening

Asta awoke, lying upon a bed of grass, the sun in her eyes. She looked around and saw nothing but mountains and trees. Slowly rising to her feet, she moved to dust herself and found she was nude. Her heart raced as she quickly scurried to a seated position.

"How did I get here?" She spoke aloud, her head swiveling. Her voice was hoarse and dried. Turning from side to side, she saw a gentle stream trickling. Running on clumsy, lifeless legs, she stumbled toward it and submerged her head.

The water was cool and burned at her coarse throat. She took in as much as she could, before feeling ill and wrenched herself from the water. Coughing heavily, her body heaved from fatigue and malnourishment. Turning her gaze up from the stream, she saw a large cluster of trees, bearing large, round and furry orbs.

Eyes desperate with hunger, Aya crawled toward them. In her dash to the stream, she had depleted what little strength she previously carried. Her arms and legs gave out on her, and she fell face first to the ground.

She lifted her head again, reaching out weakly toward the tree. A collection of the orbs, lie on the ground at its trunk, taunting her to draw near. She focused on the orbs, cursing them for not drawing closer. Growling with frustration, she looked down at the rest of her body and pawed forward.

Her hand struck something hard, though it gave beneath her fist. Her eyes flashed up once more. One of the orbs, accidentally smashed, was now within reach. Eyeing it in disbelief, the aroma it put off stuck in her nostrils. It smelt heavenly.

Without restraint or thought, Aya scooped handfuls of the strange, milky white, meat into her mouth, groaning with pleasure as it soothed her mouth and slid easily down her throat. She continued to shovel, taking no heed as to the amount of dirt and sand covering her hands, nor to the feeling of the sun, striking her bare skin.

She ate until she felt a hard pit, forming in the bottom of her stomach. An ill churning, crawled about in her belly and she feared for the nourishment she had taken in. More than feared for it, she felt greedy for it. Out of impulse, she looked around, eyes searching for anything that might threaten her newfound salvation.

She waited but saw nothing. She scooped up the remains of her orb, along with the others and slowly rose to a seated position and looked back to the stream. She found her reflection there. Her eyes stared back at her wildly. Though they were centered within her skull, in the middle of her face, they did not belong to her.

With an unsteady hand, she touched her cheek and leaned closer to the surface of the water. Blinking her eyes several times in a desperate hope to force the wild look from them. Closing her eyes, a long while and reopening them, she saw they were once again blue.

"How did I get here?" She wondered aloud, trying to search her memory for any clue. Slowing her breathing and closing her eyes, she concentrated hard on the last things she could remember.

They were on Fangor, surrounded by the enemy. She was running, Abel beside her. A great host of massive ships attacked them. Then, she was in the water.

"Vali!" She yelled out, twisting and turning, looking for any sign of the man. "Vali, where are you?" She yelled out once more but saw no one. Her strength partially restored, she rose to her feet and looked around the site of her isolation.

All around her, there was naught but cliffs, the river and trees. She could hear the screeching of animals and the buzzing of insects in the forest, but little else. Looking up to the sky, she shielded her eyes from the blinding sun.

"Where am I?" She asked aloud to no one as she continued to look about. Only the call of the wild answered her. Picking up a second of the strange, exotic orbs, she walked closer to the tree line. The sound of nearby animals intensified as she drew nearer, along with the evidence of their existence.

Feet, unlike her own, yet comparable in nature to hands, left tracks all through the sand. She turned back and looked overhead again, and seeing the darkening of clouds, entered the tree line. The instant she passed through the botanical curtain, she felt sweat trickling down her brow.

Weaving her way through the brush, Asta reached out for a large branch, suitable for use as a club. Using it to push her way through the tall vegetation, she could hear movement up above her. Something within her told her what was there. The life vibrated above her, providing a spectral outline of smaller, squirrel like beasts above.

She stared at them a moment, hungry for their meat. Her ears twitched irritably as she listened to the hastened heart rate of the beast above her. She felt something deeper within that connection. Curious, she attempted to deepen the link. As she continued to stare, the creature suddenly spasmed wildly, before falling to the ground at her feet. Startled, Asta fell to the ground and scurried backwards several lengths.

Heart hammering in her chest, she screamed inwardly as she felt heat, energy and pressure, bleeding through her veins. Her head began to throb and she sought out release from her condition. Her stomach spewed all that it held, leaving her both hungry and thirsty once more.

Slowly, she edged toward the creature which had fallen. It was nearly the size of a fox, though still appeared to be a large squirrel. She recalled the legends of Ratatoskr, the messenger of the gods. Had she just slain one of its descendants?"

Grabbing the deceptively heavy creature, she fled from the trees and sat back on the sandy beach. She looked about for a moment, in search of nearby drift wood. She found none.

She frowned, staring at the beast in front of her. She searched for a place where she might cut into the beast. Frustrated, she thrust it aside. A burst of wind cut through the air, nearly throwing Asta onto her back.

Eyes, wild with fright, she stared about for the source of the gust. The river flowed calmly, and only the sounds of startled animals could be heard. Looking about, again, Asta found herself wild with fright. The creature she had aimed to eat was eviscerated. A bloody mess, scattered across the sands.

Nausea racked her body and she found herself approaching the ruined carcass on all fours. A powerful, yet pleasant aroma reached her nostrils, smoking meat. Reaching out with shaking hands, she fought to control the survival instinct of her body and lost. The heat rising from the meat singed at her fingertips, but as wrought with hunger as she had grown, she paid it no heed.

Peeling away the small bits of fur that remained, Asta placed a large piece of the steaming meat into her mouth. Blowing between her teeth, she ignored the burning sensation of swallowing and reached for more. Only once she had eaten her fill, did she stop to consider her situation.

Her muscles ached, more so than when she had awoken. She felt deliriously tired, even though she had recently rested. Her head swooning, she moved back to the side of the river and plunged her head, drinking heavily. As she drank, she felt a soothing force, slithering about her body, providing relief to her many aches.

Pulling her head from the water, she screamed as she saw the tentacle formed of pure water, wrapping around her. The moment her concentration was broken, the tentacle collapsed.

"Have I become a Shaper?"

Chapter 18 – A Respected Enemy

"Hold too much back, Viking!" Aya yelled from the side of the circle the Kresh had drawn in the middle of the camp. Vali turned to the side, avoiding a forward thrust from a long, wooden pole and used his sword, still in its sheath, to press the weapon away from his body. The warrior Kresh, much larger and stronger than Vali, easily pushed him back by adjusting his grip.

Stumbling backwards, he narrowly recovered as another strike nearly took his head off. Vali ducked, repositioned his body in mid crouch and with a backwards sweep of his right leg, came up beside the Kresh and swung. The warrior smiled as he released his grip on the pole with his back hand, releasing the opposite edge of the weapon at Vali.

"Also, too slow!" Aya called as Vali narrowly caught the blow aimed for his nose, on the hilt of his sword. He stepped away at an angle, bringing his weapon down and around, striking the pole away from the Kresh's grip. The warrior hesitated but managed to keep his weapon as he swung wide and spun the staff.

Vali's well-trained eyes followed the weapon as it was whirled through a series of attack positions. The Kresh did not let his hands slow, instead building in speed with each pass the weapon made around his body. As the weapon spun faster still, Vali's eyes struggled to keep up with the speed of the movements and blinked.

It was then that the Kresh brought the weapon over his right shoulder and across his body toward the left, with all its force. Catching the movement, Vali brought his weapon up to defend himself and groaned as the power behind the blow traveled into his wrist and up through his arm and shoulder.

Feeling as though the right side of his body had been split like a logging tree, he dropped to the side. His weapon struck the ground several stretches away from where he did. Turning to recover his weapon, he growled again as he felt the wooden pole brought down against the back of his exposed thigh and again, as it struck him in the back.

He could hear Aya yell to him in frustration as the other Kresh warriors laughed at the pitiful Viking. Vali could only hear the ringing of his chattering bones in his ears and the pounding of his furious heart. Seven days, they had been at these exercises and each day, they were both brutally beaten.

He looked up at Aya, who sported a bruise beneath her right eye, with several more upon her arms, legs and torso. Her lips had also been split in more than one place. Being the outsider, he had taken the beatings much worse than her, and she had been keen to help him, but a week later, they were both hurting. Lately, Vali spent near most his mornings, simply counting the welts and bruises, before heading out to find more.

The Kresh warriors continued to laugh at the sport. Aya, hoping to gain ground, attempted to cheer him on in her broken understanding of his language. Vali however, was simply growing angry.

He felt the Kresh warrior plant his foot, the spirits in the soil telling him where he had placed his weight. They were harder to understand, but one who is patient and listens intently, can learn anything. The whistling in the air told him everything about the man's weapon, position, speed and destination.

Vali forced himself to the side, flinching as dirt sprayed the left side of his face. With his unblinded side, he looked to the warrior's knee and kicked it in. The Kresh howled in both agony and anger as he toppled from the weight of his own, overdeveloped body, dropping to the other knee.

Vali found his feet and weapon in the same, stumbling paces as he attempted to create space between he and his attacker. Lifting his sword, he could hear the dynamic of his audience shift. The kneeling Kresh glowered at him as he was laughed at by his own. Vali smiled and reaffirmed his fighting stance.

The warrior pounded the end of his weapon into the ground and rising to his feet, proceeded to deliver a barrage of blows at the young Viking. Vali, nearly able to match the injured Kresh's speed, tipped and back stepped where he could avoid a blow and parried where he could not. Wounded knee, the Kresh could not manage to deliver his attacks with his full strength, granting Vali an edge.

Aya's cheers coupled with his own anger and humiliation, Vali pressed his attacker back onto his wounded knee. The warrior buckled but did not collapse as Vali continuously struck from left to right, pressing more weight and direction against his enemy's debilitation. The warrior's teeth clenched as he withstood the pain from the attacks and tipped his staff.

Vali overstepped slightly and quickly recovering, brought himself beside the Kresh. Turning to face his target, he growled with irritation as a blast of sand caught him in his eyes. Stumbling back, he quickly scraped the cuff of his tunic across his face and only managed enough window of sight, to see the wooden pole collide with the side of his face.

Vali fell to the ground, too dazed to cry out. He could hear something in the distance, screaming angrily. He turned, trying to discern up from down, left from right in a sea of whirling lights and sounds. He found himself lost for an anchor, until he felt bone cracking pain, erupting through his upper back.

Everything became clear all at once, his dizziness replaced with nausea as the pole struck him hard in the upper back again. The third strike dropped him to the ground entirely. The fourth, nearly caused him to lose consciousness.

There was no way for him to tell just how long he lay there, face down in the sand. After he regained the ability to breathe, he felt a gentle pressure under each of his arms. He could hear voices, mixed in with the high-pitched wailing that filled his ears. The light faded and he feared he had slipped into unconsciousness.

"Viking, are you alright?" The sound of Aya's voice, rang like windchimes in the fog of his mind. He allowed more light to seep into his eyes, making the pain in his head far more extreme, save the portrait of a woman, before him.

"Not dead, then?" Aya smiled at him.

"No. Not dead, yet." Vali sighed, as he came to terms with his currently painful existence.

"You did well, Viking. Stood ground. Backed him into corner."

"Is that what happened? My head is still fuzzy on a few things."

"What things make fuzzy head?" Aya asked, staring down at his skull in confusion. "I wish to see fuzzy head."

"It was a jest." Vali groaned, covering his face with his hands.

"Viking, you know I no understand jest. Speak plainly or I confused." He groaned with frustration as much as pain as he lay, imitating death.

"I may have backed him into a corner, but I am the one who lost." He heard Aya make a scoffing sound, the first time he had heard it not directed toward him.

"Karn fight dirty. Cheat."

"The Comartok is not going to fight fairly."

"No. Beast fight harder in corner, too. Viking should be smarter." She chided, while gently stroking his back.

"Thank you for reminding me. Any other helpful advice?"

"Yes. Next time, protect face." He almost allowed a growl to escape as he felt her small, gentle hands placing dabs of soothing ointment on his brand new facial wounds. "Lucky Karn did not break nose. Good looking for Viking. Shame to waste." He heard a light laugh follow her words as she finished smearing the blissful concoction. He could tell through the vibrations of the earth that she had risen.

"No sleep, Viking. My turn, now." He felt another pair of hands on his left shoulder, tugging him up. He groaned, his body disagreeing with the movement. Through force of will, he slithered up the side of a log and rested his head and back against it.

"You are improving, stranger." Vali opened his eyes to see the Damaruhk, sitting beside him on the log.

"I have a long way to go, I think." He said, allowing his vision to adjust so he could watch Aya enter the drawn off circle.

"I agree, but to force Karn to employ such tactics is a sign you are growing stronger."

"Not strong enough to..."

"No. But to face the Comartok, you need patience. With the Comartok, the best course is wounding it, before you attack. Trap it. Disable it. You cannot fight a child of the gods of death on fair grounds. Make it come to you. Kill it a little at a time."

Vali watched as Aya squared off against her opponent, glaive in hand. She had secured a thick sheet of leather over the blade to keep from injuring anyone. As he watched her, a question came to him.

"Damaruhk, how did you defeat the Comartok of your time?" The elder closed her eyes as her body stiffened. It instantly became clear to Vali she did not want to answer.

"Damagoro," she sighed. "Damagoro was a mighty boar with tusks as large and thick as some of the oldest trees in these forests. It was a long while, before he was finally slain. Many warriors faced him and were trampled beneath his feet. My mate and I resorted to trickery to kill the boar."

Even though the Damaruhk was telling him of how she and one other, had managed to slay the last Comartok, Vali had other questions. He wondered more than anything at that moment, as he watched Aya, what became of the Viking before him. The elder woman sighed deeply, sensing his true inquiry.

"His name was Geir. He was like you, outsider. Full of questions. Also, like you, he often had issues with our ways."

"Damaruhk, what happened to him?" He could hear Aya hiss with anger as one of her legs was swept from beneath her.

"Viking!" She called to him, throwing him a crossed look.

"You are doing great, Aya." Vali called back, forgetting she had been quite encouraging. He was reminded that the other Kresh were not actually trying to injure her, unlike himself. "He is slower when forced on his left side." Aya nodded to him as she turned back to face the warrior, who glared at Vali.

"Come talk to me another time, Viking." Damaruhk said. "You are soon to be exiled with the last of my blood. I will grant rest to your curiosity, before your exile." He nodded his head, accepting her answer as he turned his head back toward the fight.

Aya ducked beneath the Kresh's attack as the man adjusted his left foot back and swung from the right. Aya, rolled her body near to the ground, spinning her glaive vertically and struck against the back of his weapon. As had been the case with Vali, the Kresh was knocked slightly off balance, nearly losing his weapon in the process.

Aya followed up her attack with another flick of her weapon, bringing the pommel of her glaive down in the crook of her enemy's extended elbow. As her opponent howled with pain, she spun backwards, bringing her weapon back around for the killing blow, only to be kicked in the center of her chest. Aya cried out painfully and fell backwards several paces. She remained on the ground, stunned a moment, as the other Kresh cheered for their brethren's comeback.

"Come on, Aya! You almost have him!" Vali cheered. "He does not have much left! Finish it!" Aya placed her hands beneath herself as she pressed against the ground. A small trickle of blood ran from her mouth and several scrapes. Spitting out the blood, she returned to her feet as the warrior collected his weapon.

"That's the spirit!" Vali cheered again, taking up a seat once more to find a bemused Damaruhk, smiling. Vali eyed her, waiting for her to provide the inevitable explanation.

"She has followed your example. Through you, she has studied her enemy." The Damaruhk said, watching as Aya dodged another flurry of blows. Vali could not help but notice, however that despite her attempts, Aya was wearing down far quicker than the experienced Kresh.

"Do not wait too long! Take him when you have an opening!" He called again. Aya shot him a quick glance and nodded. Tipping to the side, she narrowly dodged a vertical slash. Planting her foot on the end of the weapon, she spun her glaive down atop its haft.

The Kresh's polearm fell to the ground. Her weapon, still in front of her, she defended herself from the Kresh's counter and struck. Glaive spinning over her head, she managed two strikes on her opponent, who fell to the ground.

Aya looked to Vali excitedly as her opponent congratulated her. Visibly vibrating, she helped the other Kresh to his feet, before moving back toward Vali and the Damaruhk. The elder gazed upon the young woman a moment and nodded her head in approval.

"Well done, Aya." She said, gently examining the woman's wounds. Aya winced as the Damaruhk grazed across a long, abrasion, which had already begun to bruise. "I think that is enough for today. Clean up. Be sure to treat each other's wounds." She walked away from the two of them, leaving Aya and Vali alone.

"To the stream, then?" Vali asked, looking back over his shoulder, where beyond the tree line, the stream awaited.

"You worse shape. Go ahead. I grab more ointment." She said in a commanding voice.

"I can grab it." He offered, rising and walking toward camp, until Aya's hand stopped on his chest.

"No, I look after you. Go. I be back." She stared at him, silver eyes glittering in the sunlight. Vali nodded his head, sighing irritably as he turned away.

"Alright, then. No peeking." He grumbled, walking away into the forest. He heard the stream, before he reached it and shivered intuitively, already aware of the cold water. Stripping off his dirty clothes, he quickly washed them and hung them over a nearby branch as he stepped into the water.

He shivered as he waded deeper in, submerging himself to the waist. As he had every day, since he awoke in the Kresh's camp, he closed his eyes. Reaching out to the spirits around him, he probed at each one he could sense. A ripple moved toward him, turning his head toward its source, he saw small ripples, which flowed over the land, moving to him.

Eyes still closed, Vali focused on the ripples, trying to discern their meaning. The source of the ripples, the water and air, moved closer to him, providing a silhouette of a moving body. Vali opened his eyes, to see Aya, waist deep in the water, hand over her eyes, her body completely exposed.

"Aya, what are you doing?" He jolted with panic, quickly turning around, eyes closed, face on fire.

"I cover eyes." She answered, naïve tone in her voice.

"I can see that. But nothing else."

"I cannot see." She said, shaking her head in confusion. "You no want me see. I cover eyes."

"That is not what I meant."

"No cover eyes?" She asked, lowering her hands.

"No! Do not look either." Vali moved away, causing a splash.

"I confused." Aya said, placing her right hand back over her face. "Need to clean wounds. Cannot without eyes open." Vali let out an aggrieved sigh. They both had a long way to go, before they would be able to understand one another fully.

"You can open your eyes." He said, sinking down lower into the water. He could not see the young woman but could sense her approaching him slowly.

"Brought food," she said softly, handing several strips of dried venison to him.

"Thank you, Aya," he said accepting them. Taking a bite of the jerky, he began splashing water onto himself with his free hand.

"Karn gave many wounds." She said softly, gently splashing the scrapes on his back.

"I will beat him next time." Vali grumbled to himself, his focus drifting from the spirits around him and the woman beside him.

"Not tomorrow," she told him, splashing water on herself now. "Cana have something else planned."

"What?" He said, turning out of surprise and slowly retreating. "What do they have planned?"

"I know not. More practice for Comartok. Never mind, now. Clean wounds. Eat." She continued to splash water onto her skin, paying little mind to Vali, who still did not dare turn around. He finished consuming the strips of meat and returned to soaking his wounds.

"Aya?" He whispered, once he had finished bathing.

"Yes, Viking?"

"I am going to try and hone my grasp on the spirits, again. If I sit down over by the bank, will you stay over here."

"I can. Why?"

"It helps if there is some movement and I can reach out for things." He said, wading passed her. Moving to the edge of the stream, Vali sat down on the bank, still submerged to his upper torso as he leaned his back against an old tree, which had roots extending into the water.

He closed his eyes and focused. The sensation of whirling spirits and lights around him, returned. Reaching out, Vali attempted to touch at the spirits with his mind, only to have the first several retreat from him.

The spirits near the Kresh camps were still yet wild, having had little contact with other creatures beside those that lived in the wood. Eyes still firmly shut, he looked about, finding the spirits around Aya to be the most docile. He thought a moment, curious to the reason as he shifted his focus upon them.

"You shape, now, Viking?" Aya asked, her tone both curious and cautious.

"I am trying," he muttered back, focusing harder. "It is still quite difficult to reach out to those here in the camps. I am not so much shaping, as communing with the spirits at this point. The ones I use to reach out to before, were much calmer, more receptive to my thoughts."

"More familiar with Vikings." She suggested. Habitually, Vali shrugged his shoulders.

"It is possible," he said, again reaching out toward the spirits in the water. They swirled about lazily, the light flow of the stream as it ran down to the bay, allowing them to float by effortlessly. He watched them a moment, as they danced around the gap between he and Aya.

"What do you see, Viking?" She asked, curious of his strange ability.

"Not much, not yet." He said. "It is not the same as it was. When I was only seven or eight years old, I could do more. I can barely sense the spirits, now, where at that age, I could already shape two elements." He answered, dejectedly, following the trail of spirits back toward Aya's lightly moving body, the spirits wrapping around her.

"Keep practicing, Viking." She said to him. "You will improve. Now, need get out of water." She urged him. Rising herself, Vali caught a brief glimpse of the woman through his augmented vision, before he turned away.

He listened as Aya stepped out of the water. He could hear the water, dripping off her body and onto the walking stones. She rustled about a brief few moments, before he was certain she had left.

Rising himself, he stepped out onto the bank and began to dress, his clothes still slightly damp. He walked back into the camp, receiving numerous, mixed glances from both clans among the Kresh. Those whom he had been traveling with, nodded at him, while others even smirked. Those of the Cana clan, however, glared and scoffed as he passed by.

He decided to take a walk about the camp. Even though he had been there more than a week already, he had not taken the time to do so. The camp was quite similar to those forged by his traveling companions. Trees encircled the camp on all sides. Following in the direction of the stream, he moved toward the edge of the tiny peninsula, to look upon the woven domes he and Aya had seen before they arrived.

Moving beyond the southern tree line, he could see where the river poured into the bay. Large vines, hung from the trees in many places, anchoring large, wooden bridges, which ran through them. He found the woven domes not far ahead of him, floating on the water.

Amazed, Vali walked toward the strange vessels. There were several Kresh around and up above him, all eying him suspiciously. Slowly making his way through the camp, he stepped out onto one of the Kresh docks, which also floated on the water, opposed to being mounted on posts.

The bound boards of the bridge, swayed and rocked slightly beneath his feet. A well-traveled sailor, the sensation gave him no trouble. Stepping to the edge of the dock, he gently touched the dome. It swayed lightly, rocking on the gentle shallows of the water, but again, he was amazed. It was very nearly, a boat.

"Sometimes, it is better for us to move from place to place." Canaruhk said, having crept behind him. Vali turned to face the man, who stared out at the sea.

"I did not think the Kresh traveled much by sea?" He asked.

"We do not." He replied. "With the exception of Tharukh and the Tha, the Kresh do not much explore the seas. That is the destiny of your kin. Most Kresh are content to remain in one area or another, only traveling enough to follow the game. Beyond that, we often have little need to make large voyages across the sea."

"And yet recently, the Kresh have been traveling south, in masse." Vali pointed out.

"Yes, many Kresh have been forced from the north. The Cana are among them."

"Why, Canaruhk?" Vali asked. "Why are the Kresh being forced from their homes? My people saw it as a sign of an attack."

"Your kind often search for reasons to wage war." He replied sharply. "It is the way of the warrior races, to battle." He sighed, having been such a warrior in his youth. "It is a Kresh matter, Viking."

"I wish to understand, Canaruhk." Vali pleaded, seeking more. "I wish to help."

"Become one of the people." Canaruhk replied. "Maybe then, we will discuss such matters." He turned away from Vali, moving back toward the camp. "Come, now. While you are in the camp, the Cana will not harm you. Armed as you are however, they may grow uneasy with you wandering freely."

"Of course," Vali answered, taking one last look about the encampment, before following the elder.

"Where you go?" Aya asked, head cocked at an angle as Vali returned with Canaruhk.

"I went to the bay, to see the floating houses." He answered. Aya's eyes narrowed at him in response.

"You go without me?" She asked, a wounded tone in her voice.

"It would be better that both of you avoid that place," Canaruhk spoke. "Besides, it is not the time to explore the camp. You still have your preparations to make." Vali nodded and returned to his and Aya's tent. Walking inside, he saw a bundled lump resting on his bedroll.

Aya walked in behind him, bright smile on her face as she watched him. Vali lowered himself to the roll, resting on his knees as he lifted the leather parcel. Removing the covering from it, he found his elm branch, already carved down into the shape of a bow and stained.

"Aya, did you?" He asked, looking back at her. Smiling, the young woman nodded.

"I did. Had the time. You needed." Vali stood and walked back to her, squeezing her tightly in his arms.

"Let go, Viking," Aya squirmed against the tight grip of his lingering hug. Vali smiled as he released her, and she brushed herself off. "Your kin and their groping." She grumbled, moving away from him and sitting on her bedroll. Vali knelt beside his new bow and lifted it into his hands.

"I will have to be certain to test it, tomorrow." Aya nodded in agreement as she reached down and began grooming a pile of fletchings.

"We leave early. Cana has plan." Vali nodded his head as he looked over the delicate carving Aya had done. The bow had been stained dark brown, allowing him to see the fine grain of the wood. She had carved several, exotic and delicate features into the face of the wood, which hummed with untold significance.

"What are these?" He asked, pointing to a few of the characters on the wood, which were nested beneath the hand grip. Aya looked up at him, setting her work aside as she leaned forward. She stared at them a while and shook her head.

"Do not know." She replied, before returning to her work. Vali looked back to the carvings and then again, to Aya.

"You carved them?" Aya shrugged as she continued her work.

"Do not know them. See them. Do not know." She continued to shake her head lightly as she stuck her feathers into the ends of the arrow shafts. Staring at her in disbelief a few moments longer, he shook his head and turned his gaze upon her methodic task.

"Can I help?" He asked, leaning forward. Aya shot him a quick glance and motioned toward a separate stack of feathers.

"Use that pile. Do not mix..." She stared at the feathers in her hand, confused. She continued to eye them, racking her brain for the appropriate word.

"Feathers?" Vali asked her, lifting two or three from her pile. Aya flashed him a quick glance and nodded.

"Yes, do not mix feathers." She said, taking hers from him. "Important not to mix." She stated again for clarity and returned to her work. Vali smirked and lifting the pile from the leather rug, took them over to his bedroll. Grabbing another pile of long, wooden chutes, he began carving his own arrows, using the knife Aya had left with him days before.

"Aya?" Vali asked, striking another arrow shaft and fitting his feathers in its tip.

"Yes, Viking?"

"Can you teach me more of your language?"

"Why learn?" She asked him, not once lifting her eyes from her work.

"Well, for starters..." He paused as he attempted to think of a proper reason. He looked up at the young woman, who eyed him, awaiting his answer. "It will be useful if we can communicate, while we are hunting the Comartok."

"No need speak Kresh for that. We speak fine." Vali frowned slightly, trying to think of any other reason.

"When I am one with the people, I will need to speak with them."

"You are not. Do not have name, yet." Vali frowned at the answer. He had asked once before, why everyone, even the Rukh, who fully grasped his language, refused to call him by name. The only answer he had received was not to ask. He would learn more once he was one of the people.

"I learn more." She replied, after the long silence. He looked up at her, confused.

"Why would you need to speak my language, yet I not yours?"

"Way of Kresh." She answered, scoffing as she said it. "Will need travel. Be near your people. Die if no learn." He felt the weight of her feelings as she spoke the words. He did not understand her reasoning, and expected she would not give an answer, even if asked. Setting aside another arrow and beginning his next, he changed the subject.

"What do you think Canaruhk has planned for tomorrow?"

Do not know." She replied, setting another arrow upon her much larger pile.

"Can you guess?" She made a light clucking noise as she stared intently at her whittling knife but did not move.

"I think, we hunt." She suggested. Vali nodded his head, looking back to his bow and slowly growing supply of arrows.

"They want us to practice tracking? That should not be terribly difficult. We have both hunted before." Aya shook her head.

"No, Viking. We are hunt." Vali stared at her, mouth held slightly ajar in thought.

"You think the Cana tribe is going to hunt us? Track us down and try to capture us?" She nodded her head.

"Make us work together. Make us…" She paused. "What is word for use things around?" She motioned around the inside of the tent with both of her arms, looking to Vali in confusion.

"Only if you tell me one of your words." She scrunched her face at him.

"Zata," she finally relented, pointing at the bow in his hands.

"Zata," he repeated, feeling the word as it moved off from his tongue and pressed against the backs of his teeth. Nodding his head, he looked back up at her with a smile. "The word you are looking for, is 'resourceful.' It means to make use of your environment."

"Resourceful," she repeated, taking a brief pause after each syllable. It sounded strange coming from her. Some of the sounds, foreign to her.

"So, you believe the Cana will send us out to be hunted by the warrior Kresh, to teach us resourcefulness?"

"Learn more. But it important to think like prey. When hunting Comartok, we will be." Vali thought back to his encounter with the massive Fenrir of Fangor. His skin crawled at the thought of it and still he wondered how they might defeat such a creature, when he was without his former strength.

"Think tomorrow, Viking." She said softly, flicking her long blonde and crimson braid to the side. "Time for rest, soon. Learn from Cana, tomorrow." He nodded his head and smiled, causing her to smile in return. He finished working the fletchings into the ends of his arrows, Aya helping him to deplete the pile. She then took the collection and placed them in one of two quivers.

"Goodnight, Viking." She said to him as she laid on her bedroll and curled beneath her blanket.

"Goodnight, Aya." He repeated, though he did not make to lie down.

"You sleep." She told him, pulling the blanket over her shoulder.

"Yes, you are right." He muttered, laying down, as well. He remained motionless for a time, hands crossed over his chest, staring up but somewhere beyond the tent. His mind was running away with him, taking his thoughts to faraway places.

He could hear Aya's gentle breathing as fell into sleep and yet the phenomena held no love for him. His thoughts remained on his estranged loved ones, who presumably thought him dead. He waited several silent minutes, until he was certain the young woman, near to him had fallen asleep. Convinced that she had, he quietly rose and exited the tent.

The campgrounds were dimly lit by the low flames of the bonfire. Though he knew several of the Cana were on alert, he sighed with relief at a chance to reflect, privately. Taking up a seat near the flames, he admired their gentle dance as he dwelt on his situation.

"You should be resting." Vali quickly turned his head and rose as he heard the old chieftain speak, the elder approaching the center of the camp.

"Good evening, Canaruhk." Vali said with a respectful nod. "I am having trouble sleeping. Thought I might enjoy your fire for a moment. Clear my thoughts." The old warrior nodded his head as he stared at the flames of the central campfire. No other Kresh remained around it, but Vali knew there were those, who would not be far.

"What troubles you, Viking?" Canaruhk asked, sitting beside him. Vali resumed his seat, twirling his braided necklace, as he stared into the flames.

"I was thinking of home. My family. I am certain they believe me dead."

~ 301 ~

"No doubt you wish to return to them." Cana said.

"I do. I miss them. More importantly, they were still in danger, last I saw them. Not just my family. My entire clan."

"What sort of danger?" Vali listened to the crackling of the flames, sighed and started relaying the events that had lead him to his present predicament. Canaruhk did not once interrupt him. Not even to ask for a deeper explanation of things. He merely sat, playing sentinel as Vali told his story. When at last he was done, the old warrior spoke.

"This great enemy of yours disturbs me. They are not unlike the stories of our gods of death. However, as you said, they were nothing more than men, save the ones, which killed the land."

"Canaruhk, are there any record of these beings in any of the Kresh stories?" The elder thought some time, before answering.

"Stories of your Shaping, as you have called it, are not uncommon. The Kresh and the Vikings have long been at blade's end. There are other stories, that are far older than our war with one another. They do speak of peoples and lands, before your people but I do not know them."

"Who might?" Vali asked. Cana looked up thoughtfully, wondering.

"Once you are one of the people, you might find answers from Gararukh. Her mate was once story keeper to many of the tribes. There is little guarantee that the Gara will not try to kill you, but there is a chance they might have your answers."

"Where could I find them?" He asked. Again, Cana thought a long while.

"Only the Tha and the Gara remain to the north. It will be difficult, but should you become one of the people and you need to find them, I will help. Nothing more, can I tell an outsider with no name." There it was again, the emphasis on Vali, and his nameless status among the Kresh.

"Cana, may I ask you a question?"

"You may. I may also decide not to answer." Vali nodded his head, already prepared to walk away emptyhanded.

"Why is it I cannot be called by name among the Kresh? Is there some reason I cannot be called by my given, Viking name?" Canaruhk nodded his head, a slight crease forming between his lips from his withheld smirk.

"Is it custom for your people to know the name of your enemies?"

"Well, no, I suppose not." He said. "Though, it is not as though we do not care to know, there is simply no reason."

"Ah, yes, your kind believe they are dominant. Superior, perhaps." Vali searched for a reason to dispute such a claim but found none. The Rukh took this as a sign that Vali agreed.

"Your kin do not respect mine. Nor do they feel that they should." He continued. "Your kin hold little appreciation or respect for much of the world around them."

"That is not true, Cana." Vali rightfully argued this point. "My mother, Kari, has always taught us of the importance of honoring the old gods, of those who came before us. She taught my sister and I to show and give respect to the bounty of nature, and not to scorn its gifts. I will not argue that the Kresh seem more connected to this belief, but it is not true to claim we do not."

"A fair point. I will not argue the matter. There is much that we do not know of one another. For your kind, am I wrong to assume your names are given?"

"They are. Are all names, not given by their parents?"

"Among the Kresh, names mean more than for calling. Once one has a name among the Kresh, they are given purpose, meaning. Do your kind name the food that you eat or is it food."

"One might name an animal, raised for slaughter, I suppose." Vali suggested. Canaruhk looked at him, as if in shock.

"The Kresh do not. Food has a purpose among our people. It sustains our bodies. It is required to survive. We call them by what they are, as we do your kind, Viking."

"We do not need to remain enemies, Canaruhk. There can be peace between our people."

"You are a dreamer, Viking." Canaruhk smiled at him. "I do not disapprove of this quality, but you may be forced to learn a hard lesson."

"What lesson is that, Canaruhk?" Vali asked, no longer bothering to look back at the flames.

"You will know it, once you have learned. Just as you will be named among the people, should you become one of us. From there, perhaps a purpose you will find." Vali stood along with the elder and again, nodded respectfully.

"I thank you, Canaruhk. I understand it is not the way of your people to divulge so much to an outsider. Thank you." The elder nodded his head lightly, before turning away.

"I look forward to your naming, Viking. As an enemy, you would not be unworthy of respect." Vali watched as the man disappeared amidst the darkness of the camp. Vali sighed once more, looking up at the starry skyline, hoping beyond hope that his friends and sister, were safe. Offering up a silent prayer, to gods lost and any whom may still exist, Vali walked back to his tent, a long trial awaiting him.

Chapter 19 – To Be Hunted

Vali remained behind Aya, crouched down beneath the cover of the tall reeds. As she had suspected, they were dragged out in the early hours of the morning and taken out into the center of the forest. There, they were left behind with a warning that by sunset, the warrior Kresh, led by Karn, would be coming for them.

They ran most of the day, gathering what they could as they went. Now, as the sun began to fall, they had found a hiding place, where they might avoid detection. Per Aya's instruction, Vali had tried to catch some sleep, but had proven unsuccessful.

"If you not sleep, I will." Aya said to him, shifting slightly. He stared at the woman, who even moving in the tall grasses, made not a sound. Tucking beneath the small burrow they had dug into the side of the hill, Aya laid her bow and glaive in front of herself, and immediately fell asleep.

Vali sat, watching over the young woman as he worked to control the rate of his breathing. In the distance, every sound sent him on high alert. Daring not to move more than his eyes, Vali flicked the focus of his vision from one tussle in the brush between nighttime rodents and the 'hooting' of an owl, high up above.

He listened, as the crickets in the distance, chirped. He could hear the croaking of frogs, near to where he and Aya hid. He waited for most of the evening, until the agreed upon time, where he tapped on Aya's shoulder. She looked up at him sleepily, rapidly blinking her eyes, and nodded.

Quietly shifting from her position, she tapped him on the shoulder and readied her weapon. Vali nodded at her wearily and laid his head down, immediately allowing sleep to claim him. He was unsure how long he had been asleep, but when he awoke, he felt as though he had never done so.

"We need move." She whispered to him. Vali blinked his eyes sleepily and then realized why. The frogs, birds, crickets, and rodents, had all fallen silent. Without hesitation, he gathered his things and rolled to his knees.

Aya moved forward quietly, weapon already trained ahead of her. Vali followed, carefully pressing the tall weeds from in front of his face. He cringed inside with every rustle he heard. Aya stared back at him, worriedly, her eyes darting around them.

"Go ahead, Aya." He whispered to her, gently gripping on her shoulder. "I cannot help but make noise. I will catch up to you as I can." The young woman shook her head fiercely, thinking of a different way.

"No, Viking. Stay together." Her head twisted to the west and her body grew rigid, tense. Vali ducked down lower, trying to channel his vision in the direction she stared. He saw little more than the stalks, brushing across his face. He attempted to rise, only to have Aya latch onto him, and shake her head slowly.

"Something there." She mouthed to him, with enough exaggeration so he could read her lips.

She continued to stare out into the night, hand on her glaive, twitching. He heard the crack of a branch not far, firing all his senses into high alert. Aya darted out of sight, leaving Vali behind, nearly blind and alone.

He carefully drew his sword to his side, still in its sheath, expecting to find one of the Kresh hunters. He remained low to the ground, taking careful strides forward, holding his breath. His senses tuned in, he cringed with every blade of grass that rustled against him.

He could hear a snort from beyond the range of his sight. Another branch cracked and gave under the weight of something large. He shifted uncomfortably. The Kresh hunters could not have weighed much more than he.

Carefully, he shifted his stance, wincing with each break of the silence that threatened to suffocate him. Controlling his breathing, he steadied himself. Exhaling, he attempted to take another step back.

A bestial roar broke the silence as a large cat pounced high into the air. Vali dove sideways, rolling away and drawing his sword simultaneously. He could hear Aya call out to him, in a panic, yelling in the Kresh tongue.

He eyed the jungle cat carefully, the beast easily large enough to feast on both he and his companion. A large, black, muscled body shifted back and forth on its haunches, eying and circling him. Holding his sword to his side patiently, he waited.

He tried reaching out to the spirits around him but found nothing. Those at the Kresh camp, had begun to grow used to him. These spirits hid from him, unwilling to lend their aid. The cat pounced, and Vali found himself dashing aside, once more.

He flung his arm back, wildly, cutting nothing but the tips of the grass. The cat growled at him, a snarling laugh at his failed attempt. Blind in the darkness of the night, Vali tripped and fell when his boot snagged on a stray branch. A pain flashed into his existence as he became ensnared.

He growled, landing hard on the ground, his leg firmly entangled. Turning himself painfully to the side, he gripped his sword tightly and looked down to his leg. Slowly, the cat stalked toward him. He could see its eyes, glowing through the tall grasses, as it loomed closer.

Patiently waiting for the beast, he held the sword out to his side, ready to make the killing stroke. The cat stopped at the edge of the tall grass, its body still concealed beyond its shoulders. He stared deeply into the beast's eyes, sensing something he had never once sensed in a living creature.

The cat leaned backwards on its haunches, readying to pounce upon its victim. Vali held his breath, focusing on the strength in his arm, assuring himself of his stroke and aim. The jungle cat's frame slithered forward as it began its pounce, only it froze mid leap as a large curved blade, pierced through its chest and exited out of the back of its neck.

The predator fell without the slightest of noises, its muscles already prepped to launch it forward, pushed it limply out into the clearing. Vali stared in wonder, allowing the grip on his weapon to ease as he felt the thundering of his heart. The blade retracted from the predator's body as a small form emerged from the grasses beside it.

"You clumsy, Viking. Need try harder." Aya chided, flicking the blood from the edge of her glaive. Vali lay still, too stunned to move as the young woman went to task. Moving closer to him, she looked down at him, shaking her head.

"Get up?" She asked. Vali nodded his head.

"Of course. Just a moment." He responded, cleaving a piece of the branch free, with one swift strike of his blade. Aya nodded her head and returned to her kill.

"Coat keep warm. Meat is good." She said, both eyes focused on her prize.

"There was something different about that creature." Vali spoke, still partially within his state of shock.

"You never see Tharn?" She asked. "All same. Pounce and eat."

"No, that is not what I meant." Vali said, shaking his head. "I mean, I have never seen one, before. There was something different about this one. It had a different sense to it."

"Never been hunted, before." Aya spoke affirmatively. "Way of life for Kresh. Always something eats something else."

"It is a difficult life, I imagine." He stared into the intelligent eyes of his prey. Though they had now lost their luster, he shivered again at the overwhelming consciousness he had sensed. Dusting himself off, he removed the skinning knife from his side and helped to cut away the pelt.

"Will have to share." She told him. "Better keep one piece than two." She added.

"I understand. At least we will not need to worry about staving off the cold, without a fire."

"Need fire, cook meat." She looked around carefully. "For now, make do." She eyed a piece of the Tharn's flesh only a moment, before she scrunched her face and took a bite. Vali shot upright from shock as a small spatter of blood decorated her lips and chin. She looked away from him a minute, before cutting another strip of the meat.

"Here, eat." She said, taking another bite. Vali's stomach flipped as he watched the young woman, chewing the raw flesh and swallowing.

"You eat it raw?" He asked her, mortified.

"No fire. Eat or starve." He stared down at his stomach, which growled with emptiness. Then he looked back to the meat in Aya's hand.

"I can still manage on a bit longer." He grumbled, instead helping her to clean the body. They continued to pick at the body, until the pelt was laid aside and what extra meat they could carry was concealed inside of a bag.

"Here," Vali called back, having pulled the incisors from the beast's maw. Aya looked up at him curiously, accepting the offering.

"What for?" She asked.

"Do the Kresh not collect trophies from their hunts? Small remembrances of taking down a great predator."

"Remembrances?" She mouthed the word, it bearing no meaning to her. "We keep totems. To show great hunts. They grant strength." She eyed the teeth a moment, before looking back to him.

"How you know this?"

"We have a similar practice. Also, Canaruhk told me some things."

"Thank you, Viking." She said, depositing the fangs in her pouch, which hung beside the one filled with meat.

"We should bury what we cannot take with us." He suggested, eyeing about a moment. "It will be harder for the hunters to pick up our trail."

"This way, Viking." Aya said, grabbing onto one side of the beast. "Place in tall grass. Digging, take long time. We need run." Nodding, he grabbed onto the pieces of the carcass and helped Aya pitch it into cover.

Aya wiped her hands vigorously on her breeches as she moved back into the clearing, collecting her weapons. Vali looked down at the remains of the carcass and shuddered once more. Sheathing his sword, he noticed the cat's claws were missing.

"Come, Viking." She called back to him. "Need distance." Nodding, Vali quickly followed Aya, who had already left him trailing behind.

They ran through the night, not daring to slow, until the morning rays pierced through the tree tops. The entire time, Aya kept them traveling toward the north. Vali did not know why, but he did not question his companion's judgment.

By evening, after they had both exhausted themselves too much to climb the next hill, they rested. The sun had long since left them, leaving Vali stumbling through the jungle the past several hours. Throwing the Tharn's pelt over a collection of brambles Aya had bent down, he fell to the ground.

"How are your wounds?" She asked him, eying the scratches and scrapes he had received, tripping over and pressing through the low hanging branches and thorns.

"I will manage," he moaned, his eyes firmly shut tight. The smell beneath the pelt was indescribably unpleasant in the musky, humid air. They prayed for rain all the same. Any relief at this point was welcome.

"Need fire." Aya said, slowly rising, her body clearly as strained as his. "I grab wood."

"Stay." Vali said, rising himself. "I will gather wood. You let me rest last time."

"No need, Viking. I go." Her level of fatigue became ever more apparent to Vali, as he managed to reach the exit to their makeshift shelter, before her.

"Aya, please stay. I can gather wood." She sighed with relief, as much as she tried to hide it, and lowered herself to the ground.

"Need smoke for meat and pelt." She called back to him wearily, her eyelids already fluttering. Vali nodded and leaving his companion behind shielded himself from the weather. It had already begun to rain.

Hastily, he worked to gather up as many pieces of kindling, regardless of size, in an attempt to salvage some dry wood. Favoring the pieces, which lay beneath their patron trees, he had managed to leave a bundle undercover, before his clothes had soaked through.

Next, he charged out again, grabbing anything left over he could find, in hopes it might dry and keep them in warmth for the night. Gathering as many as he could hold, he quickly ran back to their dwelling and climbed inside the small hole they had left exposed.

His first sight was of Aya, eyes closed, breathing slowly. Carefully, he maneuvered inside the opening, laying the bundle of wood down off to the side. Next, he took to task at making a small pile of kindling to use for his flame.

He wrapped his kindling tightly and placed it over a near hollowed out branch. Placing the tip of a second stick into the hollow, he removed a leather strap from his pack and wound it around the vertical limb. Slowly, he pulled the strap back and forth, causing the two ends to rub together, the leafy bits of kindling trapped between them.

He silently focused on his work, trying to will a spark of flame, an ember, anything. He focused to the point of frustration, where only the sleeping woman beside him, kept him from throwing away his things in frustration. Instead, he took a deep breath and remembered his lessons as a boy. Those he had learned before he had become a Shaper.

First, he added a pinch of extra kindling, along with a speck of dry cotton from their pouches. Next, with increased speed, he spun the vertical twig, grinding the kindling to a fine powder within the hollow of the branch. Despite the chill which had begun to settle into their small hovel, his brow was decorated with sweat. He continued spinning, until his nostrils caught a whiff of char, and his eyes, a small ember.

Quickly, he set to work, fetching more of his kindling. Crushing them into finer pieces with the tips of his fingers, he sprinkled them over the ember, fueling it, until a tiny flame had formed. Continuously working to feed the forming embers, he blew at them gently, causing the gentle cluster of dead grasses to ignite.

Within the next several minutes, he had produced a low, gentle flame, which slowly trickled warmth into their den. Aya, still asleep, groaned with relief as she instinctively stretched her body out around the flames. Setting more fuel around his fire, Vali took the larger pieces he would not need, and built a small wall over the little hole, both blocking out more of the rain and cold, while savoring the heat and light.

He stared confidently at his work, watching as the small cloud of dark smoke blew into the pelt and flowed out of the bramble walls. It made his eyes water slightly but was not enough to cause further grief or suffocation. Removing the strips of meat from Aya's pack, he laid them out upon raised branches above the flames and allowed them to smoke and dry.

Resolving himself to keep first watch, he leaned back next to the young woman, resting his head on a moderately uncomfortable shelf in the earthworks and watched the flames. Being sure to keep his eyes wide open, he attempted a series of shapings on the fire.

The spirits around him, paid him no mind, flitting about their business, enjoying their modest meal while ignoring his presence. Focusing instead on the elements themselves, he imagined himself, pressing against the clouds of smoke. A small cloud of the smoke, broke apart from the rest, wafting toward the opposite wall, and then listlessly floated back along the current.

A bold smile crept across his lips as he again, forced a puff of smoke to separate from the main body. After several attempts, he looked down to his small fire. Eyeing the flames, he attempted to press them further, as well. He panicked when the flames nearly went out.

"No, no, no," he spoke in a worried, hushed tone. "Have more fuel, just do not go out." He continued, tossing more kindling onto the pile. The flames roared to life, once more and he found himself pressing away the smoke to keep from suffocating he or Aya.

Aya coughed gently beside him, causing him to turn quickly. She shifted begrudgingly as he did so and coughed again. Pressing forward, he willed the smoke from their shelter.

"What are you doing, Viking?" She asked groggily, blinking her eyes wearily.

"The spirits are still ignoring me." He replied. "But I am still able to shape free flowing things around me." Aya eyed him oddly, her face squinted.

"You very strange. Sleep. No hunters follow in rain." She rested her head on his thigh, immediately returning to sleep. Vali sighed as he stared down at her. Gently resting his hand on her shoulder, he closed his eyes and immediately joined her.

Chapter 20 – An Uneasy Alliance

"I understand there are risks involved, and I do not care!" Ulf roared angrily, slamming his fist down upon the table where he and the many other gathered chiefs, sat. "This is my home. The home of my people. Were it the home of any of you, I would gladly sail to your shores."

"Ulf," Crom, war chief of Ebura Island began. Like many of the war chiefs, the man's face was decorated with graying hair, which peppered his beard and skull. His brow was deeply furrowed. His grizzled hands were held close to his sagging eyelids, rubbing at the crow's feet found there.

He sat uncomfortably beneath the gaze of his peers, as he pulled at his silver and blue tunic. "I do not aim to defy your cause or deny the validity of your request. It is only that we have suffered major losses at the hands of these raiders. There were only seven of them, undefended. Not to mention they possessed Fenrir, himself, in their ranks." A general murmuring in the crowd, showed many agreed with the balding man.

"If we do not act soon, the enemy will only solidify their position!" Ulf continued to thunder at the head of the table, Finna beside him. A silence fell upon the room. Abel looked between the many people gathered, each staring ashamed to the chiefs of Ulfrost.

Those from the village however, still held a fire in their eyes, and carried a flame in their blood.

"Let us seek Uncle Grom's aid." Freyja said, standing so all could see her. Each and every head in the room turned as she came into sight. Many nodded their heads as they spoke together. Finna, however, looked mortified by the suggestion.

"I would rather we do not seek the aid of my brother." She spoke with a measure of wisdom and suspicion "As he has said before, his people are hardly fit for a war effort at present."

"That was some time ago, mother." Freyja argued. "I am certain he would help us, now. If we would only ask." Finna shot her daughter a second glance, which went ignored.

"I agree with the High Chief's daughter." A face, Abel could not see, spoke.

"And I." Another agreed.

"Surely, with all the shapers of Falkest, we would decimate this new threat." A third added. From there, the roar of agreement from the gathered crowd, grew. Abel's blood boiled at the thought of turning to the coward Grom for aid, considering his absence of late. Scanning the room, he noticed a similar response on the faces of the other citizens of Ulfrost.

"Should you enlist the aid of Chief Grom, we will come to your aid." Crom clarified. Ulf turned to his wife, and leaning in closer, whispered a few words to her. High Chief Finna eyed her husband a moment, traces of shock and outrage still on her face as she took in every word. She sighed, nodding her head as Ulf sat back in his chair.

"It shall be so. We shall seek out the aid of Chief Grom and the clan of Falkest. With their support, we will surely overthrow this threat to our way of life." A proud roar rose from the congregation, while Abel shook his head. He glanced to his right, and noticed Thala, just behind him.

"I do not trust that man." He whispered to her.

"Have you met the man?" She whispered back.

"No. From what I have heard, I had hoped I never would. The marks on his honor are as numerous as his Shapers." He added, before returning his attention to the front of the room.

Ulf and Finna rose from their seats. Freyja mirrored them as her parents addressed the room. The rest of the room grew quiet as they awaited the next order of their High Chief.

"I shall send word to Falkest, immediately. I shall now leave to consult the scrying pool. With or without his answer, I ask for everyone to be prepared to leave in the next few days." A general salute sounded, followed by Ulf and Finna leaving the room. Abel glanced up at Freyja, whom he had hardly seen since his arrival on Dumah.

She appeared worn down from the many trials of late. Her eyes were sunken and swollen from tears and fatigue. He felt poorly for the young woman, who was clearly grieving. Drawing in a deep breath, he approached her.

"Good evening, Freyja." He said.

"Oh." She replied weakly. "It is good to see you well, Abel." She half smiled at him, even though her eyes were still sunken.

"Freyja, about Vali. I am sorry." She shook her head as she looked away, lips trembling.

"It is not your fault." She whimpered, wringing her hands together as she spoke. "I know you and the others did everything that you could. You would no sooner have left him than he, you." Each head of the crewmen plunged toward the floor as they stared away, ashamed.

"What will you do next?" Abel asked, guilt heavy on his every word.

"I will send word to my uncle. I am certain that he will aid us. At least then, we can return our people to their homes. Vali and the others we have lost, would have wished for nothing less." Bowing his head and clasping his fist over his heart, Abel smiled.

"You speak truth. The Valiant and her crew shall be ready at the earliest convenience."

"I must thank you and regrettably, must also take my leave. There is no doubt in my mind that 'your' crew, shall be instrumental in reclaiming our home." The words caught in her throat as she strained to maintain her smile.

"Of course. We will see to our preparations, as well." Turning to face Thala and the others, they nodded before he could bring further thoughts to words. Paying their farewells, each left the room to tend to their various duties.

As morning came once again, Abel stood out on the beach, ankle deep in the water. He searched out far into the depths of the Tyrda Fell, in the direction of Ulfrost. The wind came up to him in gentle gusts, sending a salty spray into the air.

"Are you ready to go back out there?" Thala asked, walking up beside him. He turned slightly to see her, before setting his gaze forward, again.

"I will always return to the sea." He answered. "It is our fate. All of us, man, woman and child, return to the sea when we leave on the final voyage." The salty spray kicked up again, lightly splashing them both as they continued to stare.

"Freyja's raven has returned." Thala spoke. "Chief Grom has agreed to meet with us to discuss the matter of his aid. Should we hurry, we shall by nightfall, tomorrow. The High Chief suspects his forces could set sail, by midday tomorrow. We should anticipate his arrival off from Ulfrost's eastern shore within the next five days.

"Then it is time to return." He smiled, even at the thought of facing the black ones, again. "I am counting on you and the others."

"We are with you, captain." The crew answered. They heard a separate call from the tops of the hills to the north. Turning to face the dark-haired woman running toward them, they waited.

"I will be going with you, Abel." Brina said. "I have already cleared this with my mother and father. Will you have me?" Thala shot Abel a cross glance, which he received nervously.

"Do you have much experience?" He asked. Brina's eyes narrowed as she glared at him. Her irritation apparent.

"I only forfeited my vessel after the storms as my father's did not make it through. I will be a strong addition to your crew."

"Well, I suppose we are happy to have you." He commented. "Grab your gear. Thala, gather the others. I plan on leaving shortly."

Chapter 21 – Safe No More

Asta sat on the beach, watching as the sun rose. Over a week, she had been trapped in solitude, far from anyone or anywhere she knew. All around her, she looked upon the evidence of her trials.

Craters had been torn into the beach, from where she had attempted to seize control of her newfound power. Trees lay in ruins around her makeshift fire pit, while the nature woven path of the river, twisted out of place.

At her feet, which were buried in the sand, lay the decimated remains of her latest shaping. Shattered bits of wood, had become badly shredded as she attempted to split the wood into boards. She cursed herself angrily, which only made her control worsen.

"Vali always makes this look so easy!" She yelled to herself, suddenly remembering an unfortunate truth. Anger rose through her, jealousy for her Vali's talent and hatred for those who took him from her. The ground around her began to shake as a surge of power flowed up from her feet and into her gut.

Slamming her fists against the ground, small craters appeared in the sand, which blew out over the water in small windstorms. In a panic, she stared down at her hands, which rested over small sheets of clear material.

"Glass?" She whispered to herself. "What is happening to me?" Her eyes darted nervously about her surroundings. She fought to control the boiling of her blood, as power continued to radiate through her. She placed both palms into the sand and fought to control her breathing.

"Calm down, Asta. Breathe. You do not want to lose control, again. Again?" She repeated to herself, wondering why the thought had risen to begin with. Focusing on it, there was something else in the back of her mind, whispering to her.

"Maybe I need to lose control, again. Maybe I want to." She repeated the words she heard back in the recesses of her mind. She shook herself of the sensation. "No. Keep my head on. I need to get off from this island. Even if I do not know how I got here. A boat." She confirmed aloud to herself, looking down at the shattered bundles around her.

Rising to her feet, she treaded toward the tree line, where she aimed to procure enough wood to try again. Approaching the edge of the jungle, she could hear the voices of the indigenous primates, quieting. They had left her to herself thus far, but she wondered how long that peace might last. She only hoped their fear of her continued to keep them at bay.

"Who cares? This is my island." She heard the whisper again. "We can burn them all." Again, she shook herself, until the voice dissipated.

Staring at a particularly large, round tree, she held out her hand as she had practiced and willed the wood to bend to her will. It did as she wished and fell to the beach a moment later. Carefully, she swung her hand through the air in a chopping motion and watched as the fallen trunk responded to her commands.

From each of the four long planks of wood, which had sunk into the sand, Asta tried splitting two more. Two of her four attempts resulted in more shattered pieces. Gathering what she could salvage between the large and smaller pieces, she stepped toward the jungle.

"I need to learn what else is out there?" Rising to her feet, Asta moved back for the tree line. Slowly making her way inside, she listened to the shriek of the monkeys. Her senses half blinded by the overabundance of information provided by the spirits, Asta stumbled deeper in.

The buzz of the spirits grew louder the further she walked. Head spinning, she lowered herself to the jungle floor, and placed one hand to her pounding skull. She could see, hear, and smell everything around her.

She could tell which direction, how high, and in what tree, the chirping birds nested. Her head continued to swoon as she rose to her feet and resumed her task. Though she could not yet see it, she instinctively knew of a clearing not far ahead.

Two more steps, and the howling of the local primates returned. She stopped abruptly, utilizing her newfound senses to her best ability. She sensed a surge of life swarming about her, above and below. From the level of the ground, several large, white and silver chested primates, with elongated fangs, snarled at her.

Throwing a hand out above her head, her mind and insides screamed as she manipulated the spirits in the trees above. A shriek was all that she heard as the trees shattered, showering the vicinity with splinters.

She screamed against the chorus of primal voices, forcing the elements to spiral further out of control around her. Once she finally opened her eyes, she was alone, in the epicenter of indescribable carnage. Rising to her feet, she quickly remembered the disposition of her insides, and vomited.

"What is happening to me?" She sobbed, wiping her mouth and standing upright. Her entire body tingled with excited energy. Despite the horror she felt, she wanted to shape more, which scared her.

Through the ruined canopy of the forest, she could see the nearby mountains. Her footsteps grew less certain as she foraged further with diminishing strength. Collapsing against a nearby tree, she glimpsed through a break in the trees. Fatigue a constant companion as she traveled forward, Asta reached the clearing and dropped to the ground. Waking several hours later, by tell of the setting sun, she took her first steps upon the slope.

"A few more steps and I can learn where I am." She muttered to herself, dragging one foot behind the next. She struggled up the mountain face, often crawling on all fours, until at last, she could see above the tree tops.

"By the crows." She growled loudly to herself at the sight she beheld. Far off in the distance, visible only thanks to her enhanced vision, were the blackened sails of a massive vessel, far beyond the techniques of the Vikings. "They have found me."

Chapter 22 – Hunting the Cana

"Wake, Viking." Aya urged, prodding Vali repetitiously. He stirred, groaning as his weary muscles growled and his joints cracked.

"Has it stopped raining?" He yawned. Aya shook her head without answering as she cleared the opening of their dwelling and stepped out into the drizzle. He glanced over their campfire and looked over the gently smoking remains.

He had only just begun to crawl from the hovel, as the pelt above him, shifted. He shivered intensely as chilly rain water, poured down his back and he stood. The storm had weakened, though he hoped whatever misery they were to bear, would prove a sufficient deterrent to their pursuers.

"Will you be able to navigate under these conditions?" He asked, pulling the collar of his vest up beneath his ears.

"I can." She replied, confidently.

"I am counting on you, then." He said in a cheerful tone, though he felt the furthest he could imagine from cheery.

"I get us there. Be ready to fight."

"Where are we headed?" He asked her, the first time he had done so. Aya turned her head back to face him, at first, seeming appalled. After a few seconds, her features softened, and she stopped.

"We go to second Cana camp. I think hunters wait there."

"Wait for us to wear ourselves down, and then attack. Clever."

"Cheat, they do." Aya nearly spat. Vali had begun to glimpse at his companion's competitive love of sport. He laughed to himself, imagining he was home, once more. The delusion was quickly dissipated however, as he looked upon her exotic features, red crowned, golden hair and silver eyes.

"The Comartok will not fight fairly." He replied, thinking on Canaruhk's words.

"They are Kresh. Is different." She said again, voice filled with irritation.

"If they do not wish to fight fairly, then neither shall we." He replied. Aya's gaze snapped backwards at Vali's comment, smirk on her face.

"What you plan, Viking?" Aya asked him. Vali thought intensely a moment, considering his plan through several twists.

"How well do you know the area we are traveling too?"

"Well enough for travel. Not so well as Cana."

"Well enough you might be able to help set a trap?" Aya stared at him, curiously.

"What trap, Viking?"

"The kind my people might use, when hunting animals far larger than ourselves. The kind we might use against the Comartok." The corners of Aya's lips stretched.

"We reach Cana camp in one long day."

"Let's get an idea of what we face. Scout out. Take our time. Rest. I need for you to spy on them. You will not be detected as easily as I will. Meanwhile, I will begin to prepare a trap for them.

"When we are ready to attack, we strike, and lead them to fight on our terms." Aya nodded her head, her understanding incomplete, but not broken.

"And your trap, no kill?"

"No kill," he repeated. "Though, they might experience a great deal of discomfort." Aya smiled again.

"That, I no mind."

"Good. Let's stop early tonight. We need rest to recover our strength." Aya nodded her head, weariness still in her eyes.

"Not far from here, is cave. Cana could watch from there. We stop and rest in burrow. Search cave, tonight."

"If we find the Cana?"

"We fight them. You use Viking tricks."

"If they are not?"

"We rest. Find more meat. Hungry." Vali reached into the pouch on his hip. Inside, he still had three strips of the Tharn meat.

"Here," he said, offering one of the strips to her. "Have some of mine." Aya pondered at him a moment, looking from the offering in his hand to his face and back.

"Yours." She said.

"Do not worry about it. Take it. I still have two more."

"You not hungry?" She asked, stopping to lean against the side of a tree.

"I am used to going on a light stomach. I will be alright." She eyed him with wide, watery eyes, filled with gratitude.

"Thank you, Viking." She said, taking the jerky and chewing it with vigor. He smirked to himself as he heard a light growl emanate from the woman, who lead on.

They stopped early that night, Vali watching carefully as Aya erected a similar structure to the one she had built the night before. Again, he collected the wood for their fire, while Aya foraged for food. Gathering up a few, additional pieces, he sat them aside to fill in the entrance. Staring at his work, he shifted at the sound of something dragging behind him.

"Help me, Viking." He could hear Aya grunt nearby. Poking his head out from their burrow, his eyes grew wide at the sight of the elk she dragged. Scurrying, he quickly fled to her.

"What are we going to do with all of it?" He asked.

"Eat it." She answered, staring at him, curiously. "What else we do?"

"The two of us? All of that?" Aya looked back to the elk and then to Vali.

"Is not so much? We smoke it. Eat. No need find food. Enough until beat Cana."

"How are we going to get all of it in here?" He asked, pointing to their tiny hut, which in comparison, was little bigger than her kill.

"You help me." She said, in a tone that told him the answer should be abundantly obvious. He scratched his head, once, and looked back to their hut.

"We will need to cut it into several pieces." He suggested, turning back to face her. Aya pulled her knife from its sheath and began quartering the animal.

"At least give me a chance to help you." He said, mirroring her. As the last of the meat had been cleaned from the bones, Aya tipped back from the carcass and wiped her face on the back of her sleeve.

"Need wash." She grumbled, flicking blood from her fingertips and blade. Cleaning and sheathing his weapon, Vali looked up at her.

"You go ahead. I will start the fire and set some of the meat on. It will take some time for us to get through all of this." Aya nodded, look of gratitude on her face, which was coated with sweat. A single lock of hair, lay plastered across her face, despite how enthusiastically she blew at it.

He watched her walk away, heading south toward the water. Vali moved back into the hovel, and building his fire, threw the first of the hunks of meat upon a carefully stacked collection of branches. His task set, he looked to his own bloodied, filthy hands and flicked his fingers.

"Suppose I should wash, as well." He told himself and crawled out. Marching toward the stream, he stopped. He could see Aya down by the stream, her top pulled down as she rinsed herself with the clear waters.

Vali placed his back to her, leaning against a tree as he waited for her to finish. He stared down at the leather braid around his neck, and smiled as thoughts of Freyja and Asta, came to him. He did not dare touch the necklace, his totem, he thought, as he glanced back at the Kresh woman.

His conflictions about the Kresh rushed to the surface as he eyed his innocent and naïve companion. Her pure spirit, conviction to her people and the loyalty she had shown him, all contradicted what he knew of the Kresh. Now, he found himself in an even more unlikely situation. He found himself admiring Aya.

Shaking his head, he looked back to the strap, one of the few possessions he held, which signified him to his heritage. There was something else there, too. It lingered at the edge of his thoughts, beyond his reach. Like a star, peering down to the explorer in his heart, he reached for it, but came no closer to touching the distant glimmer.

"You wash, Viking?" Aya said, stopping near to him, her wet hair dangling down over her arms, which were crossed over her bare chest. He looked up at her and felt alarmed as she turned away.

"I will. I was just thinking." Aya caught a glimpse of the leather strap, which lay over his collarbone.

"Of your Asta. Your...Freyja." She said softly. He nodded his head and slowly rose.

"They could be across that lake now, and they would still be a world away from me." He said, forlorn smile on his face. "It does not matter, now. One day at a time, then we face Comartok." He walked away from her, without another word passing between them.

That night, they spoke very little. They munched on the last of the Tharn meat, adding in bits of the elk, until both of their stomachs were full. The crackling of the kindling in their humble fire, held their audience. They shared only the briefest of awkward glances, before Aya rolled onto her side and fell asleep.

Sitting alone in the quiet, Vali kept to his rhythmic, mindless task, switching out the strips of meat as they dried. His mind remained focused on those he fought to return to, even as the enormous distance between them, grew ever more present to him. He listened to Aya's slow breathing, and confident in the depth of her slumber, allowed his head to drop from the weight it carried.

***

The following morning, Aya left long before first light, leaving Vali behind. He quickly realized where she had gone, the moment he awoke and saw all but her glaive, still in their hollow. Stretching his body, he shuffled and pulled back the carefully stacked wood.

Crawling out to face the first rays of morning, he set out in search of his ideal ambush site. They had found it early the day before. It did not take him long to rediscover the narrow ravine cutting through the small overlook.

The ravine consisted of a long narrow tunnel. At the top of the steep path, large, thorn covered vegetation covered everything within sight. Long vines stretching from the same plants, coiled themselves within the ravine, providing a rather limited pass.

Carefully examining every path, avoiding those thorns he could, he continued to plot his trap. Traveling down the length of the ravine as it ran beneath the overlook, he found a steep drop. Not high enough to kill him, but enough for him to stop and gauge the distance. Taking his time to examine the entire terrain, he began work on his trap.

"How go preparations?" Aya asked him, near evening when he had returned to their camp.

"It will take some time, but I should be ready by tomorrow eve."

"Be best to strike them at night. Put them at disadvantage."

"The Kresh see better in the dark than I do."

"Not all Kresh." Aya corrected. "Cana clan is stronger and bigger. Aya is faster and sees in dark."

"And Vali is none of those things." He pointed out. "And I will be serving as the bait."

"Viking is good for some things."

"You think so? Anything in particular?" Aya stared at him blankly, her legs folded as she sat across the fire from him.

"I no know." She responded, offset by the question.

"But you just said that I was good for some things."

No know what things," she spoke in a defensive tone, her hands flailing at eye level. "Thought you knew." Vali shook his head and allowed his posture to slump.

"I suppose we will find out tomorrow night."

They both slept late the following morning, finally rising sometime in the afternoon. The knowledge that their enemy was not hunting them had allowed them some minor ease. Now that they had reached their inevitable encounter, that knowledge mattered little.

Vali finished the final preparations of his trap and made his way back to the lone tree on the high hill. He sat and removing another strip of his jerky, chewed while he awaited Aya.

The salty taste burned at the sores in his mouth, acquired from a diet of dried meat. He took a short swig from his waterskin and swished the water about. Swallowing, he eyed another strip and returned it to his pouch.

He eyed his hands, which were wrapped with a series of leather straps. Pulling at the knots, he secured the wrappings, before manipulating and flexing his fingers, being sure he maintained a level of dexterity. Closing his eyes, he enjoyed the breeze and dug his fingertips into the ground.

"Were I an enemy, I could have killed you." Aya spoke, approaching silently from behind him.

"Fortunately for me, you are a most trusted ally."

"We do not know. Kresh and Viking always enemies. May need to kill each other, one day." She sat near to him crossing her legs. He did not bat a single eyelash. Staring deeply into the eyes of the woman across from him, he spoke with absolute conviction.

"Aya, I could never look at you as an enemy."

"You hunt Kresh when we met."

"I found Kresh, where they should not have been. I did not attack, then." He pointed out.

"Kresh roam where they wish. It is our way."

"Since the last battle between our people, the Kresh have always honored the treaty."

"The one which slowly kills my people." She growled at him. Now, he opened his eyes and looked at Aya.

"Is that why you were on Fangor? Has something happened on the Northern Isles?" Aya turned away from him, crossing her arms as she sulked.

"It is Kresh concern." She grumbled. He imagined he felt a chill in the air.

"Aya, please tell me? Why are the Kresh moving south? Do the others plan to attack my people?" Aya shot upright and glared down at Vali.

"That all your kind care about! War. Death. Battle. Think you kill enough Kresh, Gods love you." Tears began to fall from the young woman's eyes. Her face was contorted with anger, and her body shook visibly.

"Aya, it is..."

"Kresh not like Vikings. Kresh want peace, love and be free. We no like war. Kill because must. Vikings always take, praise gods, kill more." She swept away the tears using the back of her right arm and stormed away. He watched her go. In his mind, he thought of several reasons to stop her, but couldn't. A thousand words to say, but his tongue grew too thick and heavy.

He did not leave the hilltop, until after nightfall, nor did Aya return. As the last of the sun's fading rays left the horizon and only the moon shone at its peak, Vali rose. Looking up above, he climbed the tree. Reaching the uppermost branches, he looked down the valley to bear witness to numerous flickering torches.

Less than a quarter of the distance between he and the village, Vali saw another figure. It moved swiftly, working its way toward the village. Vali sighed and quickly made his way to the ground.

"Do not worry, Aya," he said, brushing off his pants. "I will play my part." He crept toward the encampment with uncertain steps. He lost the darkness cloaked figure halfway to his destination, but continued, until he stood just outside the light set off by the flames. Focusing on the nearest of the lights, he clenched his fist as he had with the smoke. With some effort and an immense amount of patience, the torch went out.

Moving in closer, Vali reached out for the second torch and suffocated it as he had the first. Quickly dashing into the camp, he ducked beside the nearest cover. Peering out toward the center of the square camp, he focused his eyes on the central campfire. The dark figure from before darted between the blackened torches, running to the far side of the camp.

He waited patiently, keeping his breathing in check as he worked his newfound ability. He gently prodded at the flames, without provoking them into a frenzy. He focused his attention on the lowermost logs, which held the burning stack in place. Readjusting his eyes to the light, allowed him a brief glimpse of the young Kresh woman, dashing to another tent.

He smiled, so far, the plan was running soundly. A moment later, Aya darted to the next dwelling, keeping her eyes wary for any sign of the night sentry. He continued to palpate the flames as he listened. He imagined he could hear the groan of the wood, as the flames consumed it greedily. Then, a loud bellow pierced the ambience, which had previously been little more than a crackle of flame. It was now his turn to act.

Reaching deep into his gut, Vali pressed the flame with every bit of shaping he could conjure. With all the pent fury he had padded the bonfire with, the flames raged forward. The bottom of the stack, consumed far before the rest, collapsed, allowing the entire pile to topple. A cry of alarm reared out amongst the warrior camp as fuel for the fire spewed forth in every direction, allowing the fire to grow wild.

Another collection of shouts rang through the night, its voice scarcely a murmur amid the roar of the flames. Vali caught a glimpse of movement, Aya, darting from the chaotic scene. Stepping into the light, he awaited the Cana.

A deep, guttural growl sounded near to his right. Leaping back, he narrowly avoided the end of a blunted javelin. At the sight of one of the Cana, he fled.

~ 340 ~

He was no more than forty paces beyond the ring of torches, before the howls of the Kresh hunting party reached his ears. A confusing mixture of fear and exhilaration poured raw adrenaline into his blood, resulting in a grin. With eyes able to see no more than the next five to ten steps, he tore through the night.

He could hear their javelins striking the ground behind him. He only hoped he could stay ahead of them long enough to reach the ravine. As the sound of his pursuers grew nearer, he laid eyes upon the ravine, which shown in the moonlight.

His grin widened, though he was terrified. He had suspected long before Aya's warning that the Cana would be hungry for blood. Even amongst his own kind, a death was not entirely uncommon, should bouts of sport be taken too seriously. Already, he knew truth. Should the Cana catch him now, he would be dead.

He heard a swift 'whoosh' and felt his hair blow in the wind, as something not unlike a stone axe narrowly missed his head. Even in the fractured moment he had seen the weapon, he had seen enough to discern its owner. Karn had nearly caught up to him.

He entered the ravine and immediately saw the strip of thorny vine he was hoping for. Arm extended, he leapt for the wall and wretched on the rope. Bundles of vines he had spent most of an afternoon cutting, fell upon the Kresh.

A loud, echoing mob of howls echoed down toward him. Without daring to look back, he continued his flight through the narrow mouth. As he reached the choke point, he was forced to slow as his own limbs ran across the thorn coated walls.

More of the Kresh weapons struck the walls of the ravine, discarded blindly into the night. Another Kresh howl accompanied the noise, making Vali smile once more. Aya was with him.

He fled further in, eyes on the rising earthen walls as he neared his next marker. Swinging his sword, he sliced through a second cord, which allowed a net of thorny vines to fall over the gap he had just cleared. Again, he listened as numerous pained howls rang out.

He smirked confidently as his path became easier to find. The high reaching walls of the ravine alerted him to the upcoming plummet. A large form appeared at the edge of his vision. The cliff face, just above the fall.

Sheathing his sword, he reached the drop off point he had explored that morning. Pressing himself harder, he leapt blindly into the air, arms outstretched. He struck the lower edge of the overlook, his fingers barely managing to find purchase against the craggy face.

He sputtered and spat as his momentum drove both his face and chest into the stone wall. He wheezed even as he climbed, trying to capture his breath. Slowly pulling himself up, he stopped as he heard a series of aggressive, rhythmic thumps. Guessing what it could be, Vali hastened his climb, blindly searching for each handhold.

Pain exploded in his left shoulder as something heavy forced him against the cliff face. He felt warm gush flowing over his face as a series of Kresh howls escaped from the throat of the man clinging to his back. He gasped as he felt a blade being pulled from his flesh. Before the bite could return, Vali released his grip on the edge.

Both he and his attacker fell, howling with terror as they tumbled down into darkness. Vali landed painfully, his knees buckling as he collapsed to his side. He heard a groan not far from where he lay and lifted his head.

Placing his hands beneath his body, his arms shook as he raised himself. He felt warm, sticky fluid dripping from the side of his head and face. His knees rocked unsteadily beneath him as he attempted to ground himself.

His ears stopped ringing. The spinning in his head slowed. As his eyes once again drew in focus, he saw who had caused his fall. Bloody dagger in one hand, hatchet in the other, stood Karn, eyes burning with malice.

Blood dripped from the Kresh warrior, from numerous cuts decorating his face, arms, chest and legs. Vali felt pride in the effectiveness of his trap, Karn having received his wounds from charging through the walls of thorns. He gripped the leather handles of his weapons, which emitted a straining noise as the leather was compressed. With a deep, maniacal bellow, Karn raised both weapons and charged.

Vali moved to defend himself, sluggishly unsheathing his weapon. He parried Karn's downward stroke with the axe, catching the haft of the stone axe on the side of his blade. Stepping to throw the warrior's weight aside, he instead leapt back to avoid the hand holding the dagger.

Vali stumbled backwards, dabbing at the now bloody strip of flesh by his navel. As coarse as the Kresh tongue might sound from some, nothing Karn said now, came remotely palatable. Another strike from the larger, better rested and scarcely wounded Kresh, staggered the Viking further.

His left shoulder ached, the arm hanging limply at his side, nearly useless as he desperately fought against the savage style the Cana used. Blows which did not serve to destabilize Vali, came in endless flurries. Through a series of slashes, backhands and spins, Karn gave no hole for which Vali could exploit.

He winced as he moved away a half step too slowly and the knife grazed his thigh. In his stumble, he tipped enough to avoid bludgeoning, but was awarded a second, shallow cut to his face. Blood ran in Vali's left eye, blurring his vision.

He felt his chest and lungs collapse as a foot was pressed into his stomach. Next, sharp pains in his back, as he collided with the craggy cliff face. He swung blindly and froze as his sword arm was grappled and he felt a sharp point pressed to his throat.

The Kresh spoke in words, which felt better suited to a rabid dog. The dagger at Vali's throat bit in. The blade slowly rubbed against Vali's throat and was suddenly thrust away as Karn was thrown backwards.

"Viking!" He heard a feminine voice bellow, tones ringed in panic. "Viking, you all right?" Aya called again as she dropped down from above, a short distance afore.

"I'll manage," he croaked, holding his hand to his throat. "Is our trial over, now?" As if in answer, Karn leapt to his feet, howling with madness, swinging Aya's blunted javelin. Distracted by her wounded companion, Aya saw the attack a breath too late to fully block the blow to her head.

Aya dropped to a knee, her head hanging to the side as she fended off a second blow. Three more times, the massive Kresh pummeled down on her, shattering the javelin as Aya crumbled. The Cana tipped his toe into the dirt and flicked his dagger back to his hand as he moved not for Vali, but Aya.

A gurgling growl emanated from Vali as he gripped his hilt and rose. Aya groaned as she attempted to rise and gasped as she was kicked in the ribs. As he reached his full height, Vali continued to growl at the warrior, who now ignored him.

"Kachuk!" Vali yelled the best he could. He did not know the meaning of the word. He had often heard the word spat at him by Karn and his fellows. He did not know its meaning and it did not matter. Karn spun on a heel, dagger now raised, and charged.

Vali tipped sideways as he swung low. He grimaced as he felt Karn's blade peeling through the flesh on his left forearm but felt his blade strike bone. The Cana crumbled to the ground, howling in pain, while grasping at his ruined shin.

Senses overwhelmed with adrenaline, Vali kneed the warrior in the chest, before swinging his right arm back, dashing the pommel against the bridge of his nose. Karn fell to the ground helplessly as Vali, nearly blind with rage, pressed the tip of his sword over the Kresh's heart.

"Aya, are you all right?" He called into the dark.

"Kill him, Viking. He break law of the people." Aya groaned, slowly reaching her knees. "No one blame you." Vali stared down into the wild eyes of the man beneath his blade and felt the frantic beating of Karn's heart against his weapon.

Anger, fear and loathing coursed through his veins as his eyes narrowed. In Karn, he found truth to every tale he had been told in his youth. Desiring an end to the man's life, Vali gripped the handle of his sword and placed his weak second over the pommel to thrust down.

Something else flashed before his eyes. Pain, regret, loss. He saw his family and the few pleasant memories he had made with Aya. He realized Karn's life was not his to claim.

"I give you your life, Karn." Vali said, allowing the tension in his body to ease. "There are those of us who wish for an end to the bloodshed." He muttered, flicking the blood from his sword and sheathed it.

Suddenly, the various wounds on his body, burdened him, and he shuffled limply over to Aya. She held her arm across her rib cage as she stood half bent over. She shuffled alongside him, neither noticing Karn rising, weight balanced on one leg, blade in hand.

He howled once, raising his weapon over his head. Vali and Aya turned to defend themselves as Karn was toppled by another javelin, thrown from beyond the darkness. Looking up the steep slope of the ravine, they saw Canaruhk, looking down to them.

"My warriors will take you back. I will deal with Karn." The old Kresh spoke in a soft, yet threatening tone liking to a once napping predator, preparing to ravage its prey. Vali stepped away from the imposing man, whose limp showed experience, not age. Whose kind tone showed strength, instead of weakness. Aya spoke a few words in Kresh to Canaruhk. Vali caught only one word, 'Kanadesh.'

Two of the Cana approached Vali. Placing themselves beneath him, he limped alongside them. Aya near, her hand on the small of Vali's back. Making their way back through the ravine, they took the time to look upon what they had accomplished. Vali saw the Kresh reviving their own, unconscious hunters. Dozens of braves, he and Aya had managed to defeat.

"Done well, Kana," she whispered.

Chapter 23 - Unbound

Asta trampled through the bushes, charging further into the jungle. The sight of the black ones' ship marked one of the last things she could remember, before she awoke on the island. She could only imagine they had returned to finish what they started.

Reaching the jungle clearing, she quickly scaled one of the many tall trees, encircling the area. Her body flourished with energy, rapidly propelling her higher into the upper branches. Peering out from behind the natural cover, she carefully watched the ship as it weighed anchor.

Several small vessels, slowly lowered toward the water's surface, fully populated by her enemies. As the boats crept nearer to the island's shore, Asta looked back deeper into the jungle. Within the center of the island, rose the small mountain chain, where she had dealt with her primate neighbors. Gritting her teeth, she dropped from her perch and charged deeper within.

The trees swayed out of her path as she ran by. The earth rumbled as it carried her toward the mountains. It never occurred to her the same shapings might draw her enemies nearer.

She stopped at the base of the mountain and stared above. Already, a swirl of elemental energy loomed above. A crackle of thunder came from the direction of the sea. She turned her head back swiftly and nearly tripped. The forest behind her was breaking apart, wrought asunder by her godlike pursuers.

One after another, trees fell, crashing upon the next, moving in her direction. She stopped her flight and turned to face her pursuers. What she found defied her ability to reason.

The tree line burst apart, spewing debris out onto the foot of the mountain. One, black robed revenant appeared from the dust, a great mound of earth propelling its steps forward. Beside it, leaping from those trees which were left intact, a second appeared.

Both slowed their pursuit upon seeing Asta. Slowly, they stepped forward, their metal masked faces staring at her without expression. Dead slits for eyes was all she could make beneath the wraith-like beings mantles.

"Come with us." One spoke, their voice rattling from beneath the metal mask. "You are unbound. Your power is growing unstable."

"We can help, you." The earth shaper spoke, a feminine tone to the metal ring.

"Help me? You killed my Vali!" Asta roared, a guttural tone erupting from her throat like dragon's fire. Though no such flame manifested, both revenants stopped in their tracks.

"Your nature is consumption. Greed. You are a danger."

"What are we?" Asta asked, more curious than angry of those who claimed to be her fellows. "What is happening to me?" Her voice deepened as she felt her body thickening. She bent slightly at the waist as her insides rolled violently. Again, the revenants halted.

"WHAT ARE WE?" Asta yelled, this time her voice was deeper than the man across from her. The two revenants looked to one another briefly, before they charged.

The moment the two dashed forward, vines jumped from the earth and attempted to ensnare her. With a flick of her wrist, she destroyed the tips of the encroaching vines, though more followed. Asta leapt backwards, using her new found shaping prowess to both clear away more of the vines, and propel herself backwards as the revenant male approached.

The ground erupted in a spray of sparks as energy surged through the tips of the man's hands. Shrapnel, made of dirt and stone, sprayed up in Asta's face, sending a light spray of sanguine out around her. No sooner had her swift adversary struck the ground, did they kick off and prepare a second attack.

Flinging both arms to the side, Asta willed the wind to propel her opponent away. As the spritely wielder of lighting flew off course, landing hard on the ground near its fellow. They exchanged a quick glance, before the lightning user renewed his attack.

The earth shaper pressed both hands on the ground, conjuring a flurry of spikes to lunge forward. Again, Asta found herself on the defensive, avoiding the sharpened spires of earth. Her masculine opponent however, used them as a source of his advance.

Asta dove backwards, throwing herself over the nearby ledge and back into the tree line. She heard a mighty crash, not far from where she had been, followed by a burst of light, which singed the treetops. Sliding down the side of the slope, she growled in anger as her flesh was serrated on the jagged stones.

Her feet touched the bottom of the slope, jarring her forward at a run. Thrusting her hands down at the ground, she continued to run as a wall of earth rose up to her defense. She managed only a few more paces, before the male revenant landed in front of her.

"You cannot be allowed to go on. You are unbound." The man raised a single hand, producing a flicker of light.

"I do not know what that means!" Asta yelled, throwing both hands to either side of her. The forest erupted with a cacophony of violence and pandemonium, as trees, earth and sky, collided suddenly. Her opponent released his attack at the same moment, adding his own influence to the chaos.

Asta was thrown backwards, blind, deaf, and floating in a world of darkness. She struck her head and felt heat. A moment later, she felt the force in the back of her mind, clawing free.

"Quickly! Return! The serpent's spawn is breaking free!" She could hear the woman call, though she could perceive little else. She was floating freely now, surrounded by stars, in a vast ocean of emptiness.

Somewhere beyond her consciousness, there was violence, envy, greed, and lust. She looked out around her, searching for anything she might know. All she found was a chain, large, broken and composed of the same spectral light, which shaped the various constellations around her.

Floating throughout it all, signs of her broken chain, her bind, remained. Shattered links flowed from her, over everything around her and beyond. She looked upon Yggdrasil, or so she assumed, its mighty branches connecting all things.

"Vali." She whispered as the dragon's roar continued in another world. "Where are you?"

Chapter 24 – The Lord of Falkest

"How much longer to Falkest?" Halla asked. Brina, who had proven herself more than capable of enforcing her will, turned to face the woman on the oars behind her.

"We should be there by nightfall." She answered. "It is how long before we leave again, which has me curious."

"Why do you say that?" Agni, who sat across the aisle from Brina, asked.

"Chief Grom enjoys standing on ceremony." She growled. "He would avoid involving himself in unsavory matters, simply by stalling at the door. He is a terrible braggart." She concluded. Freyja, who sat at the bow of the longboat, turned her head back to glare at them.

Freyja fretted irritably in the background, checking the riggings on the ship as she muttered to herself. The sun sat just beyond its highest point. The cool breeze kept them refreshed, even beneath the scorch of its rays.

"Sounds as though you are not anxious to meet the man." Haldr laughed, serving as the fourth oar man.

"Not in the slightest. I simply wish to be at sea and involved in affairs off from Dumah." As they finished their conversation, Freyja cleared her throat, agitated look on her face.

"My uncle is a kind and generous man." She grumbled. "He has done much for his people, since the time of my grandfather. I am certain that his rare departures from Falkest, are in fact due to his devotion to his people."

"Is it so terrible on Dumah?" Abel asked from behind, changing the topic.

"Terrible? No, of course not. Not usually, at least." She said, increasing her efforts behind the oar.

"Usually?" Abel asked. Brina sighed, though she continued to row. Staring off over the side of the ship, her long, unbound hair trailed freely behind her.

"What is it that makes us Vikings?" Brina asked. Everyone assembled, stared at the back of the young woman's head, while Freyja looked to the sea.

"Pardon?" Abel asked, breaking the silence.

"What is it that makes us Vikings? Is it our heritage? Lineage? Our legacy?" Thala turned her head away from her gentle shaping, to eye the woman. Abel considered the question a moment longer, before calling forth with his answer.

"I would suppose that it is all of those things."

"Then what is our heritage? What is the legacy of our people? We were once explorers. What are we now?" Again, the answer was considered carefully, before proposed.

"We may no longer be the explorers we once were, but that does not mean we have lost our legacy. The Isles of Vala are yet undiscovered to our people. We have only begun to make this land our own."

"And yet, we have grown content to settle. We honor gods that we also believe are no more. The heart of our people came from the sea, and yet we have each buried a piece of it, on a single island."

"We had to settle somewhere, if we hoped for our people to prosper." Freyja added. "We would never have survived had we stayed adrift. Even a Viking's thoughts, ought often to be of home."

"Even if growing roots forces us to lose our way of life?" Brina asked.

"Your ancestors settled these lands at the behest of the old gods." Thala interjected. "Their guidance is what saved our people from the destruction beyond the fog. The legacy of the Viking people was not lost, because they settled the one hundred isles. It was preserved."

"I still long for adventure." Brina told them. "I long to see what lies beyond the fog." The rest of the crew rowed silently, each of them focused on their thoughts of home.

"There is nothing beyond the fog." Abel whispered, though no one heard him. He eyed his crew, who worked hard at their labors. "Perhaps we may see it, one day." He said. "For now, a different adventure awaits us."

They continued pressing against the tide the entirety of the day. Thala and Abel both took turns shaping the winds and the waves to favor their journey. By midday, their destination was in sight. Looking behind to the many other trailing ships in their party, Abel sighed.

"Let us be done with this, then." He said, eyeing the massive towers, which loomed above them. Formed by earth shapers long ago, the columns rose from the sea bed, and stood high above the island. He could see guardsmen stationed within the many watch towers, which were positioned several lengths from one another.

The island, itself, rose as a series of massive hill mounds, each level of the village built into the plateaus. Far ahead of them, beyond the towers, he could see a large pier, which wrapped around the island toward the north. From what he could see, the village began just beyond the port.

Several buildings, their construction more elaborate than those on Ulfrost, stood near one another, offering little space between. The roads winded between the many businesses and residences, snaking up the backs of the rolling hills, which climbed ever higher. At the highest peak of the hills sat a compound, nearly as large as the inner village of Ulfrost.

"Everything is so orderly." Halla commented. "Are we sure this is Falkest?"

"I am quite certain." Abel answered, eyeing the earthen constructs.

"But where are the signs of destruction?" Haldr joined in. "Were they not devastated by the storms?"

"So, they claimed." Thala added. "I suppose we will learn more once we meet with Grom." The harbor was overflowing with crazed activity as they brought the Valiant to moor. Dropping the anchor over the side of the ship, Halla jumped from the deck and tied the boat off to one of many posts.

"Brina, Freyja and I will go to meet with Grom. I want the rest of you to gather supplies for a long voyage. Once our business here is done, I wish to be far from this place as quickly as possible." Freyja turned away from her marveling and scowled at Abel.

"It is actually quite wonderful here." She protested. "You will see soon enough. There is a reason this used to be the domain of previous Viking rulers." Abel glanced again at the densely populated city, with its high earthen walls, and unforgiving shallows.

"Even so, a Viking's thoughts should often drift toward home." Freyja sighed as Brina swung her bag over her shoulder, nudging Abel's shoulder.

"Our chiefs are waiting for us to complete this assignment, remember?" Brina asked. "We need to move quickly and reclaim your island."

"You are right. We need to move swiftly." Abel agreed, walking through the port, his eyes on the high road. "The longer we wait, the longer those strangers defile our home. Chief Grom should be waiting for us."

They made their way through the busy streets of the city, passed vendors, homes, and unfamiliar faces. While aspects of their daily lives in Ulfrost were apparent, the culture of Falkest proved vastly different. Uniformed guards patrolled the streets, their arms laid across their belts for everyone to see. Children remained close to their parents, opposed to playing in large gathering circles.

Abel could hear the ring and ting of a blacksmiths forge to his left. Turning to face it, he saw the steady glow of the tradesman's workshop, and a fiercely tanned woman before it. Her raven black hair was pulled behind her head, and char decorated her apron and gloves.

A child played behind a rickety fence, just outside of the shop. A ragged cloth doll in her hands, the red and black-haired girl hummed as she played. Abel stared at the woman he saw through the open door a moment, her skin and exotic, shimmering hair rousing his curiosity.

"Kresh." Freyja growled as they strolled by. "Why uncle allows them to live here is beyond me. They should be left with their own kind. Filthy animals."

"They do not seem so different from us." Brina muttered. Abel looked to her with surprise, while Freyja's expression proved more aggressive.

"How can you say that?" Freyja gasped. "They are savage devils, who run about the wildlands, half naked and laying with animals. They have been a blight to our people since we settled the Isles of Vala."

"I know the stories about the Kresh." Brina sighed. "Believe me, half of the elders on Dumah, wish to speak of nothing more than their journeys to the savage north. It was merely an observation. I meant no harm in it."

"All the same, Brina." Abel began. "It would probably be best not to look for similarities or humanities with our sworn enemies. At least not while we are here. Who knows the beast we'll awaken?"

"Are you trying to liken the people here to them?" Freyja snapped, disapprovingly.

"I would not dream of it." He smirked. "You just never know how easily offended some people are." The incident out of sight, they quickly placed it from mind as they continued their climb. Reaching the height of the hill, the three of them stopped in wonder.

"This is the former High Chief's home?" Brina gasped, staring at the massive compound. "It could house my entire village."

"Not the former High Chief.' Freyja corrected. "Vali's father, Gram, decided to stay on Ulfrost, after earning my grandfather's approval. Grandfather, however, lead our people from here. It was also he, who chose my mother to lead, after Gram fell in the north."

"Why did Gram leave?" Brina asked. "I have never been to Ulfrost, but this place definitely gives off the feeling of authority."

"I do not know. I never met Chief Gram." Freyja spoke. "Vali never met him, either. Father has only ever told me he wishes Vali will be half of what he was." Her voice trailed off as she spoke the words.

"I am sorry, Freyja." Abel said, his voice wavering. The young woman shook her head, her crimson braid flashing between her shoulder blades.

"That is not what matters, now. I have to deliver mother's message." She reached into her sleeve and produced a small bit of parchment, sealed by the High Chief's insignia.

"Then we need not keep them waiting. Your uncle is expecting us." As the three of them walked down the road leading to Grom's sanctum, the many lanterns which lined the road, began to illuminate. Fueled by the shapings which forged the lanterns, tiny spirits of flame gathered within. Gently beginning their consumption of the food inside, the lanterns shimmered with a dull light.

"The lanterns are sealed by the light of the sun." Thala began her explanation. The light powers it throughout the day, the gathered heat feeding any spirits inside. As the rays of day fade however, the seal weakens and the tiny spirits of fire are left to consume the wood or oil that is left within.

"Why do we not use these on Ulfrost?" Abel asked, glancing at them as they walked by.

"In order to make these lanterns work such as they are, the spirits must be inside the lantern." She continued. "Some spirits would do so willingly, but it is an inefficient method. I doubt these lanterns were made with volunteers."

"Thala, why must you take something so elegant and beautiful and attempt to ruin it?" Freyja snapped.

"I only wished to convey the truth. Inconvenient or not. A shrine maiden's duty, is to pass down knowledge from one generation to the next." Abel heard another light, irritable sigh escape the woman as they reached the front gates of the manor. Standing before the doors, two guards, pikes in their hands, waited.

"We are here to see Chief Grom." Abel stated, stopping before the pike men.

"Have you an invitation?" The older of the two men asked. His nose was hooked, likely due to multiple breaks, though his body proudly displayed the strength of an earth shaping clan of warriors.

"Here," Freyja stepped forward, presenting the letter in her care. "A letter from the High Chief, my mother."

"Miss Freyja?" A tall, dark haired woman in her middle years spoke from behind. Abel and his entourage turned to face the woman, who was surrounded by four more guardsmen.

"Aunt Torunn?" Freyja gasped. "I have not seen you since I was little." She rushed toward the woman with a child's excitement, much to the chagrin of the guards. Wrapping her arms around her aunt, they shared a reassuring laugh.

"Last time I saw you, you were clung to your mother's skirts. Now here you are, two full heads taller. How have you been, dear?" Freyja pulled away slightly, as her demeanor sank.

"Of late, most harrowing, Aunt Torunn. I have come to speak with uncle about a great tragedy, which has befallen the people of Ulfrost." The woman stared up into her niece's eyes, an empathetic glaze within them. Nodding her head, she gently hooked her arm around Freyja's.

"I have heard bits from your letters to my husband." Torunn sighed. "Come now, I am sure he will be expecting you." Turning her gaze upon the guards, she spoke with authority. "You may let them through. They are friends and family." At Torunn's word, the guards inclined their heads as they opened the doors.

Mighty, wooden beams stretched far higher than the tallest buildings in Ulfrost. At the height of the beams, what appeared to be branches, spread out in all directions. From Abel's viewpoint, the halls looked as though they had been built atop the ancient trees of Falkest.

This place is even bigger inside than it looks from outside!" Brina gasped as they entered the warmly decorated hall. Just beyond where they stood, two more, giant doors awaited. Already ajar, they peered beyond them to see a massive, open space. Within, they saw statues to the old gods, along with several lengthy oaken tables.

"Through here is the great hall." Torunn spoke as she led the entourage further within. If you would, please wait here, while I fetch my lord husband."

"Thank you for your help, Aunt Torunn." Freyja said as they parted.

"Of course, dear." The woman replied. "If nothing else, what is family for?" She quickly moved to a side door and was gone, leaving Abel, Brina and Freyja alone in the empty hall.

"They have statues for most all of the gods." Brina said, as she glanced around the room.

"Near everyone I can think of is here." Abel commented. "Thor, Valkyr, Tyr. Frigg and Odin stand at the top of the king's landing. I see Baldur and Heimdall over at the base of the landing. Honestly, the only ones I do not see are the likes of Loki, and his brood."

"This is a representation of the halls of Valhalla." Freyja clarified. "All who hold good favor with the all father, dine within his halls. It was my great great grandfather who had the halls fashioned in such a way."

"And I take it your uncle sits on the landing beneath Frigg and Odin?" Brina spoke with a baiting tone.

"He does. As the leader of Falkest, it is expected for him to be able to be seen by those he sees to."

"Vali always felt it best to lead by example, but to follow from behind." Brina and Freyja turned to stare at Abel.

"As a captain at sea?" They asked.

"I believe he adopted the idea from wolves, actually. The leader stays behind, to ensure that all his pack arrive safely. His warriors know the path, while he watched over the young, old, and weak."

"A leader of compassion, then." Brina interpreted. "A fine example, I suppose. Strange for a warrior, but admirable."

"Not that it matters much." Freyja interrupted, pain in her statement.

"I am sorry, Freyja. It was inconsiderate of me to say." As they spoke, the doors at the far end of the king's landing, burst open.

"My dear, Freyja." The large, red haired and bearded man, who could only be Chief Grom, bellowed. His large, meaty and gnarled hands patted a rounded stomach as the muscular man approached. "It has only been a short while, and yet you seem to have grown so much. Quickly let us discuss these letters of yours."

"Letters?" Abel asked. "Your aunt mentioned them, as well." Freyja looked to her fellow villager with a guilty face.

"Despite my mother and father's wishes, I have been in contact with Uncle Grom for some time. It was for me that he came to the clansmeet. I have maintained contact with him, since our troubles began." Abel and Brina both stood in shock as Freyja cleared the gap between her and the lord of Falkest.

"Freyja, it is so good to see you, again." The man said, embracing his niece. "Please, tell me in detail, about these troubles plaguing you and Ulfrost."

"It is great to see you again, as well, Uncle. I only wish it were under better circumstances." As Freyja spoke, tears welled in her eyes and fell to the floor. Looking about the room, Grom brought his eyes to rest upon his niece.

"Where is young Vali? I have been eager to have a lengthier conversation with the boy. I wish to speak with him about our plans for you two." Everyone gathered, turned their heads toward the young woman, shock pouring off from their faces.

"Freyja?" Abel asked. The woman however, merely shook her head, tears flying about her person wildly.

"I am afraid your offer to make mother and father see fit to unite us is no longer an option. Uncle, I am afraid that something terrible has happened. I can scarcely admit it myself, let alone write it in a letter. You see, Vali. He has. I mean. He was lost."

"Lost?" Grom asked gently embracing his niece's shoulders. Casting a confused expression toward the others, Abel cleared his throat.

"Chief Grom. What Freyja means to tell you is that Vali, our captain, died on Fangor." To this, the war chief's gaze fell to the ground as he wrapped more tightly around his niece.

"I truly am sorry, child. I had hoped the boy might serve beside you, once it was your time to lead us. From what I have heard of the boy, you would have produced mighty Vikings." Freyja nodded her head, before taking a step back from her uncle.

"There is more, Uncle. The truth of the matter is simple. A band of men, in black robes and armor, have invaded Ulfrost. They attacked us while father and the warriors were away, fending off the Kresh.

While father and the others, are ready to battle against these invaders and force them from our lands, the fighting men and women of the other clans demand your aid. They say they will not move without the support of your shapers." Grom stared off thoughtfully for a moment, stroking his chin as he considered Freyja's request.

"It seems as though I have little choice. We have just recently recovered from our own struggles of late, and yet there are those who have need of us." He looked back to Abel and Brina, before smiling at Freyja. "You shall have our aid. I will send Urs, along with my best fighters to assist you."

Quickly, he turned away from her and placing his hand to the banister beside them, sent a surge of power through it, and the floor. Abel felt his knees rattle beneath the influence of the master earth shaper and fought to maintain his balance. A moment later, a dozen forms, clad for battle, appeared. Each dropped to a knee, before bowing their heads and clapping their right hands over their hearts.

"Summon my eldest sons, their finest captains, and the rest of my personal guard. Now." He spoke, with a voice that boomed with the strength of the earth. Each of the warriors dispersed, quickly scattering to different doorways in the hall.

Within sparse few moments, the room had filled with various faces. Among them, Abel noted the two men who could be none other than the eldest sons of the infamous chief. Urs, whom Abel knew by reputation, was a cruel faced monster of a man. He was nearly a spitting image of his father, save his larger stature and stone carved physique.

"Urs, Bram, thank you for coming so quickly." Grom began, clapping his sons on their shoulders. Bram was not unlike his father or brother, but obvious influence from another could be seen in his face. The high cheek bones and blonde hair suggested a woman who was not Freyja's Aunt Torunn.

"What is the trouble, Father?" Bram spoke, his eyes bearing actual concern.

"I am without doubt the two of you recognize your cousin, Freyja." He said, motioning toward the young woman, who smiled. Both Urs and Gram inclined their heads toward her, before turning their gaze back to their father.

"It is a pleasure to see you both, again." Freyja spoke, also staring at Grom.

"If you do not mind, Father, why have we been summoned?" Urs growled with an impatient, earthly rumble.

"Yes, of course. Time is a critical factor." Grom grumbled. "I need you two, along with my personal guard and your finest captains, to assemble. It seems my sister's people are in need of our aid and the other clans will not rise to it, without us. Prepare to embark for Ulfrost by morning."

"As you wish, Father." Bram replied, turning away and marching down the hall. Urs however, grinned wickedly as he stared at Freyja and her escorts.

"So, now the high and mighty leader of all Vikings requires the aid of those she has long spited. How amusing a turn, this is." Abel gritted his teeth as he fought the urge to reach for his weapon. Freyja stepped back in shock, while Brina gripped Abel's reaching hand.

"That is enough, Urs." Grom chuckled, patting his son on the back. "There will be plenty of time to exert that energy of yours, once you reach Ulfrost. Now go, tend to what preparations you need, and make ready." Urs turned his gaze upon the inhabitants of Ulfrost once more, the corners of his lips still hooked in a snarl.

"As you wish, Father. I will save these whelps who come groveling upon our flagstones." He turned and stamped away, paying no heed to the angrily trembling trio behind him.

"Forgive my son, if you will." Grom chuckled again, clapping Abel on the shoulder. "He is over eager to wage battle and rule, he forgets his place sometimes. It will be he, who proves your competitor when the next chief is to be chosen." He added, gently cupping Freyja's hands within his own. "Now, my dear niece. Might I offer some Falkest hospitality to you and your companions?"

"That would be most appreciated, Uncle." She responded, uneasy smile spreading her lips. "We have other companions, who await our return at the pier. Might we have a moment to fetch them?" As the words left her mouth, the doors of the great hall opened.

"Woah!" Haldr and Halla both cried as they entered the room. Thala and Agni followed, while Thala performed a silent prayer as she looked upon the magnanimous statues.

"As you can see, your friends are already here." Grom smiled and chuckled once more as he clapped Abel on the back. With two loud claps of his hands, several servants, entered the room. Each carried either platters or flagons, while some of the broader shouldered servants, carried large barrels.

Looking at each of them, Abel noticed a number of unsettling similarities between them. Each of the servants wore binds upon their wrists, ankles and necks. Some of them, wore masks, which covered portions or the entirety of their faces. Also, each of them had tanned skin, because they were Kresh.

"Come now, fellow Vikings. Drink and feast to your hearts' content. Tomorrow, you will sail along with the best of my fleet and reclaim your homes." He continued to chuckle boisterously as more servants, these clearly not of the Kresh, guided Abel and his friends toward tables.

Upon each of the tables, flagons of mead had been laid out between mass platters of food. Ham, mutton, cheeses and fruit, decorated the platters across the lengths of the large, oaken tables. Eyes watering with excitement, they each took up a place and began to eat.

"I told you Uncle would help us." Freyja said, helping herself to bits of food from the nearby platters. Agni and Haldr sat back, drinking deeply from their flagons, while Halla was perched behind a mound of smoked ham. Abel turned to see Thala, flagon in hand, staring up at the statue of Valkyr.

"I am glad that he has decided to do so, but it all seems..."

"Convenient." Brina mumbled, staring at her plate. Freyja snapped her gaze at the future chief of Dumah.

"What do you mean by that?"

"Does this not feel strange to either of you?" She asked, her eyes glancing at the nearby servants. "A month ago, they claimed to be crippled by plague and foul weather. Now, suddenly they can afford to send their finest warriors and half of their fleet?"

"I agree with you, Brina." Abel whispered.

"Abel? How can you say that?" Freyja gasped.

"Anger? Grief? I am not sure how." He sighed. "We lost a lot of men on Fangor. I lost my closest friend, who stood a few arm lengths from me.

"I witnessed horrifying creatures from the old world, resurface and wreak untold mayhem. After this, a man who turned his back on us can laugh without a care, while playing the part of a benevolent host. I apologize, Freyja, but I am a bit skeptical at the moment."

"Uncle Grom is a wonderful man." She grouched, folding her arms. "You will all see, soon enough. Before he was lost, he was even working to secure a future for Vali and I." The final sentence, spoken at a near whisper, the others let it dissipate.

"I hope so." Abel answered. "I truly hope so."

Chapter 25 – Beyond the Fog

Vali remained in the camp nearly three days, before he did much more than walk to the spring. Aya had recovered much sooner than he and left to join the hunt the following morning. Grievingly rising to his feet, he limped out from the tent and made for the stream.

As had been the case the past three days, the Kresh did little more than glance at him, while whispering in their tongue. Even Aya, who had served as his only regular confidante, had spoken no more than a few words to him. Feeling cast out, he shuffled on, solemnly hobbling to the water's edge.

A long gash remained on the left side of his face. He examined what he assumed would be a scar and shrugged, the detail looked upon handsomely among his kind. As he carefully removed his clothes, he looked back to the bandages on his left forearm and thigh. He groaned painfully as he lowered himself into the water.

"How are you feeling, Viking?" Aya asked, speaking each word slowly, as if tasting them first. He jolted slightly, causing his wounds to twinge. She flinched toward him but stopped abruptly. As Vali turned to face her, he found himself haunted.

A large, black bruise marred an otherwise flawless face. Despite this, she still carried herself at an odd angle. However, far worse than that, was her expression. Aya looked angry and worse, disappointed.

"I am fine," he spoke gruffly, feeling slighted from the callus treatment he had received for three days. He turned away from her, missing her hurt filled expression.

"That is good." She muttered in a melancholy tone, falling silent as she turned away from him slightly. Vali splashed himself with water from the stream, gently rubbing it over his body. "Scar looks good." She added, reaching toward Vali's face. Pulling his head from her reach, he ignored the compliment, instead, wondering on its source.

"What became of Karn?" He asked bluntly. "The others will not speak to me."

"He has been exiled." She answered just as bluntly as though she felt he deserved worse.

"Over me?" He asked, turning to face her. Aya shook her head lightly.

"Not your fault, Viking. Karn broke Kresh law. He has been punished."

"But by all means, I am his enemy. He was banished for almost killing an enemy of the people."

"It is more difficult than that." She said, attempting to ignore the topic.

"Explain it then." He growled.

"I cannot. You are not Kresh."

"I hear that a lot." He growled with a surmounting amount of frustration. "No wonder Damaruhk's mate turned away from the people." He knew instantly he had said something wrong and he did not care. Aya stared at him, a mixture of disbelief, shock and outrage on her face.

"You do not know what you speak of." She growled at him. He took a moment to stare at Aya, who continued to avert her eyes from him, shamefully.

"Damaruhk told me..."

"Damaruhk told you enough to ask no more questions. Does not make it truth." She stood, glaring down at him with balled fists, her body shaking.

"Then tell me the truth." Vali said, standing as well, allowing him to stare down into Aya's face.

"I cannot...you are..."

"Not one of you!" He surprised even himself as he raised his voice, angrily. Aya met his gaze briefly, eyes wide from shock and regret. If the withheld tears in her eyes were a clue to her feelings, he did not notice.

"Day after day, ever since I first set foot amongst your kind, you have reminded me. Keep your secrets, then. Maybe I do not want to be one of your people. Make it all the easier for me to leave." He marched away, walking into the forest, without looking back. Aya remained motionless, too stunned to react.

By the time the rising heat between his ears abated, Vali had realized too late what he wished he had done. Already, he attempted to replay the conversation in his mind. Angry and frustrated, he forced his way through the tall thickets and brush. Considerably lost, he stopped beneath a large tree, where he rested.

Stretching his body, he leaned his head back against the trunk. Closing his eyes, he focused his thoughts. He had already been among the Kresh over a month. Soon, he and Aya would be sent away, nothing more than their wits and what they could carry on their backs, against what the Kresh thought was a god.

He banged his left fist against a lone root and winced. Staring down to his bandaged arm and leg, he thought of the wounds received from a Kresh. Another thought occurred to Vali. Stranded in a strange place far from his home, he was going to die. He did not return to the boundaries of the camp that evening. Making himself a small hovel, such as he and Aya had recently utilized, he built a modest fire, unworried about being seen.

Leaning back against the wall of his small dome, he considered what he must yet do. Twirling his necklace in his agitation, he desperately wished to see his loved ones. As his thoughts reached one of two conclusions, running away, or facing the Comartok with Aya, he took a deep breath, knowing his choice and turned to his fire.

He lay staring into the flames, enjoying his solitude. His stomach growled, though he did his best to ignore the sensation and the discomfort it brought. A moment after, he heard a rustling outside.

"May I enter?" He heard Aya say in a testing tone.

"Yes," he muttered. The young woman entered the tiny dwelling, two bowls in her hands.

"It is cold, now. Viking walked a long way. Had to track you."

"I wished to be a long way away. Why are you not in the village?" Aya sat opposite the fire from him.

"I told you, Viking. I follow you. When you leave." She extended her arm, offering up the bowl of cooled poultry. "Eat, Viking. You will need strength to recover. Not much longer."

"Thank you," he mumbled, accepting the bowl. He stared at the bowl, sorting his many mixed feelings, continuing to play with his necklace.

Noticing that Aya was staring at him, waiting, he let the braided coil fall back to his neck and hand scooped some of the meat into his mouth. Satisfied, Aya mirrored him, folding her legs in her lap.

"Aya?" He said softly.

"Yes, Viking?"

"I know you probably cannot tell me, but I want to know. Why are you so obsessed with facing the Comartok? Does becoming one of the Rukh mean so much to you?" Aya was quiet for a long while. Vali, accepting the expected answer, nodded his head.

"When I was little, my parents left to face Comartok. They no come back." Vali's eyes opened wide. His hands balled into tight knots, digging into his thighs. Meanwhile, Aya averted her gaze, tears trickling from her silver eyes.

"I am sorry to hear that. I suppose that explains your reasons."

"Not finished," she sighed. "Dama's mate, my...grandfather, left to find them when they no return." She turned her head away, in a failed attempt to hide her tears. "Hunters returned with grandfather's body, a season later. Claimed Comartok was dead. Grandfather and Comartok, killed each other. Never found my parents."

"Your grandfather left in search of exiles. That is why Damaruhk spoke of him not learning the ways of the Kresh." Aya nodded, wiping at her streaming tears.

"Not supposed to say, even to Kresh," she murmured.

"Dama only told me, so I might understand." At long last, Vali had found an answer to one of many questions. Now that he had however, he sought to change the subject. "Your understanding of my language is getting much better." He pointed out, successfully drawing Aya's gaze and coaxing her into a smile.

"I have been practicing," she answered. "Dama and Canaruhk say it important for me to learn. I also listen to you." Her accent was still clearly that of the Kresh. However, she did hold a firmer grasp on what she said.

"Why is it so important to you?" He had avoided earning Aya's confused look she gave every time he asked an overly obvious question. His streak was now broken.

"When you leave the Kresh, so do I." She answered. "I travel with you."

~ 373 ~

"To look for your family?" Aya nodded.

"More than that, Viking." She turned away, her silver eyes glowing with sadness.

"You do not need to say anymore. I understand. I was adopted to, remember?" Aya's eyebrows raised. "Adopted?" He laughed lightly.

"I was raised by people who did not bring me into the world." Aya's contorted face remained.

"I no understand. My parents were exiled when I was small. They are still out there, somewhere." He saw hope in her eyes; the ungiving kind, which leaves one delirious in the face of proof against their desire.

"Please forgive me. I did not mean to imply they were not. For all I know, my birth family is still somewhere beyond these isles." Aya cocked her head at him slightly.

"Beyond which places?" She asked. "Kresh have traveled many islands."

"My sister and I came from outside of the Isles of Vala." Aya's eyes grew to the size and brightness of moons.

"Passed the fog?" She gasped as she asked. He stared at her a moment, before answering.

"Yes." Aya's face ignited in an unrestrained smile, filled with questions and wonder. She turned away briefly, eyed the wall of the hovel and looked back, attempting to reel herself in.

"What is beyond the fog?" She asked, silver eyes aglow.

"Nothing." Vali answered. Aya stared at him, face filled with both shock and disbelief.

"What do you mean, nothing?" She asked him. He looked around, face racked in guilt at the admission he was to make.

"About two years ago, Abel and I ventured out on a dare. We sailed out beyond the fog wall, passed where the emerald waters of the Tyrda Fell change to deep blue. Once we finally managed to navigate our way through the fog and the hellish channels within, we rolled upon waves as massive as the rolling hills and mountains but found nothing." Aya's expression was more confused than ever.

"But all that exists outside the fog, walks within the land of the gods. My people have..." She stopped herself, realizing what and to whom, she was speaking to.

"Let me guess. You cannot tell me?" Aya stared into his eyes, guiltily.

"I am sorry, Viking. I truly am." Vali sighed irritably, nodding his head as he did so.

"Are you allowed to speak with me once we are exiled?" She hesitated for a long moment, before answering.

"Not yet, Viking. Eat. You need strength." He grumbled irritably and continued to eat the cool meat. They sat in relative quiet for a long while, until both annoyed and exhausted, Vali hunkered down.

"Goodnight, Aya."

"Goodnight, Viking."

Chapter 26 - Exiled

Even a week later, when the moon had nearly vanished from the night sky, his wounds still troubled him. They sat around the evening fire, amongst the members of the Dama and Cana clans. Where his days had once been filled with song, and his evenings full of dancing and feasting, there was now only silence.

Empty faces stared back at them, eyes memorizing people whom next eve, they would not be allowed to speak of. There was no dancing, no grand feast. Instead, Vali sat alone, all his earthly possessions gathered into a pack, a satchel and two pouches.

He had spoken little to Damaruhk since their return from the wilds. Though she had promised to speak with him at length, regarding her mate and how they had conquered the Comartok of their time, Vali had grown disinterested. In fact, he felt more isolated from the Kresh than he had previously.

He thumbed the braid around his neck, absent mindedly, watching Aya. The light he had seen behind her eyes on numerous occasions was now faded. She stood beside Damaruhk, her grandmother, bearing her bravest smile, as did the elder.

Vali wished he could cry for them. The closer they came to the night of no moon, the more his thoughts dwelled on his family. Now, he watched as Aya and Damaruhk stood side by side, saying their final goodbyes. Tomorrow morning, they would be exiled, and would be dead in the eyes of the Kresh. Only once they held proof of the Comartok's death, would they be able to return.

He had asked why that was but received no answer. Again, he was reminded that he was among them, but not one of them. After making her rounds about the camp, Aya and Damaruhk both, left the fire.

"It is strange to see one sitting alone, while everyone gathers to say goodbye." Canaruhk said, resting his haunches beside Vali.

"Aya needs this time. I am not one of the Kresh. No one will mourn me, come tomorrow."

"What of your people?" He asked.

"They believe I am already dead."

"That would make sense. Have you taken this time to think of them?"

"I have."

"That is good. Far too little time to dwell on things, once you reach the Comartok's island. Are you prepared?"

"As much as can be expected." Canaruhk nodded his head as he reached behind his back.

"I have a gift for you, Viking." He said, holding out a leather wrapped handle, ending in a stone axe, the blade the length of Vali's hand. Vali looked up to the Kresh, face torn in confusion as he accepted the gift.

"I thank you, Canaruhk. However, I do not understand."

"It was meant to be Karn's, before his exile." Cana said. "He was meant to face the Comartok, before your arrival. While we may not take you as one of the people, you hold a greater sense of what the Kresh are, than he. You carry no totem, no Kresh braid," he said, flicking the greatly ornamented necklace around his throat.

"I can give you this, as well as wish you luck," said the Kresh, patting Vali on the right shoulder. "Be sure that next we meet, it is as Rukh."

"I will, Canaruhk. Thank you." Pleased with himself, the old warrior rose and began to walk away.

"And Viking." Vali turned to face him. "Damaruhk wishes me to convey that she hopes you will keep her Aya safe."

"I will. At least as safe as one can, while facing a god of death." A small crease appeared on the man's lips, and he walked away. Vali turned the stone weapon over in his hand several times over. Examining its every edge and fine detail, he came upon a painted symbol, he did not recognize. Placing the bone handled axe in his pack, he rose and moved back toward his tent.

"Stranger." Vali's head turned suddenly at the sound. Standing behind him, the young boy whom he had helped escape from his captors on Fangor. The boy stared hard at Vali, holding a small, leather pack in his hands.

"Yes?"

"A gift." He growled. "For your exile. Pay my debt." He dropped the pack, before Vali could draw near. Scurrying away, he quickly vanished behind the curtain of darkness. Curiously lifting the pack, he pulled the draw cords sealing it and gasped at its contents.

"Healing earth." He whispered, holding the priceless, emerald speckled treasure in his hands. He remembered the substance well from his studies with his mother. Through time, skill and a great deal of patience, a shaper of the earth could compress spirits of earth and water within soil, granting it healing properties.

Once rubbed into an open wound and activated with a minor shaping, the spirits could begin repairing damage to one's body. The earth had to be exceptionally rich, to nourish the spirits, once they were woken from slumber.

His hands continued to shake at a gift, which could easily save lives. He knew even his mother could not have made as much as he now held in less than a month. He presumed, the Kresh held knowledge of a natural source.

Returning to his tent, he was certain to place the healing earth among his possessions, before turning in for the night. There had never been much in the way of possessions within the tent, but now it looked barren. Only his and Aya's packs and bedrolls remained. Setting his pack beside his matt, he lowered his body to the ground and closed his eyes.

He was unsure of how long he had been asleep, when Aya returned. He remained motionless, eyes slit open, so as not to reveal himself. The young Kresh stumbled into view, unlike her typically graceful self. It took Vali only a minute to realize she was intoxicated.

She dropped to her knees near to him and stared innocently. There was a brief flicker in her eyes, before she crawled away on all fours and fell to her bedroll. Still and silent as the grave, he remained, listening.

He thought he could hear a series of light sobs but knew neither how to act or what to say. Instead, he lay awake along with her, until at last, she fell silent. Watching her still form a moment longer, he returned to sleep.

The following morning came much too swiftly. Urged on by the Cana and Dama both, their place within the camp had been vacated, before the sun rose. Eerier still, as they followed the two Rukh to the edge of the camp, belongings on their backs, the Kresh stood in a line, staring.

He looked to his left. Aya had pulled her hair into a tight bun behind her head. She stared forward fiercely, her silver eyes glowing as her lightly freckled cheeks drew attention to them. She walked, stiff chinned, shoulders back and chest out the entire length of the camp. Not once, did her eyes stray from her course, and it occurred to Vali, should her eyes falter now, she may not have the strength or courage to carry her further.

Vali did the only thing he could think of beyond remaining silent. Gently, he brushed against her hand, fingers outstretched.

Without hesitation, he felt the strong grip of her small hand on his, pulsing gratefully. He gently squeezed her hand multiple times over, attempting to send his own confidence over to bolster hers.

They moved toward the docks, which Vali felt he had visited before. As had been the case with each of the camps set by the Dama clan, each of the Cana camps, were nearly identical. Numerous, strange, Kresh canoes were docked at the edge of one of the floating piers. Less than twenty paces from the canoes, Damaruhk stopped and turned to face them. Canaruhk and his braves continued forward, while Aya and Vali stopped.

There were tears in the elder's eyes. They were drawn back by a great deal of discipline and will, but Vali could see them glisten. He saw the same in Aya's, magnified by her silver eyes.

Releasing Aya's hand, Vali stepped aside as the two Kresh wrapped their arms around one another Aya did not cry as she whispered to her grandmother in Kresh. Looking forward, he looked at Canaruhk and his braves, who had each bowed their heads, waiting patiently.

The two released one another as Damaruhk closed Aya's hands over something. Only as the young woman glared at it, did her tears fall. With one final embrace, Aya slowly walked toward the pier.

"Stranger," the elder called to him with a broken tone. He turned to face her and saw the despairing look in her eyes.

"I swear upon my ancestors and to the gods of my people. I will." He said, bowing deeply. She nodded her head to him as he followed Aya.

"Are you both ready?" Canaruhk spoke to them in a low tone. Aya and Vali nodded. "This is yours," he continued, gesturing to a lone canoe. "My braves shall take you to Comartok's last location. After that, you will be on your own. Once you leave these docks, you are exiles. You may only return, once you hold proof of the Comartok's destruction."

Vali bowed his head to the Rukh, before he stepped into the canoe and sat his belongings within. As he lowered his bag to the bed of the canoe, he noticed several other bags within.

"Gifts from the Dama clan." Canaruhk said, walking away. He smiled, looking at the added traveling supplies. Staring back toward the Dama and his companion, he bowed humbly.

Aya hesitated. She stared back to her grandmother, who bowed her head. Going rigid a moment, she joined Vali, body shaking.

Hands trembling, she slowly reached for one of the two oars. Vali turned to face her, oar already in hand. She stared back at him and he felt for her.

"I can manage for a moment. Take your time." She nodded to him and looked back to see the others already leaving. He did not understand the words she whispered over the water, nor did he need to. The emotion she conveyed, translated into every language.

As soon as the Cana camp was out of sight, Aya spun about and grabbed the second oar. Vali looked back at her with concern as Aya continued to watch the scenery. Following the river out into the open sea, they moved northwest, running along the bank.

There was another island directly north of them, which was filled with greenery, birds and various signs of flourishing life. By the second day they floated at sea, it became clear to them, where they were heading would be drastically different.

"Viking," Aya called, prodding Vali gently in the back. Opening his eyes, he saw the all too familiar craggy maw of Fangor Isle. For Vali, that was where the similarities began to diminish. Of the proud, green forests he saw nothing but large clusters of uprooted trees and pilfered earth.

Their Kresh escorts turned sideways, halting their approach. They spoke to Aya in their native tongue, pointing to the desecrated island. Aya nodded once, then twice. As the men drew up their oars once more, they paddled passed.

"We are alone, now." Aya told him.

~ 382 ~

"What else did they say?" He asked, looking back as the braves drifted away.

"They said they saw Comartok, moving about the island at last half moon. We have to find trail and follow to Comartok's den."

"Tracking, I can manage. Making ourselves invisible before a god will prove difficult."

"I help there. We need come up with plan." Vali nodded his head as they drew near the shore.

"First, we need to find shelter. Someplace where we can easily move about the island and where the Comartok cannot find us." Aya thought a moment as the boat crashed against the shore.

"There are few places where I hid elders and younglings. We can move between them."

"I want to find the stronghold. If some of my people are still there, they might be able to help us. They may even be able to provide us with supplies." Aya stared at him worriedly, without saying a word. He looked at her oddly, though she only nodded, before stepping from the canoe. Pulling the canoe ashore, he and Aya tipped it over beneath a set of trees off from the beach.

Vali reached out with his senses, searching for any signs of life. He mostly found earth spirits, always resilient, but among them, he sensed faint traces of other spirits. Taking up their things, they looked to the trail of destruction and walked.

Chapter 27 – Return to Ulfrost

"How does it feel?" Brina asked Abel, as she stared off from the deck of the Valiant, nothing but open sea ahead of them. He turned his head toward her, staring at her back as she leaned against the port side railing.

"To be on my way home?" He asked, the thought of the upcoming battle weighing heavily upon him.

"To be back at sea." She asked. "Does it not warm your soul, even as the chill air nips at you? The smell of the sea. The feel of it coursing beneath your feet."

"I suppose so. I must admit I do miss my home something terrible. I have been away far too long." She turned her head back toward him, broad smile on her face.

"I wish to feel that way, as well." She sighed, turning her loving eyes back toward the Tyrda Fell. "However, for me, leaving Dumah behind still feels liberating."

"Give it a few weeks and that will change." Agni chimed in.

"Course, the love of home dissipates after a few days, and you will long to be at sea, again." Halla commented.

"It is quite intoxicating; would you not agree?" Brina asked. To this, Abel smiled.

"It is. No matter how much we dream of home, I agree that the sea calls us back. You could not be more right. However, my love of home is much stronger at present. I look forward to having a chance of growing bored with it." All eyes save Brina's, sank to the deck at the comment.

"Aye." Agni mumbled. "Once my sisters can play in the fields and my brothers may tend to their animals, then shall I return to the sea. Until then, there can be no other mistress."

"There will be bloodshed." Abel warned. "I know how you detest it." He could hear the large man's knuckles grinding as the leather of his axe haft groaned beneath his grip.

"I will bathe in rivers of crimson as I watch the life bleed from the eyes of those who threaten my home." He growled in response.

"Well," Halla started. "When you put it that way, I am glad to be on your side."

"As am I." Brina mumbled, eyes wide. "He certainly embraces the Viking spirit when pressed."

"Save your enthusiasm for when we arrive." Abel shouted to the rest of his crew. "We will reach Ulfrost by tomorrow morning. Keep that anger for then."

"Aye, captain." The large Viking trumpeted, before returning to his duties. As silence once again sounded between the crewmen, Thala looked to Abel.

"Captain?"

"Yes, Thala?"

"Why did Freyja stay on Falkest? I thought she aimed to return along with us?"

"High Chief Finna and War Chief Ulf, wished her to remain behind, I was told. I did not argue." Thala nodded her head, though still seemed unsatisfied by the answer.

"I see. It might be for the best. She is the next chief of Ulfrost."

"That does not sound foreboding at the least." Halla commented with apparent sarcasm.

"I agree with Brina." Abel said. "Only the Old Ones know what we have signed up for. Some of us may not make it back."

"Hopefully, Urs if anyone." Brina nearly spat. "I despise that man."

"I thought you had never met Grom or his brood."

"Grom, no. Not that my first impression was great. Urs, on the other hand, has made his presence known more than once. That is a man I would not sit alone with unarmed."

"I gathered the same impression." Abel replied. "I see the others just ahead. Everyone start resting in shifts. I want everyone ready for anything, come Ulfrost."

"Aye, Captain!" All hands called. Turning his gaze back upon the fleet behind them, he considered his own concerns for the mission. Glancing back toward the flags of the various clans, which had been roused to their cause, he dwelled on his feelings.

Several hours passed, before Abel roused any of the crew. Carefully stepping around Brina, he gently nudged Thala, who was curled beside one of the few baskets on board. She shifted slightly, before her eyes fluttered, listlessly.

"Has something happened?" She asked.

"No, not yet at least. I have a bad feeling about what we might face. If anything happens, I need you to make sure the High Chief is kept safe."

"I understand. Be certain you can carry out the order, yourself. We have lost enough friends already."

"Understood." He responded, as Thala took up his station at the helm.

"Rest well, Captain. I will wake you once we are closer." With a gentle nod, Abel moved to his typical perch at the back of the vessel. Lying his head upon the deck rail, he closed his eyes, and immediately fell asleep.

***

The radiant rays of dawn, striking him full in the face, Abel awoke. Looking about carefully, he could see friendly ships on either side of them. Of his crew, everyone, save he and Brina stood, ready for battle.

"How far out are we?" Abel asked Thala, who stood at the helm.

"A falcon dropped off a note from the High Chief, moments ago. We are regrouping on Boar's Head Island, just north of Ulfrost."

"Alright, then." He said, rising to his feet. "How far out?"

"Just over there, Captain." She answered, pointing across the deck off the starboard bow. Turning to face her direction, he saw the island, just off in the distance.

"It is nearly time, Vali. Soon, we will honor you upon the mounds of our forefathers and pray for you within the barrows." He sighed, bracing himself for the battle and council to come.

***

"Thank you everyone, for coming this far." Finna spoke, her face painted with the traditional blue, black and white paint of their ancestors. "Beyond that horizon." She said, pointing off from the southern edge of Boar's Head Island. "An enemy, unknown to our people, has sought pillage against us.

"For this, I have asked your aid. Rise up and fight beside us. Help us to show them how we, Vikings, children of the Old Gods, have claimed these lands. Let us show them the strength of our people, and the consequences for crossing us."

As the gathered hordes rallied, many others cried with oaths and vulgar threats aimed at the enemy of tomorrow. Carefully watching the proceedings unfold, Abel noticed Finna and Ulf, walking

~ 388 ~

amongst the crowd. Moving toward them, he passed his crew, who conversed with their shield brothers and sisters. Beyond them, he saw the leaders of his clan, stop before the sons of Grom, whose troops alone, stood in isolation from the other clans.

"I thank you nephews, for coming to our aid." Finna spoke, extending her arm in kinship.

"An unfortunate affair, I am afraid. It is shameful it has come to this." Urs spat, ignoring the greeting.

"Aye," Finna continued, dropping her arm. "Were we not fresh from the battle of Fangor, we might take the island ourselves."

"I meant our relation." Urs's cruel smile returned. "To think my brother and I share blood from such weak clansmen. Most shameful indeed." Abel growled in his throat, even as he watched Ulf and Finna stand unaffected, with saintly patience.

"Then I suppose you will not add further shame to your burden by allowing these shameful relations outshine you." Ulf said, staring eye to eye with the man. Both had their chests pressed out, their broad shoulders and thick, corded muscles, inflated.

"That is quite enough." Finna spoke with a kind tone in her voice. "Urs, I will not chide, nor ask different of you. It is my brother's will, which has brought you, Bram and your captains, here. It would both stain the honor of your house, and bring great shame to your father, were you to fail in your duty to him."

"Just be certain your clansmen stay out of our way." Urs sniffed. "If they can manage that much, I am certain this campaign will be over quickly." He turned away from Finna and the others, pressing beyond his own crew as he returned to his ships. Abel captured a glance at them; large with black stained wood, and emerald green sails.

"Please forgive my brother, High Chief." Bram spoke, dropping to a knee, his head bowed. "He has been aggrieved by a great deal of stress of late. No less than I can imagine you have."

"Bram of Falkest, the silver-tongued brother." Finna mused, staring down at the back of her nephew's head. "Help me return my people to their homes, and there will be nothing to forgive. I have long learned my pride means little to the wellbeing of those I lead. Try to remember that when you must compete with him for leadership."

"I will, High Chief. Thank you." He called, his gaze still lowered to the grounds beneath his feet.

"Go now, play the role of your brother's keeper. You have the thanks of your High Chief." Bram bowed his head once more, before rising to his feet and chased after Urs, the rest of their fleet in tow. As the sons of Grom disembarked, Kari walked onto the scene, stopping just before the chiefs and Abel.

"Always a most unpleasant boy, that nephew of yours." She commented, staring back toward the Falkest ships.

"He has his uses. As do we all. Bram may yet have a bright future, were his brother to face an unfortunate fate." Ulf growled. Kari raised her eyebrows at the two of them.

"Harsh attitude toward your Chief's blood relation." She commented.

"Were he not of her blood, I would have killed him, myself." The man growled as Abel approached.

"You are not going as well, are you High Chief?" He asked, the concern evident.

"No, my dear boy. Kari and I shall remain behind. We will tend to the wounded as they are sent back our way."

"I am relieved to hear it." He smiled. "What does my chief command?" Finna lifted her gaze. Already, did the ships of Falkest sail south.

"To your vessels, everyone." Ulf spoke, looking about to each and every captain nearby. "Pile their corpses high upon their ships and set them ablaze upon the unforgiving Tyrda Fell." A chorus of voices roared back at the war chief as every man and woman present, charged toward their designated vessels.

"Quickly, Abel, Thala!" Halla and the others called from a distance. "It is time to go home." With a confident grin, he charged toward his crew.

Abel and his crew, disembarked upon the northern shores of Ulfrost island. Quickly darting from the beach into the dense cover of the forest, they moved in formation, bows drawn, swords at the ready. Arrow carefully nocked in place, Abel glanced back over his shoulder, and nodded to Thala.

Charging forward, they split into two groups. Abel, Thala, and Brina, broke away from the rest of their crew as they sought the advantage of the hillslopes. Others from the varying commands rallied to their cause, flowed onto the island. Within seconds, the third battle for Ulfrost had begun.

"Abel, I can see the invaders." Halla cried, pointing down toward the outskirts of the village, where a large party of armored forms was forged. A large eruption of earth and shrieks of terror roared from the village center, drawing everyone's attention.

Flames illuminated the village center, as walls of earth rose several lengths into the air. The shouts of the enemy rattled against the earthen ramparts as they were drawn into conflict with the sons of Grom. From his vantage, Abel could see the maze as it rose from the ground, allowing his squads of trained killers to surround the enemy.

"A frightening power to be sure." Brina spoke, the only one yet able to voice an opinion. "I suppose I am glad he is on our side. I would hate to be the one trapped in their right now." Abel only nodded his head in agreement as he watched the attack, unfold.

The forces occupying Ulfrost, though startled from the initial attack, responded quickly and ably. Under the howled command of their leader, his troops formed up ranks within their confines, pressing back against Urs and his fighters. Halted by the outstretched blades of their foes, the Falkest troops slowed their advance.

The two forces collided with grotesque fury, both sides spilling gore out upon the long unstained beaches of Ulfrost. It would be some time before the innocence of the land could be reclaimed. Those at his side continued to repel the advance of the enemy, though the strength of their shapings and their arms began to diminish.

"Abel." Thala called. "The spirits are answering us. They lend their voices to the battle." Abel, on the defensive, focused his senses, his consciousness probing out for the thing Thala sensed.

In answer to the unnatural forces being called to battle upon the land, the peaceful tides of Ulfrost battered the shore with a vengeance. Sensing the strength of old spirits, called from the deep emerald waters of the Tyrda Fell, Abel and Thala reached out for bolstering.

Their senses lashed out at those same forces and they answered. A large wave crashed to the shore, sending a spray of water down upon those locked in the tussle. Filtered through the trenches dug by Urs and his warriors, the water quickly overtook the forces within.

Seeing the spray flooding in, Urs raised a platform within, which encased his troops in a dome. A gale of water surged forward quickly, striking their undefended foes from their feet. As the wave receded, Urs and his men rose to their feet and finished the battle.

A cheer rang out among their troops, above and below. The warriors of Falkest, quickly advanced, allowing those defending the hill to take their first step forward. Shields and arms locked as one, as the two fronts collided time and again. The hills, drenched by the rain however, further aided the push by Abel's front.

Quickly overwhelming their enemy, they descended the hill with a renewed vengeance. Working their way to the base of the hill, he noticed the flags of Falkest on the tunics and armor of those by his side. Urs was nowhere among them.

"Where is Urs?" Abel roared over the surging chaos around them. Whirling about, axes in both hands, he knocked away an opponent's weapon as he drove his second attack, through the man's collarbone. With a sickening crunch and a dying cry, the fighter before him crumpled.

"Last I saw, they were watching the shoreline." Halla called back, releasing one arrow after another, slowing the advance of the enemy on their mound.

"Agni! Sound the horn! We need to finish the assault!" Abel called, swiping the leg out from one adversary, while plunging his axe into the belly of another. The carnage continued, Thala running lengths between the swarm of enemies and her crewmates.

Behind them, the deep bellow of Agni's war horn, tore into the night. A rallying cry swooped over the hilltop, pouring down over those who defended their ill gained conquest. Knocking another from the fight, blood spraying in a geyser across his face, Abel roared with defiance as more shield bearers roused to his side.

"Well done, lad." Bjarke called, stopping near to the young captain. Catching an axe on the head of his shield, he bellowed with laughter as he kicked his attacker down onto his fellows. "The island is nearly ours. One more push and the invaders will flee to their boats."

"Abel!" Thala yelled as she rushed across the breach in the wall, her small, agile form passing between her foes with ease. One after another, they fell beneath the strokes of her blade. "Abel, Urs' crew has returned to their ships."

"What?" He called, slashing the hamstrings of a final opponent, who tumbled over the side of the slope. He nearly froze as he heard the call of another war horn, not belonging to he, nor those fighting beside him.

In his distraction, an ally to his right, crumpled beneath an opponent's axe. Falling lifelessly to the ground, Abel growled spitefully as he lashed out again. Looking out beyond the battlefield, he could see numerous ships, landing upon the southern shore.

"Thala, what is that symbol upon their flags?" He yelled, continuing to battle tooth and nail, for every inch of soil. The young woman, swiped the legs from another, before leaping from harm's reach.

"I see only dark sails. No insignia." She yelled back, deflecting another blow.

As the chaos at the base of the hill began to thin, they were each granted a better view of the island's latest arrivals. Each wore the skin of an animal, in place of clothing and armor. Their arms and hands were wrapped in furs, bound by strips of leather. They charged toward the top of the hill swiftly, daggers and axes in each hand.

"They are with us!" The Vikings howled excitedly, slamming their weapons to their shields as the latecomers savaged the enemy from their flank. Using dagger, axe and claw, the beast cloaked, wild men moved swiftly, shredding those caught in between.

"Abel, there is another ship moving to the north." Halla called, dashing between the fallen, gathering more arrows. "They are heading for the High Chief." An eruption of earth launched spears of stone into the enemy ranks. Turning his head toward the trail left by the shaping, he saw Bram was still among them.

"Where has your brother gotten to?" Abel yelled, fighting his way nearer to the young warrior.

"I am not certain." Bram howled against the panicked wave of invaders flooding their ranks. "Last I knew, he was below, corralling the enemy." Another surge of earthen spears, erupted, dividing their foes further. Bram however, stumbled. Quickly covering the man, Abel held the line.

"Thank you." The young man panted, slowly rising to his feet. "It is difficult to perform such shapings away from my home. I can still fight." He gripped the hilt of his sword and pressed himself to his feet.

"Abel!" Brina yelled. Quickly scanning the field, he found her further down the village path, directing the flames of the burning buildings toward her foes. "They are losing ground. Push forward while you still can." She continued to funnel the flames, long whips of red and orange light slashing at those in her path.

"Quickly, everyone! We have to go after the High Chief!" Abel cried out, sprinting back toward the direction of the boat. As he tore through the familiar forest trails, he was quickly joined by the rest of his crew. As they reached the northern shores of the island, they threw their bodies at the side of the vessel and pressed it from the sands.

Scuttling on board, Haldr, Agni, Brina and Halla, all reached for the oars as Thala unbound the sails. Manning the helm, Abel pulled against the steering rudder, and quickly turned them to face Boar's Head Island. Before them, they could see the island's outline, but nothing more.

Thala stood behind the sails, pressing currents of wind into them the best she could. Coupled with the efforts of their four rowers, the Valiant quickly gained speed as it soared for their destination. Taking one hand from the oar, Abel pressed the water to offer them aid, the best he could.

"Look! A fire!" Brina yelled, pointing ahead of them toward Boar's Head Island.

"Keep rowing!" He yelled, trying himself for more strength to fuel his shaping. Their hearts all thundered within their chests. The enemy ship grew nearer as they loomed in closer. "The moment we reach the shore, have your weapons ready. There is no telling what we are about to face."

Everyone nodded, in silent agreement, the tension on board the Valiant, palpable enough to be used as a weapon on its own. They continued to row, until the boat came to a sudden and violent halt upon the shore. Their bodies forced forward by the sudden halt in movement, the momentum carried them to their feet, weapons already trained.

They charged, paying no heed to the noise they made. It hardly mattered with the noise of the battle taking place ahead. Not even one hundred paces off from the shore, they could see the evidence of a battle between powerful shapers.

"We have to hurry!" Abel called back. As the words left his lips, Thala sped passed him, blade already drawn. Brina and the others, kept pace astride him, while Agni carried the rear.

Up above them on the hill, they heard Ulf roar with rage as the earth rattled angrily. Below them, at the base of the hill, Abel came upon one of many dead men, wrapped in animal furs. He glanced at them, briefly, confused as to their meaning.

"I thought they were on our side?" He gasped as he looked above.

"There can be more than two sides to a conflict." Thala called back, stopping a few paces ahead of them, examining another body. "We can learn the details, later. We have company." She leapt backwards as another of the beast clad men, lunged toward her, swinging a clawed gauntlet at her.

Skillfully, she swatted the weapon away with her sword, and dodged to the side as the second claw swung. Abel moving to aid her, narrowly avoided the blow from an attacker, leaping from above. He rolled away, quickly catching his feet and parried another blow.

"They are in the trees!" He called. Brina, Halla, Haldr and Agni, each turning their heads skyward, warded off the oncoming ambush. The massive man, two handed axe in hand, roared with rage as he struck out against his enemy.

"They are wood shapers!" Halla called, stumbling over a root, which had wrapped its way around her ankle. She cried out in pain as the limb twisted and she fell to the ground. Bow dropping from her hand, she quickly withdrew her dagger as a man in a wolf pelt lunged at her.

Haldr, moved quickly to his sister's aid. Brina, locking blades with one opponent, and eyeing an encroaching one, sighed with agitation. Shoving back angrily against her attacker, she leapt back, and reached into the pouch at her side.

"Step away from the trees!" She cried, pulling a fistful of small pellets from the leather pouch. Throwing the pebbles at her attacker, they crackled and popped as they struck against he, and his surroundings, producing heat.

Brina, reaching out to the aroused spirits released from within, grasped onto them. Both the attacker she had repelled and his partner to the right, screamed in agony as the pelts on their backs, succumbed to the heat and ignited. With a cry of anger and exertion, Brina wrenched the hungry spirits from her attackers, flinging them toward the next available food source.

Another of the attackers cried out, as his leg caught fire, which quickly spread through the leaves and sticks upon the ground. In the distraction, Halla plunged her dagger into the foot of the man before her. Quickly withdrawing the blade, she stabbed again as the man fell. The blade piercing his temple with a sickening 'snikt!'

"Help the High Chief!" Brina yelled, throwing the flames again, creating a ring of fire between Abel, Thala and the beast clad assassins. "We can handle the rest."

"Fight bravely, my friends!" Abel yelled, turning away and charging toward the hills, Thala already half way up. Reaching the top of the hill, he first saw the ruined earth, where spears had torn their way skyward. Second, he saw the battle up ahead, working its way toward the cover of the trees.

"Hurry, Thala! It looks as though they need help!" They charged, weapons at the ready. They could hear Ulf's enraged shouts from the tree line as more pillars of earth collided into one another.

Thala reached the battle before Abel. He could hear her cry with anger as the winds roared around her. Closing the distance between them, he realized why.

Urs stood alongside no fewer than a dozen men. Among them, more of the beast cloaked men, battled against the war chief, his bride and Kari. Ulf and Finna fought back against them, using a variety of earth shapings to repel and defend against their attackers.

One axe held to his side, Abel's pace slowed slightly as he forced the minor wind shaping he could muster down to his weapon.

Guided by the tiny spirits he could call to it, he threw the axe, which quickly closed the distance between he and those who attacked his liege.

One of the men, clad in the furs of a wolf, fell to the ground, the blade of the axe buried deep between his shoulder blades. As the others turned to intercept them, Thala sprang from the shadows. With her shrine maiden's blade, she rent the flesh from their bodies, cutting through armor, skin and bone.

As three of the warriors fell to the ground, bits of their bodies, never meant to see the light of day spilled out between their feet. Their pained howls drew the attention of several more attackers as the agile woman vanished into the shadows, again. Only Abel stood in the scope of their vision, and it was he whom they charged.

Quickly drawing a long hunting knife from his boot, he stood at the ready for the four men who broke away from the main fight. As he braced himself, still crouched over from his thrown axe, he gently bumped the canteen resting on his lower back. Smile on his face, he awaited his attackers, tightly gripping the handles of his weapons.

As they drew near, he flung the dagger, which was deflected lazily by its intended target. With his free hand, however, he grabbed hold of the canteen. Pulling the cork with his teeth, he flung its contents toward the two men.

Dropping the canteen, he made a connection with the spirits within. Contorting his empty hand into a three raked claw, he swung his arm sideways. The water responded.

The water spread out into a thin streak, biting into the flesh of one of the two men, who howled with pain. Whirling about, he backhanded, swirling the water back toward the second of the four. The water cut a deep trench into the man's right shoulder.

The two lay on the ground, moaning in pain as their fellows charged. Attempting to swing once more, he found his supply of water depleted. Growling to himself, he ran toward his dagger, which lie several paces ahead.

One of the two men, flinging his arm across his body, sent a gust of strong wind toward Abel. Staggered by the sudden burst, he stumbled instead of rolled, falling short of his weapon. Scrambling to his feet, his lone axe to defend himself, he jumped back.

From out of the shadows, Thala leapt forward, swinging her sword wildly. Unseen, until it was far too late, both men fell, having received crippling wounds to their hamstrings. Staring down at her foes, she struck down at them with her blade, mercilessly, slashing the vertebrae at the base of each's neck.

"Remind me not to get on your bad side. Ever." Abel grimaced in horror as he stared at the two maimed and mortally wounded men. She regarded him with her cold, sinister eyes, and nodded.

"They should not have attacked us, were their desire mercy. The chiefs need our help." She renewed her charge as Abel gathered his belongings and followed.

Kari was in the background, dragging a bloodied Finna away from the two men. Several bodies lay between the two groups, each one of Urs's men. As Urs stepped closer to Kari, Ulf stopped in front of him, chest puffed out, face gleaming with rage.

"You damned traitor!" Ulf bellowed, sending another cluster of earthen spears toward Urs. Cruel smile still in place, the younger man swept his arm sideways, creating a moving barrier, which collapsed Ulf's attack.

"You really should have stayed behind." He laughed, staring at the weary war chief, whose brow was decorated with beads of sweat. "I only intended on killing the High Chief."

"I will not let you!" Ulf roared, drawing himself to his full height. Behind him, Kari was clinging to Finna's weak form. She herself, bled heavily, from a wound she received to the shoulder. Still, ignoring her own wounds, she tended to the chief's bloodied torso.

"You have no chance of stopping me." Urs chuckled, casually walking forward. Stepping over the bodies of his fallen men, he glanced back over his shoulder as Abel and Thala drew near.

"We made it in time." Abel said, stopping behind Urs. "How dare you betray us?"

"Betray you?" Urs scoffed, staring back at them with no small amount of disgust in his eyes. "You, who could not protect your home. Who are slowly losing your shaping. You who are too weak to proudly carry the Viking name. Your lot are nothing but filth.

"We will sail north and crush the remains of the Kresh. Their blood will serve as my offering to the Old Gods. Then, I will lead our people beyond the fog, so we might become Vikings, once more."

"You will find nothing beyond the wall of fog, Urs." Abel growled. "I have seen it."

"You lie." He seethed, staring at him. "I have seen the old maps. My grandfather told me stories of the world beyond. That fool Gram was a coward, who wished our people to remain tethered to these lands. I will be the one to reclaim it from those beyond the fog. Only then, can our people reclaim their destiny."

"Your destiny is to die, boy!" Ulf yelled, pounding both fists into the ground. Urs turned his gaze back toward his older opponent, smile on his face.

"Not before you, old man." He laughed, backhanding his fist across the rising stones, and thrusting his own fist forward. Abel and Thala both took flight at that moment, weapons drawn even as Ulf was thrown backwards.

"You blighted cur!" Abel yelled, lunging toward Urs, Thala beside him.

"You need to learn your place." Urs yelled, stepping to the side. Using his earth infused strength, he pulled back his arm and struck Thala to the side. Landing with a hard 'thud,' she rolled and skidded to a stop. Abel narrowly avoided the follow up strike and swung with his axe.

Again, moving to the side, Urs moved to strike again. Abel, smirking, lifted his arms to block the blow. His arms screamed with pain, as the attack connected. Landing on his back side, he rolled over backwards, digging in his toes as he turned about.

"Do you forget I have sparred with Vali? Next to him, your shapings are on the level of a child." Abel smiled at the appearance of anger on his opponent's face.

"Yes, a shame he died on Fangor." Urs growled. "I have long been looking forward to proving myself against him. I suppose I will have to take satisfaction in killing his sparring partner." Stepping forward, Urs continued to draw strength from the earth around him.

His movements slowed as he drew from the earth. Abel, understood this better than most, though he grimaced at his lack of a source of water. Small tremors rumbled the ground at Urs's feet. Abel continued to watch his opponent carefully, while Thala rose slowly to her feet.

"It is a shame. Now, I suppose the next High Chief will still not be you." Abel quickly made eye contact with Thala, who crept toward Kari and Finna.

"Without Finna in the way, my father shall become the next High Chief. Who, I wonder, might supplant him, should something happen?"

"Hmm. Not sure. Probably Freyja." The tremors in the ground only grew stronger as Urs neared. Abel held his ground, unwilling to take a step back, while keeping his eyes off from the retreating clansmen. As though sensing his intention, Urs stopped.

"You cannot flee from me, Finna." He growled, slowly turning to look back over his shoulder. "I can sense your movements through the earth. There is nowhere you can hide from me, so long as we touch the same earth." He lifted up his hand, causing the spirits of the earth to spring to life.

"Thala, watch out!" Abel called, as the spears slowly made their way toward the three who were fleeing. Taking his opportunity to charge, Abel ran straight for Urs exposed back, knife and axe ready.

Throwing the dagger, Urs quickly turned avoiding a fatal strike, though he took the blade in the right shoulder. He grimaced angrily, though maintained his hold on the shaping with his left hand. Abel lunged forward, preparing a follow up strike as another pillar of earth rose from the ground. Quickly backing away from the jagged spike, Abel stood firm, awaiting another opening.

"I believe you have underestimated me, boy." Ulf, having risen to his feet growled. With a wave of his hand, he shattered the trailing spears. Again, Urs yelled with anger as he watched Finna, Kari and Thala disappear into the night.

"No matter." Urs growled. "Finna is near death. Her frail body will not hold out for long. Even should she survive, she would be a fool to resurface and challenge Falkest, now." Pulling the dagger from his shoulder, he turned his body, so he could watch both of his opponents simultaneously.

"Abel." Ulf said, breathing laboriously. "With Vali gone, I need you to rouse the others. Tell Jerold what happened here. Do not let our deaths be in vain."

"Ulf." Abel yelled back. "We are both getting out of here. No one else is going to die."

"There is no shame in this death, boy." Ulf stated.

"I believe you have both forgotten I am here." Urs laughed. "Neither of you are leaving alive." Stomping on the ground, a shockwave traveled toward Ulf. At the same time, Urs sprang for Abel, who charged at him.

Ulf growled in anger as he hobbled out of the way of the attack, his left leg trailing behind him. One arm hung at his side, bleeding heavily. Abel however, swung his axe toward Urs, who smiled.

Catching the edge of Abel's axe on the blade of his pilfered dagger, Urs shoved the smaller Viking back with earth infused strength. Staggering back, unable to hold his balance against the man, he raised his arms to his defense to late. Howling in pain as he felt the tip of the dagger slicing through the flesh on the left side of his face, Abel tipped backward.

He fell to the ground, blinded by pain as the world erupted with noise around him. Something pressed him away, though he could not see what through the pain and red curtain covering his face. He could hear the battle growing ever more distant, the sounds of Urs's and Ulf's scuffle fading away.

"Ulf!" He howled deliriously, attempting to roll, even as the earth carried him away. "Ulf!" Eventually, he came to a halt. Two pairs of hands gripped him beneath the arms and lifted him to his feet.

"We have to go back!" Abel continued to howl. "Stop! We have to go back!"

"We cannot go back, Abel." He heard Brina call softly. He could feel himself being lifted into the air, resting upon something solid and unforgiving.

"I am not losing another captain." He could hear Agni from beneath him.

"Ulf needs us." Abel continued to complain.

"Abel." Brina sobbed. "Ulf is already gone."

Chapter 28 – Terror of the Old World

Vali awoke with a start, the winds on the island howling through the tunnels of the partially submerged watchtower. Thunder cracked, the sound distorted from the waterfall at the entrance. He turned himself about and found Aya's empty bedroll.

Rising from his own bed, he looked about the inside of the small cave Aya had led him to. He had been amused when she had brought him to the very same cave Asta had led them to only a short while ago. His companion nowhere to be seen, Vali stepped over toward the pool at the back of the cave.

The level of the water had dropped slightly in the month or so since his last visit and now only rose to just above his navel. Wading his way through, he stepped up into the old stone steps of the tower. A periodic flash of lightning illuminated his climb.

The howling of the wind only grew louder as he climbed higher. Reaching the top of the steps he could smell the rainwater. Aya stood beneath the lattice, leaning at the edge of the oncoming rain.

"The Comartok is still here," she whispered as he drew near. Looking out, he eyed a massive form atop one of the many mountain caps. It sat back on its haunches, head to the sky. He caught the howling of the wind once more and realized then that it was the great wolf.

Lightning pierced the sky, granting them both a clear look at what they faced. He stepped forward, walking out into the chill rain. He glared at the beast, which had once assumed the guise of a man. He imagined it too stared back at him, angry for its missing eye.

"Come back inside, Viking." Aya called. "You will be no use against the Comartok, ill. We both have a long day, tomorrow." He looked back over his shoulder and nodded, though he did not move away.

"Why do you still insist on calling me, Viking?" He said, finally relenting and moving to her.

"You are enemy to my people. We do not give names to our enemies. I thought this was obvious."

"We are both exiles, now. Surely, it will be alright to call me by name." She eyed him as she followed, returning to shelter.

"I like, Viking best. I give you a suitable Kresh name, later." She replied, turning away from him without a second thought. Moving below, they waded back through the flooded hallway and crowded the fire. Tired as they were, Vali did not even flinch when Aya disrobed, though she wrapped herself in the tharn pelt. Sitting in nothing but his breech cloth, he shivered.

"Come here, Viking." Aya said, folding her right arm over her chest as she extended her left. "No good to anyone if you catch walking death." She folded her legs over, covering the expanse between, while exposing the side of her well-toned thigh, to the hip.

Vali nodded his head, his body already shivering from the cold. Grabbing his bedroll, he laid it beside his traveling companion and sat with her. She wrapped her arm around him sharing her feverish warmth with him.

Instinctively, he wrapped his right arm around her waist and pulled the pelt tightly around them with his left. The wind, the Comartok, or possibly both, howled outside as the two shivered for warmth. They sat with their legs crossing over one another, watching their frosty breath.

"We should probably stay close tonight." Vali suggested, looking away from Aya.

"That is fine," she said, shifting herself sideways, legs straddling Vali's right thigh. "I am tired. Comartok not find us here. Safe to sleep." She tugged against the pelt as she moved to lay her body down. He allowed himself to fall beside her and only squirmed slightly as she pressed the backside of her tiny frame to his front.

He felt her burning skin against him as her legs ran between his own. She planted her feet over his and pulled his arms around herself as she wrapped her own around her chest. He focused his thoughts on home, his mother, the nearby rock; anything other than the naked woman in his arms.

"Does this bother you, Viking?" She asked, shifting against him so that her posterior pressed against that which he had attempted to prevent.

"I apologize," he gasped apologetically, turning himself slightly to keep from pressing against her in particular areas.

"I do not mind," she said, pressing tighter against him. "It cannot be helped. We both ignore it." He was grateful to her for that. His thoughts drifted back to those that he missed, and then, sleep.

They separated awkwardly come morning, neither of them making any mention of the night before. Quickly gathering up their things, they moved outside. The morning air was still chilly, the dew, partially froze.

They moved about the shattered hillsides, weaving their way through the fallen forest. Several of the trees bore claw marks left by massive paws and bite marks from monstrous jaws. They kept low the entire day, avoiding the cliffs as much as possible as they went. By the end of the day, Fangor Stronghold came into sight.

The once proud fortress was heavily battered since his last visit one month ago. The stone walls had finally succumbed to the ravages of time and ruin in most areas. Again, he sensed none but the trembling spirits of the earth and a few scattered rogues. A series of howls in the distance alerted them to nearby danger.

"We need to hide." He whispered urgently to Aya. She nodded, turning back and looked about.

"Follow me, Viking," she called as she ran deeper into the shattered woodlands. Vali followed directly behind her, batting away loose branches with the back of his hand. He could hear the wolves howling once more and realized they were being followed.

"Aya, they are tracking us." He called back to her.

"Not possible. They are north of us. Upwind."

"I am telling you they are chasing us."

"They are not normal wolves." The earthen formed beasts from his last visit leapt to mind. He chanced a look back over his shoulder and realized that Aya was right.

"We need to cross water." He called again. Aya glanced back at him, confusion on her face.

"Why?"

"I will explain, later. Just run for flowing water," he called ahead. Aya's destination shifted. She leapt over a downed tree and renewed her flight downhill.

Vali was not as quick as Aya was, nor half as agile. She tipped and hopped over, through, above and around various wooden forms, while Vali did his best to defend himself as he charged through.

"Make too much noise!" She called back, jumping to a lower slope and slid partially down its face.

Vali's knees buckled as he landed, his body bereft of the enchantments he maintained previously, and fell. Rolling down the side of the hill, he came to a stop and quickly regained his footing.

"Viking, jump!" He heard the woman cry from below. On faith alone, he kicked off from the ground and found nothing beneath him.

He yelled a number of curses as his arms and legs flailed wildly in the air. Aya clung to the side of the opposing earthen wall, looking back over her shoulder, fearfully. He heard a snarl, a snap and a whine from behind as he flew beside his companion, landing painfully against the edge of the ravine.

"I have you, Viking." She spoke lightly as Vali dug his fingers into the earth. Looking backwards, he eyed the likeness of seven wolves where he had been. They snarled hungrily at them, through doll's eyes, which were plastered to clay figures.

"Come, Viking. Get to higher ground." Aya said, tugging on his collar as she scaled the cliff edge. Vali looked down to the stream below, before lifting his gaze to the wolves, whom circled back and forth along the edge. Climbing to the top of the ledge, Aya and Vali peered back at the wolves. They were gone.

Carefully examining their surroundings, Vali recognized the familiar trail, which he had first encountered Aya upon. Turning his gaze down the path, his eyes found a large clearing. Gently tapping Aya, he pointed with a motion of his head and walked.

He stopped several paces ahead of the overlook where he had witnessed a cave troll attacking his companion. Attempting to steer away from the sight, he stopped as Aya pursued the landing. Peering down below, he watched as the woman's petite body trembled.

"My fault they die." He could hear her sniffle, her empty left hand reaching across her chest, grasping onto her right arm. She rocked lightly, while continuing to stare.

"Do not do that to yourself, Aya." Vali said softly. "There was no way you could have known."

"No matter. My responsibility. My fault. Supposed to protect. Failed." He reached out for her shoulder, wanting to offer her comfort. He hesitated, his hand vibrating half its length from her shoulder blades. Closing and reopening his fist, he placed his hand on her upper back and squeezed lightly.

"Let's go, Aya. The Comartok could easily attack at any moment." He regretted his lack of words. However, Aya turned her gaze away from the site of such a horrible tragedy and nodding her head, led the way forward.

Soon after, they reached another clearing which overlooked the valley where they had met the second time. Looking further beyond the lower vale, he saw Fangor fortress in ruins. Stunned to silence as they looked upon the once proud fortress, they could hear the howling of the clay wolves, once more.

"We need move." Aya commanded, pressing against Vali's chest. "Wolves find us soon."

"Your right. Hurry, let's head back to water." He called as they charged straight toward the river, only turning away from it once they were again safe in the waterfall cave.

"We may need to travel by boat." He suggested that night, back in their cave. "It will take longer, but I worry those things are tracking us through the earth."

"Is that possible?" She asked.

"Not only possible. For a skilled shaper, it would be easy."

"Alright, one travels by boat. What then?"

"If the Comartok is connected to the wolves, it should already know where we are. We can use that to our advantage."

"Move Comartok where we want." She concluded, smiling. "Where do we go?" Vali looked to the far southeastern edge of the island, where he and his crew had escaped through a winding channel.

"Over there. We can confine him on the peak. It is densely packed with old, deep rooted trees. It is also high up and surrounded by water. We may have an advantage if we can lure it into a trap."

~ 410 ~

"When do we spring the trap?" Vali looked up to the sky, which was still cloudy from the night before. Far in the distance, near the edge of his vision, he saw a dark curtain.

"During the next rainstorm. There are storm clouds high above. A shaper of the earth, should have difficulty performing under a torrent. That might serve as our last chance. It has already lost one eye. If it cannot track us, we will be able to take it by surprise."

"But first, we need the boat," she said, looking back in the direction of the beach.

"Can you steer through the channel?" He asked.

"Does not matter," she said confidently, handing off some of her things.

"Why?" He asked, staring at the added bundle in his arms.

"You cannot outrun the wolves." He opened his mouth to retort, but only managed to leave it agape.

"We can think of another way." He managed to blurt out as Aya began to move away from him.

"There is no other way, Viking." She spoke gruffly. "We try your plan."

"It is a bad idea." She raised an eyebrow at him as he paced back and forth.

"You do not believe I can do this?" She asked. Her question, more challenge than curiosity.

"No, it is not like that. I know that you can. You have a better chance of making it than I do."

"Then it is decided. I will go, and you take the canoe."

"No."

"Why not?"

"I cannot put you in danger such as that." He blurted out without any prior knowledge of the thought existing. He nearly stopped himself, until the anxiety and frustration accumulated over the past several weeks carried him onward. "I promised Damaruhk I would keep you safe." Aya's curious glance turned sour.

"Is that your reason? Do not bother yourself. I will be fine." She spoke angrily and stormed away from him. Vali froze helplessly in place, trying to think of any saving grace. His muse eluded him.

"Is there anything..."

"No!" She grouched without looking back. Vali's shoulders drooped. and his head hung as he followed.

They remained wary of their surroundings at all times as they made their way back to the cave, following the river. Returning to their camp for the evening, Vali sat atop the ruined tower, staring toward the peak where he had sighted his quarry.

As it had the night before, the massive beast strolled into Vali's view with the rising moon. Leaning back on its haunches, its maw erupted with an explosive yowl. The call made his flesh crawl.

He stared at the creature, breath abated. The call traveled to lands he could not see, and then, there was silence. Nearly inaudible in comparison to the Comartok, a series of higher pitched, hollow toned howls, answered.

"Do you believe it is truly a God?" Aya asked him.

"No," he answered confidently.

"Why not?" She asked, sitting beside him, legs folded.

"It was once a man," he answered, without peeling his eyes from the beast. "He was one of seven, who attacked my people at the fortress. I managed to wound him badly, when I could still shape the elements. I forced him to assume this form." Aya stared thoughtfully at the monster.

"I believe it is the Comartok." She said. "I believe you, as well." To this, Vali shifted his gaze.

"Then what exactly do you believe?"

"I believe this creature arrived a person, and then became a beast."

"Arrived from where?" Vali asked.

"Beyond the fog is where the God's dwell." She said. "I am not afraid, though." He scrunched his face as he stared at her.

"You believe we aim to kill a god and that does not bother you?"

"No," she said bluntly, listening to and watching the nighttime ambience. Long gone, were the sounds of crickets and nighttime predators. The island was essentially dead. The only sounds they heard in the long night were the weather and those made by the Comartok as it searched for their flesh.

"How does that not bother you? I know that it is no god and I am worried about us facing it."

"You say you cut out its eye. You wounded it. You forced it to shed false face. You also from outside of fog."

"Aya, I am not a higher being."

"Does not matter. You walked among them. You are different." He shook his head, argumentatively as she spoke.

"Aya, that thing is no more a god than I am. It is a shaper, different from any other I have encountered, but one in the same. I wounded it, because like me, like you, it is comprised of flesh and blood."

"I disagree, Viking, but I no argue. If you must be convinced, be it on your terms."

"All the same," he continued. "We will need to act on our plan, come morning."

"Then it wise to rest. We begin early." She advised, descending the stairwell.

Before the sun had risen, they were on the move. Vali carefully steered his canoe through the trees, placing them both on alert. She drew her glaive as Vali took up his bow. Readying an arrow to his bowstring, he waited for the beasts to show themselves.

Aya glanced back over her shoulder as she fled. Not far behind, three clay wolves bounded through the clearing, snarling and snapping as they ran. They moved quickly for earth constructs, almost too quickly, judging from his own experience. They, however, were not too fast for his bow.

Breathing normally, he trained his eye on his target, lifted his weapon, and pulled back on the string in a single, fluid motion. As he exhaled, he released his arrow and watched the missile strike its target in the right flank.

As its back-right leg crumbled, the beast toppled, shattering as it struck the ground. He drew up a second arrow as Aya charged head first through a second cropping of trees. He released his grip on the arrow, which struck the out reaching jaws of a second clay beast.

The creature shattered as it fell to the earth, leaving a trail of dust behind it. Vali reached behind his back for a third arrow as the final wolf leapt forward. Aya, with a graceful half turn, slashed her weapon wide, severing the constructs head.

Her flight uninterrupted, she sped onward as Vali sat his bow down, and took up the oar. Aya veered away from him, returning to the cover of the wood. The river arched away, taking him further from her direction.

The river itself flowed through the mass of dead trees, which crisscrossed overhead, blocking his view of the sky. Unable to determine his direction, he drew up his sword and allowed the current to take him. Another set of howls ran amok through the trees.

Their voice, distorted and omnipresent, set him on edge. He slowly shifted about, causing the canoe to rock gently away from the bank.

"Viking!" Aya called, darting into sight, again. He glanced off the left side of his vessel as she darted toward the river, another five clay constructs behind her. Sheathing his sword, he reached for his bow once more as Aya leapt into the air.

Grasping onto a low hanging branch, she swung her body and launched herself into the air. He traced her movement as she soared overhead. Landing halfway between he and the bank, she waded to the opposite side and climbed out.

He could hear the heavy paws digging into the earth as the creatures attempted to stop abruptly. Two of the beasts fell sideways, shattering one another as they kicked and flailed about. The remaining three, each stopped at the water's edge, staring at Aya, but overlooking Vali entirely.

"Hey!" He yelled, waving his arms as he floated by. The wolves paid him no mind, focused solely on the woman touching the earth. "They really are dependent on the soil." He spoke aloud, having no use for silence.

The remaining wolves stared hungrily at the young woman, who continued to flee down the bank. Even after he had drifted passed, he remained transfixed on them. At long last, they melted back into the earth. Shaking a curious thought from his mind, he lowered his weapon and paddled on.

Aya awaited him at the next bend, exhaustion apparent on her face. She sat, crouched over the roots of an old tree, watching the landscape. Using his oar to steer himself aground, he placed one foot down on the bank.

"Let's switch out for a while." He suggested. "You're only going to wear yourself down, at this pace." She looked up at him with a grateful yet resolved expression.

"I go further. I need you..." She was interrupted by the howling of the wolves, which Vali could tell were on their side of the river.

"Quickly Aya. Get on." Vali urged, holding out his hand. The Kresh however, did not take it. Looking up to the high ground, which served as their destination, she looked back, drew in a deep breath, and ran.

Vali growled with frustration, reaching for his bow. Pulling his first arrow, he set it to his string and drew back. A split second after, a rustle in the high grass alerted him to his enemy's position.

He released his grip on the missile as the first of the beasts came into sight. Shot in the ribs, the lifeless terror toppled. Vali, already poised for a second shot, pulled back on his bowstring as another dozen or more appeared.

He hesitated briefly, taken by surprise. Remembering the woman, they pursued, he quickly shook himself of doubt and fired indiscriminately. One after another, the beasts fell, until he reached back and felt the fletchings of his final arrow.

Several wolves had already sped passed, their eyes passing over him entirely. Sliding his bow back into his quiver, he did the only thing that came to mind. He drew his sword and leapt for the bank. The precise moment his hand burrowed into the malleable silt of the riverbed, two of the remaining eight sopped. Slowly, they turned to face him, yipping angrily as he thought of his friend.

"Please, spirits of the earth, help bring them to me." He pleaded, thrusting the entirety of his left hand into the dirt. With a loud howl, four more wolves spun to face him and raced for their fellows. Cautiously, he flicked his weapon through a number of steady swings.

He stared down his enemy as they closed in on him. Body still partially submerged in the water, he waited for the beasts to draw near. As predicted, they stopped just before the water's edge and glared at him.

"You cannot cross the water, can you?" He said, smiling confidently. "You can pass beneath the river, but that is all. I have found your weakness, shaper." He swiped his sword horizontally in the air, the blade passing through the creature as though it were no more substantial than the water he knelt in.

The remaining five quickly backed away, snarling at him. Vali himself, stared at the weapon in his hand and smiled. Turning his gaze back to his attackers, he swung again.

"Something wrong with iron?" He mused as they snapped at the blade. "And the Kresh think you gods." He moved closer, swinging again. Leaping back from him, again, the three in the back of the formation, began to return to the earth. His blade passed through one more, as the last turned its head sideways and melted away.

"What happened, Viking?" Aya asked, running toward him.

"These creatures have a problem with iron." He said, eying over his blade, before sheathing it.

"We need hurry to peak." Aya said, looking to the aimlessly floating canoe. "The rain is coming."

"Aya, take the canoe." Vali said, running toward their destination. Aya made a growling noise in the back of her throat, before wading over to the tiny vessel and climbing inside.

The rain began sprinkling his face, long before he reached the foothills. Already, he could hear the wolves snapping at his heels, their paws tearing at the dampening earth. He dared not look back for fear of slowing.

The rain intensified as he broke the tree line, flying nearly sideways into his face. The pathway to the peak in sight, he drew up his sword and trudged on. The stones of the slope grew slippery from the rainwater, and slick from the mud, rolling down from the upper slopes.

His feet sank and slid in the muck as the howling grew nearer. He pressed himself harder, his thighs already burning from the effort

~ 417 ~

of scaling the consuming earth. His chest heaved from the exertion, and still the sound of the wolves drew nearer.

A snarl from directly behind set his nerves on edge. Whipping his sword arm back, he severed the flesh of one beast. In his spin, he happened to look back over his shoulder. Several of earth make wolves stared at him from the base of the hill, the ground far too wet for them to approach.

As he reached the peak of the tree covered slope, he spun about, sword in his right hand, the Canaruhk's axe in his left. He stood tall, eyes narrowed, arms opened, and chest puffed out. The rain poured down in the full spray and a lone howl cut through the noise from the storm.

Vali loosed a savage call of his own, in response. With every howl from the monster that drew near, he called back with his own. The soil beneath his feet proved firmer, held together by the entangled tree roots.

Then the Comartok came, stalking into view from the same slopes he had just scaled. The beast approached alone, and much to Vali's chagrin, glared at him with two feral eyes. The beast's left eye bore a scar, proof of Vali's previous encounter. The wolf snarled angrily, glancing over Vali's mud caked form.

"You want me, beast?" Vali cried defiantly as the Comartok loomed in closer. "You are no god!" He continued to bellow. "You are flesh, the same as I, and I shall have your head!" The great wolf's upper lip receded, revealing massive canines. It leaned back on its hind legs and lunged forward.

Vali sprang forward, throwing his body weight down, allowing him to slide across the slick terrain. Flailing with the weapons he held in both hands, he garroted the Comartok's underbelly, resulting in a furious wail.

Vali scuttled beneath the wolf as it spun from side to side, attempting to find him. He continued to slash at the legs and underside of the wolf, which cried with frustration. Blood poured out of its wounds, coating he and the earth in the viscous fluid.

Swinging wildly with both arms, he continued to inflict heavy damage upon the increasingly aggravated wolf. Howling in pain and frustration, the beast continuously snapped its jaws fruitlessly at the much smaller Viking.

Body drenched in the gore of his enemy, the Viking roared with fury, weapons flailing in mad, barbaric fashion. As he chipped away at the monster's flesh, severing chunks of leg, tail and underbelly in his fury, the great wolf only wailed with threats of death. Twice it attempted to fall upon him, crushing him and twice, did Vali manage to keep clear of destruction.

Suddenly, the beast leapt sideways, spinning its body, striking Vali in the back with its hind leg. The Viking soared into the air, barely managing to keep his grip on his weapons. He landed painfully amongst the roots and stones, before rolling several times over. In an instant, his adversary was upon him, maw agape.

"Kana!" Aya cried, running up behind the Comartok. She leapt onto the beast's back, before it could react to her presence. Tearing into its flank with glaive and arrow, she stabbed repeatedly, using the deep bite of her weapons to scale the reeling monster.

The wolf flailed about heavily, expending every effort to rid the woman from its blind spot. Aya clung on for dear life, still stabbing her glaive into the beast's body. Vali fought to steady his swirling vision, swallowing down the urge to vomit as he eyed his companion.

Rising to his feet, unsteadily, Vali charged. As the wolf continued to snap at Aya, who remained out of reach, Vali brought the blade of his axe down into the wolf's shoulder. The wolf reared and striking Vali to the ground with its paw, pressed him down with one foot.

Vali's world erupted into pain as he was forced face down into the suffocating mud, slowly being crushed. A moment after, he felt a vice bite as teeth gripped into his right arm. He felt bones give as twigs and he silently screamed into the muck. Before his limb was ripped from his body, the pressure on both his arm and body released, leaving only the mind-numbing pain.

His adrenaline surged, allowing him to reach his feet. His sword lay near his right foot, which he collected in his left hand. He gripped awkwardly at the hilt and looked up to his foe.

Aya had given up her vantage. Instead, she slid to the wolf's right shoulder, where she stabbed and slashed with her glaive as she tried to remain out of reach. Fighting desperately to save her companion from death's maw, she slashed viciously, dealing as much damage with every blow as she could manage.

With one swift flick of its head, the Comartok took a thrust above its left eye, but managed to bite into the right edge of the woman's midsection. Aya cried out in pain as she was lifted into the air and shook. The wolf threw her to the ground as Vali drew near.

"Aya!" He screamed, his voice cackling as thunder. The wolf reared its head to deliver the killing blow as Vali lunged. He ran his blade through his opponent's throat, the blade wedging itself deeply into its chest.

The wolf fell sideways from the blow, releasing its hold on Aya, who did not move. Enraged beyond the limits of sanity, Vali pursued the creature. Wrenching his axe from its shoulder, Vali brought the sharp, bone axe, down repeatedly, stirring a spewing stream of gore with every strike.

The Comartok kicked at him, though Vali managed to avoid the strike. His axe jarred from his hand as he struck an exposed shoulder bone, he instead gripped the hilt of his sword and wrenched it free. He did not manage another blow.

Struck by the whirling beast's tail a moment after, he soared through the air, his sword flying free from his hand, disappearing within the falling sheets of icy water and darkness. He struck the ground forcefully and saw Aya, motionless beside him, mud spilling over top of her.

He reached out, unburying her face with his remaining useful arm. Behind him, the Comartok rolled, causing the axe to pull from its shoulder as it limped away. He checked to assure his companion still groaned as the wolf squeezed between them.

He noticed the wolf shrank slightly before realizing two more things, which horrified him. The earth was rising, forming a protective layer over the beast. Even worse, he could see his adversary's wounds recovering.

Sliding his axe into the sling on his lower back, he spun around and ran to Aya's side. She gripped tightly to her waist and stomach as Vali dropped beside her, his dangling arm swinging painfully. Wrapping his left arm beneath her armpit and across her chest, he heaved.

Aya groaned as he forced her to her feet, her arms wrenching aggressively to keep her insides intact. He placed his good shoulder beneath her, which she leaned upon, heavily. She was far smaller than he, making their flight awkward. However, he pressed toward the path, the Kresh woman's feet often dragging uselessly behind her.

Despite the steep slope and slippery footing, their descent proved equally difficult as their climb had. By the time they reached the second leg of the trail, he heard the Comartok's howl above them. The beast was back on their trail.

"Come on, Aya." He urged, pulling her along. "We have to get away."

"Run, Kana," she whimpered, her words barely audible. "I cannot." She fell forward, dragging Vali down with her. His only arm wrapped firmly around the Kresh, he fell face first into the mud. Releasing his grip on her, he lifted himself up and grabbed onto her left hand and pulled.

He dragged her through the mud, down and around to the next bend. The upper slopes shaded the path ahead, leaving it relatively dry compared to the stretch above them. He stopped in place, releasing Aya's hand and grabbing for his axe. Faces belonging to wolves reached out from the dry patches of earth and came to notice them, one after another.

The Comartok howled above them as those in front of him, snarled. He searched about for a means of escape. Again, helping Aya to her feet, he turned to face them and wrapped his one good arm around her.

"Hold onto me, tightly." He whispered to her gently, tucking her head beneath his chin. And whatever you do, do not let go." He felt her arms wrapping around him, weakly, while her fingers pressed into his back.

He clenched his jaw tightly as he looked through his peripherals at the clay beasts to his left, keeping from the rain and the supposed god, stalking nearer. He squeezed tighter, his mind drifting to thoughts of his home and the woman in his company. The Comartok loomed in closer, its yellowed eyes and drooling maw, forming a sinister smile befitting of the legendary beast. Vali closed his eyes, smiled, and tipped backwards over the edge, he and Aya plummeting to the frigid waters below.

Chapter 29 - Pursued

Abel lay upon the deck of the Valiant, growling and cursing to himself, as the rest of the crew manned the ship. The Tyrda Fell churned mercilessly, tossing their vessel about. As Abel lay upon the deck, Kari tended to both he and Finna.

"Abel, sit back down." Thala grumbled for the fourth time from behind the helm.

"Are they still following us?" He asked, taking his seat on the deck.

"Yes." Halla answered. "Brina, take a rest. It is my turn on the oars." Brina sighed appreciatively, handing over her oar, and taking up a seat beside Abel.

"Here, Haldr. Let me take a turn." Abel spoke, rising to his feet.

"Abel, lie still." Kari commanded, forcing him back with a firm hand. "I need to tend to Finna. If you hurt yourself further, there will be nothing I can do for you." Turning away from him, Kari poured herself over the High Chief, who lay motionless on the deck, covered by many blankets.

"Is the chief going to be alright?" Abel croaked, slumped over miserably. He was still half blind, the right side of his face wrapped in a heavy wad of cloth.

"She is quite weak. If she lasts the day, she will have a chance." Kari muttered the words to herself. Brina moved to Abel's side, and took up a seat beside him. Seeing his trembling hands, she gently collected one of them in her own.

"It will be alright, Abel." She spoke gently. "We will figure something out." He relaxed slightly, as she squeezed his hand. He felt her free hand, hovering just to the side of his face. Knowing the reason, he swallowed hard and licked his lips.

"How bad is it?" He asked. Brina did not answer for a long while. Turning his head to look at her, she smiled weakly.

"Well, to be honest. I think you will look quite becoming with an eyepatch." Abel turned his head to stare at her, pure shock dressing his face. Eyeing him with an uneasy stare, she gave him a nervous grin. Shaking his head, he laughed, lightly.

"You really think so?" He asked, nonchalantly. Brina laughed as well, wiping a tear from her eye.

"Ulf." He whispered, looking back toward the south.

"You cannot dwell on it, Abel." Kari snapped. "Each of us has done what we could. Instead, you can honor his sacrifice and continue on."

"Yes, ma'am." Abel sighed, staring at the crew, who all looked to him, expectantly. He stared down at his hands, which floated awkwardly with the use of one eye.

"We need to gain strength." He answered. "We need to regroup with the others. Brina, can we expect further aid from Dumah?"

"Of course. Our clan will do everything we can to see Clan Falkest is punished."

"Then I believe Dumah should be our first destination. We need to take the High Chief somewhere she can recover."

"Not to mention yourself." Kari grumbled. "Both of you need time to recover, while the rest of you need rest. We will prove little more than an annoyance to Grom and his agenda, should we exhaust ourselves beyond use."

"Thala?" Abel said, looking back.

"We are already on course for Dumah Island." She answered, not taking her eyes from her course. "We will be there tomorrow." Abel placed his arm over the railing, and slowly lifted himself to stare at the water.

"I can help us make better time." He groaned, reaching out to the spirits within.

"You most certainly will not." Brina raised her voice to him as she clasped onto his hand. "Just rest for now. We will need your strength in the days to come."

"Without Vali, Ulf, Finna, and half of the captains, we all will." Kari muttered, a stagnant tear looming in the corner of her eye. Without hesitation, she turned back to her patient, pouring over the still Finna.

"Thala, what is that?" Halla asked, staring back behind their vessel. Turning about, Brina and Abel peered back over the bow. In the distance, a looming vessel came into view.

"They are following us." Abel spat. "We need to outrun them. They must have a wind or water shaper on board."

"But all on Falkest are earth shapers." Brina said, her hand on Abel's shoulder for support and confinement. "They have bred themselves as such for as long as the Vikings have inhabited the One Hundred Isles."

"It appears as though they have some on hand." He placed his hand on the bow, and slowly rose to his feet.

"Abel, sit down!" Kari growled, staring up at him angrily.

"I am sorry, Kari." He replied. "None of us will have the chance to gain strength, if that ship catches us. Either they are rowing with earth infused strength, shaping the waves or the wind. It does not much matter. They are gaining on us." He looked down at the surface of the water and held his hand out to it.

The spirits responded to his probing mind. Eager for excitement, the ever-flowing spirits within the Tyrda Fell tussled playfully against the hull. Brina stood beside him, confident smile on her face as she extended her own hand.

"Together then." She said, pressing toward the sails, willing the vessel to move faster.

Chapter 30 - Desperation

Most of the mud had been washed away by the river as they floated. He found it exceedingly difficult to keep the two of them adrift with the use of one arm, and ever more so difficult, getting her into the canoe. Unable to manage either task, both clung to the side of the canoe as Vali kicked his legs, helping them float a safe distance from their quarry.

The oars nowhere in sight, he jumped back over the side of the canoe, and latched on with his left hand. Using his legs, he kicked as hard as his body had strength, taking them away. In the end, with the little strength they both had left, they managed.

As soon as they had reached the next island, a small little cropping, which had likely served as a now sunken peninsula, Vali made work on a shelter. Sparing no expense of effort, he managed a small den, nestled against a lone, ancient tree.

The tharn pelt, though damp from the rain, proved dry enough on the opposite side. Carefully dragging the material over top of the bent brambles, he ran back to Aya, who he had already tucked beneath the cover of the trees. Dragging her into his tiny shelter, he picked at the mud caking her body, to look at her wounds.

She had several puncture wounds, running from her right thigh, stretching over her waist and abdomen, He had seen his mother tend to worse wounds, though he lacked the majority of the healer's skill.

The mud had done well to seal her wounds temporarily. As he removed the rest of his companion's clothing, he saw just how much had been thanks to the soil. Her wounds were still coated with mud, though they bled heavily.

Aya groaned with pain as Vali went to working, tearing into the stash of supplies they had left. He fell back on his mother's teachings, cleaning the wounds, using clean, healing earth to stanch the bleeding. Placing his left hand over each wound, he offered a silent prayer to the spirits within the blackened earth. Reaching out to them the best he could, he barely managed to wake them. In the end, he managed to stop the bleeding, though Aya still shook with cold.

"Aya, I do not know if you can still hear, but I have to get you warm." He said, laying out his bedroll and dragging her to it. She continued to groan as he moved her in place but laid still once he placed the second bedroll over top of her.

Next, he looked down to his own arm, which had clearly been broken. It was also then, he noticed the damage the Comartok had wrought upon it. He had managed to stanch the bleeding earlier, allowing him to tend to his friend. However, the color left his face as he considered his need to set the bone.

First, he placed the leather grip of his bow between his teeth and clenched down. Wedging his right hand between two stones, he pressed his foot down atop, anchoring them. Closing his eyes and turning his head to the left, he pulled.

He groaned loudly as he felt the bones sliding into place. He screamed into his gag as he heard a snap, followed by a surge of pain. Vali frothed at the mouth as the last of his adrenaline abated, leaving only the compounded pain.

Tears welled in his eyes and his teeth ground against the bow. He drew a series of shallow breaths as he tried to keep himself from going into shock. Several minutes later, his breathing slowed. The violent shaking of his limbs settled. He reached for his wineskin, and after nearly gagging on the cool water, managed to swallow a mouthful.

He fashioned himself a makeshift splint and secured it tightly around his arm. Vali continued to shake with discomfort and cold as the rain continued to rage outside. Looking over to his sleeping companion, who breathed laboriously and coughed occasionally, he returned to action.

"No way to start a fire." He muttered, doing his best to rub his bare chest. Looking over to Aya, who still shivered, wet, naked and cold, he sighed.

"I am sorry, Freyja. I will return to you." He said, as he moved over to Aya's side. Instinctively, she turned her head toward him as he lay beside her, pressing herself to his chest and wrapping a bared thigh around his. She was feverishly warm. Sweat decorated her brow. He stared at her sympathetically and wrapped his arms around her.

"It's my turn to take care of you," he cooed, gently, stroking her hair.

***

He awoke the following morning, Aya still laying on his chest. He gently slid out from beneath her and looked upon her. Aya's breathing was still strained. Her forehead was still decorated with sweat.

He made certain to tuck the bed matt in tightly around her. She groaned begrudgingly as he left her side but remained. Checking to ensure his clothes had somewhat dried, he dressed with some difficulty and stepped outside.

The rain had raised the water level around the peninsula enough to flood their canoe. He tipped it over, draining the water and looked about for anything they might use. There were scarce amounts of wood on the small peninsula, only what he might pull from the lone tree. It was clear to him that they would not be able to remain long. Gathering what he could find, he returned inside and built a small fire.

Inside the den, his eyes adjusted, giving a clear vision of their desperate situation. Aya lay on one side, shivering, while her brow was coated in sweat. He had laid a small ring of stone at the center of the den for their fire. Lowering his bundle of wood, he began the difficult task of starting the fire with the use of one arm.

A gentle fire roaring, he returned to his companion's side. She still shook, while the color had drained from her face. Placing his hand on her forehead, he found her still hot with fever.

"Aya," he said, gently prodding the woman. She moaned in response as he reached for his waterskin. "Here, Aya, you need to drink." He said, holding the skin to her lips. With a groan, she turned her head away, causing a small amount to trickle down onto her neck. Cupping her head and laying it on his lap, he carefully brought the spout to her lips.

She slowly sipped as he supported her. As the water escaped the corners of her lips, he relented. Wiping her face, he gently laid her back down.

"You need to eat, as well." He said, rifling through their packs. Producing three of their strips of jerky, he held one to Aya's lips. She opened her mouth slightly, accepting the trip and chewed. She groaned with the effort, her face contorting from the strain of chewing the dried meat. Giving up, the jerky fell from her lips and onto the bedroll.

"Aya, this is all I have, and you need to eat." Vali urged, trying again with the jerky. She tried once more as Vali watched tears well up in her eyes. A memory twirled about in the back of his mind from when he was a small child. Vikings, too wounded or old to nourish themselves, lay about a small fire. Their companions and nursemaids gathered about, helping to feed them.

He looked to their equipment, which would serve inadequate to boil a broth. Looking again to the jerky in his hand, he placed a piece in his mouth, and chewed with vigor. Mincing up the meat in his mouth, he gently lifted Aya's head and brought her lips to his.

She startled at first as he transferred the chewed food from his mouth to hers. Her eyes opened to narrow slits, and then she relaxed, allowing him to care for her. Pulling away, he watched patiently as Aya chewed. He felt a tiny pressure on his hand and saw Aya gripping his left hand.

"Do not worry." He said, softly. "I will take care of you." He pulled his hand away and brought the waterskin to her lips, next. She drank a little, then he grabbed another strip of jerky.

He repeated the process, until all three strips of meat were finished. She reached for his hand again and he gave it to her. Sitting silently beside her, he waited until certain she was asleep.

Shifting out from beneath Aya, he laid her head down and shuffled out of their den. The air had already grown chilly. The force of it, billowing over the lake, caused his clothes to flutter apart, biting him.

The cold made his arm sting ever more fiercely. Still, he moved about quickly, refilling their waterskins and grabbing more wood for their fire. After he had gathered enough to keep Aya warm and from going thirsty, he returned to the den.

"You came back." He heard her gentle moan as he entered.

"Of course, I did." He said, smiling, dropping his collection of wood and allowing the waterskins to slide from his shoulder. "How are you feeling?"

"I not dead, yet." She groaned. "Where did you go?"

"I left long enough to fetch wood and water. It is already getting cold and we will need both."

"Where is Comartok?" She asked, trying to raise herself.

"Don't move. You are safe," he said, placing his left hand on her shoulder. She eyed him with scarce focus. She still looked feverish, sweating, while she shivered.

"Your arm?" She moaned, staring at his mangled right arm. Instinctively, she attempted to rise, again.

"Will heal," he spoke half-heartedly, not entirely believing his own story.

"I sorry, Kana." She said, tears in her eyes. "Thought we could do it."

"We are not finished, yet." Again, he lied. "We need to come up with a new plan." The halves of her eyes, which were still open, dripped with tears. He looked away from her, to conceal his own disparity.

"We are both still alive." He pointed out. "So long as we keep breathing, we still have a chance."

"Viking?" She groaned, her voice barely audible over the light crackling of the fire.

"Yes, Aya?" He asked, his voice shaking slightly.

"Where is Comartok?" He hesitated, formulating his response as he attempted to come to terms with his own desperation.

"Away from us, but not by much. It cannot cross the water, remember?"

"What about supplies?"

"Don't worry about that. I will manage it. Rest. You need to get better."

"I have slept. Not tired."

"Then let us talk about something else." Aya stared at him, weakly. "When you came to help me, you called me something else. You said it again, just now. Kana. What does that mean?" Aya turned her head away from him but did not shift her body.

"It is Kresh name. Thought you should have one." He smiled at her, adding a few more sticks to the pile.

"What does it mean?"

"Enough questions, Viking," she coughed. Vali checked her blankets and traded the cloth on her forehead for another. "Does Kresh name, suit you?"

"It does. Thank you, Aya." She smiled at him, before turning her head toward the fire.

"How we escape?" She asked, as she watched the dancing embers.

"I dragged you out. We wounded the Comartok badly enough, we could get away." Again, Aya stared over to Vali's right arm.

"Wasn't fast enough." She chided herself.

"You saved me, again, Aya. This," he said, gesturing toward his arm. "This was my fault. I got over confident. I made a mistake." Aya continued to stare sympathetically at his arm and lifted the blanket. Vali placed his hand over the blanket and looked her in the eye.

"Rest, Aya. Your wounds will heal, but you need rest. You are running a fever. Try to get some rest." She sighed irritably but did not argue.

Reaching out, Vali gently stroked her cheek and brushed her hair. Her labored breathing eased, and she purred lightly. Once she had fallen asleep, he rose and left the den.

In the distance, he could hear the wolves howling. First, he performed his best to patch the few holes he found in their den. Afterwards, he took up a seat on a nearby rock and stared out over the water at the rest of the isle. Within a matter of moments, a lone clay wolf formed across the lake from him and snarled.

"Yeah, I am still here." He called back. "But don't you worry, beast. Soon, I'll be coming back to finish the job." The wolf's jaws snapped angrily, before tilting its head toward the den. Vali said nothing. He only drew his axe over his lap and waited.

He continued to watch as the wolf stepped in the water. His eyes grew wide as it took a second step. By the third, he stood and readied himself to slay the beast. It did not take a fourth.

"You cannot cross, yet." He spoke aloud. "It appears you will have to wait for your meal." He heard the howling of the Comartok, once more, before he saw the beast high up on the peak.

At first glance, he thought he had only imagined that it stared at him. After several, lengthy moments however, he realized that it was. He stared back at it, forcing himself to stare, until at long last, the beast looked away.

Vali sighed with relief as he fell back to his seat and relaxed. As he sat, he took the time to address his arm, looking over the many wounds upon it. Picking at his bandages, he cringed at the sight, but breathed easily at the clean wounds left behind by the Comartok's bite.

Staring down at his hand, which shook as he laid it still, he focused on his fingers. He grimaced as he manipulated the unwieldly digits, forcing them to bend and contort. He managed a weak fist and stared at it despairingly.

Inside, Aya coughed repetitiously, pain within her breaths. Vali rose to his feet and returned inside the den. In her spasm, she had tipped to a side, body retching as she clung to her stomach. Dropping down beside her, Vali fetched the waterskin and did what he could to ease her.

"Peace, Aya. Drink." He said softly, bringing the skin to her lips. She settled after a moment and rested her head back to the bedroll.

She was burning now, hotter than ever and Vali grew fearful of sickness and infection. After coaxing her to eat a little, he returned to his study of their tiny island, and gathered what supplies he could, lopping off pieces of the tree to dry for kindling, later.

Then, his labors done, he returned to his rock, eyeing the canoe. He thought of returning to the Kresh, of fleeing for the next

~ 438 ~

island. The Comartok was still beyond sight, though he knew the beast would return.

"I could take Aya in the canoe and head further to sea." He considered, looking to the choppy waters, beyond the island. "I could fashion oars, steer us back to the north." He shook his head, interrupting himself. "I would have no way to defend her from the elements. She would only grow sicker." In the distance, he could hear the howling of the things hunting him. Vali's skin crawled, as desperation only grew in the well of his stomach.

He looked back toward their den. He stared at their dwindling store of supplies and drew up a sturdy but thin length of wood. Pinning the branch between his thighs, he used the edge of his axe to begin shaping it.

"I could leave for the next island and return with more supplies." He thought aloud, before realizing that would require him to be away far too long. He continued to whittle as he conversed with no one. "If I am away, too long, the Comartok will have already come ashore and killed Aya."

His strokes against the branch were uneven from the awkward use of his left hand. More than once, was he left growling in frustration as his edge slipped and he cut too deep or shallow. By afternoon, he had managed himself an acceptable, two-pronged fishing spear, and began his task.

By evening, he sat over their fire, tending to the strips of cod, he had roused from the pools around the island. To his great relief, the cooling, turbulent weather had left the fish in pools, clustered together. He now stared at the meat of five, his fork had found purchase with, smoking over his fire.

Aya stared weakly, as well, the light of the flames flickering within her faded, silver eyes. She did not speak, though from weakness or lack of something to say, he did not know. Worse yet, was when the young woman slept, her fevered dreams had become addled with night terrors and painful fits, which left her in tears.

Again, she ate little, before returning to sleep and Vali took only enough of the meat to sustain himself. His body ached and his stomach growled murderously from lack of sustenance. All the same, once night had fully settled above them, he sat outside, and kept watch.

Arranging a small pile of stones, he made a small fire for himself. Comprised of little more than a single, slow burning branch wrapped in ruined cloth from their packs, he huddled around it, doing his best to keep warm. The added light helped calm him, even as the nighttime howls, broke the otherwise silent eve.

At the first call, his eyes flashed toward the opposing shoreline. As it had the morning before, a lone wolf stood at the water's edge, daring to come closer. He watched patiently, counting the distance his tormentor reached, axe ready to cleave it to bits.

"Seven." He whispered to himself, the words alone producing their own, chilling air. "Four more from yesterday." He upturned his torch and smothered it in the earth, before returning to Aya's side, and claiming what sleep he might.

Come morning, a short few hours later, he rose and repeated the day before. He gathered what supplies he could; fishing with diminishing return, clipping pieces from the old tree, and refilling their waterskins. The wolves remained a constant presence, never leaving long enough for him to rest easy.

They continued to snarl and snap as they danced about in force. His nerves were sent end over end as they continuously snapped at him, while he went about his labors. The entirety of the day, they maintained an unrelenting presence.

"Shut it, you damned beasts!" He howled, grabbing hold of a loose rock on the beach with his left hand. Pitching it across the water toward them, the stone skittered to the ground in front of the beasts, who circled around it. Turning their heads back toward him, they resumed their taunting.

"Come on, then!" He yelled out, again, throwing more stones. Managing to strike several of the beasts, they finally moved on, all but one. Stopping just outside of Vali's throwing range, the wolf sat on its haunches and stared at him as he searched for food. By evening, he returned to his perch and stared upon his enemy.

"Ten." He whispered to himself, putting out his torch, and returning to the worsening Kresh's side.

Five days into his new routine, he had lost track of everything outside of his repetitive tasks. Aya, whom he could help little, remained awake for no more than a few minutes, each day. What miniscule nourishment he could force her to take in, also diminished by the day.

Day after day, he watched as his companion, whom he had grown close to, grew ever more depleted. Her fever had yet to break, and her skin had taken on a sickly color. On the morning of the sixth day, he had feared her already dead, until he noticed the gentle rise in her chest.

The wolf returned, on schedule, taking no less than twelve steps that night. Less than a quarter of the stretch between islands remained, and Vali knew he was out of time. Taking up his torch, he swung wildly at the beast, who stood little more than the reach of his torch away.

The beast snarled at the flames, backing away as his torch drew near to its clay flesh. He only managed to dry a small bit of its shoulder, which crumbled away. Sitting upon his stone, lost, defeated and exhausted, he stared at the retreating wolf. Tears of frustration running down his cheeks, he prayed.

"Old gods of the Aesir, who have long since left our world, I beseech you." He stopped to watch as a bolt of lightning, lit up the rainless sky, and a cackle of thunder, thrust against his sensitive eardrums. "I know you still look down on us from somewhere beyond. My friend and I are held prisoner, by a seemingly unconquerable enemy, and we find ourselves lacking in strength. I pray to you by name and ask for your aid.

"To Thor, please grant me your might, so I may have strength to break its bones. I pray to Tyr, that his courage may embolden me.

Heimdall, may your perception, grant me sight of a weakness, so I might prevail.

"To the mother goddess, Frigg, I ask for your guidance. To Valkyr, I pray to you for victory. And to Odin, should I fall, I pray you find me worthy of your halls, and send your ravens to the Kresh. I am lost among my kin, but Aya is not. I gladly pay sacrifice with the life I have left, but only ask that you spare her."

Vali placed his forehead to the ground, a measure of humbled prostration he had never before employed. He remained, forehead to the earth, until another flash of light, forced his attention. A cackle of thunder split the world, and again, three more bolts struck the rotting shell of Fangor Isle.

The resounding thunder proved deafening. He stumbled backwards and nearly fell as a bright light blinded him. The lightning, which had struck in the heart of the ruins of Fangor forest, had produced a swelling flame.

"Thank you." He spoke aloud, rising to his feet and lifting his head skyward. "Victory or death, life or glory, til Valhalla comes. I am Vali, Viking of Ulfrost." He chanted to himself, returning to Aya briefly.

She still drew breath, which further gave him hope. Gathering what few things he dared carry with him, he stepped out into the illuminated night, and listened to the howling of the wolves. For once, his enemy sounded just as afraid as he was.

"Victory or death."

Chapter 31 – Regaining Strength

"Crows feast upon their eyes!" Abel yelled, slamming his bloodied fist on the Valiant's ruined bow. "A blight upon them all!" He spun about, angrily kicking at the fallen debris that cluttered the deck.

"We managed to fend them off, at least." Halla spoke, wrenching a javelin from the bow.

"They will be back." Abel growled, placing his hand over the piece of black leather, which had been bound over his ruined eye. "We have only deterred them."

"Good thinking with the fire shaping, Brina." Kari spoke. "I am not so sure we would have pulled through without it." Again, Abel grumbled, looking upon the damage to the ship.

"If they are so intent on attacking us, they will only make landfall on Dumah. Will your clan be up for such an event?" Brina looked back toward their adversary, which still haunted the edge of their vision.

"One ship, without difficulty. A war between the clans however." She looked away.

"We need to consider a new destination." He offered, looking to the others onboard for guidance. A weak, shrill cough interrupted the silence. Turning their gaze to the stern, they eyed Finna, whose eyes had opened.

"High Chief!" They exclaimed as Kari fell to her side. As Finna attempted to rise, the blankets Kari had covered her with fell loose, exposing the bloodied wraps the healer had applied, firmly holding the chief's arms across her torso.

"Lie still, Finna." She said, wrapping the spare furs she used for blankets tighter around the woman. "You are not through the worst of it, yet."

"Steer northwest of Fangor." She groaned, the effort of speaking, visibly draining her. "There is an island, where we may hide." She pointed in the specified direction, before succumbing to sleep again.

"What island?" Abel asked, looking to the others. "I do not remember seeing it on any of the charts." Kari thought for a long moment, before speaking.

"Finna is right as are you." She finally spoke. "There were several islands on my husband's charts, which have not been placed on any other."

"But they could have been discovered by others. Can we at least defend ourselves, there?"

"Should we reach the island, we will be safe." Kari spoke with confidence. "Gram once told me you could only find the island if you knew it was there." She smiled, remembering her husband.

"Do you know where this island is?" He asked. Kari looked down at her lap a moment, considering the question.

"I do." Thala said.

"How do you know?" Haldr spoke up. "We have only just heard of it." Thala rolled her eyes irritably at the man, before sighing.

"Where might one store something important?" She asked. "A great number of things are stored within the shrine. Among them, I do recall pouring over an old map, which showed landforms not on any other."

"Please lead the way, then," said Abel. "Let us make sure we are not followed, though. A hidden sanctuary does us little good if we show it to someone else."

"How do we lose them?" Haldr asked.

"Fangor lies to the north, correct?" Agni broke his silence.

"Yes? Why?" Abel asked, not looking away from their pursuer.

"It is on fire." The man responded bluntly. The crew turned to face the north, and noticed the high rising plume of smoke, instantly.

"Thala, steer toward Fangor." Abel called. Perhaps whatever is going on there, will distract our enemy." Thala pulled against the oar, steering the vessel from their course toward true north.

Before the sun had begun its decline from the heavens, the island rested within sight. Flames poured off from it, scorching the sky from east coast to west. Resting high upon its lonely peak, the old Viking stronghold was also ablaze.

"What happened there?" Abel gasped, staring at the sight of it.

"Could it have been that beast?" Halla asked. "We barely escaped with our lives." Haldr and Agni, both having been absent from the battle, stared in awe.

"Not until now, did I believe your story." Agni whispered. "To think that a devil of the old world still existed."

"It is scared." Thala muttered to herself. "This fire. It is unnatural."

"How can you be certain?" Abel asked. Kari turned to face the blaze, eyes straining on the flames.

"She is right, Abel. The spirits are singing a song of vengeance and death." As they witnessed the island's cleansing, a feral howl broke apart the sound of the waves.

"It sounds afraid." Brina commented, even as her own knees quavered.

"It is not just the Fenrir." Haldr added. "I am suddenly less interested in seeing it for myself." They continued upon their course, the vessel beyond them still in pursuit.

"Keep to our task. We need to lose that ship." Abel growled. "Let the flames have that beast. I am more concerned with the living." They continued sailing toward the looming pyre, the smoke, rolling overtop the waves as they drew nearer. Soon, they were shrouded in the smoke.

"Thala. Can you manage a wind shaping to ease our breathing?" Kari commanded, more than asked.

"Yes, teacher." She answered. Immediately, the air around them thinned significantly, easing their labored breathing. The shaping cleared their vision, as well, allowing a sight of the island within the smoky curtain.

Fangor, the magnificent, mysterious wonder and historical relic of their heritage, was no more. In the short period of time he had been away, Abel could scarcely recognize where the ancient forests and proud stronghold had once been. The flames continued to leap skyward, consuming everything in their path.

The Fenrir of Fangor howled once more, rising high up above them, over the top of the far peak. Abel's heart froze in his chest as all on board gasped in horror. Halla sat still, eyes widened with horror as Thala drew her sword and turned to face the beast.

"Is that the beast what killed my son?" Kari growled. Abel felt a terrifying rumble beneath their feet. The wood groaned in protest as the petite, middle aged woman trembled with anger, causing the currents beneath them to shift. In response, the Valiant shifted nearer to the island.

"No, Kari. It was not that beast, but those who traveled with it. We cannot dwell on this, now. Let the flames consume its flesh."

"May it burn for eternity and die in immeasurable pain." She continued to seethe with hatred as the vessel carried on. The beast quickly dropped down out of sight a moment later, though its howls continued to bellow angrily at the heavens.

"May your soul find rest, my friend." Abel whispered, bowing his head in respect.

As they passed through the sheet of smoke, they lingered further north a distance, before re-charting their course. Moving due west, the oars returned to the battle against the waves. Releasing her wind shaping, Thala resumed her push against their partially collapsed sail.

Resuming their hastened pace, they sailed toward Gram's lost refuge. They stared back to view the island's cleansing once more. Hearing the death throes of the beast, which had conquered their people, each of them sighed with relief.

"I believe that we have lost them. Let us hurry to Gram's refuge."

They continued to press both the boat and themselves, throughout the entirety of the night. They neither rested nor relented, though their bodies screamed for relief. By morning, they floated listlessly, each too tired to press further. As the cover of darkness receded, they saw the island, the last concealing point before the sun filled the horizon.

"We made it." He smiled, seeing the tropical island with a high reaching mountain at its center. A large, crescent shaped formation of rock surrounded the island. Only a small, narrow strip of beach could be seen beyond the natural shield.

"We need to move toward the mountain." Kari said, carefully tucking bindings beneath the High Chief.

"What is at the base of the mountains?" Abel asked.

"A temple." Kari answered. "My husband wrote of a grand temple, built long ago when our people were still young in this world."

"It sounds as though it will be a grand place for us to start anew."

"Once we have regained our strength, we go after Grom." Abel growled, dashing his fist against the railing.

"Peace, Abel." Brina cooed, placing her hand on his shoulder blade. "First, we must find shelter and supplies. Second, I must send word back to my family. Ulfrost was merely the first of Grom's conquests. His appetite for power will not be sated for long."

"With Finna absent, he will declare himself the next High Chief. That, or he will use Freyja as a puppet." Abel bit his lip. The taste of copper ran across his tongue as the thought struck him. The coarse sand gritted against the hull, bringing the Valiant to an abrupt halt in the shallows.

"Why did we leave Freyja with that man?" He asked aloud.

"It was not your fault." Brina assured him. "We could not have known."

"But we do now." Agni growled, stepping off from the side of the longboat. "Our first duty is to the High Chief. Once she is safe, we can plot our course to liberate the people. Though." Agni stopped, noticing debris strewn across the beach.

"What is it, Agni?" Haldr asked, jumping down to the sands, as well.

"Someone else has been here. Recently." The large man grunted.

"It looks as though they attempted to build a ship." Halla commented, kneeling down near to her brother. "Do you think it is possible that Vali washed ashore?"

"Someone was or is here." Kari started, walking beside Agni, who carried the chief. "Beyond that, let us not rile our hopes. First, we need to find shelter."

"Thala, Brina and I will scout ahead." Abel said with authority. "We will search for the temple at the foot of the mountain. Halla, Haldr, please stay close to Kari and the High Chief. Also, be on the lookout for food. I believe that is your specialty?"

"It is, Captain." Haldr smiled. "We will not let you down." He turned and walked along the beach, in search of anything they might use. Abel, turning to see Brina and Thala already at the tree line, moved to follow them.

"Whoever was here, seems to have been in trouble. That, or lost control of their shaping." Brina commented, eyeing a large cluster of ruined trees, which had been violently torn asunder. Slowly, he approached, his skilled eyes tracing several sets of footprints, which traveled deeper in. Various other tracks, belonging to animals with opposable appendages on their feet, were also scattered about.

"Are you ready?"

"Just waiting for you." Brina replied, drawing her polearm. Taking up his axe, Abel followed the two into the jungle. The humidity attacked without warning. Sweat poured from his hands and brow within moments of entering the lush, green thicket.

"Stay close to each other." He cautioned, moving forward at a slow crawl, gently pressing the greenery from his path.

"There are several strange tracks, all over." Brina commented, pouring over a set of the strange footprints, which climbed up the side of a tree.

"I have seen drawings of creatures like these before." Thala said, staring at a similar pair only four paces away.

"Apes." Abel blurted. Both Thala and Brina gave him the slightest of confused looks, before he smirked. "My father has told me stories of similar creatures. They walk as we do, but they wear the guise of beasts."

"Anything else?"

"He said they can hold quite the inclination for violence when disturbed. We would do well not to give them a reason to attack us."

They continued through the jungle, hearing only sparse murmurings of the indigenous residents. Beyond them, the jungle had grown near silent. The sound of their thundering hearts and heavy breathing served as their steady companion, as they traveled toward the mountain in their sights.

"Abel, Thala, look." Brina called to them. "There are other tracks over here." As they stepped toward their comrade, a flicker of movement captured their attention up above.

"There!" Brina called, readying her weapon to strike.

"Wait!" Thala called, slapping the weapon to the side with the flat of her blade. "Brina, Abel, do not strike."

"What is it?" Abel asked, moving beside his two compatriots. Tilting their heads to the side, they attempted to glean at what rustled above them.

"Kree Reek." A chittering creature chatted at them from behind the cover of the splayed limbs of the tree. Carefully, they searched for it, though they only caught the slightest glimpses of movement. A bushy, fur covered tail, flitted into sight, followed by the scratching of tiny claws.

"Do we kill it?" Brina asked. Tauntingly thrusting her spear forward.

"Easy." Thala growled, sheathing her weapon and slowly making her way toward the tree. Carefully searching through her pockets, she found a lint covered ship's biscuit.

"Kree kree!" The creature chirped again, before springing from the cover of the trees. Abel and Brina jumped back, reflexively. Thala however, extended her arm as the creature dropped down.

It was a deep red, the same color as the bark on the Wyrd trees of Ulfrost. It had long, pointed ears, slender yet muscular limbs, and a bushy tail that was larger than the rest of its body. All in all, it stood no larger than one of their hunting hounds.

It moved about swiftly, twitching nervously as its nose attacked the air. Scuttling up and down the trunk of the tree, it continued to gaze upon them with its large, dark brown eyes. Thala returned the long stare, her lips quivering, though no one else could see.

"What is it?" Abel asked, daring to step forward. The creature quickly turned its head to face Abel, before scuttling down to the ground. He froze as it scurried about, sniffing their boot tracks as it moved closer.

Outstretching her hand, Thala knelt slightly. The vibrating nose of the creature ran laps over her palm, before it locked eyes with her once more. Without further warning, it darted around and behind Thala, latching on to the leather of her armor and pulling itself to roost on her shoulders.

"Thala, are you alright?" Brina, slightly alarmed, asked.

"It is fine." She spoke calmly. "I believe this creature here represents one of the descendants of Ratatoskr."

"The messenger god?" Brina asked.

"I do believe so. Do not worry, this is a good sign." She said, tilting her head back toward the small beast on her shoulders. "Can you show us your place of power?" As if understanding her, the creature turned to face the north and bounded from her shoulders.

"Quickly, do not lose it!" Thala said, charging after the small creature, Abel and Brina following behind her. They tore through the low hanging greenery of the jungle, shielding their faces to little avail with their hands.

Bloodied and winded, they poured out into the clearing at the far end of the forest. Several paces ahead, nearing the next outcropping of trees and foliage, the massive, hound sized rodent bounded. Thala continued the pursuit without thought to her wellbeing. Abel and Brina, stopped.

"We will catch up." Abel panted, moving at a slow jog as their sprinting, light footed companion grew ever more distant. Taking a moment to catch their breath, they resumed pace. Pressing through to the next clearing however, left them at a loss.

"Thala." Abel called, moving around the thickest parts of the obstructive plant life. Edging away from him, Brina too, placed her hands over her mouth and called.

They both turned to face the source of a nearby rustling. They could hear the bending of branches, and low reaching brambles. The sound of many somethings striking against the large leaves of the indigenous plant life, whistled in their ears.

"Brina?" Abel started, drawing up his sword once more.

"Not that I disagree, but there sounds to be quite a number of them." She said, leveraging her spear out in front of herself.

"Then perhaps we should consider running?" He suggested.

"Yes, but to where?" They turned again as another source of rustling came from behind.

"Follow me. Quickly." Thala hissed through clenched teeth as she turned away, disappearing into the high grasses. Without question or a second thought, they both poured into the tall grass behind their friend.

Their visibility proved poorer than before, immediately. The only inclination they still followed Thala was the subtle rustle of the grass ahead. Following the small parting formed when she passed through, they managed to reach the other side.

"Hurry. The temple is this way." She said, grabbing Abel's hand and leading him further in. Brina growled lightly under her breath, unnoticed by other ears.

Charging after the furry creature, they pressed along the first steps of the mountain, which were still encompassed by the trees. The forest stretched a great distance above them, while they charted along the outside edge of the lower ridge. Finally, rounding a small canyon, which tore deeper into the face of the mountain, they saw it.

"By the gods of the Aesir." Abel gasped, staring at the monolithic construct built into the mountain's flesh. It stood as high as the Wyrd trees of Ulfrost and appeared twice as ancient. No discernable features remained upon the statues, though the architecture was clearly that of their ancestors.

"We have found it." Thala exclaimed, standing near to the tiny creature, which scuttled onto her back, and draped itself over her shoulder.

"We have to go back. We need to bring Kari, the High Chief and the others here." Abel said, eying the structure for what it would soon become. "This is where we will gain our strength, and from here, we will fight back."

Chapter 32 – The Final Stand

The former forests of Fangor raged with fire, as Vali waded toward its shore. Spiraling plumes of wildfire, soared high above, engulfing everything. Even along the shoreline, far beneath the flames, he felt their embrace.

His eyes darted toward the foothills, where he could hear and see debris being tossed about as something large, rapidly made its way through the fallen forest. Reaching out with his senses, he found a host of spirits already rising in vengeance against the unnatural force, which had reft their land. They paid little attention to him as they sang their song of liberation, destruction, and rebirth.

Looking to the peak, where he and Aya had previously failed to fell the beast, Vali charged forward. He kept to the shore as long as he could, trying to stay clear of the expanding reach of the flames. At last, he came to the edge of the shore and the forest, which was still untouched by fire.

Looking back to the west, he could see the spirits rising. Spirits of flame, jumped from one tree to the next, feeding the flames as the spirits of the air, carried those of water from harm, while further aiding their feasting brethren. Their presence calmed him, emboldened him, and carried him to his enemy.

In the distance, he could see the Comartok, climbing to high ground to escape the inferno. Vali gave pursuit, charging through the fallen trees, reaching out to the spirits of the earth to guide his steps. He reached the edge of the spiraling peak, where high above, he could hear the shrill cries of the fleeing wolf.

He turned his back to the sound and instead, focused on the encroaching flames. He reached out and with what shaping he could manage, prodded at the flames. He remembered what acts he had managed at the Cana camp, and prompted the flames to surge toward him.

In a bound, the flames darted after him, racing along his given course. Whether by sense of his deed, or from fear of the flames, the Comartok above, howled in defiance. A secondary set of howls, called as well, returning Vali's attention to the path.

Axe gripped confidently in his left hand, he took his first steps toward the peak. With each step, he felt the earth trembling with anticipation beneath him, but also, he felt the presence of something far larger. The Comartok knew he was coming.

He took his time scaling the peak, waiting for the fires of Fangor to reach them. What strength the earth could afford him, he accepted gratefully as he strolled, shoulders back, head high. The air around him grew warmer, even as he climbed, and the voice of his quarry grew ever more fearsome.

At last, he stalked around the edge of the peak, eyes gleaming with madness. The Comartok stood at its center, amber eyes focused only on him. The great wolf, paced back and forth, keeping its head low, but eyes locked.

Vali stood his ground, waiting. Not for the beast that sought his heart, but for the end to arrive. Whether through divine punishment, holy judgment, or some other unnamed miracle, they had reached the end of their story. As was the way of his people, he tightened down his hold on his weapon, roared with a blood thirsty cry and dared the Fates to stop him.

His anger, fear, and determination to defend the one in his care, highlighted his every breath. Every muscle in his body, vibrated with eagerness, bred from generations of conquering the unknown. The Comartok lifted its head and howled, as its constructs pawed out from the ground beneath its feet.

Thunder roared above them, causing the beast, not Vali, to flinch. Charging forward, Vali quickly cleared the gap between he and the great wolf. The beast, dazed from the storm above, slowly turned its head to face him. Vali swung his axe, narrowly missing the Comartok's brow and instead, struck its left ear from its head.

A howling cry of pain was his answer as the fearful lord of the earth, sprang forward, striking into Vali's left side. The Viking fell on his right side, which burned with a distant agony, that was quickly smoldered by the raging blaze within. He found his feet and swung at a slowly rising pair of snapping jaws.

As one construct shattered, he made work on a second, even as dozens more, clawed at their confinement. The Comartok rounded back on him and pounced. Throwing himself sideways, Vali rolled away from the strike, and reaching his feet, ran at length around the beast.

Light now began to rise around them as the chorus of death from below, sang to them, filling both he and his quarry with foreboding. The Comartok, trapped between the flesh of the Viking and the reaching flames, continued to whirl about in indecision, having slowly become more beast than man. Much of the intelligence Vali had sensed during his previous two encounters, now seemed lost to his enemy as it continued to act indecisively.

Unabated, he sprang forward, leaping free of the wolves' reach and sank his axe blade into the monstrosity's hind leg. Expecting the coming whirl, he ducked and rolled forward, allowing him a moment of invisibility. Again, striking at the wolf's underbelly, he felt a spray of its blood, spattering him as he cleaved a line of flesh, the length of his arm.

The Comartok fell sideways, nearly crushing Vali, as it howled with pain. The wolves sprang passed him, ignoring the man entirely, as they fused with their masters wounded side. Again, rising to his feet, he charged forward, blind in his berserker state.

The wolf kicked out at him as his weapon bit down. His axe, lodged into the beast's flesh and sprang from his hand as he was knocked backwards several lengths. Immune to the pain the blow caused him, he rose again, deaf to his bodies cries.

A glimmer of light caught his eye. Turning ever so slightly, he walked with confidence toward the light provided by the flames, which now licked at the outer edges of their battleground. Sunken into the earth, halfway up the blade, was his sword, passed down to him by a faceless father, he nor anyone he knew, had ever met.

He gripped the blade in his left hand and felt as the earth pressed from it, revealing the perfectly preserved metal. His weapon shined in the light of the flames, its blade, unmarred by the earth, which had held it. The blade shined in the Comartok's eyes, and the beast snarled at him angrily, as it beheld it.

With a roar, Vali sprang forward. The Comartok reared on its haunches, preparing to pounce as its back legs sank. Quickly, it spun its head in surprise and Vali laughed triumphantly at its meaning. Reaching his quarry, he thrust forward.

Batting a single paw, Vali was flung to the left by the wolf. He felt his sword connect with flesh and felt the vibration of metal striking bone as he tore through the Comartok's forward left leg. He hit the ground and rolled, while the wolf fell forward.

Vali kicked at the ground as he squirmed out of reach. The Comartok raised itself on three legs and looked to the bloodied Viking. Blood streaked both his chest and left arm, as he stood, readying another assault. As the beast glared at him, Vali saw that the man within, was no more.

The wolf spun the best it could, breaking free of the earth spirits that held it. Choosing to face the flames over the crazed warrior, it limped away, down the path. Vali's knees buckled as he felt the world catching up to him.

He heaved, spilling out what little he had held within his belly, and leaned on the pommel of his planted weapon. His lungs retched for air. He shivered violently from the exhaustion, hunger, and pain, which the earth spirits influence, had previously shielded him from.

He heard cries of pain from below, the wolf had advanced through the flames. The cry did not come from far below but served to awake Vali for a moment. Pressing himself to his feet, he stalked toward the edge of the cliff.

He could see the Comartok below, inching toward the flames, trying to find a means of escaping them. Blade gripped tightly in his hand, Vali jumped from the edge, plummeting below. The Comartok rounded the corner as he fell.

He landed on the Comartok's side, stabbing his blade deeply into the beast's back. The wolf stumbled sideways, falling to the edge of the landing. Vali could hear the earth groaning beneath them and stared down at the fire below, as the Comartok slowly rolled.

Both he and the wolf, howled in unison as they fell to the blaze, below. Landing on the boney ribs of the wolf, Vali tumbled through the collected piles of dirt and broken branches. He landed with a heavy thud against the base of the hill, and slowly brought himself to his feet.

Heat, intense enough to make it difficult to breathe, smoldered him from all sides. The light produced by the burning giants of Fangor was blinding. Hand in front of his eyes, he searched for his weapon, which he found near the bottom of the hill.

At the top of the hill, he saw the Comartok, slowly rising to its feet. Its fur was heavily matted by mud, twigs and fallen leaves. It cried angrily as it limped away from the licking tongues of flame, which seared it. Turning its gaze back toward Vali at the bottom of the hill, it growled.

Vali was beyond exhausted. He had misjudged the strength of his enemy and expended himself, far too quickly. He had held every advantage, but now barely managed to hold his weapon. It occurred to him that no matter what fate befell him, his enemy would not survive beyond the evening, and he smiled.

The wounded wolf limped toward him, fangs dripping with long, yellow beads of saliva. The scorched earth no longer answered its call, but it was a beast of the old world, all the same. Heads held high, the two sauntered toward one another.

A crackling, not of thunder, but of a snapping branch drew their attention as a minion of the fire spirits, dashed the gap between them. The Comartok stumbled backwards, as the flames leapt at its limbs. Vali, reaching out toward the wild spirits, lent his will to theirs, and pressed them forward.

The Comartok wailed as the flames lapped at its fur. The smell of burning flesh and hair, intermixed with the burning of cedar and pine. The resulting aroma, a testament to the entropy around him, was sickening.

His body dry retched twice, before he honed himself and dashed the gap. The wild spirits did not discriminate between he and the Comartok, burning him as he passed over the fallen branch. They fed without contentment, devouring everything in their path. Still solely focused on the flames dancing about it, the Comartok did not notice Vali, until his blade swept across the side of its face.

Blinded again, the wolf shrieked with rage, whirling its body to bite at him. Its reach stunted by its crippled limb, it instead fell to the side, landing on Vali and rolling downhill. Pressed into the earth, the air was forced from Vali's lungs, and he fought desperately for another breath.

The omnipotence of the smoke and flame had begun to smother him. Its embrace had crept over him, whilst he was focused on his task. Now, the need for self-preservation threatened to strip him from his work.

His axe had fallen beside his feet, pulled from the wolf's shoulder at some point during their landing and its tumble down the hillside. He stuck his sword into the ground and quickly placed the axe in its proper place, before taking up his blade, anew. Beneath him, he saw two things; his quarry, and a narrowing opening to the tiny inlet where awaited his companion.

The Comartok noticed this, as well. Glancing up at Vali, it turned its body away and limped through the passage. Vali swore aloud, as he caught sight of a glimmer of the former intelligence the wolf had been lacking. His own life forfeit once more, he charged not for safety, but for death.

The flames bit at his legs, his arms, his face, and every other area, which still held feeling. He leapt over a burning branch, which had stretched its influence across the piles of leaves, coating the hill. Vali did not care. He charged regardless.

"Spirits of the old gods hasten to my side." He called, sword held out at arm's length. His vision had grown blurry with the lack of air flowing to his lungs. What remained, was further blurred by the stinging smoke, which watered his eyes.

Still he charged, sword held out. The Comartok was nearing salvation. It would regain its former strength and every hope he had held of saving his friend would be gone. In that moment, he had forgotten his former life, his friends, his mother, sister and coveted lover.

In a single moment, the heat of the flames, a gust of cool, salty air, and the stench of burning flesh and hair, mixed in a dizzying arrangement. His steps staggered forward, as he held his blade outward. The Comartok stopped at the water's edge, unable to cross, and unable to escape.

Slowly, it turned its head to face him, defiant until the end. It opened its jaws wide as it snapped at Vali, who narrowly listed away. He felt his blade sink into flesh and press through a hollow point. His momentum carried him forward, until he struck bone, and stopped.

The blade, edging against the stone solid innerworkings of the Comartok, jostled him aggressively, throwing him passed and face first into the river. Submerged, he rolled effortlessly, and stared at the isle of Fangor, completely engulfed in flames. He could see the Comartok roaring angrily through the bleary, shifting surface of the murky water, but could not hear its voice.

A moment later, he floated to the surface, the roar of his battle clearer than ever. His entranced rage had at long last, fizzled out, leaving him feeling naked and vulnerable. The Comartok stared at him a moment longer, blade edged to the hilt in its chest. It swooned a moment, fell into the water, and did not move.

Floating freely, no longer possessing the will to move his limbs, Vali stared at the corpse of his enemy. The immense terror he had felt from the beast eased. His own approaching death and the tranquil water sang to him of comfort, even as he stared at the flame engulfed island. Lapping at the shoreline, the waters at last claimed the flesh of his foe, which sank from his view. Triumphant smile on his face, he felt his head come to rest upon the shallows and darkness embraced him.

***

Vali awoke, the following morning, feeling numb and sick with cold, having spent the remainder of the evening, submerged in the shallows surrounding Fangor. He rose stiffly, sneezed and found his bearings. Fangor still burned, its ashes spreading out over the island and out to sea. He thanked the old gods for his luck. The isle where he and Aya had concealed themselves was left untouched.

He stumbled away from the hauntingly beautiful sight, toward his companion. He wanted more so than he imagined possible to tell her the news. The Comartok was slain.

"Aya," he croaked, his throat parched from the flames. "Aya, the Comartok is dead. We can return to the..." He stopped in midsentence. Aya lay before him, deathly still, the color drained entirely from her face.

"Aya!" He tried to yell, but instead left himself tasting blood as he fell to the ground and groveled toward her. "Aya, please do not die on me." He sobbed, pulling away her blankets, exposing her bare body and ill colored wounds. He placed his head onto her chest and his hand over her breast. She still lived, though barely.

"Hang on, Aya." He called, running out to fetch their canoe. The morning sun had already risen, granting him a clear view of their vessel. So, focused on his task, he nearly missed the obvious. A Viking ship sailed out in the distance, painted with flags, silver, green and black.

Stunned, he stopped abruptly, before reality struck him as a knife in the gut. He tried to yell, but all he managed to produce was a low toned growl. Quickly, he ran to the small pond on the peninsula and submerged his head, drinking greedily, until he felt sick to his stomach. Pulling his head from the water, he rose to his feet and ran into the shallows.

"Hey!" He cried out, flailing his one good arm, while jumping up and down. His eyes trained on the flags of the ship, he recognized the dire wolf emblem they sailed.

"Hail, Chief Grom and the Direwolves of Falkest! I am Vali, of Ulfrost!" He beckoned repeatedly. He saw a bustle of forms, surging to better look upon him. Clad in the silver, green and black of Clan Falkest, he saw a number of lady Vikings, waving back at him.

"Hail, Vali of Ulfrost. Are you responsible for this beacon?" They called back, Vali faintly seeing an arm pointing toward the great blaze of Fangor.

"I have slain the great wolf! I am run ashore, and in desperate need of aid! Will Clan Falkest help me?"

"Aye, we will!" The woman, whom he assumed was captain of the ship, called back.

"Thank you!" He yelled, charging back toward he and Aya's den. Within, he saw Aya, barely awake, staring at him weakly. "Aya!" He called, dropping to her side. "Just hang on, everything will be

~ 465 ~

alright, now." He urged, gathering up the few things they had as he began to disassemble their camp.

"The Comartok?" She groaned.

"Is dead. Aya, we can return to your people, now. They can heal you. Just hang on. My friends have found me. We can reach the Cana camp in a day, instead of three." He heard a stirring outside and rushed back from her side.

"Hurry, my friend is hurt." He froze in place as the unprecedented sight of Kresh and Viking, upon the same narrow shore came into view. He was unsure of when they had arrived, but two Cana braves and one elder stood across from his rescue party. The braves stood, spears in hand, while the elder remained behind them. The Vikings held their weapons firm, as well, staring down the much larger Kresh, ready to wage battle.

"Vali, stay back." The captain called. "We will deal with these savages." She spat, gripping the hilt of her axe with murderous intent.

"No! Wait!" Vali yelled, charging between the two forces, startling both. "They are not our enemy." He yelled, turning to the confused Vikings.

"They are Kresh, sworn enemies to all that walk upon the One Hundred Isles of Vala." Another of the crew argued.

"Not these. They are my friends. I will explain, later. Do not attack." He yelled frantically, turning around to face the Kresh, who appeared as startled as his brethren.

"As you say, Vali. Chief Grom has told us of you. We are not deaf to tell of Vali of Ulfrost. So long as they do not attack, neither shall we." She said, dropping her weapon to her side. The Kresh did not lower their arms, but they looked to Vali, faces not unkind.

"Aya is hurt." He said in a pleading tone, pointing toward the den. "Please, we must take her to the Cana." The Kresh grunted amongst one another. Seemingly understanding, they debated, pointing to Vali's clothes and the burning island. The eldest among them, stepped forward, and muttering in Kresh, shook his head.

"Exiled." He managed in the Viking tongue.

"No!" Vali yelled accidentally, startling everyone. However, weapons raised in alarm, they halted as the elder raised his hand. "The Comartok is slain." He said in a softer voice, pointing to the shallows. "Come, I will prove it." He said, delving into the shallows, where he and the great wolf had fallen.

"Stay." The Kresh barked, placing his hand on Vali's left shoulder. Turning to those in his company, he uttered a few words in Kresh. Without question, the two younger warriors with him, dove head first into the water, and quickly swam about.

Vali turned his gaze back toward his fellows, who shook impatiently, nerves on edge at what they saw. Vali looked back to the Kresh, swimming off from the shore, diving one after another, in search of Vali's proof. The elder Kresh, hand gently clasped to Vali's shoulder, tugged on him.

"Show me, Aya." He commanded.

"Please, do not do anything rash." Vali pleaded, looking back to his comrades.

"You have my word." The woman answered. Rushing inside, Vali showed the elder Kresh to his sickly companion. The elder swooped to her side with unseen agility. Peeling away the covers, he grimaced at her wounds.

"How long?" He said, gesturing to her wounds.

"Six days?" Vali questioned himself. The elder, without another word, lifted Aya, blankets and all from the ground and rose. His head pressed against the tharn pelt, which Vali made quick work to remove.

He cradled her gently in his arms, walking toward the Kresh vessel as his hunters yelled from the shallows. He could hear the Vikings calling to him, though the series of events proved too much for him to process in the moment. The elder nodded and shifting the groaning Aya, moved to their canoes.

~ 467 ~

"You speak truth, Viking." He grunted. "We take, Aya." He said, gently lowering her to rest.

"Will she be alright?" Vali asked, as the Viking captain came to his side.

"Vali, we cannot stay. There is an urgent matter."

"One minute, please?" He said, pressing away from his savior. "Elder, will she be alright?"

"Wounds bad. Do not know. Take to Cana camp" He said, after some thought. "You Ruhk, now. What do you do?" Vali twitched at hearing the man call him such. He had no answer for the man's questions. Shaking his head, he returned his attention to Aya.

"Vali," the captain spoke, grabbing his arm. "We need to be on our way. There is a war council to be held. Ulfrost is lost and the war chiefs are slain. Having found you, we must return to Falkest, quickly." Vali heard every word, though he could not process any of it. Instead, he fell to the rock he had used as a watch post the past several days.

"We need to see my friend to her people." He said.

"She is among them. Let the Kresh take care of the Kresh." One of the Vikings spat. The elder too, grumbled at Vali. One of the two braves approached the beach, Vali's sword in hand.

"We no show Viking where find Cana." He spat at him. "You Ruhk, different."

"Please, elder. We can reach the camp in less than a day. I am Kanadesh." He said, still unclear to the words meaning, but knowing its impact. The elder snapped from shock and turned back to the woman in his canoe. He seemed troubled, but instead nodded.

"Tell your people. They stay on boat." He said, lifting Aya and turning toward the Viking.

"Vali, you are not taking savages on my boat, unless they are shackled." The captain growled at him, both she and her crew, lifting their weapons.

"Captain!" Vali yelled, a sudden focus returning to the world. "I have a responsibility to this woman. I owe her a debt of life. I am bound by the honor of our people, to see her home." He walked alongside the elder, who was unfazed by the argument, or simply did not understand the language.

The captain shifted her glance from Vali, to the Kresh, to Aya, and then back. Vali stood in front of the elder, as they passed the other three crew mates. He looked at them, hands open, his face screwed up in fear for his companion.

"Please, sisters in arms. The camp is not far to the west. We can be there within the day, and then, we can move for the war council. That, or I cannot go with you. My people will sing songs of our return, if you help me."

"Get onboard, Vali. Your woman, too. I will have some questions for you, once we sort this out." The captain growled, staring daggers at the two Kresh nearing her boat.

"Viking." The Kresh brave called as he stepped from the water. "Your weapon." He said, holding out the weapon.

"Thank you." Vali said, accepting the blade and returning it to its sheath.

**

Aboard the direwolf vessel, named Fàlki, or the Hawk, Vali sat between the two Kresh and his fellow Vikings. They left the two warriors behind, on Fangor, though they had begun to unearth the corpse of the Comartok.

Much to the alarm of the elder Kresh and those onboard, the warriors each pulled against a single paw, which was nearly the size of their torsos. Grunting and groaning as they struggled to pull the beast free from the water, everyone present, save Vali gasped at the sight of the great wolf. Flashing a glance toward Vali, the crew of the Fàlki each saluted him. Now, he sat, watching the elder, who tended to the ill Aya.

"Freyja will be glad to see you." Captain Vigdis, as she had introduced herself, said.

"How is she?" Vali asked, without taking his eyes from Aya.

"She is upset, to be true. Her father, gone from this world. He will be sorely missed, along with the others."

"How did they die?" He asked, the flames of Fangor, still bright far behind them.

"During the fight to reclaim Ulfrost. The sacrifices were beyond measure." She told him, sad tone in her voice. "Til Valhalla." He nodded in agreement.

"Who, besides Ulf?" Vali asked, finally turning to face Vigdis. The captain paused a moment, as she considered the question.

"Many of the war chiefs from some of the other clans. I apologize, but I did not know their names. I was not at the Clansmeet. I was only recently, granted my vessel. Last I knew, Chief Finna still lived, though she had taken ill of late."

"What of my crew? Those boarding the Valiant?" Again, the captain sadly shook her head.

"I cannot say. I know the Valiant was present, during the attack. Beyond that, I am unsure."

"But they live?" Vali asked, the answer to this question, much more important than their present whereabouts.

"Yes, I believe they do. We may yet learn more, once we reach our destination."

"Where were you headed?" Vali asked, remembering their previous heading. "There is not much more to the north, other than the old Kresh lands."

"Not now, Vali." The captain hissed, darting a glance at the Kresh. "I cannot risk their kind, listening in on our plans. How much longer to his blasted village?"

"Not much further, now." He answered.

***

Sooner than he had expected, they arrived off the shore of the Cana camp. He was unsure as to how they knew, but as the vessel approached, Cana awaited them from their floating piers. Canaruhk, as well as Damaruhk, were there, waiting to receive the wounded Aya.

"They have us surrounded." One of the Viking crew moaned, as they stared at over one hundred Cana, weapons drawn in defense.

"May the gods curse you and yours, should this prove our deaths, Vali." The captain growled.

"Do not worry," he spoke with greater confidence than he felt. "They will not harm us. Excuse me, a moment." He said, moving out in front of the others, stepping onto the pier. The elder, carrying Aya in his arms, dashed through the crowd, Damaruhk following at his heels. A murmur rang out among the warriors, silenced only as Canaruhk raised his hand.

"Speak, honorable Fenruhk. Speak as one of the people." He barked aloud so all could hear.

"Will she live?" Vali asked. Damaruhk, Aya and the rest of the entourage had already sped away, leaving only Cana and his braves.

"I believe she will. We have tended to worse." He said, looking over to the Viking ship. "You risk much in coming here. Were you not Ruhk, you would lie dead."

"I understand, Canaruhk. I apologize for this upset. Aya needed..." Cana placed his hand on Vali's left shoulder and squeezed.

"It was the right decision, Fenruhk. You must return with your people?" He looked back to the impatiently awaiting Vikings and nodded, sorrowfully.

"I must. My home has been taken, our leaders, slain. I must find my mother and my sister." Cana nodded his head, gripping at Vali's shoulder.

"Have you any words for Aya? She has sworn herself to travel with you. What shall you tell her?" Instinctively, Vali unbound the leather cord around his neck. Taking a long look at the symbol upon it, he gently placed it into the man's hand.

"I shall never forget her kindness, nor everything she has done for me. This is not a goodbye but a promise. I will come back for this one day. Hopefully, both our peoples will be in a better place, then." Canaruhk eyed Vali's most priceless treasure in his palm with adoration.

"This gesture holds deep meaning for both our peoples." He said, looking to Vali with a smile, before placing his hand on Vali's outer shoulder. "Should we meet again, you must tell me of your travels, Fenruhk. You are Kresh and Viking, both. Responsibilities to both are now yours. Now go." Nodding his head, Vali turned away from the elder without looking back. Stepping back onto the Viking vessel, he turned his head to the captain.

"Captain, I am ready to return to my people, now."

Chapter 33 – The Fate of Those Unbound

A great beast shrieked angrily somewhere in the back of her mind. Her eyelashes fluttering, she managed to adapt to the dull lighting above her. Eyes languidly opening, Asta stared up at the iron bars of a cage.

Her last memory returning to the forefront of her mind, her body reacted with panic. Flipping to her stomach and quickly rising to her feet, she lashed out at the iron bars. Calling to her newfound powers as a shaper, she fought with earth infused strength, created searing heat within the palms of her hands and even attempted to call a swell of wind to tear the cage apart. However, no spirits heeded her call.

Tears not far from her eyes, Asta shook angrily against her confinement. The air in her lungs grew inaccessible as she felt her chest tightening. Holding her body upright, she kicked as aggressively as she could against the door, though it did no more than add to the racket she was making.

"Not going to work in that cage." A light, feminine voice told her. Asta lurched back, striking her back painfully against the bars on the opposite side. The voice said nothing more as Asta's eyes trained on the darkness ahead of her. Her heart thundering in her chest, she focused, forcing herself to calm and spoke.

"Where am I?" Asta demanded, her unnaturally deep voice scaring herself.

"Safe, for now." The voice responded. "We found you floating atop the remains of the Bound Ones' vessel." Asta's eyes continued to search for the ominous source of the voice. "It was lucky we found you."

"Why am I in a cage?" She growled, indignantly.

"We were not in love with the notion, you might wake up and change, again." The young woman answered. "I saw what you did to the last boat you got close to. Griede is not much of a swimmer and was quite concerned, as well."

"Who are you?" She asked the next question with a softer tone. Resting back against the bars of the cage, she slid back down to the bedroll and sat.

"My name is Riva. I am Unbound, similar to you." She stated. "I suppose Griede is also, but I do not much like being compared to him." Asta debated in her mind, whether she truly desired an answer to her next quandary.

"What does it mean to be Unbound?" She whispered. She could hear Riva sigh from the other side of the bars. The gentle tapping of boots on wood, drew her attention to a small, childlike form as the girl presented herself.

"I suppose first, you would need to know what it means to be a Bound One." She stated, gently toying with the short, black, split ends of her unevenly cut hair. The figure standing before Asta was for lack of better explaining, tiny. Had she not sensed a power far greater coming from the girl in front of her, she might have guessed her no more than ten winter's in age.

"Then what are the Bound Ones?" Asta asked. "I have never seen beings as powerful as they."

"Calm down, would you?" The girl pleaded, signaling with both hands for Asta to ease. "I am probably the wrong person to have that conversation with. Once we get back to the others, Henna can explain everything."

"How about letting me out of this cage, in the meantime?" Asta suggested, a hopeful tone in her voice.

"You know I cannot do that." The girl responded apologetically. "Please be patient. It will not be much longer. Soon, you will learn what we are, why the world ended and what Ageless intends for us."

We hope that you've enjoyed Unbound.

To keep up with the author, please follow on;

Facebook @jabullen

Twitter @JA_Bullen

www.jabullen.com

Now, please enjoy an excerpt from an upcoming novel

by J.A. Bullen

The Adaptables

⁇

"Agent Nelson, what do you have to say for yourself?" Counter terrorism and intelligence commander, Agent Scarlet; a tall, red haired woman, in her thirties, wearing a black and white suit spoke, staring down at the middle aged, balding man.

"I had a great run on a game of spider solitaire, this morning." The man, who was sitting at the wrong end of the interrogation table, laughed sarcastically as he loosened his cufflinks. Three agents stood behind the red head, their presence paling, in comparison to the powerful woman who was calling the shots.

"I thought that your orders were clear? Await back up, and do not engage."

"I thought they were, too. I did not order anyone to engage."

"And yet, Agents Wrath and Sable, stormed in, and nearly botched the entire mission." Her glare on him, intensified, as he continued to smile, waving his hands about, illustrating his words.

"What can I say? Dad had to go to work, and while I was away, the children misbehaved. It happens, sometimes. Doesn't help when other agencies, meddle in my operations, and try to place my balls in a vice, at every turn."

"That is not the issue, here. First, Brax and now this? Dammit Nelson, this agency cannot handle any more bad publicity. We'll be digging ourselves out of this blunder, for months." The woman continued to grow angrier, nearly knocking her brown, thick brimmed, glasses from her face. Adjusting them, she sighed deeply, and drew in a deep breath.

"Have you learned anything from the data, you found at the bunker?"

"A great deal, actually. Most disturbingly, is that the government's ruse with the Adaptables Project, was not as effective as we had hoped. It appears as though at least one other group, grew close to replicating our success."

"How close?"

"I have reason to believe that they were successful."

"What group?"

"We do not know, yet, but with new adaptables popping up, every day, it makes sense that we aren't the only ones who figured it out." Scarlet stared down at the case file, she had thrown on the table, and shook her head.

"Adaptables; government made super humans, once thought to be our salvation, have made themselves into little more than a super powered threat, tearing our nations apart. We have more civil unrest than ever before, widespread paranoia, rampant vigilantism, and all we had hoped to create, was a better soldier."

"Creating organisms, with virally mutated mitochondria; capable of altering their bodies, to produce comic book hero effects. Funny how wrong building a stronger deterrent can go." Nelson commented, eyeing the file himself.

"Yes, it would seem that while we held the biggest stick…"

"The wind blew it back, and we jabbed ourselves in the eye," Nelson interrupted.

"Any word on Codename Lucifer?" Scarlet asked. Nelson shook his head.

"Not a word. After the incident with Brax, all traces of her went silent. Nothing. Not even a rumor. Hell, we have less to go on, now, than we ever did, before."

"The one person, to whom all of this can be tied, and we cannot even prove she exists. Or determine if she was even involved." Scarlet shook her head. "If not for her domestic attacks and impassioned calls to arms, we might have been able to reveal the Adaptables, without incident, years ago."

"Do not forget Chicago," Nelson commented.

"Christ, I don't think a single day goes by, when I do not think about Chicago. Nearly twenty thousand lives, in the blink of an eye. The hell was Lucifer after?"

"War." Nelson replied.

"She may have very well gotten it." Scarlet mumbled. Staring down at the case file, she flipped the page over, showing the face of a young man with untidy black hair and hauntingly deep, blue eyes.

"Civil unrest at an all time high. Shootings in schools. A buffoon in the White House, exacerbating an already bad situation."

"Buffoon? Are you not a government appointed official? Nelson smiled candidly, tapping the table top.

"I am not concerned with my position. We are here to talk about yours."

"And Daniel Wrath." Nelson added.

"And Wrath." Scarlett agreed. "What exactly, has become of him?"

"Dead, alive, missing in action, or a clever run away; who honestly knows?" Nelson said, shaking his head.

"Is there any chance that the other questionable pick for your team assisted him? I hear that the two of them have grown quite close." Nelson's eyebrows raised at the question. Slowly, he turned his head to look at the armed men near to him.

"My honest opinion?" He asked.

"I would prefer your professional one."

"No."

"How can you be certain? Not only six months ago, your agent was buried in a hole for murdering a government asset. Her own brother, if I recall?"

"Yes, MY agent, as you so delicately put it, was locked away for tracking down and murdering a fellow, rogue agent. After the deceased went postal, lost control of his adaptation and executed forty-three unarmed civilians, MY agent, tracked him down, killed him and wiped all evidence of your agencies involvement.

"Afterwards, with great consideration to her years of service and wide array of skills, useful to my operation, I decided that it would be best to bring her on board. May I also remind you, Agent Miranda Scarlett, that Daniel Wrath is the center of this debriefing."

"Fair enough, Nelson. Back to the topic of Wrath, then." Scarlett agreed. A quizzical look flashed across Nelson's face.

"Regarding Daniel Wrath, I do have a quandary."

"Oh?" The crimson haired interrogator stared at the man seated before her.

"How did you find him, to begin with?" Nelson asked. "He never told me. He was in hiding for nearly five years, and just suddenly, he pops back up on the radar." Scarlet smiled.

"When Wrath came back into the country, he was less than subtle. I think perhaps, he had hoped to draw Codename Lucifer, to him."

"What did he do?"

"What Wrath would do. He stood in front of an embassy camera, smiling like a clown, while hitting on a female customs official." Nelson's jaw dropped. He smirked a moment, shaking his head.

"That bastard always had some balls."

"Now tell me, Nelson. What has he been up to? Your report suggests that the incident may have been planned." Nelson nodded his head, looking down at the case file, and staring at the man's photo.

"Have a seat." He told her.